Praise for *USA TODAY* bestselling author Sharon Kendrick

"[Kendrick] delivers a fiercely sensual love story
from the last two people in the world
who expected to find one another. From hot love
scenes to exotic locales to a happy ending, this book
will satisfy readers until the last page."
—*RT Book Reviews* on *The Sheikh's English Bride*

"This book is sizzling hot,
with a saucy heroine and a dynamic hero.
The scenes are full of passion and emotion."
—*RT Book Reviews* on *The Future King's Bride*

"You'll need to turn on your air-conditioning
full blast before you sit down to read
Surrender to the Sheikh! Sharon Kendrick
has penned a wonderfully passionate romance
that will curl your toes."
—*TheBestReviews.com*

All about the author

SHARON KENDRICK

When I was told off as a child for making up stories, little did I know that one day I'd earn my living by writing them!

To the horror of my parents, I left school at sixteen and did a bewildering variety of jobs. Everywhere I went I felt like a square peg—until one day I started writing again and then everything just fell into place. I felt the way Cinderella must have when the glass slipper fit!

Today I have the best job in the world—writing passionate romances for Harlequin Books. I like writing stories that are sexy and fast paced, yet packed full of emotion—stories that readers will identify with, that will make them laugh and cry.

My interests are many and varied—chocolate and music, fresh flowers and bubble baths, films and cooking, and trying to keep my home from looking as if someone's burgled it! Simple pleasures—you can't beat them!

I live in Winchester (one of the most stunning cities in the world, but don't take my word for it—come see for yourself!) and regularly visit London and Paris. Oh, and I love hearing from my readers all over the world...so I think it's over to you!

Sharon Kendrick
www.SharonKendrick.com

USA TODAY Bestselling Author

SHARON KENDRICK

Finn's Pregnant Bride

The Paternity Claim

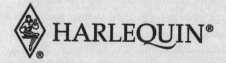

HARLEQUIN®

TORONTO • NEW YORK • LONDON
AMSTERDAM • PARIS • SYDNEY • HAMBURG
STOCKHOLM • ATHENS • TOKYO • MILAN • MADRID
PRAGUE • WARSAW • BUDAPEST • AUCKLAND

Recycling programs
for this product may
not exist in your area.

ISBN-13: 978-0-373-68808-1

FINN'S PREGNANT BRIDE & THE PATERNITY CLAIM

Copyright © 2010 by Harlequin Books S.A.

The publisher acknowledges the copyright holders of the individual works as follows:

FINN'S PREGNANT BRIDE
Copyright © 2002 by Sharon Kendrick.

THE PATERNITY CLAIM
Copyright © 2000 by Sharon Kendrick.

CONTENTS

For my wonderful aunt,
the gypsy-hearted Josephine "Dodie" Webb.

FINN'S PREGNANT BRIDE

CHAPTER ONE

AT FIRST, Catherine didn't notice the shadowy figure sitting there. She was too busy smiling at the waiter with her practised I-am-having-a-wonderful-holiday smile, instead of letting her face fall into the crestfallen lines which might have given away the fact that her boyfriend had fallen in love with another woman.

The sultry night air warmed her skin like thick Greek honey.

'*Kalispera*, Nico.'

'*Kalispera*, Dhespinis Walker,' said the waiter, his face lighting up when he saw her. 'Good day?'

'Mmm!' she enthused. 'I took the boat trip out to all the different coves, as you recommended!'

'My brother—he look after you?' questioned Nico anxiously.

'Oh, yes—he looked after me very well.' In fact, Nico's brother had tried to take more than a professional interest in ensuring that she enjoyed the magnificent sights, and Catherine had spent most of the boat-trip sitting as far away from the tiller as possible!

'My usual table, is it?' she enquired with a smile, because Nico had gone out of his way to give her the best table every evening—the faraway one, which looked out to sea.

But Nico was frowning. 'Tonight it is difficult,

dhespinis. The table is already taken. For tonight the man from Irlandia is here.'

Some odd quality changed the tone of his voice as he spoke. Catherine heard reverence. Respect. And something else which sounded awfully like a grudging kind of envy. She looked at him with a lack of comprehension. The man from *where*? 'Irlandia?' she repeated.

'Ire-land,' he translated carefully, after a moment's thought. 'He arrive this afternoon and he take your table for dinner.'

It was ridiculous to feel so disappointed, but that was exactly the way she *did* feel. Funny how quickly you established little routines on holiday. Night after night Catherine had sat at the very end of the narrow wooden deck which made up the floor of the restaurant, so close to the sea that you felt as if you were almost floating over it.

You could look down over the railing and watch the slick black waters below as they licked against the supporting struts. And the moon would spill its shimmering silver light all across the surface—its beauty so intense that for a while Catherine was able to forget all about England, forget Peter and the always busy job which awaited her.

'Can he do that?' she pleaded. 'Tomorrow is my last day.'

Nico shrugged. 'He can do anything. He is good friend of Kirios Kollitsis.'

Kirios Kollitsis. The island's very own septuagenarian tycoon—who owned not only the three hotels, but half the shops in the village, too.

Catherine strained her eyes to see a dark figure sitting in *her* chair. They said that you could judge a woman by her face and a man by his body, and, though she couldn't see much in this light, it was easy enough to tell from the taut and muscular definition of a powerful frame that this man was considerably younger than Kirios Kollitsis. By about four decades, she judged.

'I can give you next table,' said Nico placatingly. 'Is still lovely view.'

She smiled, telling herself it wasn't his fault. Silly to cling onto a routine—even a temporary one—just because her world had shattered into one she no longer recognised. Just because Peter had gone and found the 'love of his life' almost overnight, leaving Catherine wondering wryly what that said about *their* relationship of almost three years standing. 'That would be lovely. Thanks, Nico.'

Finn Delaney had been slowly sipping from a glass of ouzo and gazing out at the sunset, feeling some of the coiled tension begin to seep from his body. He had just pulled off the biggest deal in a life composed of making big deals. It had been fraught and tight and nail-biting, but—as usual—he had achieved what he had set out to do.

But for the first time in his life the success seemed empty. Another million in the bank, true—but even that seemed curiously hollow.

The ink had barely dried on the contract before he had driven on impulse to the airport and taken the first flight out to the beautiful empty Greek island he knew so well. His secretary had raised her eyebrows when he'd told her.

'But what about your diary, Finn?' she had objected. 'It's packed.'

He had shrugged his broad shoulders and felt a sudden, dizzying sense of liberation. 'Cancel it.'

'Cancel it?' she'd repeated faintly. 'Okay. You're the boss.'

Yes, he was the boss, and there was a price to be paid for that position. With power went isolation. Few spoke to Finn Delaney without an agenda these days. But, in truth, he liked the isolation—and the ability to control his own destiny which went with that. It was only when you started letting people close to you that control slipped away.

He picked up his glass of ouzo and studied the cloudy liquid with a certain sense of amusement, feeling worlds and years away from his usual self. But then, this island had always had that effect on him. It had first known him when he had nothing and had accepted him with open arms. Here he was simply 'Finn', or Kirios Delaney.

Yet for a man known in his native Dublin as The Razor—for his sharp-cutting edge in the world of business—he would have been almost unrecognisable to his many friends and rivals tonight.

The fluid suits he normally sported had been replaced by a pair of faded jeans and a thin white shirt he had bought in one of the local shops. The top three buttons were left carelessly undone, veeing down towards the honed, tanned muscle of his chest. His thick, dark hair—as usual—was in need of a cut and his long legs were stretched out lazily beneath the table.

Tonight he felt like one of the fishermen who had dragged their silver shoals up onto the beach earlier.

It was a perfect night, with a perfect moon, and he sighed as he recognised that success sometimes made you lose sight of such simple pleasures.

'This way, Dhespinis Walker,' Finn heard the waiter saying.

The sound of footsteps clip-clopping against the wooden planks made him look round almost absently, and his eyes narrowed, his heart missing a sudden and unexpected beat as a woman walked into the restaurant. He put the glass of ouzo down, and stared.

For she was beautiful. Mother of all the Saints! She was more than beautiful. Yet beautiful women abounded in his world, so what was different about this one?

Her long black hair tumbled in ebony waves over her shoulders and made her look like some kind of irresistible witch, with a face as delicate as the filmy dress which hinted at ripe, firm flesh beneath.

Yes, very beautiful indeed. His eyes glinted in assessment. And irritated, too. Her mouth was set and, very deliberately, she looked right through him as though he wasn't there. Finn experienced a moment of wry amusement. Not something which happened to him every day of the week. He spent his life fighting off women who rose to the challenge of ensnaring one of Ireland's most eligible bachelors!

He felt the stir of interest as she took her seat at the table next to his, mere inches away, and as the waiter fussed around with her napkin Finn was able to study her profile. It was a particularly attractive profile. Small, cute nose, and lips which looked like folded rose petals. Her skin was softly sheening and lightly golden, presumably from the hot Greek sun, and her limbs were long and supple.

The pulse at his temple was hammering out a primitive beat, and he felt the heated thickening of his blood. Was it the moon and the warm, lazy night air which made him look at a total stranger and wish he was taking her back to his room with him to lose himself in the sweet pleasures of the senses? Had the magic of the island made him regress to those instant clamouring desires of his late teens?

Catherine could feel the man's eyes scanning her with leisurely appraisal, and it felt positively *intrusive* in view of the fact that he was inhabiting *her* space. She studied the menu unseeingly, knowing exactly what she was planning to have.

Finn gave a half-smile, intrigued by the forbidding set of her body and the negative vibes she was sending out. It was enough of a novelty to whet his appetite.

'*Kalispera,*' he murmured.

Catherine continued to study her menu. Oh, yes, he was Irish, all right. The soft, deep and sensual lilt which was almost musical could have come from nowhere else. His voice sounded like shavings of gravel which had been steeped in honey—a voice Catherine imagined would have women in their thousands drooling.

Well, not this one.

'Good evening,' he translated.

Catherine lifted her head and turned to look at him, and wished she hadn't—because she wasn't prepared for the most remarkable pair of eyes which were trained in her direction. Even in this light it was easy to see that they were a deep, dark blue—as wine-dark as the sea she had idly floated in earlier that day. And fringed by thick, dark lashes which could not disguise the unmistakable glint in their depths.

He had a typically Irish face—rugged and craggedly handsome—with a luscious mouth whose corners were lifted in half-amused question as he waited for her to reply.

'Are you speaking to me?' she asked coolly.

He hadn't had a put-down like that in years! Finn

made a show of looking around at all the empty places in the tiny restaurant. 'Well, I'm not in the habit of talking to myself.'

'And I'm not in the habit of striking up conversations with complete strangers,' she said blandly.

'Finn Delaney.' He smiled.

She raised her brows. 'Excuse me?'

'The name's Finn Delaney.' He gave her a slow smile, unable to remember the last time he had been subjected to such an intense deep-freeze. He noticed that the smile refused to work its usual magic.

She didn't move. Nor speak. If this was a chat-up line, then she simply wasn't interested.

'Of course, I don't know yours,' he persisted.

'That's because I haven't given it to you,' she answered helpfully.

'And are you going to?'

'That depends.'

He raised dark brows. 'On?'

'On whether you'd mind moving.'

'Moving where?'

'Swapping tables.'

'Swapping tables?'

Catherine's journalist training instinctively reared its head. 'Do you always make a habit of repeating everything and turning it into a question?'

'And do you always behave so ferociously towards members of the opposite sex?'

She nearly said that she was right off the opposite sex at the moment, but decided against it. She did not want to come over as bitter—because bitter was the last thing she wanted to be. She was just getting used to the fact that her relationship had exceeded its sell-by date, that was all.

She met the mockery lurking deep in the blue eyes. 'If you *really* saw me ferocious, you'd know all about it!'

'Well, now, wouldn't that be an arresting sight to see?' he murmured. He narrowed his eyes in question. 'You aren't exactly brimming over with *bonhomie*.'

'No. That's because you're sitting at my table.' She shrugged as she saw his nonplussed expression and she couldn't really blame him. 'I know it sounds stupid, but I've been there every night and kind of got attached to it.'

'Not stupid at all,' he mused, and his voice softened into a musical caress. 'A view like this doesn't come along very often in a lifetime—not even where I come from.'

She saw a star shoot a silver trail as it blazed across the night sky. 'I know,' she sighed, her voice filled with a sudden melancholy.

'You could always come and join me,' he said. 'And that way we can both enjoy it.' He saw her indecision and it amused him. 'Why not?'

Why not, indeed? Twelve days of dining on her own had left a normally garrulous woman screaming for a little company. And sitting on her own made her all the more conscious of the thoughts spinning round in her head—of whether she could have done more to save her relationship with Peter. Even knowing that time and distance had driven impenetrable wedges between them did not stop her from having regrets.

'I won't bite,' he added softly, seeing the sudden sadness cloud her eyes and wondering what had caused it.

Catherine stared at him. He looked as though he very easily *could* bite, despite the outwardly relaxed appearance. His apparent ease did not hide the highly honed sexuality which even in her frozen emotional state she could recognise. But that was her job; she was trained to suss people out.

'Because I don't know you,' she pointed out.

'Isn't that the whole point of joining me?'

'I thought that it was to look at the view?'

'Yes. You're right. It was.' But his eyes were fixed on her face, and Catherine felt a moment halfway between pleasure and foreboding, though she couldn't for the life of her have worked out why.

Maybe it was because he had such a dangerous look about him, with his dark hair and his blue eyes and his mocking, lazy smile. He looked a bit like one of the fishermen who hauled up the nets on the beach every morning in those faded jeans and a white cotton shirt which was open at the neck. A man she would never see again. Why not indeed? 'Okay,' she agreed. 'Thanks.'

He waited until she had moved and settled in to the seat next to his, aware of a drift of scent which was a cross between roses and honey, unprepared for the way that it unsettled his senses, tiptoeing fingers of awareness over his skin. 'You still haven't told me your name.'

'It's Catherine. Catherine Walker.' She waited, supposing there was the faintest chance that Finn Delaney was an avid reader of *Pizazz!* magazine, and had happened to read her byline, but his dark face made no sign of recognition. Her lips twitched with amusement. Had she really thought that a man as masculine as this one would flick through a lightweight glossy mag?

'Good to meet you, Catherine.' He looked out to where the water was every shade of gold and pink and rose imaginable, reflected from the sky above, and then back to her, a careless question in his eyes. 'Exquisite, isn't it?' he murmured.

'Perfect.' Catherine, strangely disconcerted by that deep blue gaze, sipped her wine. 'It's not your first visit, I gather?'

Finn turned back and the blue eyes glittered in careless question. 'You've been checking up on me, have you?'

It was an arrogant thing to say, but in view of her occupation an extremely accurate one—except that in this case she had not been checking up on him. 'Why on earth should I want to? The waiter mentioned that you were a friend of Kirios Kollitsis, that's all.'

He relaxed again, his mind drifting back to a long-ago summer. 'That's right. His son and I met when we were travelling around Europe—we ended the trip here, and I guess I kind of fell in love with the place.'

'And—let me guess—you've come back here every year since?'

He smiled. 'One way or another, yes, I have. How about you?'

'First time,' said Catherine, and sipped her wine again, in case her voice wobbled. No need to tell him that it was supposed to have been a romantic holiday to make up for all the time that she and Peter had spent apart. Or that now they would be apart on a permanent basis.

'And you'll come again?'

'I doubt it.'

Her heard the finality in her voice. 'You don't like it enough to repeat the experience?'

She shook her head, knowing that Pondiki would always represent a time in her life she would prefer to forget. 'I just never like to repeat an experience.

Why should I, when the world is full of endless possibilities?'

She sounded, he thought, as though she were trying to convince herself of that. But by then Nico had appeared. 'Do you know what you're going to have?' Finn asked.

'Fish and salad,' she answered automatically. 'It's the best thing on the menu.'

'You *are* a creature of habit, aren't you?' he teased. 'The same table and the same meal every night. Are you a glutton for stability?'

How unwittingly perceptive he was! 'People always create routines when they're on holiday.'

'Because there's something comforting in routines?' he hazarded.

His dark blue eyes seemed to look deep within her, and she didn't want him probing any more. That was *her* forte. 'Something like that,' she answered slowly.

She ordered in Greek, and Nico smiled as he wrote it down. And then Finn began to speak to him with what sounded to Catherine like complete fluency.

'You speak Greek!' she observed, once the waiter had gone.

'Well, so do you!'

'Only the basics. Restaurants and shops, that kind of thing.'

'Mine isn't much beyond that.'

'How very modest of you!'

'Not modest at all. Just truthful. I certainly don't speak it well enough to be able to discuss philosophy— but since what I know about philosophy could be written on the back of a postage stamp I'm probably wise not to try.' He gazed at her spectacular green eyes and the way the wine sheened on her lips. 'So tell me about yourself, Catherine Walker.'

'Oh, I'm twenty-six. I live in London. If I didn't then I'd own a dog, but I think it's cruel to keep animals in cities. I like going to films, walking in the park, drinking cocktails on hot summer evenings—the usual thing.'

As a brief and almost brittle biography it told him very little, and Finn was more than intrigued. Ask a woman to tell you about herself and you usually had to call time on them! And less, in some cases, was definitely more. His interest captured, he raised his eyebrows. 'And what do you do in London?'

She'd had years of fudging this one. People always tended to ask the same predictable question when they found out what she did: 'Have you ever met anyone famous?' And, although Finn Delaney didn't look a predictable kind of man, work was the last thing she wanted to think about right now. 'Public relations,' she said, which was *kind* of true. 'And how about you?'

'I live and work in Dublin.'

'As?'

Finn was deliberately vague. Self-made property millionaire sounded like a boast, even if it was true, and he had seen the corrupting power of wealth enough to keep it hidden away. Especially from beautiful women. 'Oh, I dabble in a bit of this and a bit of that.'

'Strictly legal?' she shot out instinctively, and he laughed.

'Oh, strictly,' he murmured, fixing her with a mock-grave look so that she laughed too. The laugh drew attention to the fact that she had the most kissable lips he had ever seen. He found himself wondering why she was here on her own.

His eyes skimmed to the bare third finger of her left hand. No sign of a ring, present or recent. He could see Nico bearing down on them, carrying their food, and he leant forward so that the scent of roses and honey invaded his nostrils.

'How long are you staying?' he questioned.

Still reeling from the pleasure of realising that she hadn't lost the ability to laugh, Catherine let her defences down—and then instantly regretted it. Because his proximity made her heart miss a beat she blinked, startled by her reaction to the warm bronzed flesh and dazzling blue eyes. Her emotions were supposed to be suspended, weren't they? She wasn't supposed to be feeling anything other than the loss of Peter. So how come desire had briefly bewitched her with its tempting promise? 'Tomorrow's my last day.'

Oddly enough, he felt disappointed. Had he hoped that she would be staying long enough for them to forge a brief holiday romance? He must be more stressed-out than he'd thought, if that were the case. 'And how are you planning to spend it? A trip round the island?'

She shook her head. 'Been there, done that. No, I'll probably just laze around on the beach.'

'I think I might join you,' said Finn slowly. 'That's if you don't have any objections?'

CHAPTER TWO

'I THINK I might join you,' he had said.

Catherine rubbed a final bit of sun-block onto her nose and knotted a sarong around the waist of her jade-green swimsuit, aware that her heart was beating as fast as a hamster's. She was meeting Finn Delaney on the beach and was now beginning to wonder whether she should have agreed so readily.

She let a rueful smile curve her lips. She was thinking and acting like an adolescent girl! She had broken up with her long-term boyfriend, yes—but that didn't mean she had to start acting like a nun! There was no crime in spending some time with an attractive, charismatic man, was there? Especially as she had barely any time left. And if Finn Delaney decided to muscle in on her she would politely give him the brush-off.

She scrunched her dark hair back into a ponytail and grabbed her sun-hat before setting off to find some coffee. The sun was already high in the sky, but the terrace was shaded with a canopy of dark, fleshy leaves and she took her seat, trying to imprint the scene on her mind, because tomorrow she would be back in the city.

'I see you with Kirios Finn last night,' observed Nico rather plaintively as he brought her a plate of figs and some strong black coffee. Every morning he tried something new to tempt her, even though she had told him that she never ate breakfast.

'That's right,' agreed Catherine. 'I was.'

'He like you, I think—he like beautiful women.'

Catherine shook her head firmly. 'We're just passing acquaintances who speak the same language, that's all,' she said. 'I'm going home this afternoon—remember?'

'You like him?' persisted Nico.

'I hardly know him!'

'Women like Finn Delaney.'

'I can imagine,' said Catherine wryly, thinking of those compelling blue eyes, the thick, unruly hair and the spectacular body. She might not be interested in him as a man, but her journalistic eye could appreciate his obvious attributes.

'He brave man, too,' added Nico mournfully.

Catherine paused in the act of lifting her cup and looked up. Brave was not a commonly used word, unless someone had been sick, or fought in a war, and her interest was aroused. 'How come?'

Nico pushed the figs into her line of vision. 'The son of Kirios Kollitsis—he nearly die. And Kirios Delaney—he save him.'

'How?'

'The two of them take scooters across the island and Iannis, he crash. So much blood.' He paused. 'I was young. They brought him here. The man from Irlandia carry him in in his arms and they wait for the doctor.' Nico narrowed his eyes in memory. 'Kirios Delaney had white shirt, but now it was red.' And he closed his eyes. 'Red and wet.'

Oh, the power of language, thought Catherine, her coffee forgotten. For some reason the stark words, spoken in broken English, conjured up a far more vivid impression of life and death than a fluent description of the accident could ever have done. She thought of the wet and bloody shirt clinging to Finn Delaney's torso and she gave a shiver.

'They say without Kirios Delaney then Iannis would be dead. His father—he never forget.'

Catherine nodded. No, she imagined that he wouldn't forget. A son's life saved was worth more than a king's ransom. But even if he hadn't acted as he had Finn Delaney was still an unforgettable man, she realised, and suddenly the casually arranged meeting on the beach didn't seem so casual at all.

She should have said no, she thought.

But her reservations didn't stop her from picking her way down the stone steps which led to the beach. When she had reached the bottom she stood motionless. And breathless.

The beach—a narrow ribbon of white bleached sand—was empty, save for Finn himself. His back was the colour of the sweetest toffee and the lean, hard body was wearing nothing but a pair of navy Lycra shorts. Catherine's mouth felt like dust and she shook herself, as if trying to recapture the melancholy of yesterday.

What the hell was the matter with her? Peter had been her life. Her *future*. She had never strayed, nor even looked at another man, and yet now she felt as though this dark, beautiful stranger had the power to cast some kind of spell over her.

He was lost in thought, looking out over the limitless horizon across the sea, but he must have heard or sensed her approach, for he turned slowly and Catherine suddenly found that she could not move. As if that piercing,

blue-eyed stare had turned her to stone, like one of t..
statues which guarded Pondiki's tiny churches.

'Hi!' he called.

'H-hello,' she called back, stumbling uncharacter-
istically on the word. But didn't his voice sound even
more sensual today? Or had the discovery that another
man could set her senses alight made her view him in
a completely different light?

Finn watched her, thinking how perfect she looked—
as though she was some kind of beautiful apparition
who had suddenly appeared and might just as suddenly
fade away again. A faery lady. 'Come on over,' he said
huskily.

Catherine found moving the most difficult thing she
had ever had to do, taking each step carefully, one in
front of the other, like a child learning how to walk.

Still, he watched her. No, no ghost she—far too vivid
to be lacking in substance. The black hair was scraped
back and barely visible beneath her hat, emphasising
the delicate structure of her face, the wariness in the
huge emerald eyes.

The swimsuit she wore was a shade darker than those
eyes, and it clothed a body which was more magnificent
than he had been expecting. The lush breasts looked
deliciously cuppable, and the curve of her hips was just
crying out for the lingering caress of a man's palm.

Realising that his heart was thundering like a boy's
on the brink of sexual discovery, and aware that he
must just be staring at her as if he'd never seen a woman
before, Finn forced his mouth to relax into a smile as
she grew closer.

'Hi,' he said again.

She felt strangely shy—but what woman wouldn't,
alone with such a man on a deserted beach? 'Hi.' She

managed a bright smile. She wasn't a gauche young thing but a sophisticated and successful woman who was slowly recovering from a broken romance. And as soon as the opportunity arose she would tell him that she was interested in nothing more than a pleasant and companionable last day on Pondiki.

Finn smiled, so that those big green eyes would lose some of their wariness. 'Sleep well?'

She shook her head. 'Not really. Too hot. Even with the air-conditioning I felt as though I was a piece of dough which had been left in a low oven all night!'

He laughed. 'Don't you have one of those big old-fashioned fans in your room?'

'You mean the ones which sound as though a small plane has just landed beside the bed?'

'Yeah.' He wanted something to occupy himself, something which would stop him from feasting his eyes on her delicious breasts, afraid that the stirring in his body would begin to make itself shown. 'What would you like to do?'

The words swam vaguely into the haze of her thoughts. In swimming trunks, he looked like a pin-up come to life, with his bright blue eyes and dark, untidy hair.

Broad shoulders, lean hips and long, muscled legs. Men like Finn Delaney should be forbidden from wearing swimming trunks! More to distract herself than because she really cared what they did, she shrugged and smiled. 'What's on offer?'

Finn bit back the crazy response that he'd like to peel the swimsuit from her body and get close to her in the most elemental way possible. Instead, he waved a hand towards the rocks. 'I've made a camp,' he said conspiratorially.

'What kind of camp?'

'The usual kind. We've got shelter. Provisions. Come and see.'

In the distance, she could see a sun-umbrella, two loungers and a cool-box. An oasis of comfort against the barren rocks which edged the sand, with the umbrella providing the cool promise of relief from the beating sun. 'Okay.'

'Follow me,' he said, his voice sounding husky, and for a moment he felt like a man from earlier, primitive times, leading a woman off to his lair.

Catherine walked next to him, the hot sand spraying up and burning her toes through her sandals.

The sound of the sea was rhythmical and soothing, and she caught the faint scent of pine on the air, for Pondiki was crammed full of pine trees. Through the protective covering of her sun-hat she could feel the merciless penetration of the sun, and, trying to ignore the fact that all her senses felt acutely honed, she stared down instead at the sizeable amount of equipment which lay before her.

'How the hell did you get all this stuff down here?' she asked in wonder.

'I carried it.' He flexed an arm jokingly. 'Nothing more than brute strength!'

Memory assailed her. She thought of him carrying his wounded friend, his white shirt wet with the blood of life. Wet and red. She swallowed. 'It looks…it looks very inviting.'

'Sit down,' he said, and gestured to one of the loungers. 'Have you eaten breakfast?'

She sank into the cushions. She never ate breakfast, but, most peculiarly, she had an appetite now. Or rather, other pervasive appetites were threatening to upset her equilibrium, so she decided to sublimate them by opting for food.

'Not yet.'

'Good. Me neither.'

She watched as he opened the cool-box and pulled out rough bread and chilled grapes, and local cheese wrapped in vine leaves, laying them down on a chequered cloth. With what looked like a Swiss Army knife he began tearing and cutting her off portions of this and that.

'Here. Eat.' He narrowed his eyes critically. 'You look like you could do with a little feeding up.'

She sat up and grabbed the crude sandwich and accepted a handful of grapes, preferring to look at the chilled claret-coloured fruit than meet that disturbing blue stare. 'You make me sound like a waif and stray!'

He thought she was perfect, but that now was neither the time nor the place to tell her. 'You look like you haven't eaten much lately,' he observed.

'I've eaten well on Pondiki,' she protested.

'For how long—two weeks, maybe?'

She nodded.

'But not before that, I guess,' he mused.

Well, of course she hadn't! What woman on the planet ate food when she had been dumped by a man? 'How can you tell?'

It gave him just the excuse he needed to study her face. 'Your cheeks have the slightly angular look of a woman who's been skipping meals.'

'Pre-holiday diet,' she lied.

'No need for it,' he responded quietly, his eyes glittering as he sank his teeth into the bread.

He made eating look like an art-form. In fact, he

made eating look like the most sensual act she had ever seen—with his white teeth biting into the unresisting flesh of the grapes, licking their juice away with the tip of his tongue—and Catherine was horrified by the progression of her thoughts.

When she'd been with Peter she hadn't been interested in other men, and yet now she found herself wondering whether that had been because there had been no man like Finn Delaney around.

'This is very good,' she murmured.

'Mmm.' He gave her a lazy smile and relaxed back, the sun beating down like a caress on his skin. There was silence for a moment, broken only by the lapping of the waves on the sand. 'Will you be sorry to leave?' he asked, at last.

'Isn't everyone, at the end of a holiday?'

'Everyone's different.'

'I guess in a way I wish I could stay.' But that was the coward's way out—not wanting to face up to the new-found emptiness of her life back home. The sooner she got back, the sooner she could get on with the process of living. Yet this moment seemed like living. Real, simple and unfettered living, more vital than living had ever been.

Finn raised his head slightly and narrowed his eyes at her. 'Something you don't want to go back to?' he questioned perceptively. 'Or someone?'

'Neither,' she answered, because the truth was far more complex than that, and she was not the type of person to unburden herself to someone she barely knew. She had seen too much in her job of confidences made and then later regretted.

And she didn't want to think about her new role in life—as a single girl out on the town, having to reinvent herself and start all over again. With Peter away on assignments so much, she had felt comfortable staying in and slouching around in tracksuits while watching a movie and ploughing her way through a box of popcorn. She guessed that now those evenings would no longer be guilt-free and enjoyable. There would be pressure to go out with her girlfriends. And nights in would seem as though life was passing her by.

'I suppose I've just fallen in love with this island,' she said softly. Because that much was true. A place as simple and as beautiful as Pondiki made it easy to forget that any other world existed.

'Yeah.' His voice was equally soft, and he took advantage of the fact that she was busy brushing crumbs from her bare brown thighs to watch her again, then wished he hadn't. For the movement was making her breasts move in a way which was making him feel the heavy pull of longing, deep in his groin. He turned over onto his stomach. 'It's easy to do.'

Catherine removed a grape pip from her mouth and flicked it onto the white sand. 'And what about you? Will you be sorry to leave?'

He thought of the new project which was already mounting back home in Ireland, and the opposition to it. And of all the demands on his time which having his fingers in so many pies inevitably brought. When had he last taken a holiday? Sat in such solitude, in such simplicity and with such a—his heart missed another unexpected beat—such a beautiful companion? He pressed himself into the sand, ruefully observing his body's reaction to his thoughts and just hoping that she hadn't.

Her legs were slap-bang in front of his line of vision, and he let his lashes float down over his eyes, hoping that lack of visual stimulation might ease the ache in his groin. 'Yeah,' he said thickly. 'I'll be sorry.'

She heard the slurred quality of his voice and suspected that he wanted to sleep. So she said nothing further—but then silence was easy in such a perfect setting.

She feasted her eyes on the deep blue of the sea, and the paler blue of the sky above it. Remember this, she told herself. Keep it stored in your mind, to bring out on a grey wet day in England, as you would a favourite snapshot.

She flicked a glance over to where Finn lay, watching the rise and fall of his broad back as it became gradually slower and steadier. Yes, he was definitely asleep.

His dark tousled head was pillowed on hair-roughened forearms, and the image of the sleeping man was oddly and disturbingly intimate. Very disturbing. She found herself picturing his bronzed body contrasted against rumpled white sheets and the resulting flush of awareness made Catherine get abruptly to her feet. She needed to cool off!

The sea beckoned invitingly, and she pulled off her sun-hat and ran towards it, her feet sinking into the heavy wet sand by the water's edge. She splashed her way in, waiting until she was out of her depth before she began to strike out.

The sea was as warm as milk, and not in the least bit invigorating, but the water lapped like silk over her heated skin. Catherine continued to swim quite happily in line with the shore, and was just thinking about going in when she experienced a gut-wrenchingly sharp spasm in her leg. She squealed aloud with the shock and the pain.

She tried to keep swimming, but her leg was

stubbornly refusing to work. She opened her mouth to call out, but as she did salt water gushed in and she began to choke.

Don't panic, she told herself—but her body was refusing to obey her. And the more the leg stiffened, the more water poured into her mouth, and she began to flail her arms uselessly and helplessly as control slipped away...

Finn was lost in a warm world of sensation, inhabited by a green-eyed siren with a cascade of black hair, when his dream was punctured by a sound he could not recognise. His eyes snapped open to find Catherine gone.

Instinct immediately warned him of danger and he leapt to his feet, his blue eyes scanning the horizon until he saw the disturbed water and the thrash of limbs which told him that she was in the sea.

And in trouble.

He ran full-pelt into the sea, his muscular legs jumping the waves, breaking out into a powerful crawl which ate up the distance between them.

'Catherine!' he called. 'For God's sake, keep still—I'm on my way!'

She barely heard him, even though she registered the command somewhere in her subconscious. But her body was not taking orders from her tired and confused mind and she felt herself slipping deeper...ever deeper...choking and gagging on the sour, salty taste.

'Catherine!' He reached her and grabbed hold of her, hauling her from beneath the surface and throwing her over his shoulder. He slapped the flat of his palm hard between her shoulder blades and she spat and retched water out of her mouth, sobbing with relief as she clung onto him.

'Easy now,' he soothed. 'Easy.' He ran his hands experimentally down over her body until he found the stiffened and cramped leg.

'Ouch!' she moaned.

'I'm going to swim back to shore with you. Just hold onto me very tightly.'

'You c-c-can't manage me!' she protested through chattering teeth.

'Shut up,' he said kindly, and turned her onto her back, slipping his arm around her waist.

Catherine had little memory of the journey back, or of much that followed. She remembered him sinking into the sand and lowering her gently down, and the humiliation of spewing up the last few drops of salt water. And then he was rubbing her leg briskly between his hands until the spasm ebbed away.

She must have dozed, for when she came to it was to find herself still on the sand, the fine, white grains sticking to her skin, leaning back against Finn's chest.

'You're okay?' he murmured.

She coughed, then nodded, a sob forming in her throat as she thought just how lucky she had been.

He felt her shudder. 'Don't cry. You'll live.'

She couldn't move. She felt as if her limbs had been weighted with lead. 'But I feel so…so *stupid*!' she choked.

'Well, you were a little,' he agreed gently. 'To go swimming straight after you'd eaten. Whatever made you do that, Catherine?'

She closed her eyes. She couldn't possibly tell him that the sight of his near-naked body had been doing things to her equilibrium that she had wanted to wipe clean away. She shook her head.

'Want me to carry you back to the lounger?'

'I'll w-walk.'

'Oh, no, you won't,' he demurred. 'Come here.' And he rose to his feet and picked her up as easily as if she'd been made of feathers.

Catherine was not the type of woman who would normally expect to be picked up and carried by a man—indeed, she had never been the recipient of such strong-arm tactics before. The men she knew would consider it a sexist insult to behave in such a way! So was it?

No.

And no again.

She felt so helpless, but even in her demoralised state she recognised that it was a pleasurable helplessness. And the pleasure was enhanced by the sensation of his warm skin brushing and tingling against hers where their bodies touched. Like electricity.

'Finn?' she said weakly.

He looked down at her, feeling he could drown in those big green eyes, and then the word imprinted itself on his subconscious and he flinched. Drown. Sweet Lord—the woman could have *drowned*. A pain split right through him. 'What is it?' he whispered, laying her gently down on the sun-bed.

She pushed a damp lock of hair back from her face, and even that seemed to take every last bit of strength she had. But then it wasn't just her near escape which was making her weak, it was something about the way the blue eyes had softened into a warm blaze.

'Thank you,' she whispered back, thinking how inadequate those two words were in view of what he had just done.

A smile lifted the corners of his mouth as some of the tension left him.

Some.

'Don't mention it,' he said, his Irish accent edged with irresistible velvet. But he wished that she wouldn't look at him that way. All wide-eyed and vulnerable, with the pale sand sugaring her skin, making him long to brush each grain away one by one, and her lips slightly parted, as if begging to be kissed. 'Rest for a while, and then I'll take you back up to the hotel.'

She nodded, feeling strangely bereft. She would have to pack. Organise herself. Mentally gear herself up for switching back into her role of cool, intrepid Catherine Walker—doyenne of *Pizazz!* magazine. Yet the soft, vulnerable Catherine who was gazing up into the strong, handsome face of her rescuer seemed infinitely more preferable at that moment.

Peter? prompted a voice in her head. Have you forgotten Peter so quickly and replaced him with a man you scarcely know? Bewitched by the caveman tactics of someone who just happened to have an aptitude for saving lives?

She licked her bottom lip and tasted salt. 'You save a lot of lives, don't you, Finn Delaney?'

Finn looked at her, his eyes narrowing as her remark caught him off-guard. 'Meaning?'

She heard the element of caution which had crept into his voice. 'I heard what you did for the son of Kirios Kollitsis.'

His face became shuttered. 'You were discussing me? With whom?'

She felt on the defensive. 'Only with Nico—the waiter. He happened to mention it.'

'Well, he had no right to mention it—it happened a long time ago. It's forgotten.'

But people didn't forget things like that. Catherine knew that *she* would never forget what he had done

even if she never saw him again—and she very probably wouldn't. They were destined to be—to use that
old cliché—ships that passed in the night, and, like all
clichés, it was true.

He accompanied her back to the hotel, and she was
glad of his supporting arm because her legs still felt
wobbly. When he let her go, she missed that firm, warm
contact.

'What time are you leaving?' he asked.

'The taxi's coming at three.'

He nodded. 'Go and do your packing.'

Catherine was normally a neat and organised packer,
but for once she was reckless—throwing her holiday
clothes haphazardly into the suitcase as if she didn't
care whether she would ever wear them again. And she
didn't. For there was an ache in her heart which seemed
to have nothing to do with Peter and she despised herself for her fickleness.

She told herself that *of course* a man like Finn Delaney would inspire a kind of wistful devotion in the
heart of any normal female. That *of course* it would be
doubled or tripled in intensity after what had just happened. He had acted the part of hero, and there were
too few of those outside the pages of romantic fiction,
she told herself wryly. That was all.

Nevertheless, she was disappointed to find the small
foyer empty, save for Nico, who bade her his own wistful farewell.

No, disappointment was too bland a word. Her heart
actually lurched as she looked around, while trying
not to look as though she was searching for anyone
in particular. But there was no sign of the tall, broad-
shouldered Irishman.

Her suitcase had been loaded into the boot of the

rather ramshackle taxi, and Catherine had climbed reluctantly into the back, when she saw him. Swiftly moving through the bougainvillaea-covered arch, making a stunning vision against the riotous backdrop of purple blooms.

He reached the car with a few strides of those long legs and smiled.

'You made it?'

'Just about.'

'Got your passport? And your ticket?'

If anyone else had asked her this she would have fixed them with a wry look and informed them that she travelled solo most of the time, that she didn't need anyone checking up on her. So why did she feel so secretly pleased—protected, almost? 'Yes, I have.'

He ran his long fingers over the handle of the door. 'Safe journey, Catherine,' he said softly.

She nodded, wondering if her own words would come out as anything intelligible. 'Thanks. I will.'

'Goodbye.'

She nodded again. Why hadn't he just done the decent thing and not bothered to come down if that was all he was going to say? She tried to make light of it. 'I'll probably be stuck in the terminal until next week—that's if this taxi ever gets me there!'

He raised his dark brows as he observed the bonnet, which was attached to the car with a piece of string. 'Hmmm. The jury's out on that one!'

There was a moment's silence, where Catherine thought he was going to say something else, but he didn't. On impulse, she reached into her bag for her camera and lifted it to her eye. 'Smile,' she coaxed.

He eyed the camera as warily as he would a poisonous snake. 'I never pose for photos.'

No, she didn't imagine that he would. He was not the kind of man who would smile to order. 'Well, carry on glowering and I'll remember you like that!' she teased.

A slow smile broke out like the sun, and she caught it with a click. 'There's one for the album!'

He caught the glimpse of mischief in her green eyes and it disarmed him. He reached into the back pocket of his snug-fitting denims. He'd never had a holiday romance in his life, but...

'Here—' He leant forward and put his head through the window. She could smell soap, see the still-damp black hair and the tiny droplets of water which clung to it, making him a halo.

For one mad and crazy moment she thought that he was going to kiss her—and didn't she long for him to do just that? But instead he handed her a card, a thick cream business card.

'Look me up if ever you're in Dublin,' he said casually, smacking the door of the car as if it was a horse. The driver took this as a signal and began to rev up the noisy engine. 'It's the most beautiful city in the world.'

As the car roared away in a cloud of dust she clutched the card tightly, as if afraid that she might drop it, then risked one last glance over her shoulder. But he had gone. No lasting image of black hair and white shirt and long, long legs in faded denim.

Just an empty arch of purple blooms.

CHAPTER THREE

'CATHERINE, you look *fabulous*!'

Catherine stood in her editor's office, feeling that she didn't want to be there, but—as she'd told herself—it was her first day back at work after her holiday, so she was bound to feel like that. 'Do I?'

Miranda Fosse gave her a gimlet-eyed look. '*Do* you?' She snorted. 'Of course you do! Bronzed and stunning—if still a little on the thin side of slender!' She narrowed her eyes. 'Good holiday, was it?'

'Great.'

'Get Peter out of your system, did you?'

If Miranda had asked her this question halfway into the holiday Catherine would have bristled with indignation and disbelief. But the pain of losing Peter was significantly less than it had been. Significantly less than it should be she thought—with a slight feeling of guilt. And you wouldn't need to be an expert in human behaviour to know the reason why. Reasons came in different shapes and forms, and this one had a very human form indeed.

Catherine swallowed, wondering if she was going very slightly crazy. Finn Delaney had been on her mind ever since she had driven away from the small hotel on Pondiki, and the mind was a funny thing. How could you possibly dream so much and so vividly of a man you barely knew?

The only tangible thing she had of him was his card, which was now well-thumbed and reclining like a guilty secret at the back of her purse.

'Got any photos?' demanded Miranda as she nodded towards the chair opposite her.

Catherine sat down and fished a wallet from her handbag. It was a magazine tradition that you brought your holiday snaps in for everyone else to look at. 'A few. Want to see?'

'Just so long as they're not all boring landscapes!' joked Miranda, and proceeded to flick through the selection which Catherine handed her. 'Hmmm. Beautiful beach. Beautiful sunset. Close-up of lemon trees. Blah, blah, blah—hang on.' Behind her huge spectacles, her eyes goggled. 'Well, looky-here! Who the hell is *this*?'

Catherine glanced across the desk, though it wasn't really necessary. No prizes for guessing that Miranda hadn't pounced on the photo of Nico grinning shyly into the lens. Or his brother flexing his biceps at the helm of the pleasure-cruiser. No, the tousled black hair and searing blue eyes of Finn Delaney were visible from here—though, if she was being honest, Catherine felt that she knew that particular picture by heart. She had almost considered buying a frame for it and putting it on her bedside table!

'Oh, that's just a man I met,' she said casually.

'Just a man I met?' repeated Miranda disbelievingly. 'Well, if I'd met a man like this I'd never have wanted to come home! No wonder you're over Peter!'

'I am *not* over Peter!' said Catherine defensively. 'He's just someone I met the night before I left.' Who saved my life. And made me realise that I *could* feel something for another man.

Miranda screwed her eyes up. 'He looks kind of familiar,' she mused slowly.

'I don't think so.'

'What's his name?'

'Finn Delaney.'

'Finn Delaney...Finn Delaney,' repeated Miranda, and frowned. 'Do I know the name?'

'I don't know, do you? He's Irish.'

Miranda began clicking onto the search engine of her computer. 'Finn Delaney.' A slow smile swiftly turned to an expression of glee. 'And you say you've never heard of him?'

'Of course I haven't!' said Catherine crossly. 'Why, what have you found?'

'Come here,' purred Miranda.

Catherine went round to Miranda's side of the desk, prepared and yet not prepared for the image of Finn staring out at her from the computer. It was clearly a snatched shot, and it looked like a picture of a man who did not enjoy being on the end of a camera. Come to think of it, he had been very reluctant to have *her* take his picture, hadn't he?

It was a three-quarter-length pose, and his hair was slightly shorter. Instead of the casual clothes he had been wearing in Pondiki, he was wearing some kind of beautiful grey suit. He looked frowning and preoccupied—a million miles away from the man relaxing with his ouzo at the restaurant table with the dark, lapping sea as a backdrop.

'Has he got his own website, then?' Catherine asked, unable to keep the surprise out of her voice. He hadn't looked like that sort of person.

Miranda was busy scrolling down the page. 'There's his business one. This one is the Finn Delaney Appreciation Society.'

'You're kidding!'

'Nope. Apparently, he was recently voted number three in Ireland's Most Eligible Bachelor list.'

Catherine wondered just how gorgeous numbers one and two might be! She leant closer as she scanned her eyes down the list of his many business interests. 'And he has fingers in many pies,' she observed.

'And thumbs, by the look of it. Good grief! He's the money behind some huge new shopping complex with a state-of-the-art theatre.'

'Really?' Catherine blinked. He had certainly not looked in the tycoon class. Her first thought had been fisherman, her second had been pin-up.

'Yes, really. He's thirty-five, he's single and he looks like a fallen angel.' Miranda looked up. 'Why haven't we heard of him before?'

'You know what Ireland's like.' Catherine smiled. 'A little kingdom all of its own, but with no king! It keeps itself to itself.'

But Miranda didn't appear to be listening. Instead she was continuing to read out loud. '"Finn Delaney's keen brain and driving talent have led to suggestions that he might be considering a career in politics." Wow!' Her face took on a hungry look. 'Are you seeing him again, Catherine?'

'I—I hadn't planned to.' He had told her to drop by if ever she was in Dublin—but you couldn't really get more offhand than that, could you? Besides, if he had his very own appreciation society then she was likely to have to join a very long queue indeed!

'Did he ask you out?'

Catherine shook her head. 'No. He just gave me his card and said to call by if I happened to be passing, but—'

'But?'

'I don't think I'll bother.'

From behind her spectacles Miranda's eyes were boring into her. 'And why not?'

'Millions of reasons, but the main one being that it's not so long since I finished with Peter. Or rather,' she corrected painfully, 'Peter finished with me. It went on for three years and I need to get over it properly.' She shrugged, trying to rid her mind of the image of black hair and piercing blue eyes and that body. Trying in vain to imprint Peter's there instead. 'A sensible person doesn't leap straight from one love affair to another.'

'No one's asking you to have a love affair!' exploded Miranda. 'Whatever happened to simple friendship?'

Catherine couldn't explain without giving herself away that a woman did not look at a man like Finn Delaney and think friendship. No, appallingly, her overriding thought connected with Finn Delaney happened to be long, passionate nights together. 'I'm not flying to Dublin to start a tenuous new friendship,' she objected.

'But this man could be a future prime minister of Ireland!' objected Miranda with unaccustomed passion. 'Imagine! Catherine, you *have* to follow it up! You're an attractive woman, he gave you his card—I'm sure he'd be delighted to see you!'

Catherine narrowed her eyes suspiciously. 'It isn't like you to play matchmaker, Miranda—you once said that single people gave more to their job! Why are you so keen for me to see Finn Delaney?'

'I'm thinking about our readers—'

Everything slotted into place. 'Then don't,' warned Catherine. 'Don't even *think* about it. Even if I was— even if I *was* planning to call in on him—there's no way that I would dream of writing up a piece about it, if that's the way your devious mind is working!'

Miranda bared her teeth in a smile. 'Oh, don't take things so seriously, girl! Why don't you just go?' she coaxed. 'Give yourself a treat for a change.'

'But I've only just got back from my holiday!'

'We can do a feature on the city itself—the whole world loves Dublin at the moment—you know it does! The single girl's guide! How about if we call it an assignment? And if you want to call in on Finn Delaney while you're there—then so much the better!'

'I'm not writing anything about him,' said Catherine stubbornly, even while her heart gave a sudden leap of excitement at the thought of seeing him again.

'And nobody's asking you to—not if you don't want to,' soothed Miranda. 'Tell our readers all about the shops and the restaurants and the bands and who goes where. That's all.'

That's all, Catherine told herself as her flight touched down at Dublin airport.

That's all, she told herself as she checked into the MacCormack Hotel.

That's all, she told herself again, as she lifted the phone and then banged it straight down again.

It took three attempts for the normally confident Catherine to dial Finn Delaney's number with a shaking finger.

First of all she got the switchboard.

'I'd like to speak to Finn Delaney, please.'

'Hold the line, please,' said a pleasantly spoken girl

with a lilting Dublin accent. 'I'll put you through to his assistant.'

There were several clicks on the line before a connection was made. This time the female voice did not sound quite so lilting, and was more brisk than pleasant.

'Finn Delaney's office.'

'Hello. Is he there, please? My name is Catherine Walker.'

There was a pause. 'May I ask what it is concerning, Miss Walker?'

She didn't want to come over as some desperado, but didn't the truth *sound* a little that way? 'I met Finn—Mr Delaney—on holiday recently. He told me to look him up if I happened to be in Dublin and...' Catherine swallowed, realising how flimsy her explanation sounded. 'And, well, here I am,' she finished lamely.

There was a pause which Catherine definitely decided was disapproving, though she accepted that might simply be paranoia on her part.

'I see,' said the brisk voice. 'Well, if you'd like to hold the line I'll see if Mr Delaney is available...though his diary *is* very full today.'

Which Catherine suspected was a gentle way of telling her that it was unlikely the great man would deign to speak to her. Regretting ever having shown Miranda his photo, or having foolhardily agreed to get on a plane in the first place, she pressed the receiver to her ear.

Another click.

'Catherine?'

It was the lilting voice of honey pouring over shaved gravel which she remembered so well. 'Hi, Finn—it's me—remember?'

Of course he remembered. He'd remembered her for several sweat-sheened and restless nights. A few nights too long. And that had been that. He'd moved on, hadn't expected to hear from her again. Nor, it had to be said, had he particularly wanted to. The completion of one deal made room for another, and he had the devil of a project to cope with now. Finn dealt with his life by compartmentalising it, and Catherine Walker belonged in a compartment which was little more than a mildly pleasing memory. The last thing he needed at the moment was feminine distraction.

'Of course I remember,' he said cautiously. 'This is a surprise.'

A stupid, stupid surprise, thought Catherine as she mentally kicked herself. 'Well, you did say to get in touch if I happened to be in Dublin—'

'And you're in Dublin now?'

'I am.' She waited.

Finn leaned back in his chair. 'For how long?'

'Just the weekend. I…er…I picked up a cheap flight and just flew out on a whim.'

Maybe it wasn't the wisest thing in the world, but he could do absolutely nothing about his body's reaction. And his body, it seemed, reacted very strongly to the sound of Catherine Walker's crisp English accent, coupled with the memory of her soft, curved body pressed against his chest.

'And you want a guide? Am I right?'

'Oh, I'm quite capable of discovering a city on my own,' answered Catherine. 'Your secretary said that you were busy.'

He looked at the packed page in front of him. 'And so I am,' he breathed with both regret and relief, glad that she hadn't expected him to suddenly drop everything. 'But I'm free later. How about if we meet for dinner tonight? Or are you busy?'

For one sane and sensible moment Catherine felt like saying that, yes, she was busy. Terribly busy, thank you very much. She need not see him, nor lay herself open to his particular brand of devastating charm. In fact, she could go away and write up Miranda's article, and...

'No, I'm free for dinner,' she heard herself saying.

He resisted a small sigh. She had been aloof on Pondiki, and that had whetted an appetite jaded by the acquiescence of women in general. For a man unused to having a woman say no to him, the novelty had stirred his interest. And yet here she was—as keen and as eager as the next woman.

But he thought of her big green eyes, hair which was as black as his own, and the small sigh became a small smile.

'Where are you staying?'

'MacCormack's.'

'I'll pick you up around seven.'

Catherine waited for him to say, Does that suit you? But he didn't. In fact, there was nothing further than a short, almost terse 'Bye' and the connection was severed.

She replaced the receiver thoughtfully. He sounded different. Though of course he would. People on holiday were less stressed, more relaxed. So was the fisherman with the lazy smile and sexy eyes simply a one-day wonder?

For her sanity's sake, she hoped so.

The morning she assigned to culture, and then she ate lunch in the requisite recommended restaurant. The rest of the afternoon she spent soaking up the city— marvelling at the shops in Grafton Street, studying the sparkling waters of the Liffey, just getting a feel for

Ireland's beautiful capital city—before going back to the hotel to write up her copy.

It certainly has a buzz, she thought, as she reluctantly dragged her body from a bath which was filled right up to the top with scented bubbles.

She dressed with more care than usual. She wanted to appear all things. Demure, yet sexy. Casual, yet smart. To look as though she hadn't gone to any trouble, yet as though she'd stepped out from one of the pages of her own magazine! You ask too much of yourself, Catherine, she told herself sternly.

She decided on an ankle-length dress of cream linen, stark and simple, yet deliciously cut. Understated, stylish, and not designed to appear vampish. Not in the least.

Her black hair she caught up in a topknot, to show long jade earrings dangling down her neck, and at just gone seven she went down to the foyer with a fast-beating heart.

He wasn't there.

The fast beat became a slam of disappointment, and her mind worked through a tragic little scenario.

What if he had stood her up?

Well, more fool her for her impetuosity!

Catherine walked across the marbled space and went to gaze at the fish tank. The exotic striped fish swam in leisurely fashion around the illuminated waters, and she watched their graceful tails undulating like a breeze on a cornfield. How uncomplicated life as a fish must be, she thought.

'Catherine?'

She turned around, startled and yet not startled to hear the rich Irish brogue which broke into her thoughts, and there stood Finn Delaney—looking the same and yet not the same. Some impossibly beautiful and yet impossibly remote stranger. Which, let's face it, she reminded herself, was exactly what he was.

He was dressed similarly to the shot she had seen on the website, only the suit was darker. Navy. Which somehow emphasised the blue of his eyes. And with a silk tie, blue as well—almost an Aegean blue. The tie had been impatiently pulled away from the collar of his shirt so that it was slightly askew—and that was the only thing which detracted from the formal look he was wearing.

Even his hair had been cut. Not short—certainly not short—but the dark, wayward black locks had been tidied up.

Gone was the fisherman in the clinging, faded denim and the gauze-thin shirt. And gone too was the careless smile. Instead his luscious lips were curved into something which was mid-way between welcoming and wary.

'Well, hi,' he murmured.

Oh, hell—if ever she'd wished she could magic herself away from a situation it was now. What the hell had possessed her to come? To ring him? To arrange to meet him when clearly he was regretting ever having handed her his wretched business card in the first place?

'Hi,' she said back, trying very hard not to let the rich Irish brogue melt over her.

He gave a little shake of his shoulders as he heard the faint reprimand in her voice. 'Sorry I'm late—I was tied up. You know how frantic Friday afternoons can be before the weekend—and the traffic was a nightmare.'

He was trotting out age-old excuses like an unfaithful husband! 'I should have given you my mobile number—then you could have cancelled.' She raised her eyebrows, giving him the opt-out clause. 'You still could.'

Finn relaxed, and not just because by offering to retreat she had made herself that little bit more desirable. No, the renewed sight of her had a lot to do with it. He *had* been regretting asking her to call by, but mainly because he hadn't imagined that she would. Not this soon.

Yet seeing her again reminded him of the heart-stopping effect she seemed to have on him. With an ache he remembered her in that stretchy green swimsuit, which had clung like honey to the lush curves of her breasts and hips. He remembered the heated cool of her flesh as the droplets of sea-water had dried on contact with his own. And the dark hair which had been plastered to her face, sticking to its perfect oval, like glue.

Yet tonight, in the spacious foyer of the up-market hotel, she couldn't have looked more different. She looked cool and untouchable and—perversely—all the more touchable just for that.

Her hair was caught back in some stark and sleek style which drew attention to the pure lines of her features. The small, straight nose. The heart-shaped bow of a mouth which provoked him with its subtle gleam. High cheekbones which cast dark, mysterious shadows over the faintly tanned skin, and of course the enormous green eyes—fathomless as the sea itself.

'What? Turn you away when you've travelled so far?' he teased her mockingly.

She raised her eyebrows. 'From London, you mean, Finn? It's not exactly at the far end of the globe.'

'Is that so?' he smiled. 'Well, thanks for the geography lesson!'

His voice was so low and so rich and so beguiling that she thought he would instantly get a career in voice-overs if he ever needed money quickly. Though, judging by the information on the website, he wasn't exactly short of cash.

Reluctantly, she found herself smiling back. 'You're welcome.'

Finn's blue eyes gleamed. 'Do I take that to mean you don't want Finn Delaney's tour of Dublin's fair city?'

No. She meant that she was beginning to regret having come, but she understood exactly what had brought her so irresistibly. Or rather, who. In a plush Dublin hotel foyer Finn Delaney's attraction was no less potent than when he had hauled her flailing from the sea. When she had clung to his nearly naked body on a sun-baked Greek beach.

She swallowed. 'I thought we were having dinner. Not playing tourist.'

'Sure,' he said slowly. 'Are you hungry?'

'Starving.' It wasn't really the truth, nor even close to it, but she was here now, and at least dinner would provide distraction techniques. She could busy herself with her napkin and sip at her wine and hope that the buzz of the restaurant would dilute his overpowering presence. Then maybe the evening would be quickly over and she could forget all about him.

'Then let's go.'

'Finn—'

The hesitant note in her voice stilled him. 'What?'

'You must let *me* buy *you* dinner.'

His eyes narrowed. 'Why?'

She shrugged awkwardly. Surely in some small way she could repay the debt she owed him, and in doing so give herself a legitimate reason for being here? 'I owe you. Don't forget, you saved my—'

'No!'

The single word cut across her stumbled sentence and in that moment she got an inkling of what it would be like to cross this man, was glad that she wouldn't.

'*I'm* buying dinner,' he said unequivocally. '*I* invited you and it's my territory.' His eyes narrowed. 'Oh, and Catherine—it was no big deal. You had a little cramp and I pulled you out of the water, okay? Let's draw a line under it and forget it, right?'

She wondered if there was anything more attractive than a modest hero, but she heard the determination which underpinned the deep voice and nodded her head with an obedience which was unusual for her. 'Right,' she agreed.

His face relaxed into a smile and his gaze was drawn to the direction of her feet. Flat heels, he noted. 'You wore sensible shoes, I see.'

He made her feel like Little Miss Frump! 'I didn't wear spindly stilettos in case we were walking to the restaurant!' she returned.

'Good. Good because we are walking,' he replied evenly, though the thought of her wearing sexy high heels momentarily drove his blood pressure through the ceiling. 'Come on, let's go.'

They walked out into a warm summer evening, where the streets of Dublin were filled with people strolling with presumably the same purpose in mind.

'Have you booked somewhere?' asked Catherine.

Surely it would sound arrogant to say that he didn't need to? 'Don't worry, I've got us a table.'

He took her to St Stephen's Green—stunning and grand and as beautiful as anything Catherine had ever seen. And tucked away, almost out of sight of all the splendour, was a small restaurant whose lack of menu in the darkened windows spoke volumes for its exclusivity.

But they knew Finn Delaney, all right, and greeted him like the Prodigal Son.

'It's your first time here? In Ireland, I mean, and in Dublin in particular?' he asked, when they were seated at a window table which gave them a ringside seat for people watching. And people-watching was what Catherine normally loved to do. Normally. Except now she was finding her normal interest had waned and she was much more interested in watching just one person.

Trying not to, she shook her napkin out over her lap instead. 'Yes, it is.' Did he think she had flown out especially to see him? Some kind of explanation seemed in order. She shrugged. 'You said it was the most beautiful city in the world, and I thought I'd come and see for myself.'

He gave a low laugh. 'I'm flattered that you took my word for it.' Dark eyebrows were raised, and blue eyes sizzled into hers with a mocking question. 'And is it?'

'Haven't seen enough yet,' she said promptly.

'Haven't you?' His eyes were drawn to the curve of her breasts. 'Well, we'll have to see what we can do about that.'

CHAPTER FOUR

WHICH WAS HOW Catherine came to be sitting in Finn Delaney's sports-car late the following morning, with the breeze turning her cheeks to roses and the sky like a blue vault above her head.

'Don't forget to tie your hair back,' he had murmured as he had dropped her back at her hotel and bade her goodnight.

So she'd woven a ribbon into a tight French plait and was glad she had—because the wind from the open-top car would have left her hair completely knotted. A bit like her stomach.

'Where are we going?' she asked as she slid into the passenger seat beside him.

He turned the ignition key and gave a small smile. How cool she looked. And how perfect—with the amber ribbon glowing against her black hair. He couldn't remember the last time he had seen a grown woman tie a ribbon in her hair, and the result was a devastating combination of innocence and sensuality. 'To Glendalough. Ever heard of it?'

She shook her head. The way he said the name made it sound like music.

'Okay—here's your little bit of tourist information. It's a sixteenth-century Christian settlement about an hour outside Dublin—famous for its monastery. The name Glendalough comes from its setting—an idyllic valley in between two lakes.'

Idyllic.

Well, wasn't this idyllic enough? she wondered, casting a glance at the dark profile as he looked into his driving mirror.

Dinner had been bliss—there was no other way to describe it—though she supposed that this should have come as no surprise. Finn Delaney had been amusing, provocative, contentious and teasing, in turn. And if she had been expecting him to quiz her about her life and her loves and her career, she had—for once—been widely off the mark. He seemed more interested in the general rather than the specific.

Maybe that was a lucky escape—for she doubted whether he would have been so hospitable if he had discovered that she was a journalist. People had so many preconceived ideas about meeting journalists—usually negative—which was the main reason why Catherine had fallen into the habit of never revealing that she was a member of a despised tribe! At least, not until she got to know someone better.

No, it had been more like having dinner with the brightest tutor at university. Except that no tutor she had ever met looked quite as delectable as Finn Delaney. He had argued politics and he had argued religion.

'Both taboo,' she had remarked with a smile as she'd sipped her wine, though that hadn't stopped her from arguing back.

'Says who?'

'Says just about every book on social etiquette.'

'Who cares about etiquette?' he challenged, sizzling her with a provocative blue stare.

At which point she felt consumed by a feeling of

desire so strong that it made her throat constrict with fear and guilt.

Surely it must be more than Finn himself that was having this effect on her? She'd met handsome, charming and successful men before—lots of them— but she couldn't remember ever being enticed quite so effectively.

And what about Peter? taunted the suddenly confused voice in her head. *Peter.* The man you expected to spend the rest of your life with.

Was the vulnerability which followed a break-up making her more susceptible than usual? Catherine squirmed uncomfortably in her seat, but Finn didn't appear to have noticed her self-consciousness.

Thank God.

Because he was looking at some squashy chocolate cake with a gleam of unfettered delight in the blue eyes.

'Wouldn't you just think that chocolate should carry a health warning?' he sighed.

'I thought it did—certainly if you eat too much of it!' She averted her eyes from the washboard-flat stomach.

He licked a melting spoonful with an instinctive sensuality which was making Catherine's stomach turn to mush.

'So everything in moderation, then? Is that right?' he observed softly, but the blue eyes were sparking with what looked like simple mischief.

'That wasn't what I said at all,' remarked Catherine tartly—but even so she could barely get her fork through her summer pudding.

Some men made deliberate remarks which were overtly sexual and which somehow made you end up being completely turned off by them. Whereas Finn made remarks which seemed to all intents and purposes completely innocent. So how come she didn't believe a word of the moderation bit? She'd bet that in the bedroom he was the least moderate person on the planet.

And Peter seemed a very long way away. In fact, the world seemed to have telescoped down into one place—and that was this place, with this man, eating a delicious dinner which was completely wasted on her...

The road to Glendalough passed through some of the most spectacular countryside that Catherine had ever seen.

'Oh, but this is glorious,' she sighed.

He shot her a faintly reproving glance. 'You sound surprised, but you shouldn't be. The beauty of Ireland is one of the best-kept secrets in the world. Didn't you know that, Catherine?'

And so were Ireland's men, if this one was anything to go by. 'I live to learn,' she said lightly.

And how he enjoyed teaching her, he thought, desire knifing through him in a way which made him put his foot down very hard on the accelerator.

She intrigued him, and he couldn't for the life of him work out why. Surely it couldn't *just* be a passing resemblance to a woman he had known so long ago that it now seemed like another lifetime. Or her cool, unflappable manner, or the way she parried his remarks with witty little retorts of her own, the way women so rarely did. But then, she did not know him, did she? Finn's reputation went before him in the land of his birth, and he was used to women—even intelligent ones—being slightly intimidated by that.

'Are you English?' he asked suddenly, as he slowed the car to a halt in Glendalough.

She turned to look at him. 'What an extraordinary question! You know I am!'

'It's that combination of jet hair and green eyes and pale skin,' he observed slowly. 'It isn't a typically English combination, is it?'

Catherine reached for her handbag, the movement hiding her face. Any minute and he would start asking her about her parentage, and she couldn't bear that. Not that she was ashamed—she wasn't. Of course she wasn't. But the moment you told someone that you might be descended from almost anyone but that you would never know—well, their attitude towards you changed. Inevitably. They pitied you, or looked at you with some kind of amazed horror, as if you were invariably going to be damaged by the circumstances of your upbringing.

'Oh, I'm a hybrid,' she said lightly. 'They always make for the most interesting specimens.' Her eyes met his in question. 'What about you, Finn?'

'Irish, true and true,' he murmured.

The expression in his eyes was making her feel rather dizzy, and her throat felt so dry that she had to force her words out. 'So when is my guided tour going to begin?'

'Right now.' He held the door of the car open, his hand briefly brushing against her bare forearm as he helped her out, feeling the shivering tension in response to the brief contact. Instinctive, he thought, and found his mind playing out wicked and tantalising scenes, wondering if she was an instinctive lover, if she gave and received pleasure in equal measure.

Through the backdrop of mountains she saw low streams with stepping-stone rocks, and Celtic crosses which were really burial stones. She stared hard at the primitive carvings.

'You don't like graves?' he quizzed, watching her reaction.

'Who does?' But the question still lay glinting in the depths of his blue eyes and she answered truthfully, even though it sounded a little fanciful. 'I guess that looking at them makes you realise just how short life is.'

'Yes. Very short.' And if his life were to end in the next ten minutes, how would he like to spend it? He stared at the lush folds of her lips and longed to feel them tremble beneath the hard, seeking outline of his. 'Let's walk for a while,' he said abruptly.

They walked until Catherine's legs ached, and she thought what a wimp living in a city had made her. Which just went to show that the machines at the gym were no substitute for honest-to-goodness exercise! 'Can we stop for a moment?' she asked breathlessly.

'Sure.'

They sat side by side on a large black rock in companionable silence and then he took her to a simple greystone building where refectory tables were laid out and lots of students sat drinking tea and eating big, buttered slices of what looked like fruitcake. It wasn't what she had been expecting.

'Ever eaten Champ?' he enquired, as they sat down.

She shook her head. 'What is it?' she asked.

'Potato.'

'Just potato?' She threw her head back and laughed. So much for eating out with a millionaire! 'You're giving me potato?'

He gave a slow smile. 'Well, no—there's chopped

shallots added, and it's served in a mound, and you melt a great big lump of butter in the centre. Try some.'

It was pure nursery food—warm and comforting, with a golden puddle of butter seeping into the creamy mashed potato.

'It's good,' said Catherine, as she dipped her fork into it.

'Isn't it?' Their eyes met in a long, unspoken moment. 'Where would the Irish be without the humble potato?'

'Where indeed?' she echoed, thinking how uncomplicated life felt, sitting here with him. For a moment all the stresses of Catherine's London life seemed like a half-remembered dream. There was a sense of timelessness in this place which seemed to give her a sense of being of this world and yet not of it.

And Finn seemed timeless, too—his clever eyes watching her, the tension in his body hinting at things she would prefer not to think about. Their mouths were making words which passed for conversation, but seemed so at odds with the unspoken interaction which was taking place between them.

After she had drunk a cup of tea as black as tar itself he leaned across the table towards her, smelling not of fancy aftershave but of soap and the undeniable scent of virile male.

'Would you like to see the Wicklow Bay?' he asked softly.

If he'd promised to show her the end of the rainbow she would have agreed to it at that precise moment. 'Yes, please.'

They drove through countryside as green as all the songs said it was, until Finn drew to a halt next to a spectacular seascape and switched the engine off. 'Let's get out. You can't appreciate it properly from here.'

They stood in silence for a moment, watching and listening as the waves crashed down onto the beach.

'There,' he murmured. 'What do you think to that?'

She thought of the view from her bedroom window back in Clerkenwell and how this paled in comparison. 'Oh, it's stunning!'

'But not a patch on Greece?'

She shook her head. 'On the contrary—it's just as beautiful. But wilder. More elemental.' Just like him, she thought, stealing a glance at him.

He stood like an immovable figurehead as he gazed out to sea, the wind whipping his black hair into dark little tendrils. He turned to look at her and something in the uninhibited pleasure in her eyes quite took his breath away.

'So, do you have a sense of adventure, Catherine?' he murmured.

'Why do you ask?'

'I'll guess you haven't been in the sea since your holiday?'

'Well, no. There isn't a lot of it in London!'

'And you know what they say about getting straight back on a horse after it's thrown you?'

'Just what are you suggesting, Finn?'

His eyes burned into her.

'Shall we let the waves catch us between the toes as we sink into the sand?' he asked, in a lilting voice. 'Take our shoes off and walk on the edge?'

It sounded unspeakably sensual, and unbelievably echoed the way she was feeling right then. On the edge. Yes. But the edge of what she didn't know.

'And you call *that* being adventurous?' she teased, because at least that way she could disguise the sudden helplessness she was experiencing. 'What a boring life you must have led!'

And she kicked off her sandals and took them in her hand, leaving her legs bare and brown as she looked at him with a touch of defiance. 'Come on, then! What are you waiting for?'

He was waiting for the ache in his groin to subside, but he gave a wry smile as he bent to roll his jeans up, wondering how she would react if he said what was *really* on his mind. That she might like to slip that dress right off, and her bra and panties, too, and go skinny-dipping with him and let him make love to her in the icy water? God, yes! Now that really *would* be adventurous!

Then he drew himself up, appalled. He didn't have sex in public with women he barely knew!

She ran ahead of him, wanting to break the sudden tight tension, and the sea was icy enough to achieve that. 'Yeow!' she squealed, as frothy white waves sucked up between her toes and rocked her. 'I'm going back!'

'*Now* who's the unadventurous one?' He held out his hand to her. 'Here.'

Feeling suddenly shy, she took it as trustingly as a child would, safe and secure in that strong, warm grasp. But a child would not have had a skittering heart and a dry mouth and a fizzing, almost unbearable excitement churning away inside her, surely?

'Blowing the cobwebs away?' he asked, as they re-traced their steps.

'Blown away,' she answered. And so was she. Completely.

Her hand was still in his, and he guessed that to the

eyes of an outsider they would look like a pair of lovers, killing time beautifully before bed.

He moved fractionally closer and whispered into her ear, as if afraid that the words might be lost on the wind. His whole world seemed to hinge on his next question and what her response to it would be. 'Would you like to see where I live, Catherine?'

She jerked her head back, startled. 'What. Now?'

He had not planned to say it. He kept his home territory notoriously private, like a jungle cat protecting its lair. In fact, he had thought no further than a scenic trip to Glendalough. But something about her had got beneath his skin.

He raised his eyebrows at her questioningly. 'Why not?' He looked at the goosebumps on her bare legs and arms and suppressed a small shiver as the tension began to build and mount in his body. 'You're cold. You look like you could do with some warming up.'

Catherine supposed that the drawled suggestion could have sounded like a variation on Come up and see my etchings, but somehow the rich, Irish brogue made it sound like the most wonderful invitation she'd ever heard.

He was right—she *was* cold. And something else, too. She was slowly fizzing with a sense of expectation and excitement—her nerve-endings raw and on fire with it.

Not the way that Catherine Walker normally behaved, but—so what? Surely it was just natural and acceptable curiosity to want to see his home? At least, that was what she told herself as she heard herself replying, 'Yes, I'd like that, Finn. I'd like that very much.'

CHAPTER FIVE

'SO THIS IS where you live, is it?' asked Catherine, rather stupidly stating the obvious and wondering if she sounded as nervous as she suddenly felt.

What was she doing here, alone in a strange flat with this gorgeous black-haired and blue-eyed Irishman? Setting herself up for some kind of seduction scene? Waiting for Finn to put his arms around her and kiss her? To discover whether that kiss would really be as wonderful as she'd spent far too much time imagining?

And isn't that what you really want? questioned a rogue voice inside her head. Isn't that why your heart is pumping in your chest and your cheeks are on fire, even though you're supposedly cold?

Finn smiled. 'I bought it for the view.' But he wasn't looking out of the window.

'I can see why.' She swallowed, tearing her eyes away from that piercing sapphire gaze with difficulty.

The lit-up Georgian buildings in the square outside predominated, but she could see the sparkle of the Liffey, too, reflecting the darkening sky and the first faint gleam of the moon.

'Shall I make you something warm to drink?' he questioned softly.

She smiled. 'The cold's all gone.'

The walls of his huge flat seemed to be closing in

on him, and he knew that if he didn't move he might do something both of them would regret. 'Then come outside, onto the terrace—you can see for miles.' He unlocked a door which led out onto a plant-filled balcony. 'The moon is huge tonight. Big as a golden dinner-plate and fit for a king.'

She thought how Irishmen had the ability to speak romantically without it detracting one iota from their masculinity. And he hadn't lied about the moon. It dazzled down on them. 'It looks close enough to touch,' whispered Catherine.

'Yes.' And so did she.

She forced herself to look at the pinpricks of silver stars, to listen to the muted sound of the city, knowing all the while that his eyes were on her, and eventually she turned to face the silent, brooding figure.

'It's lovely,' she said lamely.

'Yes.' He narrowed his eyes as he saw her shiver. 'You're cold again?'

'Yes. No. Not really.'

'Coffee,' he said emphatically. But he could see the tremble of her lips, and the tension which had slowly been building up inside him suddenly spilt over into the realisation that he could no more walk out into his kitchen and make her some coffee than he could resist what he was about to do next. 'But it's not coffee you want, is it, Catherine?' he questioned, and pulled her gently into his arms. 'Is it?'

Her world spun out of focus and then clicked back into perfection. 'Finn!' she said breathlessly. 'Wh-what do you think you're doing?'

He laughed softly at the predictable question, noting in a last moment of sanity that there was no reproach in it. 'Just this. What you want me to do. What those big green eyes of yours have been asking me to do from the moment I met you.' And he lowered his mouth, brushing his lips against the sudden wild tremble of hers.

She swayed against him, opening her mouth to his and feeling as though she had been born for this kiss, thinking that nothing had ever felt quite like this—not even with Peter.

Is this what all the books and magazines write about? she wondered dazedly. Is this why *Pizazz!* has such a massive and growing readership?

'Oh, Finn. Finn Delaney,' she breathed against the warmth of his breath, and the kiss went on and on and on.

He lifted his mouth away by a fraction, seeing the look on her face and feeling pretty dazed himself. As though he had drunk a glass of champagne very quickly, and yet he had drunk nothing stronger than tea. 'You were born to be kissed, Catherine,' he observed unsteadily.

'Was I?' she questioned, with equally unsteady delight.

'Mmm.' He pulled a pin from her hair so that it tumbled free, black as the sky above them. 'To be made love to beneath the stars, with the light of the moon gilding your skin to pure gold.'

'I've never been made love to beneath the stars,' she admitted, without shyness.

He smiled as he took her hand, raised it to his lips, his eyes unreadable. 'It's too cold out here, but you can see them from my bedroom.'

She didn't remember making any assent, only that her hand was moved from his mouth to his hand and that he was leading her through the splendour of his Georgian flat into his bedroom.

'See,' he said softly, and pointed to the huge windows where outside the night sky dazzled.

'It's like the London Planetarium!' she said. 'You're very lucky.'

'Very,' he agreed, but both of them knew he wasn't talking about the stars. 'You're a long way away, Catherine.'

'A-am I?'

'Yes, indeed. Come here.'

She knew a moment's apprehension as she walked straight into his arms. And now she *could* see his eyes, and read the hectic glitter in their velvet blue. What in the world was she *doing*?

But by then he was sliding the zip of her dress down in one fluid movement, as if he had done such a thing many, many times before. And Catherine supposed that he had.

'I should feel shy,' she murmured.

'But you don't?'

'You've seen me with less on than this.'

But underwear was always a million times more decadent than a bikini, however brief. 'So I have,' he agreed thickly, as he surveyed her lace-clad body. 'Only this looks a whole lot better.'

He bent his head to touch his lips against the tip of one breast which strained impatiently against the flimsy lace of her brassière.

And Catherine closed her eyes, giving herself up to sensation instead of thought. A soft, sweet aching overwhelmed and startled her, and she wound her arms tightly around his neck, as if afraid that he might suddenly disappear. As if this—and him—might be all some figment of a fevered longing. 'Oh, Finn,' she sighed.

He lifted his head and looked at her questioningly. 'Should we be doing this?' Her green eyes opened very wide.

He felt like saying that this was something she should have asked herself earlier than now, that his body was growing unbearably hard.

'That's up to you, sweetheart.' His mouth immediately stopped grazing the long line of her neck, the restraint nearly killing him. 'It's make-your-mind-up time. Stop me if that's what you want.'

Was he aware that he was asking the impossible?

'Do you want to?' he murmured.

'God, no. No,' she breathed. A thousand times no. She moved her mouth to rove over the rough shadow of his chin, her hands on the broad bank of his shoulders for support, her knees threatening to buckle.

He gave a low, uneven laugh as the moonlight shafted through the window and illuminated the ebony strands of her hair. Her undisguised need only fuelled him further, and he gave in to the overwhelming desire to possess her. His hand reached round to snap open her brassière, as though they were old and familiar lovers, and she clung to him wearing nothing but a tiny little thong.

'I want to make love to you, Catherine,' he said urgently.

She didn't reply, just burrowed her hands beneath his sweater, finding the silken skin there, her fingernails tracing faint lines against it, hearing him suck in a ragged breath.

'I want to make love to you,' he repeated. 'Come to bed.' He didn't wait for an answer, just led her over to the king-sized canopied bed and pulled back the cover.

'Get in, sweetheart,' he instructed shakily. 'You're shivering.'

Shivering? She felt in a fever of need, was glad to slip beneath the duvet—glad for its protection and for the opportunity to watch him throw his clothes carelessly to the floor, until he was completely and powerfully naked. All golden skin and dark shadows and hewn, strong limbs.

'Move over,' he whispered as he climbed in beside her, encountering the soft folds of her flesh, and he moved to lie over her. 'No, on second thoughts,' he drawled as the warmth of her body met his, 'stay exactly where you are.'

'Are you asleep?'

Finn opened his eyes. No, he hadn't been asleep. He had been lying there, alternating between revelling in the sated exhaustion of his flesh and wondering what the hell he had done. 'Not any more.' He yawned.

'Did I wake you?' She wondered if that sounded defensive, and then swiftly made up her mind that she was not going to lie around analysing what had happened. He had made love to her and she had enjoyed it. More than enjoyed it. End of story in this modern age. Not well-thought-out, not necessarily wise, but it had happened, and there was no point in trying to turn the clock back and regret it.

Finn smiled, his reservations banished by the sight of her wide green eyes and the dark, dark hair which tumbled down in disarray over her lush, rose-tipped breasts. He gave a rueful glance down at his already stirring body. 'Kind of.'

Catherine swallowed as she saw the involuntary movement beneath the thin sheet and felt an answering rush of a warmth. Oh, God! How did he make her feel the way he did? And then she looked at him, every glorious pore of him, and the answer was there, before her eyes.

To her horror she found herself asking the worst question since the beginning of time. 'So how come you've never married, Finn?'

He repressed a sigh. Silent acquiescence was what his chauvinistic heart most longed for. He reached and pulled her down against his bare chest. 'Is that a proposal?' he teased. 'Because surely it's a little early for that kind of thing?'

She felt her breasts pressing against him, but suddenly she wanted more than this. She had spent the night making love to him. She knew his body. But what did she know of the man himself? He might have made her cry out his name time and time again, but a girl had her pride.

'Are you always so evasive?' she teased.

'I am when my mind is on other things. Like now.'

'Finn!'

'Mmm?'

He was stroking her bottom now, running the flat of his hand over it with the appreciation that a horse-lover might give to a particularly prize filly. And though her mind began to form a protest it was too late, because he had slid his fingers right inside her still-sticky warmth.

Her eyes opened very wide. 'Finn!' she said again, only she could hear the helpless pleasure in her own voice.

'What?'

'Stop it.'

'You don't want me to stop it.'

'Yes, I do!'

'Then why are you moving your hips like that?' he purred suggestively as his fingers continued to stroke and play with her.

'You know damned well why!' she moaned, feeling the sweet tension building, building.

'Still want me to stop?' He stilled his hand and looked at her half-closed eyes and parted lips.

She shook her head wildly. 'No!' she whimpered, and just the renewed touch of him was enough to make her splinter into a thousand ecstatic pieces.

He thrust into her warm, still-tight flesh, the sensation nearly blowing his mind, and his last thought before the earth spun on its axis was that nothing had ever felt this good. Nothing. He felt the violent beckoning of sweet release just as he heard her give another choked moan of disbelief, and then his blood thundered and he moaned.

She rolled off his sweat-sheened body and collapsed on the bed beside him. It took a moment for her breath to return to anything approaching normality. 'Wow,' she said eventually.

'Wow, indeed,' he echoed drily. But he felt shaken. Was it simply *because* they were virtual strangers that their lovemaking had been the best of his life? He stared sightlessly at the ceiling.

And now what? Catherine dozed for a moment or two, then opened her eyes again. 'I guess I'd better think about going.' She held her breath almost imperceptibly, wondering whether he would beg her to stay. She gave a half-smile. No, not beg. Men like Finn Delaney didn't beg—didn't ever *need* to beg, she would hazard.

'Must you?' he questioned idly.

Well, there she had it in a nutshell. He wasn't exactly

kicking her out of bed, but neither was he working out a busy timetable for the rest of the day.

''Fraid so,' she fibbed. 'I have a plane to catch.'

'What time?'

'Five o'clock.'

He glanced at the wristwatch he had had neither the time nor the inclination to remove last night. 'It's only ten now.'

And?

'You'll have some breakfast first?' He turned onto his side and gave a slow smile. 'I make great eggs!'

He made great love, too. But she was damned if she was going to go through his thanks-very-much-for-the-memory routine. Dispatched with eggs and a shower, and perhaps another bout of uninhibited sex if she was lucky. Catherine Walker might have behaved recklessly last night, but at least she still had her pride.

And no way was she going to hang around like an abandoned puppy, desperate for affection!

'I'll skip,' she said casually, and slid her bare legs over the mattress. 'I never eat breakfast.'

'You should,' he reprimanded.

Perhaps she should. Like perhaps she should have thought twice about allowing herself to get into a situation like this.

'Coffee will be fine. Mind if I use the shower?'

'Of course not.'

How bizarre to be asking his permission for something like that when she had allowed him the total freedom of her body during that long and blissful night.

Had she just been feeling love-starved and rejected? she wondered as she stood beneath the steaming jets of water in his typically masculine bathroom. And how often did he entertain women in such a spontaneous and intimate way?

It was a one-off for *her*, sure—but maybe she was just one of a long line of willing women who were so easily turned on by his captivating blend of Irish charm and drop-dead sexuality.

Catherine repressed a shudder as she dried herself. She didn't want to know.

She came out of the bathroom looking as cool and as aloof as a mannequin, and Finn blinked. To look at her now you would never have believed that she could be such a little *wildcat* in bed. He felt another tug of desire and despaired.

Catherine picked up her bag and went over to where he was standing by the window, watching her with an unreadable expression. She wondered how many hearts he had broken in his time. Scores, undoubtedly—but hers would not be among them. She would extricate herself as gracefully and as graciously as possible.

'What about coffee?' He frowned.

She shook her head. She would not cling. Last night had just happened; she must put it down to experience. And at least, she thought wryly, at least it had got Peter well and truly out of her system. 'I'll get some back at my hotel.' She gave him what she hoped was a cool, calm smile. 'Thanks for a great evening, Finn.' She raised herself up on tiptoe to kiss his cheek. 'A great night, I should say,' she added, braving it out.

'The pleasure was all mine,' he murmured.

Ruthlessly, she eradicated any trace of awkwardness or vulnerability from her voice, but it wasn't easy—not when confronted by the glittering blue eyes which reminded her of things which were making her pulses race. Even now. 'Bye, then.'

Once again her coolness intrigued him, particularly in view of what had happened—she was behaving as though she had just been introduced to him at a formal drinks party! Maybe she was trying to slow the pace down, and in view of the speed with which things had happened wasn't that the best thing to do under the circumstances? So why did he want to drag her straight back to bed?

He was just about to suggest running her back to her hotel when the telephone began to ring. He gave a small click of irritation.

'Answer it,' she urged, as this evidence of a life of which she knew nothing drove reality home. She was eager now to make her escape, to put it all down to a wonderful never-to-be-repeated experience.

'Don't worry, it's on the Ansaphone—'

It was also echoing out over the flat, and after his drawled and lilting message came the sound of a female voice. 'Finn, it's Aisling—where the hell were *you* last night?'

He leaned over and clicked off the machine, but by then Catherine was by the door, her features closed and shuttered.

'Look me up if ever you're in London,' she said, and walked out without a backward glance. She wondered who Aisling was, and where he was supposed to have been last night, before telling herself that her behaviour guaranteed nothing other than a night to remember—certainly not the right to question him.

Finn stood staring after her for a long, indefinable moment as the sound of the lift outside whirred into action, taking her out of his life just as quickly as she had burst into it.

And it occurred to him that he didn't have a clue where she lived.

CHAPTER SIX

CATHERINE SPENT the whole evening pacing the flat, tempted to smoke a cigarette—which she hadn't done in almost three years now. She kept telling herself that it had been out of character. True. Telling herself that it had been a terrible, terrible mistake. But unfortunately the jury was still out on that one.

Because the mind could play all kinds of tricks on you, and at the moment her mind seemed very fond of sending tantalising images of black hair, a bare, bronzed body and a pair of beautiful, glittering blue eyes. Images which kicked her conscience into touch.

She didn't want to think about him! Not when there was no future in it—and there was definitely no future in it. He hadn't exactly been distraught at the thought of her leaving, had he? Demanding to know her phone number and asking when he could fly out to London to see her?

But what did she expect? The pay-off for acting on instinct rather than reason was never going to be love and respect.

She forced herself to go through her photo albums and look at pictures of her and Peter, but instead of pain ripping through her there was merely a kind of horrified acceptance that Finn had been able to transport her to realms of fantasy which Peter never had.

So what did that say about their long-standing relationship? More importantly, what did it say about *her*?

She had only just sat down at her desk on Monday when there was a telephone call from Miranda.

'Can you get up here right now, Catherine? I want to talk to you about Dublin.'

'Sure,' answered Catherine, in a voice which was made calm only by sheer effort of will. 'I've written the piece.'

'Never mind about that,' Miranda answered mysteriously. 'Just get your butt up here!'

There was a quivering air of expectancy and excitement on the editor's face.

'Did you meet him?'

'Who?'

'Who? *Who?* Finn Delaney, of course!'

'Oh, him,' answered Catherine with monumental calm, though inside her heart was crashing painfully against her ribcage. She wondered what Miranda would say if she told her that she had spent most of her time in Dublin being made love to by Finn Delaney. Not a lot, most probably. Miranda had been a journalist for long enough not to be shocked by *anything*. Her throat felt too dry for her to be able to speak, but she managed. 'Er, yes, I saw him. Why?'

'And did he seem interested in you? I mean, like, *really* interested in you?'

It wasn't just the odd way that the last question was phrased, or that it was mildly inappropriate. No, something in Miranda's tone alerted Catherine to the fact that this was not simply idle curiosity, and she felt the first whispering of foreboding. She played for time. 'Interested in what way, exactly?'

Miranda snorted. 'Don't be so dense, Catherine—it doesn't suit you! Sexually. Romantically. Whatever you like to call it.'

'No comment.' But Catherine gave it away with the deep blush which darkened her cheeks.

Miranda looked even more excited. Everyone in the business knew what 'no comment' meant and immediately Catherine could have kicked herself for saying it. It implied guilt, and guilt was pretty close to what she was feeling.

'So he was?' observed Miranda.

'No!'

'I'd recognise that look on a woman's face anywhere—'

'What look?' asked Catherine, alarmed.

'That cat-got-the-cream look. The kind of look which speaks volumes about just how you spent your weekend!'

'Just leave it, Miranda, won't you?' Suddenly Catherine was feeling flustered, out of her depth. Her boss was the last person to make a value judgement about her behaviour, but what about the way she was judging *herself*? 'I don't want to talk about it!'

'Well, let me show you something,' said Miranda slowly, and picked up a clutch of photos which were lying on her desk, 'which might just change your mind.'

'If it's photos of Finn, you've already shown me—remember? I know he's loaded, and I know he's powerful and the next-best thing to sliced bread, but if you're looking for a kiss-and-tell story then you're wasting your time, Miranda.'

'No—look,' said Miranda with unusual brevity, and handed her one of the photos.

Catherine stared at it, and her blood ran cold as time seemed to suspend itself.

For it was like looking into a mirror. Seeing herself, only not quite seeing herself. The same and yet remarkably different. She blinked. The woman in the photo had jet-black hair and huge green eyes, and a certain resemblance around the mouth, but there the similarities ended.

It was like comparing a piece of crude mineral deposit to the finished, highly polished diamond it would one day become.

Because the woman in the photo had all the pampered glamour of someone who spent absolute riches on herself. Someone who indulged, and indulged, and indulged.

'Who is this?' breathed Catherine.

'Deirdra O'Shea,' said Miranda instantly. 'Heard of her?'

'N-no.'

'Bit before your time, I guess—though I'd only vaguely heard of her myself. She's Irish—well, the name speaks for itself, doesn't it?—starred in a couple of forgettable films about ten years ago and has been living in Hollywood trying to make it big ever since but never quite managing it. She's your spitting image, isn't she?'

Something close to fear was making breathing suddenly very difficult. 'Why are you bothering to show me this?'

Miranda shrugged, and thrust another photo into Catherine's frozen fingers. 'Just that she was Finn Delaney's sweetheart.'

It was a curiously old-fashioned word to use, especially about a man like Finn, and it hurt Catherine more than it had any right to. 'What do you mean, his *sweetheart*?'

'He was smitten, apparently—completely and utterly smitten. They met before either of them had really made it—and you know what that kind of love is like. Fierce and elemental. Love without the trappings.' Miranda sighed, sounding for a moment almost wistful. 'The real thing.'

'I still don't understand what this has got to do with me!' said Catherine crossly, but she was beginning to get a very good idea.

'He's a notoriously private man, right?'

Catherine shrugged. 'Apparently.'

'Yet he meets you on a Greek island and tells you to look him up.'

'Lots of people do things like that on holiday.'

'And you fly out there and have some kind of red-hot weekend with him—'

'I didn't say that!'

'You didn't have to, Catherine—like I said, I can read it all over your face.' Miranda paused. 'Are you seeing him again?'

Now she felt worse than reckless—she felt stupid, too. 'I—hadn't—planned to.'

'He didn't ask you?'

No, he hadn't asked her. The truth slammed home like a blunt fist and defensiveness seemed her only rational form of protection. 'Miranda—what the hell is this all about? Some kind of Spanish Inquisition?'

'All I'm saying is that if he used you as some kind of substitute for the woman who broke his heart—'

Catherine opened her mouth to say that it wasn't like that. But what *had* it been like, then? He hadn't struck her as the kind of man who would normally make mad, passionate love to a complete stranger. A notoriously private man...

So what could have been his motivation?

She, at least, could blame her reeling emotions on having been dropped by Peter. But—dear God—had Finn Delaney spent the whole time imagining that she was *someone else*?

Her ego, already severely punctured, underwent a complete deflation.

When he'd told her she was beautiful, and how it was a crime against society for a body like hers to be seen wearing any clothes at all, had he been thinking about Deirdra? When he'd driven deep inside her, had he been pretending that it was another woman's soft flesh he was penetrating?

Inwardly she crumpled as she realised just what she had done. But most of all what *he* had done. He had used his Irish charm in the most manipulative and calculating way imaginable. He had guided her into his bed with all the ease of a consummate seducer, had made love to her and then let her walk out of his flat without a care in the world.

He hadn't even asked for her phone number, she remembered bitterly.

She came out of her painful little reverie to find Miranda's eyes fixed on her thoughtfully—with something approaching kindness in them. And Catherine was badly in need of a little kindness right then.

'Why don't you tell me all about it?' Miranda suggested softly.

Maybe if she'd eaten breakfast, or maybe if her body hadn't still been aching with the sweet memories of his lovemaking which now seemed to mock and wound her, then Catherine might have given a more thoughtful and considered response.

But memories of betrayal—her mother's and now her own—fused into a blurred, salty haze before her eyes, and she nodded, biting her lips to prevent her voice from disintegrating into helpless sobs.

'Oh, Miranda!' she gulped. 'I've been so stupid.'

'Do you want to tell me what happened?'

She needed to tell *someone* about it. To unload her guilt. To make some kind of sense of it all. She shook her head. 'There's nothing to tell.'

'Try me.'

Distractedly, Catherine began voicing her thoughts out loud. 'Maybe it was a reaction to Peter—I *don't know*—I just know that I behaved in a way which was completely alien to me!'

'You slept with him?'

Catherine nodded. She supposed that was one way of putting it. 'Yes, I slept with him! I fell into his arms like the ripest plum on the tree. I spent the night with him. Me! *Me!* I still can't believe it!' Her voice rose in disbelief. 'I went out with Peter for three years and never even *looked* at another man.' But then, no man like Finn Delaney had come along for her to look at, had he? 'And before that there was only one significant other. I was too busy building up my career to be interested in men. And I've certainly never—*never*—been quite so free and easy. Not even with Peter.'

Especially not with Peter. Quite the opposite, in fact. Peter had been surprised that she had held out so long before letting them get intimate. He'd said it was a refreshing change to find a woman who played hard to get. But it hadn't been a game—it had been a necessity. Born out of a need for self-respect which her mother had drummed into her and a desire to have him respect *her*.

Which made her wonder what Finn Delaney must be thinking about her now.

'Maybe he has something special—this Finn Delaney.'

'Oh, he has something *special* all right!' burst out Catherine. 'Bucketfuls of charm and sex-appeal—and the ability to pitch it at just the right level to make himself irresistible to women!'

Miranda, not normally given to looking fazed, raised her eyebrows. 'That's some testimony, Catherine,' she murmured. 'I take it that he was a good lover?'

'The best,' said Catherine, before she had time to think about it. And with those two words she seemed to have managed to invalidate everything she had had with Peter, too. 'He was unbelievable.'

There was a long silence.

'You'll get over it,' said Miranda at last.

Catherine raised a defiant face, but her green eyes were full of a tell-tale glittering. 'I'll have to,' she said staunchly. 'I don't have any choice, do I?'

His face almost obscured by the creamy bloom of flowers and dark green foliage, Finn narrowed his eyes as he surveyed the names next to the doorbells.

Walker. Flat 3. He shifted the flowers onto one shoulder, as if he was winding a baby, and jammed his thumb on the bell.

Inside the flat, the bell pealed, and Catherine frowned, then stifled a small groan. Bad that someone should call unannounced after this week when she had lost almost everything. What had remained of her self-respect. Her pride. And now her job.

Miranda hadn't even had the grace to look ashamed when Catherine had marched straight into her office and slammed the latest copy of *Pizazz!* on her desk.

'What the hell is *this* supposed to mean, Miranda?' she demanded.

Miranda's face was a picture of unconvincing innocence. 'You don't like the piece? I thought we did Dublin justice.'

'I'm not talking about the piece on Dublin and you know it, Miranda!'

'Yes.' Miranda's face turned into one of editorial defiance. 'The story was too good not to tell.'

'But there *was* no story, Miranda!' protested Catherine. 'You know there wasn't.' Except that there was. Of course there was. And it was the oldest trick in the journalist's book. Being creative with the facts.

The only facts that Miranda had gleaned from Catherine were that she had spent a wild night with Finn Delaney and that he had not asked to see her again. Miranda had discovered for herself that Catherine looked uncannily like an ex-lover of his, and from this had mushroomed a stomach-churningly awful piece all about Finn Delaney underneath Catherine's article on Dublin.

It described him as an 'unbelievable' lover, and hinted that his sexual appetite was as gargantuan as his appetite for success. It described the view from his bedroom in loving detail—and she didn't even remember telling Miranda about *that*! It did not actually come out and name Catherine as having been the recipient of his sexual favours, but it didn't need to. Catherine knew. And a few others had guessed.

But the person she had been astonished not to hear from was Finn Delaney—and she thanked God for the silence from that quarter, and the fact that *Pizazz!* didn't have a big circulation across the water.

'You deceived me, Miranda,' she told her editor quietly. 'You've threatened my journalistic integrity! I should bloody well go to the Press Complaints Commission—and so will Finn Delaney if he ever reads it and if he has an ounce of sense!'

'But it was in the public interest!' crowed Miranda triumphantly. 'A man who could be running a country—it's our *duty* to inform our readers what he's really like!'

'You don't have a clue what he's really like!' stormed Catherine. Though neither, in truth, did she. 'You've just succeeded in making him sound like some kind of vacuous stud with his brain stuffed down the front of his trousers!'

And with that Catherine had flung down her letter of resignation and stomped out of the office into an unknown future, her stomach sinking as she told herself that she could always go freelance.

The doorbell rang again.

Now, who the hell was bothering her at this hour in the morning? At nine o'clock on a Saturday morning most people were in bed, surely?

'Hello?' she said into the intercom, in a go-away kind of voice.

Downstairs, the petals of the scented flowers brushing against his cheek, Finn felt the slow build-up of tension. He had tried to pick a time when she would be in and it seemed that he had struck lucky.

His eyes glittered. He wanted to surprise her.

'Catherine?'

A maelstrom of emotions swirled around like a whirlpool in her befuddled brain as that single word instantly gave her the identity of her caller. But of course it would. She would recognise that rich Irish brogue from a hundred miles away, even if her guilty conscience hadn't been fighting a war with a suddenly stirring body.

Finn?

Finn?

Here?

He must have seen the article!

A fit of nerves assailed her. Catherine pressed her forehead against the door and closed her eyes. Oh, why the hell had she answered the wretched door in the first place? He knew now that she was here, and short of ignoring it and hoping he might go away…

She opened her eyes. Tried to imagine him shrugging those broad, powerful shoulders and just quietly leaving and failed miserably. She was trapped.

Presumably Finn Delaney had come here to wipe the floor with her. To tell her exactly what he thought of women who blabbed their tacky stories to middle-of-the-road magazines.

'Catherine?'

She tried to work out if he sounded furiously angry or just quietly seething, but the rich, lilting voice sounded nothing more than deeply irresistible.

'C-come up, Finn,' she suggested falteringly.

The words stayed in his mind as he rode up in the lift, and an odd sort of smile twisted his lips. Of course everything she said would drip with sexual innuendo—because it sure as hell was pretty much all they had really shared.

Sex.

But still he felt the unwilling burn of excitement just thinking about it.

Catherine had enough time to zip round her mouth with her electric toothbrush and then drag a comb through her long, mussed-up hair. The over-sized tee shirt which fell to an unflattering length at mid-knee she would just have to live with.

She cast a despairing glance in the mirror. At least she couldn't be accused of being a *femme fatale*.

Then her face paled as she heard the lift door open, and all flippancy fled as she remembered just why he was here. *Femme fatale,* indeed. As if he would look at her with anything but contempt after what had happened!

She opened the door before he had time to knock, and the first thing he thought was how pale her face looked without make-up. The second was that the baggy tee shirt did absolutely nothing to conceal the tight little buds of her nipples which thrust against the soft material. He felt himself harden.

'How lovely to see you!' she said brightly—which was true. Because he looked heart-stoppingly gorgeous in a pair of faded jeans and a sweater in a washed-out blue colour which made his eyes seem even more intense than usual. Her heart started crashing in her chest and she tensed in expectation, wondering how he was going to express himself.

Withering contempt? she wondered. Or blistering invective? But as she waited for the storm to rage over her, her pulse began to race in response to the confusing messages she was getting. He was carrying flowers. Strange, beautiful flowers, the like of which she had never seen before. With long white-green petals and dark leaves.

Flowers?

Finn gave a rueful shrug of his shoulders. 'Sorry. It's

a pretty unsociable hour to call, I know,' he murmured. 'And it looks like I just got you out of bed.'

She found herself blushing and hated herself for it. Why draw attention to a remembered intimacy which now seemed as false as a mirage? 'No, no—I've been awake for hours.' Which also was true; she certainly hadn't slept more than a couple of hours at a stretch since she had returned from her fateful trip to Dublin.

'Aren't you going to invite me in, Catherine?' His tone was as soft as the paw of a tiger moving stealthily through the jungle.

'You want to come in?' she questioned stupidly. Well, of course he did—no doubt a man of his status would object to a slanging match where the occupants of the nearby apartments were in danger of hearing!

He gave a half-smile. 'Is this how you usually react when lovers appear on your doorstep offering you flowers?'

He handed her the flowers but she barely registered their beauty—because all her attention had focused on that one hopeful word he had uttered.

Lovers.

That didn't sound past tense, did it? Which meant not one, but two things. That he couldn't possibly have read the article, and that possibly—just possibly—he wanted to carry on where they had left off in Ireland. But did *she*?

Of course she did! Just the sight of him was making her mind take flight into a flower-filled fantasy world where it was just her and Finn. Finn and her. Uttering a silent prayer of thanks, she swallowed down her excitement as she stared at the exotic blooms.

'They're for me?' she asked, even more stupidly.

He raised his eyebrows. 'Did you think I'd be so

insensitive as to turn up here carrying flowers for someone else?'

'I suppose not.' She smiled, hardly daring to acknowledge the growing pleasure which was slowly
warming her blood, so that she felt as if she was standing in front of a roaring fire. 'Come in,' she said, and
drew the door open. She thrust her nose into the forgotten blooms as the most delicious and beguiling scent
filled her nostrils. 'These are absolutely gorgeous,' she
breathed. 'Just gorgeous. And so unusual.' She turned
wide green eyes to his. 'What are they?'

His voice was careless. 'Mock orange blossom.'

'You mean as opposed to real orange blossom?' she
joked.

'Something like that.'

She'd never seen mock orange blossom on the stalls
of her local flower market, but perhaps Finn Delaney
had stopped to buy them in one of the more exclusive
department stores. She smiled again, not bothering to
hide her delight. 'I'll go and put them in water—please,
make yourself at home.' Did that sound too keen?
she wondered as she went off to the kitchen to find a
vase.

Oh, who cared? Wasn't a man who turned up on
your doorstep first thing on a Saturday morning bearing
flowers being more than a little keen himself?

Maybe he felt the same as she did, deep down. That
the time they had shared in Greece, and then in Dublin,
hinted at a promise too good to just let go.

Humming happily beneath her breath, she filled a
vase with water.

Finn prowled around the sitting room like a caged
tiger, noting the decor with the eye of a man used to
registering detail and analysing it.

The curtains were still drawn—soft gold things, through which the morning sun filtered, gilding the subdued light and giving the room a slightly surreal feel.

Lots of books, he noted. Run-of-the-mill furniture. Two fairly ordinary sofas transformed from the mundane by the addition of two exotic throws. A couple of framed prints and a collection of small china cats. Not enough to tell him anything much about the real Catherine Walker. His mouth flattened as she walked back into the room and deposited the flowers in the centre of a small pine coffee table. Their scent filled the room.

Now what? wondered Catherine. Were they going to carry on as if nothing had happened between them? 'Coffee?' she asked.

He shook his head and moved towards her, driven on by some primeval urge deep within him. His eyes were shuttered as he pulled her into his arms, feeling her soft flesh pliant against the hard lines of his body, which sprang into instant life in response. 'I haven't come here for coffee.'

She opened her mouth to protest that he might at least adhere to a *few* conventional social niceties before he moved in for the kill, but by then he had lowered his mouth onto hers, and she was so hungry for his kiss that she let him. How long had it been? Four weeks that felt like a lifetime…

'God, Finn—'

'What?' He cupped her breast with arrogant possession, liking the way that the nipple instantly reacted, pressing like a little rock against his hand.

To be in his arms once more was even better than she remembered, and the honeyed pleasure which was invading her senses was driving every thought out of her head other than the overriding one—which was how much she wanted this. Him.

'Mmm? You were saying?'

'W-was I? I can't remember.' Catherine's hands roved beneath the washed-out blue sweater, greedily alighting on the silken skin there. 'Oh, it's so good to see you.'

'And you, too. And this is certainly the kind of welcome I was hoping for.' His voice sounded thickened, slurred. He drew his mouth away from hers and his eyes were glittering with blue fire. 'My only objection is that I'm not seeing quite enough of you, Catherine. Don't you think it's time to remedy that situation?'

And with a single fluid movement he peeled the tee shirt off her body, over her head, and threw it to the ground, so that she was standing naked before him.

'Finn!' She felt the air cool her already heated body, but any consternation fled just as soon as he touched his lips to her nipple, and she began to shake as she clutched his dark head further against her breast. 'Oh, God!'

That shuddered cry of pure, undiluted desire fuelled his already overwhelming hunger, and he yanked his sweater over his head, kicked off his deck shoes, pulled roughly at the belt of his jeans and unzipped them. 'Take them off,' he commanded unsteadily.

On fire with her need for him, Catherine sank to her knees and slid the denim down over the hard, muscular shaft of his thighs, burying her head in the very cradle of his masculinity, her tongue flicking out to touch him where he was burningly hard. He groaned.

'Are you always like this?' he demanded, once the jeans were discarded, and he drew her down with an urgent need onto the carpet, their naked bodies colliding and merging with a mutual greed.

'Like what?' Hungrily she nipped at a hard brown nipple and he shuddered.

'So responsive.' So bloody easy to turn on, and so fiendishly good at turning *him* on until he thought he might explode with need.

Only with you, she thought, but that seemed too frighteningly vulnerable a thing to say. She licked instead.

He moved over her, his eyes burningly bright—a strange, shining combination of blue and black. In the heat of the moment his mind went blank and he forgot everything other than the sweet temptation of her flesh.

'God, Catherine, I want you so badly.' He slipped his hand between her thighs, where she was as wet as he had known she would be, and a wild kind of fever heated his blood. He moved and then groaned, then groaned again as he thrust into her, deep and hard and long, and she gave a low, exultant scream of pleasure.

'Is that good?' he ground out. 'Because—sweet God in heaven—it feels good to me!'

She gave herself up to the delicious rhythm, feeling control beginning to slip away.

'Is it, Catherine?' he urged, wanting to hear the surrender he could feel in her fast-shivering flesh. 'Is it good?'

Through dry lips she managed to say the very word she had said to Miranda. 'Unbelievable,' she groaned, as he filled her and moved inside her. 'Unbelievable.'

It happened so quickly, and her orgasm seemed to make Catherine's world explode. For a moment consciousness actually receded, and she was lost in a dreamy, perfect world of feeling and sensation, then it slowly ebbed back and reality was just as good. She smiled. That was if reality was lying naked in Finn's arms with the whole day—maybe even the weekend—ahead of them.

And this time they would do things other than make love. She could cook him lunch—had she got enough food to produce something impressive?—and then afterwards she could take him to the park. Maybe an early film, and then supper... Sooner rather than later she was going to have to come clean about her job, and very probably the mix-up about the article, but she could deal with that. She was certain she could...

'Mmm,' she breathed in anticipation. *'Mmm!'*

Her ecstatic response shattered his equilibrium and a sudden icy chill shivered its way over his bare flesh.

Finn withdrew from her and rolled away, and the physical deprivation of his presence made her whimper like a lost little animal.

'What are you doing?' she murmured sleepily, watching through half-slitted eyes the graceful, muscular body as he reached for his jeans.

'What does it look like? I'm getting dressed.'

He pulled the jeans back on and zipped them up before replying, and suddenly his face was shuttered. This was a new, hard Finn she didn't recognise, with a new, hard voice she didn't recognise either.

'Wh-where are you going?'

'I don't think that's really any of your business, do you?'

Catherine screwed up her eyes as she sat up, thinking that she must have misheard him—or that perhaps she had slipped unknowingly into a nightmare made uncannily real by his expressionless face. 'What?'

The movement which curved his lips was a bitter parody of a smile. 'Shall I repeat it for you in words of

one syllable, Catherine?' he questioned cruelly. 'I said
it's none of your business. Got that?' And he slipped his
feet into the deck shoes, jerked on the blue sweater.

Her mind was spinning as it strove to make sense
of this bizarre ending to what had just happened. Perhaps if she wasn't so befuddled by the aftermath of her
orgasm then she might have made sense of it sooner.
'Finn, I don't understand—'

'Oh, don't you?' His mouth twisted and the blue eyes
were as cold as ice. 'Then you can't be very good at
your job, can you? If you lack the ability to understand
the implication behind a simple sentence like that!'

The penny dropped. Her job, he had said. Yes,
of course. Her job—her wretched, wretched job!
Oh, God—he *had* seen the article! 'Finn, I want to
explain—'

'Oh, please—spare me your lies. Just don't
bother!'

Realising that she was completely naked, Catherine
grabbed at her tee shirt and wriggled it over her head as
she scrambled to her feet, aware of the movement of her
breasts and aware too that Finn wasn't oblivious to their
movement either. She turned to him with a face full of
appeal, and suddenly nothing was more important than
establishing the truth. 'You owe me the right to explain
what happened,' she said in a low voice.

'I owe you *nothing*!' he spat back, and the temper
which had been simmering away came boiling over,
words spilling out of his mouth without thought or care.
'In fact, quite the contrary—I felt that in view of the
fact I'd been paid nothing for an article about me which
I did not agree to, then I should take my payment *in
kind*!'

It took a moment or two for the meaning behind his

words to sink in, and when it did Catherine felt sick. Physically sick. And even worse was the look in his eyes...

So here was the look of blistering contempt she had been anticipating at the very beginning but had conveniently forgotten when he had given her flowers and put his arms around her. And it was even worse than in her most fevered imaginings...

She swallowed down the bitter taste in her mouth, barely able to believe what he was implying. 'Y-you mean...you mean...you came here today *deliberately* to have sex with me—'

'Sure,' he answered arrogantly. 'It wasn't difficult—but why should it be? It was as easy as pie the last time.'

She wanted to hit him, to shout, to scream at him—but still she forced herself to question him, because surely there was some kind of ghastly mistake. 'To get your own back for some stupid magazine article?' she finished faintly.

'"Some stupid magazine article"?' Two high lines of colour ran across his cheekbones, and his Irish accent seemed even more pronounced. 'It may be just some stupid article to you, sweetheart, but it has very effectively sent my credibility flying!'

'You mean that you wanted to look whiter than white because you hope to run for government?' she demanded.

'That has nothing to do with it!' His voice became a low hiss. 'Other people put labels on me that I do not seek for myself! I couldn't give a stuff about politics, but I *do* care what my friends and family read about me!'

And he fixed her with a look of such utter scorn that Catherine actually flinched.

Her own look matched his for scorn now. 'And the flowers? Such an elaborate masquerade, Finn,' she said bitterly. 'Did you really have to go to so much trouble to ensure my seduction? Did you think that your powers of persuasion were slipping?'

'I never doubted that for a minute, sweetheart,' he drawled, and then his eyes gleamed and his voice softened. 'No, the bouquet was to send you a silent message.'

She stared at him uncomprehendingly.

'Did you never hear of the language of flowers, Catherine?'

The question and the way he asked it were so close to the image of the poetic Irishman who had swept her off her feet that for a moment Catherine was lulled into imagining that the things he had said were not real.

She shook her head.

'Every flower carries its own message,' he continued softly.

'And the mock orange blossom?' she asked shakily. 'What does that stand for?'

'Can't you guess?' He paused, and raised his dark eyebrows. 'Not got it yet, Catherine? Deceit,' he said finally, with a cruel, hard smile.

She supposed that as a gesture it deserved some kind of accolade, but it felt like a knife being twisted over and over in her gut.

'Just tell me one thing,' he said, and his eyes were piercingly clear. 'When you came to Dublin did your editor send you? Was it just coincidence that brought you? Or did she tell you to get something on me?'

Catherine opened her mouth. 'Well, she told me to, yes. But—'

'But what? The article just wrote itself, did it?' he questioned witheringly.

She wanted to say, It wasn't like that! But she knew that no words in the dictionary could ever make things right between them now.

'Please go,' she said quietly.

But he was already by the door. 'Nothing would give me greater pleasure,' he grated.

And with that he was gone.

CHAPTER SEVEN

THE moment the door had shut behind him, Catherine snatched the flowers from out of the vase and took them to the kitchen sink, where she squashed them ruthlessly with a rolling pin, bashing and bashing at them until they were made pulp.

That should relieve some of her pent-up frustration, she thought, with a fleeting feeling of triumph which evaporated almost immediately. Except that she wasn't feeling frustrated—not in the physical sense, in any case. No, her frustration was born out of the random and cruel tricks of fate which had led her into this situation. The man whom she had fallen for, hook, line and sinker, would never trust her again.

But he didn't even give you a chance to explain yourself, she reminded herself bitterly—and in the heat of the moment she had forgotten to ask him about Deirdra O'Shea. Finn Delaney himself was no saint, she thought. And there had been a reason why she had been so indiscreet with Miranda.

Tears began to slide down her cheeks just as the telephone rang.

She snatched it up, despising herself for the eagerness which prompted her, thinking that maybe Finn had had a change of heart—was ringing her to apologise for his unbelievably cruel behaviour.

'H-hello?'

But it was her mother. 'Catherine? Are you all right?'

Catherine wiped the tears away with a bunched fist. 'Of course I'm all right, Mum.'

'Well, you don't sound it.' Her mother's voice sounded worried, but of course it would. Mothers were notoriously good at detecting when their daughters were crying, particularly when they were as close as Catherine and her mother. 'Have you been crying?'

'Not really.' Sniff.

'Not really?' Her mother's voice softened. 'Do you want to tell me about it?'

'I can't! You'll hate me for it!'

'Catherine, stop it. Tell me what's happened.'

Such was her distress that the story came tumbling out—or rather an edited version designed to cause the least hurt to her mother. Catherine did not mention that she barely knew the man, nor the shockingly short time scale involved. She just told her the simple truth of the matter, which was that she had leapt into a foolish and inconsidered relationship straight after Peter and that it was now over.

'Oh, Mum!' she wailed. 'How could I have done it?'

'You did it on the rebound,' her mother said firmly. 'Lots of people do. It isn't the end of the world! Just try to put it out of your mind and forget about it.'

'And I hadn't seen Peter for months and months!' Catherine found herself saying, which again was true. She didn't want her mother thinking that she was about to start taking lovers at the drop of a hat.

'I'm not making any value judgements, darling. I know the sort of person you are. I've never doubted you for a moment, and anyone who does needs their head examining!' she finished fiercely. 'Who is this man—is he married?'

Catherine heard the slightly raw tone. Even now her mother still hurt. She had had her own cross to bear. Loving a married man had brought with it nothing but pain and heartache. And a baby, of course. Mustn't forget the baby. For Catherine had been one of those fatherless children—a child who had never known her father. 'No, he's not married.'

'Thank God for that!'

'I shouldn't have worried you by telling you about it, Mum.'

'I'm more worried about the fact that you don't have a job any more,' her mother was saying. 'Any luck on the freelance front?'

'I haven't really been looking—'

'Well, better start, Catherine—you have to keep a roof over your head and food in your mouth and clothes on your back, remember?'

Oh, yes, she remembered all right. Independence had been another lesson drummed into her from an early age by a woman who had always had to fend for herself and bring up her child. Catherine's mother had initially been wary of her daughter's chosen career, seeing it as precarious—and for Catherine to now be freelance must be her idea of a nightmare.

'Oh, I'll find something—I've got plenty of contacts.'

'Why don't you come down this weekend? It'd be lovely to see you.'

Catherine hesitated, tempted. She couldn't think of anything nicer than to escape to her mother's tiny cottage, surrounded by fields and trees, with a distant peep of the sea. Under normal circumstances she would have been scooting straight out of the door to buy her ticket at the train station.

But these were not normal circumstances. No, indeed. Catherine cast a disgusted look down at her baggy tee shirt.

'No, Mum,' she replied. 'I have a heap of things to do here. Maybe next weekend.'

'All right, darling. You will take care of yourself, won't you?'

'Of course I will!'

Her mother's words came back to haunt her during the next few weeks as Catherine scouted around many publications angling for assignments. She had a mixed bag of luck. Some people knew her work and respected it, and were keen to hire her. But the market was full of freelance journalists—some of them talented and hungry and straight out of college—and Catherine knew that she was going to have to work very hard to keep up with the competition. Suddenly the staff job she had had at *Pizazz!* seemed terribly comfortable, and she wondered why she had bothered throwing it in.

As a defiant gesture it had been rather wasted. She had lost Finn anyway—though she reminded herself that he had never been hers to have.

And what else had her mother said?

'Take care of yourself.'

Had she known that the stress of everything that had happened would leave Catherine feeling distinctly peaky?

Stress had all kinds of insidious effects on the human body, she knew that as well as the next person. It played havoc with her appetite, for example. One minute she would be feeling so nauseous that just the thought of food would make her feel sick. The next she would be diving for the biscuit tin and thickly spreading yeast extract on a pile of digestive biscuits.

It wasn't until one afternoon when Sally—her best friend on *Pizazz!* and the only person she had kept in touch with from there—commented that she was putting on weight that Catherine's safe reality finally crumbled into dust.

She waited until Sally had gone and then shut the door behind her with a shaking hand. She went into the bathroom to stare at her white, haunted face with frightened eyes. Knowing deep down and yet denying it. Not wanting to know, nor daring to.

The thought that she might be pregnant simply hadn't occurred to her. But as she allowed the facts to assemble logically in her head she wondered how she could have been so stupid.

The next day she went through the rituals of confirmation, knowing that they were unnecessary, but until concrete proof confirmed her worst fears she might really be able to put it down to stress.

The blue line on the indicator was a fact. Just as was the faint tingling in her breasts. The missed periods. The nausea. The compulsive and compensatory eating. It all added up—and you wouldn't need to be Doctor of the Year to work out why.

Catherine sat back on her heels and took a deep breath, hugged her arms protectively around her heavy breasts.

Now what?

Her breathing short and shallow and low, she tried to flick her mind through her options. But nothing she thought of seemed to make any sense because it didn't seem real. It couldn't be real, could it?

She went into denial. Threw her energy into an article on pet cemeteries and spent days researching it. Managed to agree to an almighty fee for a piece on London's newest wannabe club and spent a queasy evening in a smoke-filled room regretting it.

She denied it all over Christmas by wearing baggy jumpers and telling her bemused mother that she was trying to 'cut down' when asked why she wasn't drinking.

And still the days ticked by—until one morning, after dashing to the bathroom to be sick, she gripped the washbasin with still-shaking hands and stared at her white-green reflection in the mirror.

She was pregnant with Finn Delaney's baby!

A man who despised her, a man she barely knew—a man, moreover, who had walked out of her life with the clear wish of never setting eyes on her again.

She was going to have a baby.

And with that one focused thought all her options and choices dissolved into one unassailable fact.

She was going to have a baby.

She booked an appointment with her doctor, who raised her eyebrows questioningly at Catherine when she'd finished her examination.

'Yes, you're pregnant, though you're fine—fit and healthy.' The doctor frowned. 'You really should have come to see me sooner, you know.'

'Yes, I know.'

The doctor appeared to choose her words delicately. 'And you're going to go ahead with the pregnancy? Because if you're not…'

Catherine didn't even have to think about it. Some

things you just knew, with a bone-deep certainty. She drew a deep breath, scared yet sure. Very, very sure. 'Oh, yes. Very definitely.'

The doctor nodded. 'How about the father? Will he be able to support you?'

Another pause. There was no doubt that he would be *able* to. But... 'I'm not expecting him to. We're not... together any more.' How was that for managing to make the truth sound respectable?

'But you'll tell him?'

Catherine sat back in her chair. 'I don't know.' She didn't feel she knew anything any more.

The doctor straightened the papers on her desk and looked at her. 'A man has a right to know, Catherine—I really believe that.'

Catherine walked back to her flat, scarcely noticing the light drizzle which slowly seeped into her skin and clothes. The doctor's question refused to go away. *Should* she tell him? Did he really have a right to know that he had fathered a baby?

She sat in the sitting room, nursing a cup of tea which grew cold and unnoticed, while the floor where she and Finn had made love seemed to mock her nearly as much as her idealistic thoughts.

Made love, indeed!

She might have been swept away with the passion of seeing him again, but Finn's seduction had been cold-blooded in thought, if not in deed.

And yet the responsibility was just as much his as hers, surely?

She could be proud and vow never to tell him that his child was growing inside her womb, but what of the child itself?

Was she going to subject him or her to a lifetime of

what she had had to endure? The terrible insecurity of not knowing who your father was? Of growing up with one vital half of the gene jigsaw missing? And with her having to nurse some terrible, pointless secret?

So did she pick up the telephone and tell him? Or write him a letter detailing the consequences of their moment of madness? She winced as she attempted to compose a clumsy paragraph inside her head. Impossible.

The sun began to dip in the sky and she put the cup of untouched tea down on the coffee table as tears began to slide down her cheeks. She angrily brushed them away, her heart aching for the new life inside her. Why should her baby suffer just because two adults had acted without thought?

She needed courage, more courage than she had ever needed before, because there was only one way to tell him something like this.

Face to face.

CHAPTER EIGHT

'I'M SENDING Miss Walker through, Finn.'

'Thanks, Sandra.' Finn flicked off the intercom and waited, sitting very still behind the huge desk as the door to his office opened and Catherine walked in, an indefinable expression in her green eyes. She wore a black velvet coat—a loose, swingy sort of thing—and with its contrast against her pale face and black hair she looked liked a beautiful sorceress.

'Come in, Catherine,' he said evenly, and rose to his feet. 'Shut the door behind you.'

As if she needed telling! As if she wanted his assistant to hear what she was about to say to him—and the ensuing discussion which would inevitably follow it. She shut it.

'Sit down, won't you?' He sat down himself and gestured to the chair opposite his, but Catherine shook her head.

'I'll stand, if you don't mind. I've been cooped up on a flight and in a cab,' she said. And although she knew that the flutterings in her stomach were due to nerves, and not the baby, she wasn't going to risk sitting in front of him and squirming. She met his gaze. 'I'm surprised that you agreed to see me.'

'I'm surprised that you want to.'

In his unmoving face only his blue eyes showed signs

of life. His features looked as cold and as motionless as if they had been hewn from rock as old as the stone of Glendalough, where he had taken her that day which now seemed an age ago. And it was. It had been a different Catherine who looked up and laughed into his eyes that day.

The Catherine who was here was on a mission. To give him the truth—a truth which she felt honour-bound to tell him. But wasn't it funny how you could practise saying something over and over again, yet when the opportunity came the words just wouldn't seem to come?

Finn watched her as he waited, thinking that somehow she looked different—and not just because her face was closed and wary and pale. No, there was something he couldn't quite put his finger on, something which alerted his sixth sense. The same sense which told him that a beautiful woman like Catherine Walker must have her pride. A pride which would have no time for a man who had acted as he had done. Yet she had phoned asking to speak to him. Personally and urgently.

'I'm all yours, Catherine,' he said, and then wished he hadn't, for the irony hadn't escaped him—nor her either, to judge from her brief, bitter smile.

No need to preface it with anything as humiliating as, Do you remember when we last met in London...? Such a distortion of the truth would only embarrass them.

'I'm pregnant,' she said baldly.

There was a long, long silence, but not a flicker of emotion crossed his face. 'I see.'

'It's yours!' she declared wildly, wanting to shatter the tense expectation in the air, to breathe some life into that unmoving face of his.

'Yes.'

Catherine stared at him, and delayed shock, together with his cold and monosyllabic reply, made her legs feel like water. She sank into the chair he had originally offered and stared at him with wide, uncomprehending eyes.

'You aren't going to deny it?'

'What would be the point? I can't imagine that I would be your first choice as father to your child. What we had between us hardly qualifies as the greatest love affair of all time, does it? So why would you lie about something as important as that? And if you aren't lying then the logical conclusion is that you must be telling the truth.'

It was a cold and analytical assessment and, oddly enough, seemed to hurt far more than if he had just lost his temper and flatly denied it—called her all names under the sun and told her to get out of his office and his life. For a start, it would have given her a let-out clause.

And it would have shown passion. Feelings. *Something* other than this cold and distant look in his eyes. As if he were a scientist surveying some rather odd-looking specimen in a test-tube. But then, what had she expected? 'You don't seem surprised,' she said heavily.

He shrugged. 'A simple case of cause and effect.'

'How very cynical, Finn.'

'Cynical, but true,' he mocked, then drew a deep breath as he thought back to that mad and tempestuous morning in her London flat. He gave a long and heavy sigh. 'That's what comes of forgetting to wear a condom, I suppose.'

Reduced to the lowest possible denominator.

Catherine flinched, as though he had hit her. And he might as well have hit her, the pain in her heart was so intense. She remembered the frantic way they had fallen to the floor, the wild hunger she had felt for him, and he, apparently, for her.

Yet he had come there that day with just such a seduction—if such a word could be used to describe something so basic—in mind. But he had not protected himself, and she had been too caught up in the mood and the magic—yes, magic—to notice.

She could deny it until she was blue in the face, but Finn Delaney had completely had her in his thrall. Then, and before. But now she saw the so-called magic for what it was—an illusion—like a trick of the light.

'Was your lack of care simply an omission on your part?' she questioned.

'What do you think?' he demanded. 'That I did it deliberately? That I somehow hoped for this particular little scenario?' His blue gaze bored into her. 'What was I *thinking*?' He gave a low, bitter laugh. 'That's the trouble, you see, Catherine—I wanted you so badly that I wasn't thinking at all.'

'A wanting fuelled by contempt,' she observed bitterly, noticing that he didn't deny it.

'And when is the—?'

His deep, musical Irish voice faltered just a little.

He stared down at the figures he had been working on, and she noticed that it was the first time he had let any emotion creep in.

He looked up again. 'When is the baby due?'

'They aren't sure.'

The blue gaze became more intense. Quizzical. Silently demanding some kind of explanation. And of course he was entitled to one. She was here, wasn't she?

She had foisted paternity on him and with that he had earned certain entitlements.

'I wasn't really sure about my dates myself, that's all. June—they think.'

'June.' He stared unseeingly out at the panoramic view from the window. 'So I'm to be a father some time in June?'

'Not necessarily.'

Now it was *his* turn to flinch, the dark-featured face looking both pained and quietly thunderous, and she realised that he had grossly misinterpreted her words.

'No, no, no!' she defended instantly. 'I didn't mean *that*. What I mean is that you don't have to have anything to do with this baby. Not if you don't want to.' He had not sought fatherhood, and therefore he should not be shackled by it.

'So why exactly are you here, Catherine?' He narrowed his eyes at her thoughtfully. 'Is it money you want?'

His mercenary judgement was like a slap to the face, and Catherine blanched as she shakily tried to rise to her feet. But there seemed to be no power to her legs. How much more hurt could he inflict on her?

'How dare you say that?' she hissed with an angry pride. 'You may be a big, powerful, rich businessman, but if you think I've come here today begging—*begging* for your largesse,' she repeated on a shuddering breath, 'then you are very much mistaken, Finn Delaney!'

'So just what *do* you want? A ring on your finger?'

'Hardly!' she contradicted witheringly. 'Strange as it may seem, I have no desire to tie myself to a man who thinks so badly of me that he believes I would treat my child as a commodity! Actually, I came here today to tell you about the baby simply because I felt that as an intelligent human being you would want to accept your share of responsibility for what has happened.'

'Catherine—'

'No!' Anger was giving her strength—beautiful, restorative strength. 'You've made your views perfectly clear. Don't worry, I won't be troubling you again!'

'I guess you could always sell your story to the highest bidder,' he said consideringly, and then ducked instinctively as something whizzed across the room.

Catherine had picked up the nearest object to her on his desk, which happened to be a large and very heavy paperweight, and it flew a foot wide of him and bounced deafeningly against the wall, bringing a marvellous landscape painting shattering down beside it, the glass breaking into a million shards.

The office door flew open and Sandra, his assistant, ran in, her eyes taking in the scene in front of her with disbelief. 'Oh, my God! Is everything all right, Finn?' she asked, her soft Irish accent rising in alarm. 'Would you have me call Security?' She stared at a white-faced and mutinous Catherine. 'Or the police?'

But Finn, astonishingly, was laughing—a low, gravelly laugh.

He shook his head. 'No, no—leave it, Sandra,' he said. 'Everything's fine. Miss Walker was just getting in a bit of target practice!'

'But unfortunately I missed!' said Catherine, her voice tinged with a slight hysteria. Her chair scraped back as she struggled to her feet.

'That will be all, thanks, Sandra,' said Finn quickly.

Sandra gave him one last, mystified stare before exiting the room and shutting the door behind her, just as Catherine reached it.

But Finn was quicker, beside her in a moment, where he caught hold of her shoulder. 'You're not going anywhere!'

'Let go of me!'

'No.' He moved her away from the door and whirled her round. He could see that she was very, very angry indeed. 'You could have killed me, you know,' he observed slowly.

'I wasn't aiming at you!' she snapped. 'But I wish to God I had!'

'What, and leave your child without a father?'

'You're not fit to be a father!'

He saw how distressingly white her face was and his whole manner altered. No matter what his feelings on the subject, the fact remained that she was pregnant. With his baby. And this kind of scene could surely not be doing her any good.

'Come and sit down and have some tea.'

'I don't want any tea! I want to go home!'

'To London? I think not. You're in no fit state to be flying back today. Not in your condition.'

It was that time-honoured phrase which did it. Which finally broke down the barriers she had tried to erect around her heart. *In your condition.* Someone should have been saying that to her with tender loving care. Preferably a husband who adored her, worshipped the ground she walked on, wanted to rub the small of her back and wait on her. Not a man who had had sex with her as some primitive kind of revenge and got so carried away with himself that he hadn't stopped to think about the consequences.

Though neither had she.

And instead she was about to replicate exactly what she had spent her whole life vowing not to do. Becoming a single mother, with all the emotional and financial hardship which went with that role.

She thought back to her own childhood. Her mother doing two and sometimes three jobs to make ends meet, so that Catherine should never feel different from the other children. Of course, she *had* felt different—some of the other children had made sure of that—but she had always been fed and clothed and loved and warm enough.

She had prayed that her mother would meet someone, but when eventually she had he had regarded Catherine as an encumbrance. Someone who was in the way and would always be in the way of his new wife and himself. He hadn't been outwardly horrible to her, but she had seen the hostility in his eyes sometimes, and it had frightened her.

Her mother must have seen it, too—for one day she had greeted Catherine at the school gates, a little pale and a little trembling, and told her that she was no longer going to marry Johnny. Catherine had laughed with delight and hugged her mother, and they had gone out and eaten tea and scones in a small café. His name had never been mentioned again.

How often had she hoped to repay her mother for her hard work and sacrifice by providing lavishly for her as she became older? Hadn't she dreamed of being one of the most snapped-up journalists in the land? Of maybe one day even writing a novel—a novel which would be a bestseller, naturally. She would buy her mother's cottage for her, make her old age secure.

Instead of which she must now go and destroy her mother's hopes and dreams for her. And her own, too.

She wanted to go away and just howl in some dark

and private corner, but she saw that Finn was effectively barring the door.

'Are you going to let me leave?'

'What do you think?'

She fixed him with an icy look. 'I could scream the place down—that would get "Security" up here in a flash—if they thought you were raping me!'

He opened his mouth to say something, but thought better of it. Now was not the time to make a cheap and clever remark. 'Sit down, Catherine.'

'No, I w-won't.'

'Sit *down*, will you, woman? Or do I have to pick you up and carry you?'

It was like a brand-new sapling trying to withstand the full force of a hurricane. Catherine gave a weary sigh. She could see that he meant business, and besides, sitting down was what she wanted to do more than anything else in the world. Though lying down would have been better. Much better.

She sat down in the chair and closed her eyes. 'Go away,' she mumbled. 'Leave me alone.'

'Your logic is failing you,' he said drily. 'This is *my* office, remember.' He flicked on the intercom again. 'Sandra, will you have us sent in some tea? Good, strong tea. Oh, and something to eat?'

'Cake, Finn? Your favourite chocolate?' purred Sandra.

'Something more substantial than cake,' he replied, with a swift, assessing look at Catherine's fined-down cheekbones. 'A big, thick sandwich with a bit of protein in the middle.'

'Did you not have your lunch, Finn?' giggled Sandra.

'*Now*, please, Sandra!' he snapped.

'Why, *certainly*!' his assistant replied, in a hurt and huffy voice.

His face was stern as he looked down at Catherine, who was still sitting in the chair with her eyes closed. 'Are you asleep?' he asked quietly.

'No. Just trying to block out the sight of your face!'

'And what if the baby looks like me?' he questioned. 'Won't that be a terrible problem?'

Catherine opened her eyes and steeled herself against the impact of his handsome, mocking features. 'I hope it's a girl,' she said frostily. 'Who looks as little like you as possible! And even if he or she *does* look like you—'

'Yes?'

'I'll still love them!' she declared fiercely. 'I may not have a lot to offer, but I can give this baby love, Finn Delaney! Now, are you please going to let me go? Or am I a prisoner here?'

He spoke using the soothing voice of a psychiatrist who was trying to placate an extremely mad patient. 'You're not going anywhere until you've calmed down.'

'Then get me as far away from you as possible— that's the only way to guarantee *that*!'

There was a light tap on the door. 'Come in, Sandra,' called Finn rather drily, noting how circumstances could change routine. Sandra never, ever knocked. But then he never, ever had women turning up at his headquarters hurling paperweights against the wall!

A frosty-looking Sandra deposited a loaded tray on the low table in one corner of the room.

'Will there be anything else, Finn?'

He shook his head. 'No—thanks, Sandra.'

'You're welcome.'

He couldn't miss the trace of sarcasm, but then maybe it wasn't so very surprising. Sandra had been with him for years, had seen him run his affairs with cool-headed acumen and detachment.

'Catherine?'

'What?'

'Do you take sugar?'

She almost laughed aloud at the irony of it all—until she remembered that it wasn't in the least bit funny. Her green eyes blazed with a kind of furious indignation, directed at him, but felt deeply by herself.

'What a funny old world it is, don't you think, Finn? Here I am carrying your baby, and you don't even know whether I take sugar in my tea! Or milk, either, for that matter!' she finished wildly, wondering if she could put these sudden, violent mood swings down to fluctuating hormones. Or the bizarre situation she found herself in.

'So, do you or don't you?' he questioned calmly. 'Have sugar?'

'Usually I don't, no! But for now I'll have two!' she declared, experiencing a sudden desire for hot, sweet tea. 'And milk. Lots of it.'

He poured the tea and handed her a hefty-looking sandwich.

'I don't want anything to eat.'

'Suit yourself.'

But the bread and the ham looked mouthwateringly good, and Catherine remembered that she had eaten nothing since a midnight craving had sent her to the fruit bowl last night and she had demolished the last three remaining apples. Her stomach rumbled and her hand reached out for the sandwich. She began to eat, looking at him defiantly, daring him to say something. But to his credit he simply took his own tea and sat down in front of her.

He waited until she had finished, relieved to see that the food and drink had brought a little colour into her cheeks. 'So now what? Where do we go from here?'

'I told you—I'm going back to London.'

He shook his head. 'I don't think so,' he demurred. 'You can't just arrive on my doorstep like the good fairy, impart a momentous piece of news like that, then take off again.'

'You can't stop me!'

'No, I can't stop you. But you still haven't told me why you came here today.'

'I would have thought that was pretty obvious.'

'Not really. You could have phoned me. Or written me a letter.' The blue eyes challenged her. 'So why didn't you?'

What was the point of hiding anything now? If she hadn't kept her job secret then he probably wouldn't have given her his card, and she wouldn't have gone to see him, and then this would never...

But she shook her head. What was the point of wasting time by thinking of what might have been? Or what might *not* have been, in this case.

'I wasn't sure that you'd believe me.'

'You thought that seeing me in person would convince me?' He frowned. 'But why? You don't *look* pregnant—' With that she opened the buttons of her coat and stared at him defiantly. He stilled.

For there, giving a smooth contour to her slim body, was the curve of pregnancy, and Finn stared at it, utterly speechless.

'I just knew I had to tell you face to face, and show

you that it's real, it's happening,' she said, meeting that shocked stare. 'Besides, it isn't the easiest thing in the world to write, is it?'

He forced himself to remember that she had betrayed him. 'Even for a journalist?' he questioned sarcastically.

'Even for a journalist,' she echoed, but she felt the prick of tears at the back of her eyes and bit her lip again, knowing that whatever happened he had to hear *this* truth, too. He might not believe her, but she had to tell him.

'Finn, my editor *did* send me to Dublin when she found out we'd met—and she *did* try to get a story on you. But I said no.'

'So the story was just a figment of my imagination?' he queried sarcastically.

'No, but I didn't write that piece about you, and neither did I receive any money.'

'Oh?' he queried cynically. 'So they just happened to guess what the inside of my apartment is like, did they? And the fact that you obviously rate me in bed?'

'I was upset, and I blurted a few things out to my editor, not expecting her to use them.'

'What very naive behaviour for a journalist,' he said coldly, but his heart had begun to beat very fast. If she had been tricked into giving a confidence, then didn't that put an entirely different complexion on matters? And didn't that, by default, make his subsequent behaviour absolutely intolerable?

'Oh, what's the point in all this?' she sighed. 'Don't worry about it, Finn. I'm not asking you to have anything to do with this baby.'

'But it's not just down to *you*, is it?' he asked quietly.

A cloud of apprehension cast its shadow. 'What do you mean?'

'Just that I want to,' he said grimly. 'This is my baby, too, you know, Catherine. By choosing to tell me you have irrevocably involved me—and believe me, sweetheart, I *intend* to be involved!

CHAPTER NINE

CATHERINE stared at Finn in shock and alarm.

'Well, what did you expect?' he demanded. 'That I would say, Okay—fine—you're having my baby? Here's a cheque and goodbye?'

'I told you—I did *not* come here asking you for money!' she said furiously.

'No? But you still haven't told me why you *did* come here.'

Catherine stared down at her lap, then looked back up at him, her eyes bright. 'Because I didn't know my own father.'

There was an odd, brittle kind of pause. 'You mean he died?' he questioned slowly.

She shook her head, met his eyes squarely. Defiantly. 'I'm illegitimate, Finn.'

'Come on now, Catherine,' he said gently. 'That isn't such a terrible thing to be.'

'Maybe not today it isn't—but things were different when I was a child.'

'Did you never meet him?'

'Never. I don't know whether he's alive or dead,' she said simply. 'He was married to someone, and it wasn't my mother. Like I said, I didn't know him and he didn't want to know me.' Her eyes were bright now. 'And I didn't want to inflict that on my own child.'

He caught a sense of the rejection she must have felt, and again was filled with a pang of remorse. 'I'm sorry—'

'No!' Fierce pride made her bunch her fists to wipe away the first tell-tale sign of tears, and she set her shoulders back. 'I don't want or need your sympathy for my upbringing, Finn, because it was a perfectly happy upbringing. It's just—'

'Not for your childhood,' he said heavily. 'For my recklessness.'

Their eyes met. 'You don't have the monopoly on recklessness,' she said quietly. 'The difference is that our motivations were different. You came round hell-bent on revenge, and you extracted it in the most basic form possible, didn't you?'

Had he? Had he really been that cold-blooded? It was surely no defence to say that all he had planned to do was to deliver the flowers with a blistering denouncement, but that all rational thought and reason had been driven clean out of his mind by the sight and the touch and the feel of her. Was that the truth, or just a way of making events more palatable for his conscience?

'You have a very powerful effect on me, Catherine,' he said unsteadily. Because even now, God forgive him—even with all this going on—he was thinking that she looked like some kind of exquisite domesticated witch, with that tumble of ebony hair and the wide-spaced green eyes. Or a cat, he thought thickly. A minxy little feline who could sinuously make him do her will.

What kind of child would they produce together? he found himself wondering. An ebony-haired child with passion running deep in its veins? 'A very powerful effect,' he finished, and met her eyes.

She steeled herself against his charm, the soft, sizzling look in his eyes. 'Yes, and we all know why, don't we? Why I have such an effect on you.'

His eyes narrowed. 'You're attempting to define chemistry?'

'I'm not defining anything—I'm describing something else entirely.' She threw him a challenging look and he matched it with one of his own.

'Go on,' he said. 'I'm intrigued.'

'We both know why such a famously private man should act in such an injudicious way.'

That one word assumed dominance inside his head. It wasn't a handle which had ever been applied to him before. 'Injudicious?'

'Well, wasn't it? If you'd bothered to find out a little bit more about me then you would have discovered that I was a journalist and presumably would have run in the opposite direction.'

'You were being deliberately evasive, Catherine. You know you were.'

'Yes, I was. I always am about my job, because people hold such strong prejudices.'

'Can you wonder why?' he questioned sarcastically.

'But it all happened so quickly—there was no time for an extended getting-to-know-you, was there, Finn? Tell me, do you normally leap into bed quite so quickly?'

'Not at all,' he countered, fixing her with a mocking blue look. 'Do you?'

'Never.' She drew a deep breath, not caring whether he believed her or not. His moral opinion of her did not matter. He would learn soon enough that she intended to be the mother to end all mothers. 'But maybe you didn't *need* to get to know me.'

'Now you've lost me.'

'Have I? Well, then, let me spell it out for you! We both know that the reason you couldn't wait to take me to bed was because I reminded you of your childhood sweetheart!'

'My childhood sweetheart?' he repeated incredulously.

'Deidra O'Shea! Are you denying that I look like her?'

It took a moment for her words to register, and when they did his accompanying feeling of rage was tempered only by the reminder that she was pregnant.

'You have a look of her about you,' he said carefully. 'But so what?'

'So *what*?' Catherine turned a furious face to him. 'Don't you realise how insulting that is for a woman?'

'What? That I happen to be attracted to dark-haired women with green eyes? Where's the crime in that, Catherine? Don't you normally lust after men who look like me? Isn't that what human nature is all about? That we're conditioned to respond to certain stimuli?'

What would it reveal about her if she admitted that she didn't usually lust after men at all? That Peter had been the very opposite of Finn in looks and character. Peter didn't dominate a room, nor did his charisma light it up just as surely as if it had been some glorious, glowing beacon. Peter had not been able to make her melt so instantly and so responsively with just a glimmering look from his eyes.

'Did you pretend I was her?' she demanded heatedly. 'Close your eyes and think it was her?'

'But I didn't close my eyes, Catherine,' he answered seriously. 'I was looking at you all the time. Remember?'

Oh, yes, she remembered. She remembered all too well. The way his eyes had caressed her just as surely as his fingertips had. The things he had said about her body. He had compared her skin to silk and cream, in that musical and lilting Irish accent.

'And what about you?' he questioned suddenly. 'What's the justification for your behaviour? Was it perhaps a way of striking out at a man who had hurt you badly?'

Her mouth opened, but no sound came out.

'Peter,' he said deliberately. 'The man who left you.'

'How on earth did you find out about Peter?' she breathed.

'Oh, come on, Catherine! When the article was brought to my attention by my cuttings service, I had a check run on you. Suddenly everything made sense. Why a woman, seemingly so aloof, should go to bed with me without me really having to try. You wanted to get back at your ex-boyfriend, didn't you?'

She let him believe it. Because the truth was even more disturbing than his accusation. That she had been so besotted by Finn she had scarcely given Peter a thought. Didn't that fact damn her more than redeem her?

Catherine felt tired. Weary. Unable to cope with any more.

'Oh, what's the point in remembering? What's done is done and we just have to live with the consequences.'

'Don't go back to London today,' he said suddenly.

She looked at him. 'Can you give me a good reason why not?'

'You're tired. And we have things to discuss.' His blue eyes gleamed with resolve, and he continued in a quieter voice, 'Just as there are consequences to what happened between us, there are also consequences to your visit here. Come on.' He stood up. 'Let's go.'

'Go where?'

'I'll take you back to the flat. You can rest there, and then we can talk.'

It wasn't so much his strength or his determination which made Catherine weakly nod her head. She was pregnant, she told herself. She was allowed to be persuaded.

'Okay,' she agreed.

Finn stared out of the window at the distant waters of the Liffey—grey today, to match the sky. And to match his mood, he thought, with a heart which was heavy.

He turned silently to look at where Catherine lay, asleep on the king-sized sofa. She had been fighting sleep ever since he had brought her back here and at long last she had given up the battle.

Her hair lay in tousled silken strands of black, contrasted against a Chinese silk cushion, and her dark lashes feathered into two perfect arcs on her high cheekbones. She slept as peacefully and as innocently as a child, he thought. He stared at the curve of her belly as his thoughts repeated themselves in his mind.

A child.

A wild leap of something like joy jumped unexpectedly in his chest.

A child!

And not just any child. This was *his* child.

And, no matter what the circumstances, wasn't the procreation of life always a miracle? Didn't the tiny heart of his child beat inside this woman?

This stranger.

And yet he felt he knew her body more intimately than that of any woman who had gone before.

Catherine opened her eyes to find Finn standing, staring down at her. For a moment she was muddled and confused, wondering just where she was and what had happened. And then it all came back to her in one great jolting rush.

She was in his flat, and she had told him, and his reaction had been—unexpectedly—one of immediate acceptance, not suspicion.

She sat up and yawned. 'I fell asleep,' she said unnecessarily.

'You certainly did.' He glanced at his watch. 'For almost an hour. Looked like you needed it.'

An hour! 'Good grief.' She yawned again. When was the last time she'd slept so soundly in the middle of the day? Better start getting used to changes, she thought, as she ran her hand through her rumpled hair. She looked up into the imposing, impassive face. 'What are we going to do?'

He gave an almost imperceptible nod. *We*, she had said, acknowledging the power in a single word. He realised that already they were a unit. If you were lovers, even married, then no matter how long you were in a relationship a certain question-mark of impermanence always hovered unspoken in the air. But not any more. He and Catherine were fact. Chained together for the rest of their lives. The mother, the father and the baby.

'Tell me about what your life in London is like,' he

said suddenly, and seated himself on the sofa opposite hers, stretching his long legs out in front of him.

Catherine blinked. 'Like what? You know where I live.'

'Yes. A one-bedroomed flat in the middle of the city. Not the most ideal place for bringing up a baby,' he observed.

She was intelligent enough not to argue with that. 'No,' she agreed quietly. 'It's not.'

'And your job?' he questioned. 'On *Pizazz!*.' He spat the word out as though it was a bitter pill. 'Will they give you paid maternity leave?'

Catherine hesitated. Of course. He didn't know—but then how would he? 'I don't have a job any more,' she said slowly, and saw his head jerk upwards in surprise. 'Or rather, I do, but it's certainly not one which will give me paid maternity leave. I'm...I've gone freelance,' she said at last.

'Since when?' he demanded. 'Since before you knew you were pregnant?'

'Of course! I'm not *completely* stupid!'

Guilt twisted a knife in his gut. 'You can't get another staff job?'

'Not like this! Who's going to take someone on at this stage of pregnancy? I can just see it now—Welcome, Catherine, we'd love to employ you. And, yes, we'd be delighted to give you paid leave in a few months' time!'

He studied her, trying to be dispassionate, to block out her blinding beauty. 'So how exactly are you planning to bring up this baby, in Clerkenwell, with no regular income?'

'I haven't decided.'

'You make it sound as though you have the luxury of choice, Catherine—which it seems to me you don't.'

'I'll think of something.' Her mother had managed, hadn't she? Well, *so would she*!

He looked at her closely, this beautiful woman he had been unable to resist, recognising that their lives would never be the same again.

'Where does your mother live?' he questioned, so uncannily that for one mad moment she wondered if he was capable of reading her thoughts.

'Devon.'

'Would you consider going there?'

Catherine shuddered. What, and let the village watch history repeating itself? The conquering daughter returning home vanquished, pregnant, and trying to eke out a living? Could she possibly land herself on her mother—who was happy with her independent life and her charity work? Would she want to go through the whole thing yet again?

'It would be too much for my mother to cope with,' she said truthfully.

That was one option dealt with. 'And do you know many people in London?'

She shrugged. 'Kind of—though I've only been there a couple of years. Colleagues, of course. Well, ex-colleagues, mainly,' she amended. And work friendships were never the same once you'd left a job, were they? Everyone knew that. 'I've got some good close friends, too.'

'Any with children?'

'Good grief—no! Career women to a fault.'

'Sounds a pretty isolated and lonely place for a woman to be child-rearing.'

'Like I said, I'll manage.'

His eyes narrowed. 'Commendable pride, Catherine,' he said drily. 'But it isn't just you to think about now, is it? Do you really think it's fair to foist that kind of lifestyle on a poor, defenceless baby?'

'You're making it sound like cruelty!' she protested. 'Lots and lots of women have babies in cities and all of them are perfectly happy!'

'Most probably have supporting partners and extended families!' he snapped. 'Which you don't!'

'Well—'

'And most do not have a credible alternative,' he said, cutting right across her protests. 'Like you do,' he finished deliberately.

There was something so solemn and profound in his voice that Catherine instinctively sat up straight, half fearful and half hopeful of what his next words might be. 'Like what?' she whispered.

'You could come and live here, in Dublin.'

She stared at him as if he had suddenly sprouted horns. 'Are you out of your mind?'

'I don't think that my thinking could be described as normal, no. Though that's hardly surprising, given the topic,' he answered drily. 'But it's certainly rational. Consider it,' he said, seeing her begin to mouth another protest.

'I have, and it took me all of three seconds to reject it!' she answered crossly, despising the sudden rapid race in her heart-rate.

'Listen,' he continued, as though she hadn't spoken, 'Dublin is a great city—'

'That's hardly the point! I can't live here with you, Finn—surely you can see that would be impossible?'

There was a long, rather strange pause. 'I wasn't suggesting that you live here with me, Catherine.'

Oh, if only the floor could have opened up and swallowed her! 'Well, thank God for that,' she said, rather weakly, and hoped that her voice didn't lack conviction. 'Where did you have in mind, then? Is there some home for unmarried mothers on the outskirts of the city?'

He had the grace to wince. 'I have a cottage by the sea. It's in Wicklow, close to Glendalough and a relatively short drive away. Fresh air and village life. It would be perfect for you. And the baby.'

It sounded like an oasis. 'I don't know.'

He heard her indecision and, like a barrister moving in for the kill with his closing argument, fluently outlined his case. 'You live on your own in London—what's the difference? And I can come and see you at weekends.'

Once again, she despaired at the sudden race of her pulse. He meant grudging duty visits, nothing else. She shook her head. 'No.'

'There are other factors, too, Catherine.'

She looked up, wishing that it wasn't such painful pleasure to stare into the eyes of the man who had fathered her child. 'Such as?'

'I have some friends who live there—Patrick and Aisling. I can introduce you to Aisling—she'd love to meet you, I'm sure. They've three children of their own—it would be good to have someone like that around.'

Aisling?

The name rang a bell and Catherine remembered the morning she had left Finn's flat. A woman called Aisling had been talking on the answer-machine, asking where the hell he had been. She had assumed that it was someone he had stood up because he'd had a better offer.

'Do you know more than one Aisling?' she asked.

'No. Why?'

She shook her head. 'It doesn't matter.'

He carried on trying to sell the delights of Grey-stones, knowing that if she could see the place for herself she'd be sold. 'And my aunt lives there, too.'

'Your aunt?'

'That's right. She's…well, she's a very special lady.'

Catherine swallowed. She could just imagine what a protective relative would have to say about some conniving woman tricking her darling nephew into fatherhood.

'I don't think so, Finn,' she said uncertainly. 'Wouldn't everyone find the situation a little odd?'

'Well, of course they would. No one's ever heard me mention you before, and suddenly here you are—pregnant with my child!'

'Could do your street-cred a lot of harm?' she hazarded sarcastically.

'It's not my reputation I'm thinking about, Catherine,' he said softly. 'It's yours.' His eyes glittered as the spectre of responsibility reared its head. He did not baulk, but faced it head-on. 'There is, of course, one solution which would guarantee you all the respect a woman in your condition warrants.'

Utterly confused now, she stared at him in perplexity. 'What solution?'

'Marry me.'

There was a long, deafening silence and Catherine's heart clenched in her chest. 'Is this some kind of joke?' she demanded hoarsely.

He shook his head. 'Think about it, Catherine—see

what sense it makes. It gives you security, for a start. And not just for you, for the baby.'

Perhaps someone else might have considered that offer in a purely mercenary way, but that someone else was not Catherine, with Catherine's experience of the world.

She had never thought about her own mortality much, but right now it was foremost in her mind. New life automatically made you think of the other end of the spectrum.

What would happen to her if she died suddenly? Who would look after and care for the baby? Not her mother, that was for sure.

But if she married Finn...

She stared at him with clear, bright eyes. 'And what's in it for you?'

'Can't a clever journalist like you work it out?' he answered flippantly, but then his voice sobered. 'As an ex-lover I can be sidelined, but as your husband I would have a say in the baby's life. It legitimises everything.' His eyes met hers with sudden understanding. 'And didn't you say that you didn't want what you had to endure yourself for your baby? Whatever happens, Catherine, this child will have my name—and one day will inherit my wealth.'

'An old-fashioned marriage of convenience, you mean?'

'Or a very modern one,' he amended quietly.

It was a deliberately ambiguous statement. 'And what's that supposed to mean?'

'It means whatever you want it to mean. We can make the rules up as we go along.'

'And how long is this marriage supposed to last—presumably not for life?'

'Presumably not.'

'And if you want out?'

'Or you do?' he countered coolly.

'Either. If the situation between us is untenable in any way, then—'

'Aren't you jumping the gun a little? Why don't we save the big decisions until after the baby is born?'

He gave the glimmer of a smile, and Catherine felt her stomach turn over. Did he have any idea how that smile could turn a normally sensible woman's head? In spite of everything.

'What do you say, Catherine?'

She thought of going through it all alone, and suddenly felt the first tremblings of fear. For a moment she felt small and helpless and vulnerable—though surely that was natural enough?

While Finn was big and strong and dependable. It didn't matter what his feelings for her were, he would protect her, instinct told her that. And instinct was a very powerful influence where pregnant women were concerned.

She looked at him. He had stated that she didn't really have the luxury of choice, and in a way he was right. For what right-minded and responsible woman in her situation could give any answer other than the one which now came from between her dry lips.

'Very well, Finn. I'll marry you.'

CHAPTER TEN

AS WEDDINGS went, it was bizarre. The ceremony had to be quick and it had to be discreet—any sign of a hugely pregnant bride would have the press sniffing around in droves, and Finn didn't want that. Neither did Catherine.

And organising a wedding wasn't as easy as they made out in the films.

'Ireland's out,' he'd said grimly, as he replaced the telephone receiver. 'You need three months' written notice.'

'You didn't know that?' The question came out without her thinking.

'Why would I?' His eyes had sparked icy blue fire. 'I've never got married before.'

And wouldn't be now, she'd reminded herself painfully. Not if he hadn't been in such an invidious situation.

'It'll have to be in England, and I have to be resident for seven days prior to giving notice,' he'd said flatly. 'It's fifteen days minimum after that.'

He'd made it sound as if he was to undergo a protracted kind of operation. Catherine had turned away.

They'd flown back to England, where Finn had booked in to a hotel, and by some unspoken agreement they had not seen one another until the day of the wedding itself—although they'd had a few brief, uncomfortable conversations.

Catherine had spent the three weeks trying to behave as normally as possible—seeing her friends, trying to write—even once visiting her mother. And all the while her great big secret had burned so strongly within her that she was astonished no one else noticed.

When the day of the wedding finally dawned, her most overwhelming emotion was one of relief—that soon the subterfuge would be over.

Catherine glanced at her watch as she waited for her reluctant husband-to-be. She hadn't bought anything new—because that also seemed to go against the mood of the arrangement. Her favourite clingy violet dress made her look voluptuous, and she was grateful for the long jacket which covered most of the evidence.

But when she opened the door to him, her face drawn and tense, Finn felt his heart miss a beat.

'Smile for me, Catherine,' he whispered.

Obediently she curved her lips upwards into a smile, trying not to be enticed by the blue gleam of his eyes.

'You look like a gypsy,' he observed softly, as she pinned two large silver hoops to her ears.

'Is that bad, or good?'

'It's good,' he replied evenly, but he had to force himself to walk away and stare sightlessly out of the window. The trouble was that he still wanted her, and yet there now seemed to be an unbreachable emotional gulf which made intimacy out of the question. He glanced down at his watch. 'Almost ready to go?'

Nerves assailed her for the hundredth time that morning. He looked so devastating in his dark suit and snowy shirt that she was having difficulty remembering that this was all make-believe. He wasn't a *real* groom any more than she was a *real* bride. 'Finn, it's still not too late to back out, you know.'

'You want to?'

Of course she did. Part of her would have loved to be able to wave a magic wand and wish her old life back. While another part wished that this gorgeous man would sweep her into his arms and kiss all her make-up off and tell her that he couldn't bear *not* to marry her.

But of course he wouldn't. It wasn't that kind of deal. This was, to use her own expression—and it was one which had the power to make her giggle in a slight hysteria which she put down to hormones—a marriage of convenience. Modern or otherwise.

'Are you wishing it was Peter?' he asked suddenly.

'Peter?' To her horror she actually had to pause and think who he was talking about.

He heard the tone of her voice and his mouth thinned. That said a lot about her level of commitment, didn't it? 'Yeah, Peter—the man you went out with for—how long was it, Catherine? Four years?'

'Three.' She heard his disapproval and she couldn't bear that he might think she had just leapt from Peter's bed into his. 'We hadn't seen each other for six months before he ended it,' she said slowly. 'And I accepted that it was over.' She turned wide green eyes up to his. 'There was certainly no motive of getting my own back.'

'I see.' But he felt his body relax a little.

'And besides, what about you?' she challenged. 'Are you sorry that it's not Deirdra you're marrying?'

There was a pause. 'Deirdra's history.'

'That doesn't answer my question, Finn.'

He supposed it didn't. 'It happened a long time ago.' He shrugged. 'We were both seventeen and discovering sex for the first time. It burnt itself out and then she went to Hollywood. End of story.'

He was describing first love, thought Catherine with a pang. And maybe for him—as for so many people—no one would ever live up to that idealised state. First love. There was nothing like it—even hard-bitten Miranda had said that.

'Oh, I see,' she said slowly.

He looked at her assessingly. 'Back out now, if you want to, Catherine.'

'No, I'm happy to go ahead with it,' she said.

'Well, you don't look it,' he said softly. 'You'll have to work harder than that to convince anyone.'

She fixed a smile to her glossy lips. 'How's that?'

'Perfect,' he answered, feeling an ache in his groin which he knew would not be satisfied by a traditional post-wedding night.

For directly after the ceremony they were taking the first flight back to Ireland. A car would be waiting at the airport and he was driving her to Greystones, to settle her into the house.

And after the weekend he would return to Dublin. Alone.

Finn thought how vulnerable she looked on the plane, shaking her head and refusing his offer of a glass of champagne, her face telling him that she had nothing to celebrate.

He had to keep telling himself not to be sucked in by a pair of green eyes and a rose-pink mouth, tell himself instead that Catherine Walker had a bewitching power which hid her true nature. And that beauty combined with burgeoning life could fool a man into thinking she was something different. And, while she might not have conspired to humiliate him publicly, she had still deliberately kept from him the fact that she was a journalist.

'Won't your mother think it strange that you didn't tell her about the wedding?' he asked, as the car left Dublin and began to eat up the miles leading towards the coast.

'Lots of people go away and get married without telling anyone these days.'

'She won't pry?'

'I'll have to tell her the truth—that I'm pregnant,' she said flatly. 'She'll understand.' Oh, yes—her mother would understand *that* all right.

'And when are you going to inform her that you've acquired a husband?'

Acquired a husband! He made it sound like something from a Victorian novel! 'When I'm…settled.'

'Soon?' he demanded.

She nodded. 'Once I've been at Greystones for a couple of days.' Catherine stole a look at Finn's dark profile. 'Have you told your aunt, or any of your friends?'

He shook his head, easing his foot down on the accelerator. 'They'd only have wanted to join in and make a big fuss of it.'

And, presumably, turn the day into something it wasn't.

But repeating her marriage lines after the registrar had made Catherine feel heartbreakingly wistful, and only the stirring flutter in her stomach had kept her voice steady enough to speak in a voice as devoid of emotion as Finn's.

'What a lovely couple you make!' the registrar had

cooed, and then said with a twinkle, 'You may now kiss your wife.'

Finn had looked down at Catherine, a wry smile touching the corners of his lips as he saw the startled look which widened her green eyes. 'Mustn't disappoint, must we?' he'd murmured, and bent his head to brush his mouth against hers.

As kisses went, it had been almost chaste. Not deep and hungry and greedy, like the kisses they had shared before they had made love. But, in its way, the most poignant kiss of all—gentle and full of false promise. His lips were like honey and just the touch of them had sent little shivers of longing all the way down her spine. And yet it had mocked her with all that it could have been and was not.

Not for them the urgent and giggling drive to the nearest bed to consummate the marriage. Instead she would be delivered to a house which—although it sounded quite lovely—was to be hers alone during the week, while the baby grew inside her belly.

And after that?

Resisting the urge to wrap her arms around his neck, Catherine had pulled away, giving the watching registrar an awkward smile.

They arrived at Greystones late in the afternoon, through sleepy-looking streets and past stone houses. Finn's cottage stood at the far end of the small town, an unprepossessing low stone building which looked as though it had been there since the beginning of time.

'Oh, it's beautiful, Finn,' she said, breathing in the sea-air and thinking what a healthy place this was to be when she compared it to her tiny flat in London.

And she was healthy, too—the bloom of pregnancy

making her face seem to glow from within. She looked
both fragile and strong, and on an impulse Finn bent
and scooped her up into his arms, his eyes glittering
blue fire as he looked down into her face.

'What the h-hell do you think you're doing?' she
spluttered.

'Bowing to tradition, as well as bowing my head,'
he said softly, as he bent his head to carry her through
the low door. 'By carrying you over the threshold.'

He placed her down carefully, seeming reluctant to
remove his hands from her waist, and Catherine stared
up into his face. 'Why did you do that?'

'It'll soon get round that I've married you. We ought
to maintain at least a modicum of pretence that it's the
real thing.'

She pulled away. It hurt just as much as it was probably intended to, and Catherine had to remind herself
that she had walked into this with her eyes open. She
had agreed to marry him for the sake of her baby and
her baby alone—but that didn't stop her from having the
occasional foolish fantasy, did it? Didn't stop her from
wishing that they didn't have to go through a hypocriti-
cal stage-managed act just in case anyone happened to
be watching them.

In an attempt to distract herself she looked around
her instead. The cottage was comfortably furnished
with squashy sofas, and paintings of wild and wonderful Wicklow were hung everywhere. But the walls were
surprisingly faded—indeed, the whole room looked as
though it could do with a coat of paint.

'Come through here,' said Finn, looking at the stiff
and defensive set of her shoulders. 'I've something to
show you.'

The smaller room which led off the sitting room

looked similarly tired, but Catherine's attention was soon drawn from the state of the walls by a desk overlooking the big garden at the back of the house. Because what was on it stood out like a sore thumb. A desk with a high-tech computer, fax and telephone and state-of-the-art printer—all obviously and gleamingly new.

'For you,' he said simply.

Catherine looked longingly at the computer, which made her own look as if it had been invented around the same time as the wheel, then lifted her face up to him. 'Why?'

'A wedding present.'

'I've bought nothing for you—'

He shook his head. 'You write, don't you? I thought that as you were going to be living in a remote place you might as well have the most modern stuff on the market to keep you in touch with the big world outside.'

'I've brought my own computer,' said Catherine stubbornly.

'I imagined you would have done—but I doubt it has anything like the speed or the power of this one.'

She turned on him furiously. 'You don't have to *buy* me, you know, Finn!'

'For God's sake—do you have to be so damned defensive? You wouldn't *be* here if I had been thinking with my head instead—'

'You don't have to spell it out for me,' she said in a hollow voice, feeling quite sick. 'And there's no need for you to play the martyr, either.'

'I am not playing the martyr,' he retorted. 'I am just taking responsibility for your predicament—'

'Stop it! Just stop it!' she interrupted, even angrier now. 'I will not, *not* have this baby described as a "predicament". It wasn't planned, no—but it's happened and

I intend to make the best of it. This baby is going to be a *happy* baby, whatever happens. And you shan't take the lion's share of the responsibility, either. We're both to blame, if you like.'

'Blame?' He gave an odd smile. 'Now who's using loaded words, Catherine?' But he forced himself to draw back, to blot out lips which when furiously parted like that made him want to crush them beneath his own. And to try to put out of his mind the fact that to spend the rest of the afternoon in bed might just rid them both of some of their pent-up anger.

And frustration, he thought achingly.

'Would you like to get changed?' he asked, eyeing the purple dress which clung so provocatively to her blossoming body and wondering how he was going to get through the weekend with any degree of sanity.

Catherine nodded. 'Please.'

'Come on, I'll show you upstairs.'

There were four bedrooms, though one was almost too tiny to qualify.

Finn put her suitcase on the bed of the largest room, which suddenly seemed like the smallest to her, when he was close enough to touch and she was beguiled by a faint, evocative trace of his aftershave.

'The bathroom's along the corridor,' he said quickly. 'You'll find everything you need.'

She had a quick bath and then struggled into her jeans, throwing a baggy jumper over the top. When she came downstairs she found that Finn had changed as well.

He saw her frowning. 'What's up?'

'My jeans won't do up!' she exclaimed, pointing at the waistband.

He hid a smile. 'That's generally what happens,

Catherine. We'll have to buy you some pregnancy clothes—though God knows where around here!'

'Big tent-like dresses with Peter Pan collars!' she groaned.

'No, not any more,' he said knowledgeably.

Her eyes narrowed. 'How do you know that?'

'I remember Aisling telling me, the last time she was pregnant. Come on and I'll make you tea,' he said. 'And then I'll light a fire.'

She followed him into a kitchen which had most definitely not been modernised, and Catherine raised her eyebrows in surprise at the old-fashioned units and the brown lino on the floor. Even the ugly windows hadn't been replaced!

'How long have you owned this place, Finn?'

He turned the tap on and filled up the kettle, his back to her. 'It came on the market about five years ago.'

She heard the evasion in his voice and wondered what he wasn't telling her. She raised her eyebrows. 'It's not the kind of place I imagined you buying. It's... well, it's nothing like your place in Dublin.'

'No.' He had forgotten for a moment that she was a journalist, with a journalist's instinct for a story. *His* instinct would be not to tell it. But they were married now, even if it was in name only. And if she was going to give birth to his baby then what was the point in keeping everything locked in? 'It's where I was born. Where I lived until the age of seven.'

Catherine studied him. There was something else here, too—something which made his voice deepen with a bleak, remembered pain. She wondered what had happened to him at the age of seven.

He saw the question in her eyes and sighed, knowing that he had to tell her. She carried his baby, and that

gave her the right to know about a past he had grown
used to locking away. 'My mother died,' he said, in
stark explanation, bending down to light the gas with
a match.

'I'm sorry—'

'She'd been widowed when I was a baby—there was
no one left to look after me and so I went to live with
my aunt.'

'Oh, Finn.' Her heart went out to him, and she
wanted to put her arms tightly round him and hug away
his pain, but the emotional shutters had been banged
tightly shut. She could read that in the abrupt way he
had turned away, putting cups and saucers upon a tray
with an air of finality. Catherine understood the need
for defence against probing into pain. The time was
not right—indeed, it might never be right. But that was
Finn's decision, not hers.

'Have you such a thing as a biscuit?' she asked, with
a smile. 'I'm starving!'

He let out a barely perceptible sigh. 'There's enough
food to sink a battleship. I asked Aisling to come in
and stock up on groceries. We don't have to go out all
weekend, if we don't want to.'

Catherine's smile faded and she couldn't quite work
out whether she felt excitement or terror. What did that
mean? she wondered, with a slight tinge of hysteria.
That play-acting as honeymooners was going to extend
as far as the bedroom?

'Go and sit down, Catherine,' he commanded softly.
'And I'll bring this through.'

His face was unreadable in the dying light of the
day, and rather dazedly Catherine obeyed him, sinking
down onto one of the squashy sofas while she struggled
not to project too much. There was no point in working

out what she would do if he suggested bed when the circumstance might never arise!

He brought the tea in and poured her a cup.

'Is today a sugar day, or not?' he asked gravely.

She bit back a smile, stupidly pleased that he had remembered. 'Not. My cravings seem to have settled down into something approaching a normal appetite.' She waited until she had drunk some of the tea, then put the cup down. 'Finn?'

'Catherine?'

'How often do you come to stay here?'

'Not often enough,' he admitted. 'I keep meaning to spend weekends here, to get a breath of sea-air and a bit of simple living to blow the cobwebs away, but...' His words tailed off.

'But?'

'Oh, you know what it's like. Life seems to get in the way of plans.'

Yes, she knew what it was like—or rather what it *had* been like. But she was beginning a whole new life now, and a whole new future. And not just in terms of the baby. She was going to be living in Finn's cottage as his quasi-wife and she didn't have a clue about what role she was supposed—or wanted—to fulfil! Make up the rules as we go along, he had said, but surely that was easier than he suggested?

But for the baby's sake she cleared her thoughts of concern and settled down to drink her tea.

He saw the softening of her face, and the look of serenity which made a Madonna of her, and found himself wondering how many different masks she wore. Or was her pregnancy just making him project his own idealised version of her as the future mother of his child?

That she was soft and caring and vulnerable...rather than the cynical and go-getting journalist.

Life is evidence-based, Finn, he reminded himself grimly. Just think of the evidence. She wears different masks, that's all. Just as all women do.

He stood up. 'I'll light the fire,' he said shortly.

Catherine felt unreal and disconnected as he created a roaring blaze from the logs in the basket, and warmth and light transformed the room just as dusk crept upon the early evening air. The flames cast shadows which flickered over the long, denim-clad thighs and she remembered their powerful strength in different guises. Running through a Greek sea. Naked and entwined with hers.

He looked up to find her watching him, her slim body sprawled comfortably on the sofa, and the temptation to join her and to kiss her almost overwhelmed him. He knew that in her arms he could forget all his doubts and misgivings about the bizarre situation they had created for themselves.

But wouldn't being intimate with her tonight make a bizarre situation even more so? Confuse and muddy the waters?

He caught her eye but she quickly looked away, as if uncomfortable, and Finn was forced to acknowledge that things had changed, that there was no guarantee that Catherine wanted him in that way any more. Not after everything that had happened.

Later she unpacked, and Finn cooked them supper, and afterwards they listened to Irish radio until she began to yawn and escaped to her bedroom. Her senses and thoughts were full of him. All she could think about was how much she wanted him.

And how much easier everything would be if she didn't.

But, after a surprisingly sleep-filled night alone on the big, soft feather mattress, the morning dawned bright and sunny. After breakfast Finn took her down to the beach to look at the boats and to walk along the sand, then afterwards to meet his aunt.

Her heart was beating nervously as they approached the house. 'What's her name?'

'Finola.'

'I bet she'll take an instant dislike to me.'

'Don't be silly, Catherine—she's hardly going to hate a woman I bring home and introduce as my wife, now, is she? She loves me; she wants me to be happy.'

Happy? What an ironic choice of word.

'So what's your definition of happiness, Finn?'

He stooped down for a pebble and hurled it out at the blue sea before turning to look at her with eyes which rivalled the ocean's hue.

'It's a way of travelling, Catherine,' he said slowly. 'Not a destination.'

So, was she happy at this precise moment? She thought about it. Actually, yes, she was. Though contented was probably a better description. She was healthy and pregnant and walking along a beautiful beach with a beautiful man. And if she defined happiness in a futile wish that their relationship went deeper than that, then she was heading for a big disappointment. You couldn't look for happiness in another person. First you had to find it within yourself.

She thought that to the outside world they probably made a very striking couple—both tall and slim, with matching heads of jet-black, and her gleaming and brand-new gold band proclaiming very definitely that she was a newly-wed.

But there were several giveaway signs that all was not as it appeared. Finn did not smile down into her face with the conspiratorial air of a lover, nor hold her hand as if he couldn't bear to let it go.

Not, that was, until they arrived at his aunt's house. Then he caught her fingers in his and squeezed them reassuringly. 'It'll be okay,' he whispered.

The door was opened by a grey-haired woman in her late sixties, whose faded eyes were a blue a few shades less intense than those of her nephew. She only came up to the middle of his chest, but she flung her arms around him all the same and Catherine's heart clenched as he hugged her back. She'd never seen him so openly affectionate and demonstrative.

'Why, it's the divil himself!' she exclaimed. 'Finn! Finn Delaney!' She fixed him with a look of admonishment, but anyone could see her heart wasn't in it. 'And why haven't you been round to see me sooner?' Without waiting for an answer, she moved the blue eyes curiously from Finn to Catherine. 'And who might this be?'

Catherine was feeling as nervous as a child on the first day of school, recognising how much this woman meant to Finn and desperately not wanting to start off on the wrong foot.

'I'm Catherine,' she said simply. 'I'm Finn's wife.'

CHAPTER ELEVEN

Finn's wife.

The first and only time she had said it had been to Finn's aunt, but she thought it often enough, running the words sweetly through her mind like chocolate melting over ice-cream.

She had thought it the first morning he had driven back to Dublin, standing in the doorway just like a proper wife, watching his car disappear over the horizon, leaving her alone with her thoughts and her writing and her growing baby. And the big bed in which she slept alone.

The car had become a distant dot and she'd slowly closed the door on it, telling herself that she was glad he had made no move to consummate the marriage.

It would have only complicated things. Made the inevitable split more difficult—for her, certainly. Because women grew much closer to a man when they had sex with him. Even more so when that man's child grew bigger with every day that passed.

But being off limits had forced them together in a way which had its own kind of intimacy. For what did you do when you were closeted together every weekend and unable to do the one thing you most wanted to do?

Well, they seemed to go for an awful lot of walks.

Brisk, bracing walks along the unimaginably beautiful coastline. He would feed her cream and scones, and afterwards take her back to the cottage and insist that she put her feet up for the inevitable sleep which would follow. Sometimes she would wake up to find him watching her, the blue eyes so blazing and intent. And for one brief and blissful moment she would almost forget herself, want to hold her arms out towards him, to draw him close against the fullness of her breasts.

But the moment would be lost when he turned away, as if something he saw in her disturbed him, and she wondered if he felt uncomfortable with this masquerade of marriage. Did he find himself wanting to tell the aunt who was more like a mother to him that it was not all it seemed? That he had made her pregnant and was simply doing the right thing by her? Was he now perhaps regretting that decision?

He'd taken her to meet his friends who lived at the far end of the small town. Apparently he had known Patrick 'for ever', and Patrick's wife, Aisling, was an energetic redhead who squealed with delight when they told her the news.

'At last!' she exclaimed. 'You've done it at last! Oh, Finn—there'll be legions of women weeping all over Ireland!'

'And legions of men sighing with relief,' commented Patrick wryly as he reached into the fridge for a bottle of champagne.

'Shut up.' Finn smiled.

'So you went and got married *without telling anyone*?' Patrick demanded as he eased the cork out of the bottle. 'Even us?'

'Especially you,' murmured Finn. 'We didn't want the

whole of Wicklow knowing!' He paused. 'Catherine's pregnant, you see.'

'Oh, Patrick,' said Aisling softly. 'Will you listen to the man? "Catherine's pregnant," he says. As if we didn't have eyes in our heads, Finn Delaney! Congratulations! To both of you!'

She hugged them both in turn and Catherine felt a great lump rise in her throat, glad to have her face enveloped in Aisling's thick-knit sweater. I don't deserve this, she thought. I can't go through with it. Pretending to these nice people that all is what it seems.

But she looked up, her eyes bright, and met a sudden warm understanding in Finn's, and she drew an odd sort of comfort from that.

'Will you look after Catherine for me while I'm away in Dublin, Aisling?' he said, his voice suddenly urgent.

'But I don't need looking after!' protested Catherine, slightly terrified that this attractive woman with the warm smile might ask questions which would be impossible not to answer truthfully.

'You can see me as much or as little as you wish to, Catherine—I won't mind in the least,' said Aisling firmly. 'But won't you be terribly lonesome with Finn away?'

'Catherine wanted peace and quiet,' put in Finn. 'So Dublin's out. And she wants to write.'

'Yes.' Catherine swallowed. 'I'm a journalist.'

'So I believe,' said Aisling lightly, leaving Catherine wondering whether she had read the article. But even if she had she didn't seem to hold it against her, not judging by the genuine warmth of her welcome, anyway.

A small boy came running in, closely followed by an older sister, his face covered in sand and the sticky remains of a crab. 'Jack Casey! Just what have you been doing to yourself?'

'He tried to eat the crab, Mammy!' crowed the little girl. 'Even though I told him not to!'

'And you just let him, did you?' asked her mother, deftly picking up a cloth and beginning to scrub at her protesting son. 'Does this not put you off what you're about to go through, Catherine?'

'Well, I'll have a few years to prepare myself,' said Catherine, as Jack deposited a chubby handful of shells into her lap.

'Jack! Please don't put sand all over Catherine's dress!' scolded Aisling.

'I don't mind—honestly, I don't.'

Finn sat and watched the interaction of everyday family life and felt a great clench of his heart. How easy and uncomplicated it all seemed on the surface. With Catherine sitting there laughing as a sticky hand was shoved towards her hair, which today she had woven into two thick plaits which fell over her breasts.

Pregnancy suited her, he thought unwillingly, and her growing body seemed just as sexy as the pre-pregnancy one had done.

Thank God he was going back to Dublin in the morning!

The weeks slid by and Catherine settled into her new life, taking to the slow, easy pace like a duck to water.

She rose early and walked along the seashore, tracing her route back via the shops, where she bought freshly baked bread and milk which tasted better than any milk she had ever drunk before.

Then she settled down to write, but found that her writing had changed. She no longer had the desire nor the contacts to produce the punchy, easy-read features which had defined her career up until this point.

The flat in Clerkenwell was being rented out at an exorbitant fee, and so for the first time in her life there were no pressing money worries. She could enjoy her pregnancy and give in to what she most wanted to do.

She began to write a book.

'You're the only person I've told!' she said on the phone to her mother one night.

'What, not even Finn?'

'No. It's a surprise,' said Catherine truthfully. Or was she scared of trying and failing in his eyes?

'And when am I going to meet this husband of yours?' asked her mother. 'Everybody's asking me what he's like and I have to tell them that I don't know!'

This was a difficult one—more than difficult. Catherine had the means to fly her mother out—and knew how much she wanted to see her and how much her mother would enjoy life in the small Irish village. But— and it was a monumental but—how did she begin to explain the situation?

If her mother came she would either have to tell the truth or she would have to pretend, and she didn't know how long she could keep that up in front of the person who knew her so well.

For a start she and Finn would be expected to share a bedroom, and she knew for a fact that she couldn't do it. Couldn't sleep with him and not be climbing the walls with a terrible yearning to have him close to her in a way he did not want to be. It was bad enough on her nights alone, and the ones when he was sleeping just along the corridor—being in an enclosed space with a bed in it would be almost impossible.

'Soon, Mum,' she said lamely.

'If you leave it much longer, then I'll be a grand-mother!'

And that might be the best solution all round. Wait until the baby was born and the disruption he or she would cause would detract from what was actually going on in Finn and Catherine's so-called relationship. And besides, no one expected a new mother to be energetically making love to her husband every night!

Having another person in the house would mean that Finn would be able to focus on the best thing to do. And so would she. They could come to an amicable agreement about access, and all the other things people had to discuss when they were no longer together.

Not that she and Finn had ever been together. Not really. Not in the true sense of the word, anyway.

But it was funny how you could grow close to someone, even though your head was telling you that it was sheer madness to do so. She didn't want to find him funny and sexy and engaging. She wanted to be able to pick holes in his character, to tell herself that actually he was a cold and power-hungry maniac and that she would never have been happy with him anyway.

But she couldn't.

She told herself that it was easy to get on well with someone over the course of a weekend—that if they lived together all the time they would irritate the hell out of each other. But she couldn't quite believe that, either.

Energy flowed through her like lifeblood. She wrote throughout the day, sometimes well into the evening, and when Finn rang she would tell him how her day had been. They would talk with an ease and familiarity which was poignant in itself.

One night she told him how she'd been over and

helped Aisling with her baking, and that Aunt Finola had taken her to a bingo session at the church hall and Catherine had won an ironing board!

'What are you going to do with it?'

'I gave it to the priest's housekeeper. It seems silly to have two.'

'Could come in useful,' he said gravely.

'As an extra table, perhaps?' she suggested helpfully.

She told herself that of course it was easy to talk to someone on the phone, because you couldn't see the expression on their face or the look in their eyes. She told herself that it was important they remained on good terms because she would need to be in touch with Finn for the rest of her life. The baby would always connect them.

And she told herself that she would be okay when the day came—perhaps sooner than she would hope for—when he would tell her gently that the time had come for the parting of the ways. That they had done their best for the baby and now they were both free.

But she didn't want to be free. Or was that simply sneaky Mother Nature again—tying her emotionally to the biological father of her child?

It didn't seem to matter how much logic warned her that she mustn't embrace her new-wife role too enthusiastically, because try as she might she couldn't help herself.

Every Friday night she felt like a woman whose husband was coming home like a conquering hero. She would see the city-strain etched on his face as he opened the front door and she would pour him a gin and tonic—just like a real wife.

Finn found he couldn't wait to be out of the city on

Friday nights, tying up his work as early as possible so that he could be roaring out of Dublin and heading for the sea.

His apartment now seemed very empty in a way that the cottage never did. But Catherine did girly things; maybe that was why. She put flowers in vases and she baked cakes. Any day now he was fully expecting her to have acquired a new puppy!

She's just playing another role—a domestic role this time, he told himself, as the glitter of the distant sea told him he was almost home. But surely she wouldn't be able to keep it up for ever?

He walked into the cottage one night and frowned. Something was different, and it took a moment or two to figure out what it was.

'You've painted the walls!'

'So I have.' She gave a serene smile as she walked over to the drinks tray, pleased with the soft-peach wash which had transformed the dingy room. 'Do you like it?'

He looked around, his expression closed yet edgy, trying to distract himself from the pink V-necked sweater she wore, which showed far too much of the heavy swell of her breasts and seemed far too provocative for a cold Friday night in Wicklow!

'You should have asked me first!' he ground out.

The smile died on her lips. 'I'm sorry, Finn,' she said stiffly. 'I was mistakenly using the place as my home, perhaps fooling myself a little too convincingly that we were a married couple!'

'Even if we were,' he came back bitingly, 'surely decorating is something a couple would discuss together?'

'I wanted to surprise you—'

gave a little shudder as he drew her into the circle of his arms. Could she still wear skimpy underwear like that, even though she was pregnant? He guessed that he was about to find out.

Still holding her with his hands, he pushed her away. 'I've never undressed a pregnant woman before,' he murmured.

'I should hope not!'

'I'll be very careful,' he promised, as he peeled her sweater over her head.

She looped her arms around his neck and followed with the nuzzle of her lips. 'Not too careful, I hope. And besides, it doesn't matter now!'

He smiled. 'That wasn't what I was talking about, and you know it. I meant because you're pregnant.'

'Pregnant women are very resilient—or hadn't you noticed?'

Oh, yes—he'd noticed all right. She wasn't one of those women who lay around like an invalid, expecting to be waited on. Why, just the other day he had had to forcibly remove a spade from her hand and tell her that it was too cold to be digging. She had become huffy and stomped off, and told him that it was a crime not to foster love on such a beautiful garden.

He sucked in a breath as her body was revealed to him. Her breasts were glorious, ripe and bursting as they pushed against ivory-coloured lace. And the matching lacy thong left very little to the imagination.

'God,' he moaned. 'I'd no idea that a pregnant woman could look so sexy!'

'Well, that's a relief,' she offered drily.

He unclipped her bra and the heavy breasts came spilling out. He bent his head and his tongue licked luxuriantly against one hard, dark nipple. Catherine clutched at him, dizzy with the sheer sensation of it.

'Finn,' she said weakly.

'Mmm?'

He tugged at the little lacy thong, sliding it down over her thighs, and laid his hand softly on the dark fuzz of hair which concealed the very core of her femininity. He felt her jerk with pleasure. Wanted to give her yet more pleasure.

He knelt in front of her as if in homage, then dipped his tongue to delve into her honeyed warmth. She clutched his head to her, catching sight of their reflected image in the mirror. The sight of it turned her on even more. It seemed outrageously provocative to see her naked, pregnant body and the dark-haired man working such magic with his mouth.

'I'd better get horizontal,' she groaned. 'Before I fall over.'

He lifted his head and saw the smoky look in her eyes. 'Yeah. I think you'd better.'

He carried her, protesting, but only half-heartedly.

'Finn, stop it—I'm much too heavy these days.'

'But I like it. I like carrying you.'

'I'd noticed!'

'And you're still light enough not to trouble me.'

'You're a very strong man, Finn Delaney,' she sighed.

'I know I am,' he teased.

But he felt as weak as a pussycat as he tore his clothes off and lost himself in the warmth of her embrace.

He kissed her long and hard, smoothing his hand reverentially over her belly, and was just about to move it along, down to the inviting softness of her thighs, when she shook her head.

'Wait,' she whispered.

'I don't think I *can*—'

'Your baby, Finn. He's going to kick.'

'How can you tell?'

'I just can—ouch!'

Finn felt the hefty swipe of a small heel as it connected with the flat of his hand, and he stared down into Catherine's eyes, more shaken than he would have imagined.

'You think it's a boy?' he questioned thickly.

'I think so.'

'How?'

'I don't know...I just... Oh, *Finn*!'

'Do you like that?'

He wasn't feeling the baby any more. 'Mmm.' She slipped her hand down luxuriously, to capture the silken-steel of him, exultant to feel him shudder helplessly beneath her caress. 'Do *you* like that?'

'It's not me I'm thinking of right now—I don't want to hurt you, Catherine.'

For a moment she closed her eyes. If only he knew that the only way he was going to hurt her was by leaving her. And this is only going to make it harder, whispered the voice of reason. You should stop it right now.

But how could she possibly stop him when she wanted him so badly?

'What shall we do?' he whispered.

For a moment she thought he was asking about their future—but his fingers were playing with her breasts, sending little shivers of exquisite sensation rippling like warm sun across her skin. 'You mean *how* shall we...?'

'Mmm.'

'Use your imagination, Finn—I'm as much of a novice at this kind of thing as you are. I—oh, *Finn*!' She gave an expectant wriggle as Finn turned her onto her side and began to stroke her bottom, the other hand sliding up around her waist and from there to cup a swollen breast. She felt him pressing against her, so hard and so ready.

He felt her heat, sensed her urgency. He would never normally have asked a woman if she was ready, but he needed to be sure. And not just because she was pregnant.

'Catherine?' he questioned unsteadily.

'Oh, yes, Finn. Yes!'

Her senses seemed more highly tuned than they had ever been, and she was not sure whether that was down to abstinence or pregnancy. But as he entered her Catherine's mind cleared and she identified the emotion she had not before dared analyse.

For it was love, pure and simple. She loved this man. This man who could never truly be hers. She closed her eyes tightly. Stopped thinking and started feeling. Less pain that way.

Afterwards they lay exactly as they were, like sweat-sheened spoons, their heartbeats gradually slowing along with their breathing.

He looped a careless arm around her belly and felt another kick. He smiled against her shoulder. 'Ouch, again!'

'You should feel it from inside!'

He levered himself up onto one elbow to stare down at her, brushing back a strand of black hair, his eyes serious. 'I'm sorry I snapped at you.'

'You were frustrated, I expect. Don't worry about it, Finn—so was I.'

His face darkened. 'You think that's what it was all about? Frustration?'

'I don't know, do I? I'm trying to be practical.' Trying not to read too much into this situation and having to fight very hard with herself not to. 'What was it about, if not frustration?'

He turned onto his back, noticing for the first time the old-fashioned embossed wallpaper which covered the ceiling. Would she have ripped *that* down, the next time he came home—and would it really matter if she did? 'You just happened to touch a raw nerve.'

'Because I went ahead and decorated without asking you? Because I took control away from you?'

Would it sound crazy to tell her? Was it crazier still to have her think that he was the kind of intolerant tyrant who insisted on being privy to every decision made inside the home?

He shook his head, wondering if she had become a journalist because she was perceptive, or whether perception had come as a by-product of her career. Or was this just what happened naturally when a man and a woman started living together—started to know one another inside and out? Surely it weakened your defences to let someone get inside your head? Strengthened the relationship, yes, but at what cost?

'What, Finn?' she persisted softly.

'More a case of burying my head in the sand, I guess. Arrested development—call it what you like. A crazy urge to hang on to the past—I'm not sure, Catherine.'

She rested her head on his shoulder. 'You're talking in riddles.'

He smoothed her hair absently. 'I never changed this house at all, you see. I wanted to have it exactly the way it was.'

She thought about this for a moment. 'Like Miss Havisham in *Great Expectations*, you mean?'

'Well, I haven't got a wedding dress covered in cobwebs, if that's what you're implying!' He wound a strand of hair around his finger. 'I suppose this place always represented where I came from. I felt it would be a kind of betrayal if I decorated the interior so that it looked like something you'd find in a magazine.'

'If you applied that theory to everything then we'd still be travelling by horse and cart,' she said reasonably.

He laughed. 'Perhaps.'

She looked at his pensive profile. Was it only in bed that a man like this let his guard down? 'You don't need material things to remind you of your roots, Finn,' she told him softly. 'The values you learned are what matters, and you keep those deep in your heart.'

He nodded. This felt close. Dangerously close. A warm haven far away from the rest of the world. He forced himself to return to reality—because reality was the one thing he was equipped to deal with. He turned to face her and ran a lazy finger down her side, enjoying her responsive shiver. 'So I guess this means we'll be sharing a bedroom from now on?'

It felt like one step forward and two steps back, and all her zing and fizz and exhilaration evaporated. The brightness dimmed and Catherine felt curiously and ridiculously disappointed at his matter-of-fact assessment. Until she reminded herself that nothing had changed—not really.

Their situation was no different from what it had been before, except that now sex had been introduced into the equation. She shouldn't start confusing post-coital confidences with real, true and lasting intimacy.

'I guess we will,' she said lightly. 'Now, are you going to go down and make me my supper? I have a ferocious appetite on me!'

'Ferocious, hmm?' He smiled as he swung his naked body out of bed and looked down at her. 'You know, Catherine, you're sounding more Irish by the day.'

She nodded. She needed to. Her baby was going to be born in Ireland and have an Irish father.

She, too, needed roots.

CHAPTER TWELVE

'CATHERINE! For God's sake, come in here and sit down.'

'I can't! I'm sorting out the kitchen cupboards!'

Finn levered himself up from the sofa and came and stood in the doorway, watching while she bent to work, wondering how a woman eight months into her pregnancy could possibly have such a delectable bottom. He walked over to where she crouched and cupped her buttocks.

'Finn, stop it—'

He bent his head to nuzzle her ear. 'Don't you like it?'

'That's not the point—'

'No?' He kissed the back of her neck. 'The point being what, precisely?'

'I told you—I'm trying to get everything sorted out for when the baby comes.'

'But the baby isn't due for another month,' he objected. 'And I'm flying to London tomorrow. Leave it, Catherine. You won't see me all week.'

'I don't see you all week as it is.' She straightened up with difficulty and allowed him to help her to her feet. 'So what's the difference?'

'A whole sea dividing us?' he teased. 'Won't you miss me?'

She wound her arms around his neck. 'A bit.'

He touched his lips to hers. 'Only a bit?'

Much, much more. 'Stop fishing for compliments!'

'Then come and sit down and have a drink and watch some television.'

She sank onto the sofa. 'What an exciting life we lead, Mr Delaney!'

'Are you complaining?' he asked seriously, as he handed her a glass of sparkling water.

'No, I love it,' she said simply. Just as she loved him. How cosy it all was on the outside. She took a sip and looked at him over the rim of the glass. She had been fidgety over the past few days. Perhaps it was because he was travelling to England. It *was* different, him being in London. A whole plane-ride away. Maybe now was the time to stop pretending that the future was never going to happen.

'Finn?'

'Mmm?'

'There are so many things we haven't discussed.'

'Such as?'

'Well, what happens when the baby's born. What we're going to do—'

'I thought we were taking it a day at a time?'

'And we are.' She drew a deep breath. 'But we can't go on like that for ever, can we?'

He put his glass down. 'I think we could.'

Her heart started beating frantically. 'You do?'

'I can't see any reason why not.' He smiled. 'My sweet Catherine! We've discovered that we like one another. That we can live together without wanting to throw things.' His eyes glittered. 'Thankfully, you seem to have got all that out of your system!' He smiled again as she giggled. 'See! We make each other laugh.

We're compatible sexually—though that was never in any question, was it? That's not bad to be going along with.'

'And you think that's enough?'

He got up and threw a log on the fire, because the May weather had taken a sudden, unseasonable dip. It fizzed like a golden firework in the grate and he turned to look down at her, his face all light and shadows cast by the flicker of the flames.

'It's more than a lot of people have,' he said quietly. 'But you must decide whether it's enough for you. Whether you want to go chasing rainbows, or settle for giving this baby the security it deserves. Think about it, Catherine.'

Chasing rainbows. He made the search for love sound so insubstantial. And of course love had been the glaring omission from his list.

'And fidelity?' she asked, because that was more tangible than love.

'I could not tolerate infidelity,' he said slowly. 'And I would not expect you to either.'

Which was not quite the same as saying that the situation would never arise, was it? That if someone came along and captured Finn's heart he wouldn't be off?

'It's up to you, Catherine,' he said. 'The choice is yours. I'm being honest in what I'm offering you.'

Choice. There it was again, that infernal word he was so fond of using and which she was so wary of. Because choice meant coming to a decision, and there was always the chance that she would make the wrong one.

She could give her baby security—and not just the security of being legitimate and being cared for. The security of having a father around. A father who, she was certain, would love the baby as much as she did, who would be the kind of role-model that any small boy would give his eye-teeth for.

He was not offering her rose-tinted dreams and an impossibly romantic future together, but surely that was just practical. And honest, as he had said.

She considered the alternative. Going back out there as a single mother and consigning herself to a life alone with her baby. Or foolishly hoping that she might meet another man who would capture her heart as Finn had done—knowing, deep down, that no other man would ever come close to holding a candle to him.

If they had been different people, with different upbringings and in different circumstances, then both of them might have gone chasing those elusive rainbows.

But they were not different people. They were Finn and Catherine. And their pasts had made them into the people they were today. The past was powerful, she recognised—it sent far-reaching repercussions down through the ages.

'I'll think about it,' she said.

Their lovemaking seemed especially close that night, and they held each other very tightly afterwards for what seemed like a long time.

When Catherine went to the door to wave Finn off in the morning, her heart felt as heavy as the sky.

Finn glanced up at the leaden grey clouds and frowned. 'Feels like snow.'

'You can't have snow in May,' she protested.

'Who says we can't? One year we had a frosting in June!'

'You're kidding?'

'No, sweetheart, I'm not.' He caught her in his arms. 'You will take care, won't you?'

'Of course I will! What do you think I'm going to do? Start snow-boarding? Cross-country skiing?'

'I'm serious.'

She rose up on tiptoe to touch her lips to his. 'And so am I,' she whispered. 'I'll be fine. Ring me when you get to London.'

'Get Aunt Finola to move in if the weather turns bad or if you're worried. Or go and stay with Aisling and Patrick. When are you seeing the doctor next?'

'The day after tomorrow. Finn, stop fussing, will you? Just go!'

His mouth lingered on hers until he drew away reluctantly. 'Better go. Plane to catch.' He held her one last time. 'I'll see you Friday.'

Love you, she thought silently as his car roared away, and she shivered and shut the door.

He rang her from the airport. 'What's the weather like?'

She glanced out at the sky. 'Same.'

'I'll ring you just as soon as I get there.'

'Finn, what's wrong with you? Why are you so worried?'

'What's *wrong* with me? My wife's pregnant and I'm leaving the country! Why on earth should I be worried, Catherine?' he questioned wryly. But he *was* worried. Uneasy. Did every father-to-be feel like a cat on a hot tin roof at a time like this?

Catherine put the phone down and made herself some tea. She glanced at her watch to see that Finn's flight would now be airborne. Keep him safe for me, she prayed, while outside the sky grew darker and the first snowflakes began to flutter down.

It snowed all afternoon, becoming whiter and thicker, until the garden looked just like a Christmas card. Catherine had just lit a fire when there was a loud banging on the door, and there stood Aunt Finola, scarcely recognisable beneath hood and scarf, a rain-mac worn over a thick overcoat and countless sweaters!

'Come in.' Catherine smiled. 'What are you doing out on an afternoon like this?'

'Finn rang me,' explained Finola, shaking snow off her boots. 'Told me to drop in and keep my eye on you.'

'He keeps fussing and fussing!'

'He's worried about you. And the baby.'

'I'm fine.'

'Yes.' Aunt Finola sat down and held her hands out to the heat before sending Catherine a shrewd look. 'You're looking much better these days. Less peaky. More…at peace with yourself,' she finished.

It was an ironic choice of word. 'Well, I'm pleased that's the way I look,' said Catherine slowly.

'You mean it's not the way you feel inside?'

She hesitated. This was Finn's aunt, after all—and in some ways his mother, too. 'I'm fine,' she repeated carefully. 'Honestly.'

'Things seem better between you these days,' observed Aunt Finola carefully. 'You seem more relaxed these past few weeks. The two of yous seemed terrible tense a lot of the time before that.'

Catherine did some sums in her head, and blushed. Oh, God—was it that obvious? That the moment they had starting having sex their relationship had settled down?

'You really love my boy, don't you?' asked Aunt Finola suddenly.

Catherine met her eyes in surprise. But what was the point in lying to someone who loved him, too? Wouldn't she then be guilty of false pride? 'Yes, I love him. Really love him.'

'So why the long face?'

Catherine shook her head. 'I can't talk about it.'

'Well, maybe you can't—but I can. I don't know what went on before Finn brought you here, and I don't want to know, but I assume that he married you because you were pregnant.'

Catherine went very pink. 'Yes,' she whispered. 'Are you shocked?'

Aunt Finola gave a cross between a laugh and a snort. 'Shocked? I'd be a very strange woman indeed to have reached my age and be shocked by something like that! It's been going on since the beginning of time! But Finn's a good man. He'll care for you, stand by you.'

'Yes, but…' Catherine's words tailed away.

'You want more than that, is that it?' Finola nodded her head. 'Tell me, Catherine—is the relationship good, generally?'

'Very good,' Catherine realised, unconsciously beginning to list all the things he had said to her on the eve of his departure. 'We get on, we make each other laugh…' Her cheeks went pink again. 'Oh, lots of things, really. But—'

'But?'

It sounded so stupid to say it. 'He doesn't love me!'

Finola digested this for a moment or two in silence. 'Doesn't he? Are you sure?'

'He never says he does!'

Finola shook her head. 'Oh, you young women today!' she said exasperatedly. 'Fed a diet of unrealistic expectations by magazines and books! How many smooth-tongued chancers have you met for whom words are cheap—who tell you they love you one minute and are busy looking over your shoulder at another woman the next? It's not what you say that matters, Catherine, it's what you *do* that counts.'

'You mean you think that Finn loves me?'

'I've no idea what Finn thinks—he never lets me in. He's let no one in, not really—not since he lost his mother.' Her brow criss-crossed in lines of sadness. 'Think about it, Catherine. They'd been everything to each other and suddenly she was taken away, without warning. What child wouldn't have grown wary of love after something like that? Or of expressing it?'

Why had she never looked at it that way before? Her thoughts came tumbling out as words. 'You think I'm being selfish?'

Finola shook her head. 'I think you're not counting your blessings and thinking of all the good things you *do* have. Love doesn't always happen in a blinding flash, Catherine. Sometimes it grows slowly—like a great big oak tree from out of a tiny acorn. And marriages based on that kind of love are sometimes the best in the world. Solid and grounded.' She caught the look on Catherine's face. 'Which doesn't mean to say that they're without passion.'

No. It didn't.

'It all boils down to whether you want instant gratification or whether you are prepared to work for something,' finished Finola gently. 'It's not the modern way, I know.'

'An old-fashioned marriage?' questioned Catherine wryly.

'There was a lot less divorce in those days.' Aunt

Finola shrugged. 'People stuck by each other through the good times and the bad times. For richer for poorer. In sickness and in health. Forsaking all others.'

'We got married in a register office,' commented Catherine absently.

'I know you did. But you still made vows, didn't you? Even if you didn't mean them at the time, that doesn't mean they can't be true in the future.'

Catherine nodded. 'Thank you.'

'For?'

'For talking sense to me. For making me realise what's important. I think I really needed to hear it!' She smiled. 'Shall I go and put the kettle on?'

'Now you're talking!'

By morning the world was silent and white, but at least the snow had stopped. Catherine got up as soon as it was light, peering out of the window at the frozen scene with pleasure—until she realised that the path to the gate was completely impassable. Someone could break their leg on that, she thought, especially if it became icy. And so, after a flurry of solicitous phone calls from Finn, Finola and Aisling, Catherine decided to clear the snow away.

She wrapped up warmly and set to work, and several people stopped to talk to her as she cleared the path—most of them asking when the baby was due.

'Not until June,' she told them.

'You've a bit of a wait, then!' said the postman's wife, who had six herself. 'The last month or so's always the worst!'

No one seemed to think it odd that a pregnant woman should be working physically, but that was because, Catherine realised, it wasn't. Not at all. And especially not in rural areas. For centuries women had been working in the fields until they had their babies, and what she was doing wasn't so very different. That morning she felt strong, capable and really *alive*—as if she could conquer the world.

The path was almost cleared when the first pain came, so sharp and so unexpected that Catherine dropped her shovel and held her hands to her tight belly, her breath coming in clouds on the frozen air.

It couldn't possibly be the baby, she reassured herself as the tight spasm receded. The baby wasn't due yet. These pains were nature's way of warning you what the real thing was like.

But the spasms continued throughout the night, and by three o'clock in the morning Catherine could stand it no longer and rang Finola.

'I think it's the baby!' she gasped. 'I think it's coming!'

'Jesus, Mary and Joseph! Don't do a thing. I'm on my way!'

'I couldn't do anything,' said Catherine weakly, and clutched at her middle. 'Even if I wanted to.'

Finola arrived and took one look at her. 'Let's get you straight up those stairs,' she said, 'and then I'm calling the doctor!'

'But I'm supposed to be having the baby in hospital!'

Aunt Finola snorted. 'And how do you suppose we're going to get you to hospital? On a sledge?'

Catherine giggled, and then groaned. 'Don't!' Her mouth fell open. 'And Finn's supposed to be here! I want Finn here with me.'

'Finn's in London,' said Finola gently. 'Just think about him. Pretend he's here. He'll get here eventually.'

And so he did, by which time Catherine was propped up on the pillows, illuminated by the sunshine which was fast melting the snow, cradling a black-haired baby who was not as tiny as she should have been.

He burst in through the bedroom door, his face a stricken mixture of panic and joy, and was beside the bed in seconds, kissing her nose, her lips, her forehead.

'Catherine! Oh, sweetheart. Sweetheart! Thank God!'

Both Finola and Catherine heard the break in his voice and for one brief moment their eyes met across the room. The expression in the older woman's said as much as, Are you completely *mad*? and Catherine knew that she mustn't wish for the stars. Stars were all very well, but they were a million miles away. This was here. And now. Grounded and safe. Far more accessible than stars.

'You're okay?' he was questioning urgently.

'More than okay,' she said, with the first stirrings of a new-found serenity she suspected came hand in hand with motherhood.

'And is this my daughter?' he was saying in wonder as he stared down at the ebony-dark head and then slowly raised his head to look at his wife. 'My beautiful daughter.'

The soft blue blaze dazzled her, enveloped her in its warmth and wonder. 'Meet Mollie,' she said, and handed him the bundle who immediately began to squeak. 'Miss Mollie Delaney. She hasn't got a middle name yet—we hadn't agreed on one and I thought you might like to—'

'Mary,' he said firmly, as she had known he would. His mother's name.

Finn looked down at the baby in his arms.

'Hello, Mollie,' he said thoughtfully, and when he looked up again his eyes were suspiciously bright.

Aunt Finola made a great show of blowing her nose noisily.

He had come full circle, Catherine realised. Mollie had given him back something of himself. His own childhood had been snatched away from him by the death of his mother and now having his own baby gave him a little of that childhood back.

'What can I say, Catherine?' he said softly. 'Other than thank you.'

At which point his aunt got abruptly to her feet and glared at him. 'I'm off!' she said briskly. 'I'll be back tomorrow!'

After she had gone, the two of them just gazed at their sleeping infant for long, peaceful seconds.

He put the baby down gently in the crib and then sat on the edge of the bed, taking Catherine into his arms as though she was a fragile piece of porcelain which might shatter if he held her too hard.

'Catherine,' he said shakily.

She wanted him closer than this. 'I won't break, you know.'

He pulled her against him and kissed her then, soothed and excited her with just the expert caress of his lips. Catherine sighed with pleasure and then with slight irritation when he stopped, and opened her eyes to find him looking at her rather sternly.

'This changes everything, you know.'

'I know it does. No more sleep, for a start!'

But he shook his head. 'You know what I'm talking about, Catherine.'

That was just the problem. She didn't. Or rather,

she didn't dare think about it. Hence her attempt at a joke.

His eyes were burning into her with such intensity—so blue, so beguiling. 'This baby cements what we have between us. You know that, don't you?'

It wasn't the most romantic way he could have put it, but then, whoever said anything about romance? She and Finn were about compatibility and maturity and making the best of a situation they had not chosen. And making the best of things was surely a sound bedrock from which to work?

She recognised, too, that Finn would do all in his power to make sure their relationship flourished—for the sake of Mollie if for nothing else.

She nodded, her eyelids dropping to hide her eyes, afraid that he might see traces of wistful longing there.

'Catherine,' he commanded. 'Look at me.'

She lifted her head and met the soft blue stare.

'Living with you is so easy,' he murmured. 'In so many ways.' There was a pause. 'You make me happy,' he added simply, and he lifted her fingertips to his lips and kissed them.

And if Catherine's heart ached to hear more then she was just being greedy. She made him happy—he had said so. And he made *her* happy. Which was more than most people had. Expecting those three little words said more about society's conventions and ex-pectations than anything else. For how many people said 'I love you' and then proceeded to act as if they didn't? Why, Peter had said it, and then he had run off with someone else!

No, she would count her blessings—and they were legion.

They made each other happy.

Who could ask for anything more than that?

EPILOGUE

CATHERINE sighed a contented sigh. 'Not exactly a conventional honeymoon, is it?'

Finn glanced up from sleepy eyes. In the distance, the dark blue waters lapped rhythmically onto the sand. 'Well, it was never a conventional relationship, was it, sweetheart?' he asked sleepily.

'Finn Delaney, will you wake up and talk to me properly?'

He rolled over onto his back, screwing his eyes up against the bright sunshine, and gave a lazy smile. 'It's all your fault, Mrs Delaney—if you didn't make such outrageous demands on me every minute of every day, then I might be able to keep my eyes open!'

Catherine rubbed a bit more sun-cream onto her tanned arm. 'And you honestly think that Mollie will be okay?'

He propped himself up on one elbow. 'With your mother and Finola looking after her? And Aisling having to be forcibly restrained from dragging her off to the beach every second? Are you kidding, sweetheart? Sounds like bliss for a two-year-old, to me!'

'Mmm. I guess you're right.'

'And anyway—' he pulled her into his arms, feeling the stickiness of the lotion on her skin and pushing his hips against hers in a decidedly provocative way '—I thought we'd decided to do things more conventionally from now on?'

She kissed his neck. 'Mmm.' The church wedding had been conventional enough—even though she had balked at wearing full white bridal regalia. But the snazzy silk suit in softest ivory, purchased from a shop in Grafton Street, had certainly won Finn's approval! And so had the miniature duplicate she had secretly ordered for Mollie!

They had flown out to Pondiki that same afternoon, to discover that Nico had himself found a bride, and was soon to be a father!

Finn gazed at her. 'Are you happy, Catherine?'

'It's a way of travelling, Finn,' she reminded him. 'Not a—Finn!' For he had pulled her onto her back and was lying above her, his gorgeous face only an inch away.

'Are you?' he whispered, his breath warm against her face.

'Blissfully.'

And she was.

Finn now worked from home two days a week—though he claimed that she and his daughter distracted him far too much.

'So what?' she had asked him airily. 'You've enough in the bank, and a bit more besides!'

'Have you a shameless disregard for your future, woman?' he had demanded sternly.

Catherine's mother was a frequent visitor, and she and Finola had struck up a firm friendship.

'Would you ever listen to those two?' Finn would often say, when the rise of their laughter made Mollie giggle. 'What the hell do you think they're concocting now?'

And Mollie continued to thrive. The most beautiful child on the entire planet, as her adoring parents were so fond of saying when they looked at her sleeping every night.

Her early birth, while unexpected, had soon been explained by Catherine's gynaecologist. It seemed that Catherine really *had* got her dates wrong, and that Mollie had been conceived in Dublin, not London, which made her heart lift with pleasure.

'You know what that means, don't you, Finn?' she had asked him.

He certainly did. It meant that their child *had* been conceived in passion, not anger—thank God.

Catherine had abandoned the book she had been writing; she found motherhood much more rewarding. 'Doesn't mean that I'll never write again,' she'd told Finn. 'Just not now.'

And Finn had taken to helping her in the garden sometimes—a plot which she had so transformed that word had spread of its beauty through Wicklow and beyond. Last year she had opened it up to the public, charging entry to those who could afford to pay and selling tea and cakes to raise money for the local library.

Finn called it 'helping' her in the garden, but in reality he just planted things occasionally. Primroses and roses and hollyhocks, and an unusual variegated tulip. And a peach tree, and the arbutus which did so well in that part of Ireland and which was known affectionately as the strawberry tree.

She had leaned on her spade one day and looked at him. 'Odd choice of plants, Finn.'

'Mmm.'

Something in his tone had set her thinking, set a distant memory jangling in her head, and she'd gone to her computer that evening, when he had gone up to the pub for a pint with Patrick. She'd browsed through her search-engine and had looked up the language of flowers. And there it all was, in black and white before her eyes.

Primrose—fidelity.

Variegated tulip—beautiful eyes.

Peach tree—my heart is thine.

And most lovely of all was the arbutus, which meant esteemed love.

Her eyes had been moist when she'd opened the door to him later.

'You've been crying!' he accused.

'Oh, you stupid man!' she exclaimed, flinging her arms around him. 'Why didn't you tell me?'

'Tell you what?'

'The garden! All those things you planted and I never knew why! Why didn't you just come out and say so?'

'That I love you?' he said tenderly. 'Is that what you want to hear, my sweet, beautiful Catherine?'

'Of course it is!'

They ended up in bed, and afterwards she rolled over to lie on top of him, a fierce look in her eyes. 'Finn?'

'Catherine?'

'Did you ever give another woman flowers with a message?'

'Never.'

'So why me?'

He shrugged, and gave a contented smile which still somehow managed to be edged with sensuality.

'I never wanted to before.'

'Tell me you love me again,' she begged.

'I'll tell you that every day for the rest of our lives,' he promised.

He did. But Catherine had more than words to warm her. She had only to look out at her garden to see Finn's love for her growing every day.

* * * * *

THE PATERNITY CLAIM

CHAPTER ONE

COME on, come *on*! With a frustration born out of fear, Isabella jammed her thumb on the doorbell one last time and let it ring and ring, long enough to wake the dead—and certainly long enough to rouse the occupant of the elegant London townhouse. Just in case he hadn't heard her the first time round.

But there was nothing other than the sound of the bell echoing and her hand fell to her side as she forced herself to accept the unthinkable. That he wasn't there. That she would have to make a return journey—if she could summon up the courage to come here for a second time.

And then the door was flung open with a force of a powerhouse—and one very angry man stood looking down at her, his crisp dark head still damp and shining from the shower. Tiny droplets of water sparkled among the brown-black waves of his hair. Lit from behind, it almost looked as though he were wearing a halo—though the expression on his face was about as unangelic as you could get.

His black eyes glittered with irritation at this unwelcome intrusion and Isabella felt her heart begin to race. Because even in her current nerve-jangled state of crisis his physical impact was like a shock to the senses.

He was wearing nothing but a deep blue towel which

was slung low around narrow olive hips and came to midway down a pair of impressively muscled thighs. Half of his chin was covered with shaving foam and in his hand he held an old-fashioned cut-throat razor which glinted silver beneath the gleam of the chandelier overhead.

Isabella swallowed. She had seen his magnificent body in swimming trunks many, many times—but never quite so *intimately* naked.

'Yes?' he snapped, in an accent which did not match the Brazilian ancestry of his looks and a tone which suggested that he was not the kind of man to tolerate interruption. 'Where's the fire?'

'Hello, Paulo,' she said quietly.

For the split second before his brain started making sense of the information it was receiving, Paulo stared impatiently at the woman who was standing on his doorstep looking up at him with such wary expectation in her eyes.

He ignored the sensual, subliminal messages which her sultry beauty was hot-wiring to his body, because his overriding impression was how ridiculously *exotic* she looked.

She wore a brand-new raincoat which came right down to a pair of slender ankles, so that only her face was on show. A face covered with droplets of rain from the summer shower, her dark hair plastered to her head. Huge, golden-brown eyes—like lumps of old and expensive amber—were fringed with the longest, blackest lashes he had ever seen. Her lips were lush, and unpainted. And trembling, he thought with a sudden frown.

Trembling... She looked like a lost and beautiful waif, and a warning bell clanged deep within the recesses of his mind. He knew her, and yet somehow he also knew that she shouldn't be here.

Wrong place. Definitely.

'Hello,' he murmured, while his mind raced ahead to slot her into her rightful place.

'Why, Paulo,' she said softly, thinking for one unimaginable moment that he actually didn't *recognize* her. 'I wrote and told you that I was coming—didn't you get my letter?'

The moment she spoke a complete sentence, the facts fell into place. Her accent matched her dark, Latin looks—although her English was as fluent as his. The almond-shaped eyes set in a skin which was the seamless colour of cappuccino. The quiet gleam of black hair which lay plastered against her skull by the rain.

The last time he had seen her, she had been standing illuminated by the brilliant sunshine of a South American day. Her silk shirt had been stretched with outrageous provocation over her ripe, young breasts and there had been the dark stain of sweat beneath her arms. He had wanted her in that moment. And maybe before that, too.

Resolutely he pushed that particular thought away, even as his eyes began to soften with affection. No wonder he hadn't recognised her, against the grey and teaming backdrop of an English summer day, looking cold and hunched. And dejected.

'Isabella! *Meu Deus!* I can't believe it!' he exclaimed, and he leaned forward to kiss her on each cheek. The normal and formal Latin American greeting, but rather bizarre and unsettling—considering that he was wearing next to nothing. He noticed that although she offered him each cool cheek, she shrank away from any contact with his bare skin. And he offered up a silent prayer of thanks.

'Come *in*,' he urged. 'Are you on your own?'

'M-my own?'

He frowned. 'Is your father here with you?'

Isabella swallowed. 'No. No, he's not.'

He opened the door wider and she stepped inside.

'Why on earth didn't you tell me you were coming?' he demanded. 'This is so—'

'Unexpected?' she put in quickly. 'Yes, I know it is.' She nodded her head in rapid agreement—but then she was prepared to agree to almost anything if he would only help her. She didn't know how—she just knew that Paulo Dantas was the kind of man who could cope with anything that life threw at him. 'But you got my letter, didn't you?' she asked.

He nodded thoughtfully. It had been an oddly disjointed letter mentioning that she might be coming to England sometime soon. But he had thought of soon in terms of years. He certainly wasn't expecting her *now*, not yet—when she was still at university. 'Yeah, I got your letter. But that was a couple of months back.'

She had written it the day she had found out for sure.

The day she realised the trouble she was in. 'I shouldn't have just burst in on you like this. I tried ringing, but the line was engaged and so I knew you were here and I...I...'

Her voice faded away, unsure where to go from here.

In her mind she had practised what she was going to say over and over again, but the disturbing sight of a near-naked Paulo had startled her, and the carefully rehearsed words were stubbornly refusing to come. Not, she thought grimly, that it was the kind of thing you could just blurt out on somebody's doorstep.

'I thought it might be nice to surprise you,' she finished lamely.

'Well, you've certainly done that.'

But Isabella saw his sudden swift, assessing frown.

'I'm sorry, I've come at an awkward time—'

'Well, I can't deny that I was busy—' he murmured, as the hand which wasn't holding the razor strayed down to touch the towel at his hips, as if checking that the knot remained secure. 'But I can dress and shave in a couple of minutes.'

'Or I could come back later?'

'What, send you away when you've travelled thousands of miles?' He shook his crisp, dark head. 'No, no! I'm intrigued to discover what brings Isabella Fernandes to England in such dramatic style.'

Isabella paled, as she tried to imagine what his reaction would be when she told him her momentous piece of news. But there was one more obstacle to overcome before she dared accept his offer of hospitality. What she had to tell him was for his ears alone. 'Is Eduardo here?'

And some sort of transformation occurred. A face which was fundamentally hard and uncompromising underwent a dramatic softening, and a smile of pure pleasure lifted the corners of his mouth—making him look even more outrageously handsome than he had done before.

'Eduardo? Unfortunately, no.' The mouth curved into a heart-stopping grin. 'Ten-year-old boys prefer to play football with their friends rather than keep their father company—and my son is no exception. He won't be back until later. A—' Inexplicably, he hesitated. 'A friend of mine is bringing him home.'

'Oh.' The word came out with just the right amount of disappointment, but Isabella wondered if the relief showed on her face. She also wondered who the friend was, as she quickly wiped a raindrop off her cheek.

Paulo watched the jerky little movement of her hand.

She seemed nervous, he thought. Excessively nervous.

Not a quality he had ever associated with Isabella. She could outshoot most men—and ride a horse with more grace than he had ever seen in another human being. He had watched her grow from child to woman—in the condensed, snap-shot way you did when you only saw someone once a year.

'You'll see him later. Come on—take off that wet raincoat. You're shivering.'

She was shivering for a variety of reasons—and coldness was the least of them.

'Th-thank you.' She stood blinking beneath the glow of the artificial light which danced overhead, frozen by the strangeness of this new environment. And the fact that Paulo was standing next to her, still wearing next to nothing, a faint drift of lemon about him—as indolently at ease with his semi-naked state as if he had been wearing a three-piece suit.

With numb fingers, she began fumbling with the buttons of her coat and Paulo felt the strongest urge to unbutton it for her, as you would a child—except that the first lush glimpse of her T-shirted breasts reinforced the fact that she was anything but a child. And that if he didn't put some decent clothes on in a minute...

'I can't believe you didn't buy an umbrella, Bella?'

he teased, in an attempt to divert his uncomfortable thoughts. 'Did nobody tell you that in England it rains and rains? And then it rains some more—even in summer!'

'I thought I'd buy one when I got here, and then I... well, I forgot,' she finished lamely, although an umbrella had been the very last thing on her mind. She had spent weeks and weeks just wearing her father down.

Telling him that it was *her* life and her decision. And that lots of people of her age dropped out of university. She had told him that it wasn't the end of the world, but the look on his face had told her otherwise. Isabella shivered. And he didn't the know the half of it.

He felt the slight tremor in her body as he tugged the cuff of her jacket over her wrist and hung the garment on a peg above a radiator. 'There. You're dry underneath. Come into the sitting room.'

Reaction set in. He was letting her stay. Her teeth started to chatter but she clamped them shut. 'Thank you.'

'Need a towel for your hair?' he asked, shooting her a quick glance. 'Or maybe borrow a sweater?'

'No. Honestly. I'll be fine.' But she didn't feel fine.

Her limbs felt stiff and icy as he led her along a wide, deep hallway and into a large, high-ceilinged room, its cool, classic lines made warmly informal by the pulsating colours he had chosen.

Isabella looked around her. It was a very *Latino* colour scheme.

The walls were painted a rich, burnt orange colour and deepest red and covered with vibrant pictures— there was one she instantly recognised as the work of an up-and-coming Brazilian painter. Two giant sofas were strewn with scatter cushions and a low table contained magazines and papers and a book about football. Dotted around the place were photographs of a young boy in various stages of growing up—Paulo's son—and a black and white studio portrait of a cool, beautiful blonde, her pale shining hair held close to a little baby. And that, Isabella knew, was Elizabeth—Paulo's wife.

'Make yourself comfortable,' he instructed, 'while I get dressed and then I'll make you some coffee—how does that sound?'

'Coffee would be lovely,' she replied automatically. Paulo went back upstairs and into the bathroom to finish shaving and frowned at himself in the mirror. Something was different about her. Something. And not just that she'd put on a little weight. Something had changed. Something indefinable… And it was something more than the dramatic sexual flowering he had noticed a few short months ago. He moved the blade swiftly over the curved line of his jaw.

He had known her for ever. Their fathers had been friends—and the friendship had survived separation when Paulo's father had eventually settled in England, the home of his new wife. Paulo had been born in Brazil, but had been brought to live in London at the age of six and his father had insisted he make an annual pilgrimage back to his homeland. It was a pilgrimage Paulo had carried on after the deaths of his parents and the birth of his own son.

Every year, just before Carnival erupted in a blaze of colour, he and Eduardo would travel to the Fernandes ranch for a couple of weeks and Paulo had seen Isabella grow up before his eyes.

He had watched with interest as the little girl had blossomed to embrace the whole spectrum of teenage behaviour. She had been stubborn and sassy and sulky, like all teenage girls. By seventeen she had begun to develop a soft, voluptuous beauty all of her own, but at seventeen she had still seemed so *young*. Certainly to him. Even at eighteen and nineteen she had seemed a different generation to a man who was, after all, a decade older, already widowed and with a young son of his own.

But something had happened to Isabella in her twentieth year. In the blinking of an eye, her sexuality had exploded into vibrant, throbbing life and Paulo had been touched by it; his senses had been scorched by it.

He had lifted her down from her horse and there had been a split-second of suspended movement as he held her in his arms. He had felt the indentation of her waist and the dampness of her shirt as it clung to her sweat-sheened skin. Their laughter had stilled and he had seen the suddening darkening of her pupils as she had looked into his eyes with a hunger which had matched his own.

Desire. Potent as any drug.

And his conscience had made him want no part of it.

He removed the towel from his hips, staring down at himself with flushed disbelief as he observed the first stirring of arousal. He scowled. Because that was the whole damned trouble with sexual attraction—once you'd felt it, you could never go back to how it was before. His easy, innocent relationship with Isabella had been annihilated in that one brief flash of desire. *That* was what was different.

His mouth twisted as he crumpled up the towel and hurled it with vicious accuracy into the linen basket, then gingerly stepped into a pair of silken boxer shorts.

Isabella wandered distractedly around the sitting room, going over in her head what she was going to say to him, forcing herself to be strong because only her strength would sustain her through this. 'Paulo, I'm...'

No, she couldn't come straight out with it. She would have to lead in with a casual yet suitably serious statement. No matter that deep down she felt like howling her heart out with shock and disbelief...because indulging her feelings at the moment would benefit no one.

'Paulo, I need your help...'

She heard the jangle of cups and looked up, relieved to find that he had covered up with a pair of jeans and a T-shirt. On his chin sat a tiny, glistening bead of scarlet and it drew her attention like a magnet.

He saw the amber brilliance of her eyes as she stared at him and felt the dull pounding of his heart in response.

'What is it?' he asked huskily.

'You've cut yourself,' she whispered, and the bright sight of his blood seemed like a portent of what was to come.

Paulo frowned, lifting a fingertip to his chin. 'Where?'

'To the right. Yes. There.' The finger brushed against the newly shaven surface and drew it away; he looked at it with a frown. Had his hand been shaking? He couldn't remember the last time he'd cut his face.

'Right,' he said, absently licking the finger with a gesture which was unintentionally erotic.

'Coffee.'

She tried for the light touch but it wasn't easy when all the time she felt the weight of the great burden she carried. 'I haven't had a decent cup since I left home.'

'I can imagine.' He smiled.

She watched as he slid onto the sofa, moving with the inborn grace of an alley cat. Back home they always called him *gato*, and it was easy to understand why. The word in Portuguese meant 'cat' but it also meant a sexy and beautiful man—and no one in the world could deny that Paulo Dantas was just that.

Tall, dark and statuesque, he was a matchless mix of English mother and Brazilian father. His was a spectacular face, with an arrogant sweep of cheekbones which could have been sculpted from some gold-tinted stone and hooded eyes more black than brown. The luscious mouth hinted at a deeply sensual nature, its starkly defined curves making it look as if it had been created to inflict both pleasure and pain in equal measures.

She took the coffee that he offered her with a hand which was threatening to tremble. 'Thank you.'

This was *crazy*, thought Paulo, as he observed her unfamiliar, frozen smile and her self-conscious movements. It was like being in a room with a stranger. What the hell had happened to her? 'How is your father?' he enquired politely.

'He—he's very well, thank you.' She tried to lift the coffee cup to her lips but now her fingers were shaking so much that she was obliged to put it down with a clatter. 'He says to say hello to you.'

'Say hello back,' he said evenly, but it was difficult to concentrate when that shaky movement made the lush curves of her body move so uninhibitedly beneath the T-shirt.

Isabella wondered if she was going mad with imagining, or had his gaze just flickered over her breasts? She wondered how much he had seen—and Paulo was an astute man, no one could deny that. Had he begun to guess at her secret already? Unobtrusively she glanced down at herself.

No, she was safe. The hot-pink T-shirt was relatively loose and the matching jeans were far from skin-tight. Nothing clung to the contours of her body. And besides, there was no visible bump yet. Nothing to show that there was a baby on the way, bar the aching new fullness of her breasts and the sudden nausea which could strike her at any time. And frequently did.

She tried a smile, but felt it wobble on her lips. 'I expect you're wondering why I'm here.'

At last! 'Well, the thought *had* crossed my mind,' he said, managing to turn curiosity into a teasing little comment. 'People don't just turn up from Brazil unannounced—not as a rule. Not without phoning first. And it's a pretty long way from Vitória da Conquista.'

Isabella turned her head to glance out of the uncurtained window into the rain-lashed sky. It certainly was. Back home the temperature would be as warm as kisses, the land caressed by a soft and sultry breeze.

'And shouldn't you be at college? It's still term-time, isn't it?'

She started to tell the story, though not the whole story. Not yet. 'Actually, I've dropped out of college.'

His body shifted imperceptibly from relaxed to watchful. 'Why?' he drawled coldly. 'Is that what every fashionable student is doing this year?'

She didn't like the way his mouth had flattened, nor the chilly displeasure in his eyes. 'No, not exactly.'

'Then why?' he demanded. 'Don't you know how important qualifications are in an insecure world? What are you planning to do that's so important that it can't wait until the end of your course?'

She opened her mouth to tell him about her dreams

of travelling, of seeing a world outside the one she had grown up in—and then she remembered, and hastily shut it again. Because that would never happen now. She had forfeited her right to do any of that. 'I had to…get away.'

Paulo frowned. Her anxiety was almost palpable, and he leaned forward to study her, finding his nostrils suddenly filled with the warm, musky note of her perfume. He moved out of its seductive and dangerous range. 'What's the matter with you, Bella?' he asked softly. 'What's happened?'

Now was the time to tell him everything. But one look at the disquiet on his face, and the words stuck in her throat. 'Nothing has happened,' she floundered. 'Other than the fact I've left.'

'So you said.' He felt another flicker of irritation and made sure that it showed. 'But you still haven't come up with a good reason why—' A pause, while the black eyes bored into her. 'Mainly, I suspect, because you don't have one.' Normally, he wouldn't have been so rude to her—but then this was not a normal situation. 'So, Isabella,' he said silkily. 'I'm still waiting for some kind of explanation.'

Tell him. But, faced with the iron disapproval in the black eyes, she found that her nerve had crumbled again.

'I was bored.'

'*You were bored.*' He tapped the arm of his chair with a furious finger.

'OK, stressed then.'

'*Stressed?*' He looked at her with disbelief. 'What the hell has a beautiful young woman of twenty got to be stressed about? Is it a man?'

'No. There is no man.' And that *was* the truth.

'For God's sake, Bella—it isn't like you to be so fickle! I can't believe that an intelligent girl—*woman*—' he corrected immediately and a pulse began a slow, rhythmical dance at his temple, 'like you should throw everything away because you're "bored"! So what? Stick it out for a few months more—because believe me, *querida*,' he added grimly, 'there's nothing quite so "boring" as a dead-end job—which is all you'll get if you drop out of college!'

And suddenly she knew that she couldn't tell him. Not now. Not in ten minutes' time—maybe not ever. How could she risk the contempt which would follow as surely as night followed day? Not from Paulo, whom she'd adored as long as she could remember.

'I wasn't looking for your approval,' she said woodenly.

'You don't seem to be looking further than the end of your nose!' he snapped. 'And just how are you planning to support yourself? Expecting Daddy to chip in, I suppose?'

She glared at him. 'Of course not! I'll take whatever I can get—I'm young and fit. I can cook. I'm good with children. Fluent in English and Portuguese.'

'A very commendable CV,' he remarked drily.

'So you'd recommend me for a job, would you, Paulo?'

'No, I damned well wouldn't!' His voice deepened into a husky caress. 'But I would do everything in my power to make you change your mind.' There was a pause, and then he spoke to her with the ease and affection which had always existed between them, until temptation had reared its ugly head.

'Go home, Bella. Complete your studies. Come back in a couple of years.' His eyes glittered as he imagined what two years would do to her. 'And *then* I'll find a job for you—on that I give you my word.'

She glanced down at her hands, unable to meet his eyes as his voice gentled. In a couple of years her world would have altered out of all recognition, in a way that she still found utterly unimaginable. 'Yes, you're probably right,' she lied.

'So you'll go back to college?'

'I'll…think about it.' She made a pantomime of looking at her watch, affecting a look of surprise. 'Oh, look—it's time I was going.'

'You're not going anywhere,' he protested. 'You've only just arrived. Stay and see Eddie—he'll be back soon.'

'No, I don't think I will.' She rose to her feet, anxious now to get away. Before he guessed. 'Maybe another day.'

'Where are you staying?'

'Just down the road,' she said evasively.

'Where?'

'At the Merton.'

'At the Merton,' he repeated thoughtfully.

He walked her to the front door just as they heard the sound of a key being slotted into the lock, and for some reason Paulo felt extraordinarily guilty as the door opened and there stood Judy—so cool and so blonde, wearing something soft and clinging in pale-blue cashmere, and a faint look of irritation on her face. Next to her stood his son, and the moment the boy saw Isabella his dark eyes lit up like lanterns.

'Bella!' he exclaimed, and immediately started speaking in Portuguese as he hurled himself into her arms. 'What are you doing here? Papa didn't tell me you were coming!'

'That's because Papa didn't know himself,' said Paulo, in the same language. 'Bella just turned up un-announced while you were out!'

'Are you coming to stay with us?' demanded Eddie.

'*Please*, Bella! Please!'

'Eduardo, I can't,' answered Bella, her smile one of genuine regret. She had bonded with Eduardo from the word go—maybe because they had both had motherless childhoods. She had helped him with his riding and with his Portuguese and seen him grow from toddler-hood to a healthy young boy. And before very long, he would be towering above her as much as his father did. 'I'm going to be travelling around. I want to see as much of the country as I can.'

'Is this a private conversation,' asked the woman in blue, 'or can anyone join in?'

Paulo gave an apologetic smile and immediately switched to English. 'Judy! Forgive me! This is Isabella Fernandes. She's visiting England from Brazil. Isabella, this is Judy Jacob. She's—'

'I'm his girlfriend,' put in Judy helpfully.

Isabella prayed that her smile wouldn't crumple.

'Hello. It's nice to meet you.'

Paulo shot Judy a look which demanded co-operation.

'Isabella is a very old friend of the family—'

'Not *that* old,' corrected Judy softly, as she chose to ignore his silent request. 'In fact, she looks incredibly young to me.'

'Our fathers were at school together,' explained Paulo smoothly. 'And I've known Isabella all my life.'

'How very sweet.' Judy flashed a brief smile at Isa-bella and then leaned forward to plant a light kiss on

Paulo's lips. 'Well, I hate to break the party up, sweet-heart, but the show starts at—'

'And I really must go,' said Isabella hastily, because the sight of that proprietorial kiss was making her feel ill. 'Goodbye, Paulo. Goodbye, Judy—nice to have met you.' Her voice barely faltered over the insincere words. 'Goodbye, Eduardo.' She ruffled the boy's dark head and smiled down at him.

'But when will we see you?' Eduardo demanded.

'Oh, I'll be in touch,' she lied, but as she looked into the black glitter of Paulo's eyes she suspected that he knew as well as she did that she would not come back again. Because there was no place for her in his life here. No convenient slot she could fill—pregnant or otherwise. And if there had been the tiniest, most pathetic hope that she meant something more to him than just friendship... Well, that hope had been extinguished by a girlfriend who was the image of his late wife. A girlfriend who called him 'sweetheart' and who owned a key to his flat.

But then, what had she honestly expected? That she could turn up unannounced and tell him she'd run away from home—pregnant and alone—and that he would give that slow, lazy smile and solve all her problems for her?

She didn't stop for the traditional kissing of the cheeks—she didn't want to annoy Judy more than she already seemed to have done. Instead, she wrapped her coat tightly around her as she stepped out into the early evening and wondered just where she went from here.

CHAPTER TWO

'ISABELLA!' screamed a female voice from the bottom
of the stairs. 'Can you get down here straight away?'

In her room at the top of the ugly, mock-Georgian
house which stood in an 'upmarket estate', Isabella
sighed. She was supposed to be off duty. Getting the rest
which her body craved, and the doctor had demanded
on her last visit to him. But that was easier said than
done.

What did they want from her now, this noisy and
dysfunctional family? she wondered tiredly. A pound
of her flesh—would that be enough to keep them off
her back for more than five minutes?

Wasn't it enough that she worked from dawn to
dusk, looking after the lively twins who belonged to the
Stafford family? Au pairs were supposed to *help* look
after the children and engage in a little light housework,
weren't they? And to have enough time for their own
studies and recreation. They weren't supposed to cook
and clean and iron and sew and babysit night after night
for no extra money.

Sometimes Isabella found herself wondering just
why she put up with treatment which clearly broke every
employment law in the book. Was she weak? Or simply
a fool?

But it didn't take long for her to realise exactly why

she was willing to put up with such shoddy behaviour—one look in the mirror reassured her that she was not in any position to be choosy. The curve of her belly was as ripe as a watermelon about to burst, and Mrs Stafford—for all her faults—was the only prospective employer who'd agreed to take her baby on, as well.

Of course, there'd always been the option of going home to Brazil, or returning to the ranch. But how could she face her father like this?

When her furtively conducted pregnancy test had turned out to be positive, she'd been so stunned by disbelief that she hadn't felt strong enough to present her father with the unwelcome news.

And the longer she put off telling him—the more difficult the task had seemed. So that in the end it had seemed easier to run to England. To Paulo. Never dreaming that her life-long infatuation with the man would render her too proud to tell *him*, either.

Coming to the Staffords had seemed the only decision which made any sense at the time, but she'd lived to regret it since.

Or maybe the regret had something to do with letting down the two men who she knew adored her.

'Isa-*bella*!' Resisting the urge to yell back at her boss to go away, Isabella levered herself off the bed and slipped her stockinged feet into a pair of comfortable slippers. If there was one thing she enjoyed about being pregnant—and so far it was the only thing she had enjoyed—it was allowing herself the freedom to dress purely for comfort. Elasticated waists and thick socks may have made her resemble an enormous sack of rice, but she felt too cumbersome to care.

'Coming!' she called, as she carefully made her way downstairs.

The twins came running out of the sitting room, their faces working with excitement. Charlie and Richie were seven year-old twins whose mission in life seemed to be to make their au pair's life as difficult as possible. But she'd grown fond of these two boys, with their big eyes and mischievous grins and excessively high energy levels.

Rosemary Stafford's methods of childcare had not been the ones Isabella would have chosen, but at least she was able to have a little influence on their lives.

She had tried to steer them away from the video games and television shows which had been their daily entertainment diet. At first, they'd protested loudly when she had insisted on sitting down and reading with them each evening, but they had grown to accept the ritual—even, she suspected, to secretly enjoy it.

'You've gotta vis'tor, Bella!' said Richie.

'Oh? Who is it?' asked Isabella.

'It's a *man*!'

Isabella blinked. Like who? 'But I don't know any men!' she protested.

Richie's mother appeared at the sitting room door.

'Well, that's a *bit* of an exaggeration, surely!' she said in a low voice, looking pointedly at Isabella's swollen belly. 'You must have known at least one.'

Isabella refused to rise to the remark—but then she'd had a lot of practice at ignoring her boss's barbed comments.

Ever since she'd first moved in, Rosemary Stafford had made constant references to Isabella's pregnant and unmarried state, slipping easily into the role of some kind of moral guardian.

Isabella thought this was rather surprising, considering that Mrs Stafford had become pregnant with the twins while her husband was still living with his first wife!

She gave a thin smile. 'Who is it?'

Mrs. Stafford was trying hard not to look impressed.

'He *says* he's a friend of the family.'

She could see Charlie and Richie staring up at her, but Isabella's smile didn't slip. Even though a thousand warning notes were playing a symphony in her subconscious. 'Did he give his name?'

'He did.'

'And?'

'It's Paulo somebody-or-other.'

Isabella's mouth froze. 'Paulo D-Dantas?' she managed.

'That's the one,' said Mrs Stafford briskly. 'He's in the drawing room. You'd better come along and speak to him—he doesn't seem like the kind of man who likes to be kept waiting.'

Isabella's hand strayed anxiously to her hair. What was he doing here? And what must she look like? Her eyes flickered over to where the hall mirror told its own story.

Her thick dark brown hair had been carelessly heaped on top of her head, secured by a tortoiseshell comb. Her face was pale, thanks to the English winter—a pallor made more intense by the fact that she wasn't wearing a scrap of make-up.

'Why on earth didn't you tell me?' hissed Mrs Stafford.

'Tell you what?'

'That a man like *that* was the father of your child?' Isabella opened her mouth to protest, but by then her employer was throwing open the door to the sitting room and it was too late to do anything other than go in and face the music.

The room seemed darker than usual and Isabella wondered why, until she saw that Paulo was standing staring out of the window and seemed to be blocking out much of the light.

He turned slowly as she came into the room and she saw his relaxed pose stiffen into one of complete disbelief as he took in her physical condition. The exaggerated bulge of her stomach. The heavy weight of her breasts.

She saw his black eyes glitter as they hovered on the unfamiliar swell, and she tried to read what was written in them. Shock. Horror. Disdain. Yes, all of those. And she found herself wishing that she could turn around and run out of the room again or, better still, turn back the clock completely. Something—anything—other than have to face that bitter look in this sorry and vulnerable state.

'Isabella.' He inclined his head in formal greeting, but the low-pitched voice sounded oddly flat.

He was wearing a dark suit—as if he had come straight from some high-powered business meeting without bothering to change first. The sleekly cut trousers made the most of lean, long legs and the double-breasted jacket hugged the broad shoulders and chest. Against the brilliant whiteness of his shirt, his skin gleamed softly olive. She had never seen him so formally dressed before, and the conventional clothes seemed to add to the distance between them.

Isabella felt the first flutterings of apprehension.

'Hello, Paulo,' she said steadily. 'You should have warned me you were coming.'

'And if I had?' His voice was deadly soft. 'Would you still have received me like this?'

She saw from the dark stare which lanced through her like a laser that it was not a rhetorical question. 'No. Probably not,' she admitted.

Mrs Stafford, who had been gazing up at Paulo like a star-struck schoolgirl, now turned to Isabella with a look of reprimand. 'Isabella—where are your manners? Aren't you going to introduce me to your friend?' She gave Paulo the benefit of a sickly smile.

Isabella swallowed. 'Paulo, this is Rosemary Stafford—my boss. Paulo is—'

'Very welcome,' purred Mrs Stafford. 'Very welcome indeed. Perhaps we can offer you a little refreshment after your journey? Isabella, why don't you go and make Mr Dantas a drink?'

Paulo said, in Portuguese. 'Get rid of her.'

Isabella felt inexplicably nervous. And certainly not up to defying him. 'I wonder if you'd mind leaving us, Mrs Stafford? It's just that I'd like to talk to my... friend—' she hesitated over a word which did not seem appropriate '—in private.'

Rosemary Stafford's pretty, painted mouth became a petulant-looking pout. 'Yes, I expect you do. I expect you have many issues to resolve,' she said, with stiff emphasis, and swept out of the sitting room, past where Charlie and Richie were hovering by the door, trying to listen to the conversation inside.

Paulo walked over to the door and gave the boys a slight, almost apologetic shrug of his shoulders, before quietly closing the door on them. And when he turned to face Isabella—she almost recoiled from the look of fury which burned from his eyes.

As though she were some insect he had just found

squashed beneath his heel and he wished she would crawl right back where she had come from. But what right did he have to judge her? She thought of all she'd endured since arriving in England, and suddenly Paulo's anger seemed little to bear, in comparison. She drew her shoulders back to meet his gaze without flinching.

'You'd better start explaining,' he said flatly.

'I owe you no explanation.' A pulse began a slow beat in his temple.

'You don't think so?' he said quietly.

'My pregnancy has nothing whatsoever to do with you, Paulo.'

He gave a hollow, bitter laugh. 'Maybe in the conventional sense it doesn't—but you involved me the moment you told your father that you were going to pay me a visit.'

She screwed her eyes up and stared at him in confusion. 'But that was months ago! Before I left Brazil. And I did visit you. Remember? That day I came to see you in your flat?'

'Oh, I most certainly do,' he said, grimly resurrecting the memory he had spent months trying to forget. 'I wondered then why you seemed so anxious. So jumpy.' He had been intensely aroused by her that day, and had thought that the feeling was mutual—it had seemed the only rational explanation for the incredible tension between them. But he wasn't going to tell her that. Not now. 'I also sensed that you were holding back— something you weren't telling me. And so you were.' He shook his head. 'My God!' he said slowly.

'And now you know!'

'Yes, now I know,' he agreed acidly. 'I put your tiredness down to jet-lag—when all the time...' He looked over at her swollen stomach with renewed amazement.

'All the time you were pregnant. Pregnant! Carrying a *baby*.' The word came out on a breath of disbelief. 'How can this have happened, Bella?'

She met his accusing gaze and then she *did* flinch.

'Do you really want me to answer that?'

'No. You're right. I don't!' He sucked in a hot, angry breath. 'Don't you realise that your father is worried *sick* about you?'

'How can you know that?'

'Because he rang me yesterday from Brazil.'

'W-why should he ring *you*?' she stumbled in confusion.

'Think about it,' he grated. 'He asked me to come and see you, to find out what the problem is. Why your letters have been so vague, your phone-calls so infrequent.' He shook his head and the black eyes lanced through her with withering contempt. 'I certainly don't relish telling him the reason why.'

'So he still doesn't know?' she questioned urgently.

'About the baby?'

'It would seem not,' he answered coldly. 'Unless he's a very good actor indeed. His main anxiety seemed to stem from the fact that he could not understand why you had chosen to flunk university to become an au pair.'

'But he knew all that! I wrote to him—and told him that living in England was an education in itself!' she protested.

She'd kept her father supplied with regular and fairly chatty letters—though carefully omitting to mention her momentous piece of news. As far as he knew, she would probably go back and repeat her final year at college. She hadn't mentioned when she was going home and he hadn't asked. And she thought that she'd convinced him that she was sophisticated enough to want to see the world. 'I've been writing to him every single week!'

The chill did not leave his voice. 'So he said. But unfortunately letters sent from abroad are read and re-read and scoured for hidden meanings. Your father suspected that you were not happy, though he couldn't put his finger on why that was. He asked me to come to see whether all was well.' Another cold, hollow laugh. 'And here I am.'

'You needn't have bothered!'

'No, you're right. I needn't.' His mouth curved with disdain as he gazed around the bland room, with its unadorned walls and rows of videos where there should have been books. Littered on the thick, cream carpet were empty chocolate wrappers. 'My, my, my—this is certainly some *classy* hide-out you've chosen, Isabella!' he drawled sarcastically.

His criticism was valid, but no less infuriating because of that. She struggled to find something positive to say about it. 'I like the boys,' she came up with finally. 'I've grown very fond of them.'

'You mean the two hooligans who nearly rode their skateboards straight into the path of my car?'

Isabella went white. 'But they aren't supposed to play with them in the road!' How was she supposed to watch them twenty-four hours a day? 'They *know* that!'

Paulo narrowed his eyes as he took a look at her pale, thin face, which seemed so at odds with her bloated body and felt adrenaline rush to fire his blood. He'd felt a powerful sense of injustice once before in his life, when his wife had died, but the feeling which enveloped him now came a pretty close second.

And this time he was not powerless to act. 'Answer me one question,' he commanded.

Isabella shook her head. This one she'd been anticipating. 'I'm not telling you the name of the baby's father, if that's your question.'

'It's not.' He almost smiled. Almost. He had somehow known that she would proudly deny him that. But he was glad. Knowledge could be a dangerous thing—and if he knew, then he might just be tempted to find the bastard responsible, and to…to… 'Is there anything special keeping you in this house, this particular area?'

'Not really. Just…the twins.' Which told him more than she probably intended.

That the father of her baby did not live locally. Nor live in this house. It wasn't probable—but it was possible. His mouth tightened. Thank God. 'Then go upstairs and get your things together,' he ordered curtly. 'We're going.'

It was one more bizarre experience in a long line of bizarre experiences. She stared at him blankly. 'Going where?'

'Anywhere,' he gritted. 'Just so long as it's out of here!'

Automatically, Isabella shook her head, as practical difficulties momentarily obscured the fact that he was being so high-handed with her. 'I can't leave—'

'Oh, yes, you can!'

'But the boys need me!'

'Maybe they do,' he agreed. 'But your baby needs you more. And right at this moment you look as if you could do with a decent meal and a good night's sleep!' He steadied his breath with difficulty. 'So just go and get your things together.'

'I'm not going anywhere!' she said, with a stubbornness which smacked of raging hormones.

Paulo gave a faint, regretful smile. He had hoped that

it would not come to this, but he could be as ruthless as the next man when he believed in what he was fighting for. 'I'm afraid that you are,' he disagreed grimly.

Suddenly she wondered why she was tolerating that clipped, flat command. She lifted her chin in a defiant thrust. 'You can't *make* me, Paulo!'

'I agree that it might not be wise to be seen carrying a heavily pregnant woman out to my car—though I am quite prepared to, if that's what it takes,' he told her, a soft threat underpinning his words. 'You can fight me every inch of the way if you want, Isabella, but I hope it won't come to that. Because whatever happens, I will win. I always do.'

'And if I refuse?' Her eyes asked him a question, a question he had no desire to answer—but maybe it was the only way to make her see that he was deadly serious.

'Then I could threaten to tell your father the truth about why you left Brazil. But the truth might set in motion all kinds of repercussions which you may prefer not to have to deal with at the moment. Am I right?'

'You wouldn't do that?' she breathed.

'Oh, yes. Be assured that I would!'

She stared back at him with helpless rage. 'Bastard!' she hissed.

'Please do not use that particular term as an insult!' he snapped. 'It is entirely inappropriate, given your cur-rent condition.' His eyes flickered coldly over her bare fingers. 'Unless you have an undisclosed wedding to add to your list of secrets?' He read her answer in the proud tremble of her lips. 'No? Well, then my dear Isabella—that leaves you little option other than to come away with me, doesn't it?'

It was far too easy. Far too tempting. But what use

would it serve? Could she bear to grow used to that cold judgement which had hardened his face so that he didn't look like Paulo any more, but some dark and disapproving stranger? 'I can't just leave without notice! What will the boys do?'

He refrained from telling her that her priorities were in shockingly bad order. 'They have their mother, don't they? And she will just have to look after them for a change. Does she work?'

Isabella shook her head. 'Not outside the home,' she answered automatically, as her employer had taught her to. In fact, Mrs Stafford had made leisure into an Olympic sport. She shopped. She had coffee. She lunched. And very occasionally she lay in bed all day, making telephone calls to her friends...

'Run upstairs—'

She turned on him then, moving her bulky body awkwardly as the emotion of having borne her secret alone for so long finally took its toll. She blinked back the tears which welled up saltily in her eyes. 'I can't run anywhere at the moment!' She swallowed.

He resisted the urge to draw her into his arms and to give her the physical comfort he suspected that she badly needed. It was not his place to give it. Not now and certainly not here. 'I know you can't—that's why I'm offering to help you. If you go and pack, I will deal with your employer for you.'

'Shouldn't I tell her myself?' He thought how naive and innocent she could look and sound—despite the very physical evidence to the contrary. He shook his head impatiently. 'She's going to be angry, isn't she?'

Isabella pushed a dark strand of hair away from her face with the back of her hand. 'Furious.'

'Well, then—you can do without her fury. Let her take it out on me instead. Go on, *querida*. Go now.'

The familiar word made her heart clench and she had to put her hand onto the back of a chair to steady herself. She had not heard her mother-tongue spoken for months, and it penetrated a chink in the protective armour she had attempted to build around herself. She nodded, then did as he asked, lumbering up to her room at the top of the house with as much speed as she could manage.

She did not have many things to pack. She'd brought few clothes with her to England, and what few she had no longer fitted her. Instead, she'd bought garments which were suitable for this cold, new climate and the ungainly new shape of her body.

Big, sloppy jumpers, two dresses and a couple of pairs of trousers with huge, elasticated waists which she was currently stretching to just about as far as they could go.

She had been forced to buy new underwear, too—and had felt like an outcast in the shop. As if everyone knew she was all alone with her pregnancy. And that no man would ever feast his eyes with love and pride on the huge, pendulous breasts which strained against the functional bra she'd been forced to purchase.

She swept the clothes and her few toiletries into the suitcase and located her passport. On the windowsill stood a wedding-day photo of her parents and, with a heavy heart, she added it to the rest of her possessions.

And then, with a final glance round at the box-room which had been her home for the last five months, she quietly shut the door behind her.

At the foot of the stairs, a deputation was awaiting her. Towering over the small group was Paulo, his hair as black as ebony, when viewed from above. Next to him stood Rosemary Stafford, her fury almost palpable as she attempted to control the two boys.

'Will you keep *still*?' she was yelling, but they were taking no notice of her.

Charlie and Richie were buzzing around the hallway like demented flies—whipped up by the unexpected excitement of what was happening, and yet looking vaguely uncertain. As if they could anticipate that changes would shortly be made to their young lives. And correctly guessing that they would not like those changes at all.

Isabella reached the bottom of the stairs and Paulo took the suitcase from her hand. 'I'll put this in the car for you.'

She felt like calling after him, Please don't leave me! but that *would* be weak and cowardly. Instead, she turned to Rosemary Stafford and forced herself to remember just how many times she had helped the older woman out. All the occasions when she had agreed to babysit with little more than a moment's notice. And never complained. Not once. 'I'm sorry to have to leave so suddenly—'

'Oh, spare me your lies!' hissed Rosemary Stafford venomously.

'But they're *not* lies!' Isabella protested. 'It isn't practical to carry on like this. Honestly. The truth is that I *have* been getting awfully tired—'

'Oh? And what about other, earlier so-called "truths"?' Rosemary Stafford's glossy pink lips gaped uglily. 'Like your assurance that the father of your baby wasn't going to turn up out of the blue and start creating havoc with my routine?'

Isabella was about to explain that Paulo was not the father of her baby—but what was the point? What could she say? The boys were standing there, wide-eyed and listening to every word. Trying to make two seven-year-old boys understand the reality of the whole bizarre situation was more than she felt prepared to take on right then.

Instead, she reached out an unsteady hand and ruffled Richie's blond hair. Of the two boys, he'd been the one who had crept the furthest into her heart, and she didn't want to hurt him. 'I'll write,' she began uncertainly.

'Take your hands away from him, and don't be so *stupid*!' spat out Mrs Stafford. 'What will you write to a seven-year-old boy about? The birth? Or the *conception*?'

Isabella shuddered, wondering how Mrs Stafford could possibly say things like that in front of her children.

'It's time to leave, Isabella,' came a low voice from behind them, and Isabella turned to see Paulo framed in the neo-Georgian doorway. His face was shadowed, the features so still that they might have been carved from some rare, pitch-dark marble. Only the eyes glittered—hard and black and icy-cold.

She wondered how long he had been standing there, listening, whether he had heard Mrs Stafford's assumption that he was the father of her baby.

And her own refusal to deny it.

'Isabella,' prompted Paulo softly. 'Come.' Impulsively she bent and briefly put her arms round both boys. Richie was crying, and it took every bit of Isabella's willpower not to join in with his tears, knowing that it would be self-indulgent to break down and confuse them even more. Instead, she contented herself with a swift and fierce kiss on the top of each sweet, blond head.

'I *will* write!' she reaffirmed in an urgent whisper, as Paulo took her elbow like an invalid, and guided her out to the car.

CHAPTER THREE

As soon as the front door had shut behind them, Paulo let go of Isabella's elbow and she found herself missing its warmth and support immediately.

'The car is a little way up the street,' he said, still in that same flat tone which she'd never heard him use before.

He'd parked it there deliberately. Just in case. He had not known what he expected to find. Or who. He hadn't known if she would come willingly. And how he would've coped, had she refused. Because some instinct had told him even then, that he would not be leaving without her.

Isabella walked beside him towards the car, suspecting that he'd slowed his normal pace down in order for her to keep pace with him. She got out of breath so easily these days. 'Where are you taking me?'

'Taking implies force,' he corrected, looking down at her dark head, which only reached up to his shoulder. She seemed much too tiny to be bursting ripe with pregnancy. 'And you seem to be accompanying me willingly enough.'

What woman wouldn't? she thought, with another wistful pang. 'Where?' she repeated huskily.

A plane droned overhead, and he briefly lifted his face to stare at it. 'For now, you will have to come home with me—' He sent her a searing glance as if he anticipated her objection. 'Think about it before you say anything, Bella. It makes the most sense.'

If anything could be said to make sense at that precise moment, then yes, she supposed that it did. And hadn't that been her first choice? Before she'd seen him prowling half-naked around his own territory—like some sleek and beautiful cat? *Gato*. Before she'd seen the beautiful woman who'd frozen her out so effectively. Before she'd decided that she could not face him with her terrible secret. 'Doesn't it?'

Isabella nodded, wondering what Judy was going to say *this* time. 'I suppose so.'

'As to what happens after that…' A silky pause.

'There are a number of options open to you.'

'I'm not going back to Brazil!' she declared quietly.

'And you can't make me!'

He let that one go. For the moment. 'Here's my car.' A midnight-blue sports car was parked with precision close to the kerb, and Isabella stared at the low, gleaming bodywork in dismay.

'What's the matter?' She glanced up to find that the black eyes were fixed intently on her face. He must have noticed her hesitation. She gestured to her stomach, placing her hands on either side of her bump, to draw his attention to it. 'Look—'

'I'm looking,' he replied, taken aback by the sudden hurl of his heart as one of her hands strayed dangerously close to the heavy swell of her breast.

'I'm so big and so bulky, and your car is so streamlined.'

He held the door open for her. 'You think you won't fit?'

'Look away,' she said. 'It won't be a graceful sight.' She began to ease her legs inside and his face grew grim as he turned back to look at the house they had just left—where two small boys forlornly watched them from an upstairs window. He did not know what lay ahead, beyond offering her temporary refuge, but already he suspected that his loyalties might be torn. How could they not be?

He'd known Isabella's father for years—ever since he was a boy himself. And for the last ten summers since his wife's death had accepted Luis's hospitality for both himself and his son.

Eddie had been just a baby when his mother had died so needlessly and so tragically in a hit-and-run accident that had produced national revulsion, but no conviction. The man—or woman—who had killed Elizabeth remained free to this day. In the lonely and insecure days following her death, it had seemed vital to Paulo that Eddie should know something of his South American roots.

As a father himself, Paulo felt duty-bound to inform Luis Fernandes what was happening to his daughter. But Isabella was not a child. Far from it. Would she expect him to collude with *her*? To keep quiet about the baby?

And for how long?

He waited until they'd eased away from the kerb, before jerking his head back in the direction of the house.

'How long were you planning to stay there?'

'I don't know.' She stared at the road ahead. 'I just took it day by day. Mrs Stafford said that I could work the baby into my routine.'

Paulo's long fingers dug into the steering wheel. 'But

you must have *some* idea, Isabella! Until the baby was…
what…how old? Six months? A year? Would you then
have returned to Brazil with a grandchild for your father
to see? Or were you planning to keep it hidden from
him forever?'

'I told you,' she answered tiredly, wishing that he
wouldn't keep asking her these questions—though she
noted that he'd refrained from asking the most fundamental question of all. 'I honestly *don't know*. And not
because I hadn't thought about it, either. Believe me,
I'd thought about it so much that the thoughts seemed
to just go round and round inside my head, until sometimes I felt like I would burst—'

Paulo's mouth hardened. Hadn't he felt exactly like
that after Elizabeth's death? When the world seemed to
make no sense at all? He stole a glance at her strained,
white face and felt an unwilling surge of compassion.
'But the more you thought about it, the more confused
you got—so that you were still no closer to deciding
what to do? Is that right?'

His perception disarmed her, just as the warmth and
comfort of the car soothed her more than she'd expected
to be soothed. Isabella felt her mouth begin to tremble,
and she turned to look out of the window at the city
speeding by, so that he wouldn't see. 'Yes. How could I
be?' She kept her voice low. 'Because whatever decision
I reach—is bound to hurt someone, somewhere.'

Her words were so quiet that he could barely hear,
but Paulo could sense that she was close to tears. A deep
vein of disquiet ran through him. Now was not the time
to fire questions at her—not when she looked so little
and pale and vulnerable.

He thought how spare the flesh looked on her
bones—all her old voluptuousness gone. As if, despite

the absurdly swollen bump of her pregnancy, a puff of wind could blow her away.

'You haven't been eating properly,' he accused.

'There isn't a lot of room for food these days.'

'Have you had supper?'

'Well, no,' she admitted. She'd been seeking refuge in her room: too tired to bother going downstairs to hunt through the junk food in the Staffords' fridge for something which looked vaguely nutritional.

'Your baby needs sustenance,' he growled. 'And so, for that matter, do you. I'm taking you for something to eat.'

Nausea welled up in her throat. She shook her head.

'I can't face the thought of food at the moment. Too much has happened—surely you can understand that?'

'You can try.' His mouth twisted into a mocking smile. 'For me.'

She knotted her fingers together in her lap. 'I suppose I'm not going to get any peace unless I agree?'

'No, you're not,' he agreed. 'Just console yourself with the thought that I'm doing it for your own good.'

'You're so kind, Paulo.' He heard the tentative attempt at sarcasm and oddly enough it made him smile. At least her spirit hadn't been entirely extinguished.

'More practical than kind,' he murmured. 'We need to talk and you need to decide your future. And we can't do that in private at my house.'

'Because of Eduardo?'

'That's right.' He wondered how he could possibly explain away her pregnancy to the son who idolised the ground she walked on. 'He'll be curious to know why you're here—and we can't give him any answers if we don't know what they are ourselves. And it might just come as a shock for him to see you so—' the words tasted bitter on his lips '—so heavily pregnant.'

She remembered the cool, blonde beauty who had let herself in and forced herself to ask the question. 'What about Judy? Won't she mind me landing myself on you?'

'I shouldn't think so.'

There was an odd kind of pause and she turned her head to stare at the darkened profile.

'I'm not seeing her any more,' he said.

'Oh.' Isabella was unprepared for the sudden warm rush of relief, but she tried not to let it show in her voice. 'Oh, dear. What happened?'

Paulo compressed his lips, resisting the urge to tell her that it was none of her business. Because it was. Because somehow—unknowingly and unwittingly—Isabella had exposed him to doubts about his relationship with Judy which had led to its eventual demise.

He'd thought that shared interests and a mutually satisfactory sex-life were all that he needed from a relationship. But Isabella's visit had made him aware that there was no real *spark* between him and Judy. And something which he'd thought suited him suddenly seemed like an awful waste of time. 'We kind of drifted apart,' he said.

'But you're still friends?'

'I suppose so,' he answered reluctantly. Because that was what Judy had wanted. She'd settled for 'friendship' once she realised he'd meant it when he told her it was over. But he knew deep down that they could never be true friends—she still wanted him too badly for that. 'We're not supposed to be discussing *my* love-life, Isabella.'

'Well, I don't want to discuss mine,' she said quietly.

'Does that mean you aren't going to tell who the father of your baby is?'

Isabella flinched. 'That's right.'

'Do I know him?'

'What makes you think I would tell you, if even you did?'

He found her misplaced loyalty both exasperating and admirable. 'And what if I made you tell me?' he challenged.

The streetlights flickered strange shadows over his face and Isabella felt suddenly uncertain. 'You couldn't.'

'Want to bet?'

'I n-never bet.'

'I'm not sure that I believe you,' he said softly. 'When you are living, walking proof that you took a *huge* gamble.' And lost, he thought—though he didn't say it. The look on her face told him he didn't have to. The car came to a stop at some traffic lights and he shifted in his seat to get a better look at her.

And Isabella forgot the baby. Forgot everything.

Through the dim light, all she could see in that moment were his eyes. Dark, like chocolate, and rich like chocolate, and sexy like chocolate. And chocolate was what Isabella had been craving for the past eight months.

'Paulo—'

But he'd turned his attention back to the road ahead.

'We're here,' he said grimly.

She heaved a sigh of relief as he pulled up outside an Italian pasta bar. Heaven only knew what she'd been about to blurt out when she had whispered his name like that. At least the activity of eating might distract him from his interrogation—and maybe she was hungrier than she had previously thought. It would certainly make a change to have a meal cooked for her.

The restaurant was small and lit by candles, and almost full—and Isabella was certain that they would be turned away. But no. It seemed that here they knew him well. Paulo asked for, and got, a table in one of the recesses of the room—well away from the other customers.

She glanced down at the menu she'd been given, at the meaningless swirl of words there. And when she looked up again, it was to find him studying her intently.

'Do you know what you want?'

She shook her head. 'No.'

He jabbed a finger halfway down his menu. 'Why don't you try some spinach lasagne?' he suggested. 'Lots of nutrients to build you up. And you, *querida*, could certainly do with some building up.'

She nodded obediently. 'All right.'

He wasn't used to such passivity—not from Isabella—and thought how wan her face looked as the waiter came over to their table. 'Drink some tomato juice,' he instructed, almost roughly. 'You like that, don't you?'

'Thanks. I will.' She shook out her napkin and smoothed it out carefully on her lap as he gave their order.

'So.' He traced a thoughtful finger on the crisp, white cloth and leaned across the table towards her. 'We—or rather *you*—have a few big decisions to make.'

'I'm not going home!'

'No. So you said.' His mouth hardened. 'Anyway,

your objection is academic, isn't it, Bella? No airline will allow you to fly in such an advanced stage of pregnancy.' He paused, his dark gaze on her belly, as if he could estimate the gestation just by looking. 'And you're…how many weeks?'

She hesitated. 'Thirty-seven.'

'Only three weeks to go,' he observed, his eyes burning into her. 'So when did you conceive?'

Isabella blushed. 'I don't have to answer that.'

'No, you don't,' he agreed. 'But I can work it out for myself in any case.' His eyes shuttered to dark slits as he did a few rapid sums in his head, then flickered open to stare at her with astonishment. 'That takes us back to just around Carnival time.'

'Paulo, *must* you?'

He ignored her objection, still frowning. 'That means you must have become pregnant just after I left.'

She supposed that there was no point in denying it. 'Yes.'

'Or maybe it was *during* my visit?' he suggested, unprepared for the lightning-bolt of jealousy.

'No!' she shot back.

He frowned again, not seeming to care that the waiter was depositing their food and wine before them. 'So who is it? I don't remember seeing you with anyone. No ardent lover hanging around the place. I don't remember you rushing off every minute to be with someone.'

Quite the opposite, in fact. She had been at *his* side most minutes of the day. Her father had even made a joke about it. *She has become your little shadow, Paulo,* the older man had laughed and Isabella had aimed a mock-punch at her father's stomach while Paulo had watched the movement of her lush breasts with hungry eyes and a guilty heart. And been very sure that if his host knew what was going on in his mind, then he would have kicked him off the ranch there and then.

'So who is it?' he asked again, only this time his voice sounded brittle.

Isabella mechanically ate a mouthful of pasta, forcing herself to meet his eyes. 'Is my coming to stay with you conditional on me telling you who the father is?'

'I don't need to know his name. I'm certainly not going to try to wring it out of you.' There was a long and dangerous pause. 'But if he turns up, demanding to see you—'

'He won't,' she put in hurriedly. 'It won't happen. I give you my word, Paulo.'

'You sound very sure,' he observed. He looked over the rim of his wineglass, fixing her with a dark gaze which was as intense as his next soft question. 'Does that mean that the affair is definitely over?'

The *affair*? If only he knew! 'Yes.' Isabella swallowed. She owed him the truth. Or as much of the truth as she dared give without making herself sound like the biggest fool who ever walked the earth. 'It's over. It never really got off the ground, if you must know.' Her eyes glittered with a defiant kind of pride as she stared at the man she had idolised for as long as she could remember.

'But I can't come to stay with you, not even for a minute—not if you despise me for what I've done, Paulo.'

'Despise you?' He looked across the table, saw the stubborn little tilt of her chin, and felt a wave of anger wash over him. What a way to have a first baby, he thought bitterly. It shouldn't be like this—not for any woman—but especially not for Isabella.

He remembered Eduardo's impending arrival, when

Elizabeth had planned everything right down to the very last detail. Nothing had been left to chance, save chance itself. He had joked that her hospital bag had been packed almost from the moment of conception, and Elizabeth had laughed, too. His voice softened. 'Why on earth would I despise you?'

'Why do you think?' Isabella stared down at her plate with eyes which were suddenly bright. 'Because I'm going to have a baby. I'm going to be an unmarried mother! I've let my father down,' she said huskily. 'And myself!'

He leaned further across the table towards her, so that the flame of the candle was reflected in the black eyes. 'Now listen to me, Isabella Fernandes, and stop beating yourself up!' he whispered fiercely. 'We aren't living in the Dark Ages. You'll be bringing a baby up on your own—so what? A third of the population in England is *divorced*, for God's sake—and there are countless children who are the casualties of broken marriages. At least your child won't have to witness the deterioration of a relationship.'

'But I didn't *want* to have a baby like this!'

'I know you didn't.' He took her hand in his, staring down at it as it lay inertly in his palm. It felt small and cold and lifeless and he began to massage the palm with the pad of his thumb, stroking some kind of warmth back into it. He felt her trembling response and found himself filled with a sudden fierce need to comfort her. Protect her.

'There is no Merton Hotel, is there?' he asked suddenly.

She glanced up. 'How do you know that?'

His mouth twisted into a strange kind of smile. 'How do you think? I came looking for you.'

'*Did* you?'

'Sure I did.' After she'd left his house so abruptly, he'd gone to the theatre with Judy. He had sat through the show feeling distracted and bored and had been forced to endure all kinds of intrusive questions afterwards at supper, when Judy had been determined to find out everything she could about Isabella.

Too much wine had made Judy tearful and very slightly hysterical as she'd accused him of concealing something about his relationship with the Brazilian girl.

She'd made accusations about Isabella which had appalled him nearly as much as they had aroused him... Grim-faced, he'd driven her home and resisted all her attempts to seduce him. Afterwards, he had gone home and phoned Directory Enquiries for the number of the Merton Hotel, only to discover that no such place existed.

So Isabella had not wanted him to find her, he remembered thinking, with faint surprise, because women usually made it easy for him to contact them—not the opposite. But that, he had decided reluctantly, was her prerogative.

And now he knew why.

He stared at her. 'Just why *did* you come to see me that day, Bella?' he asked. 'Was it to ask for my help?'

She hesitated. 'I... Yes. Yes, it was.'

'But something changed your mind. I wonder what it was.' His eyes narrowed with interest. 'Why did you go away without telling me?'

'I couldn't go through with it. When it came down to it, I just couldn't face telling you.'

'And that's it?' he demanded.

Again, she hesitated, but she knew she couldn't admit that she'd been intimidated by his girlfriend. And by the very fact that he had one. 'That's it.' She turned her face up to his and stumbled out his name. 'Oh, Paulo!' she sighed. 'Whatever have I *done*?'

The choked little words stabbed at him, and he gave her hand one final squeeze. 'There's nothing you can do about it. You've been unlucky, that's all—'

'No, please don't say that.' She kept her voice low. 'This is a baby we're talking about! Not a piece of bad luck!'

'That's not what I meant. You took a risk—and you've paid the ultimate price for that risk.' He gave a bitter laugh. 'Didn't anyone ever tell you, Bella, that there's no such thing as safe sex?'

But he found that his words produced unwanted images—images of Isabella being intimate with another man, her dark hair spread in a shining fan across a stranger's pillow and a bitter taste began to taint his mouth. He put his napkin down on the table and threw her a look of dark challenge. 'I just hope it was worth it, *querida*.'

Worth it? Isabella stared down at her plate, but all she could see was a blur of tears. If only he knew, she thought. If only he knew.

CHAPTER FOUR

IT WAS getting on for nine o'clock when Paulo drew up in the quiet, tree-lined crescent. It was a cold, clear night and moonlight washed over the tall town houses, making them silvery-pale and ghost-like.

'Will Eduardo be asleep?' whispered Isabella, sleepy herself after the meal which she had surprised herself— and him—by almost finishing.

'You obviously have idealistic views on children's bedtime,' he answered drily as he put his key in the lock. 'He'll be playing on his computer, I imagine.' He opened the front door and ushered her inside, dumping Isabella's bag on the floor just inside the hall. 'Hello!' he called softly.

There was the sound of dishes being stacked some-where, and then a woman of about fifty appeared, wiping her damp hands down the sides of her trousers. She had short, curly red hair which was flecked with grey and a freckled face which was completely bare of make-up. Her navy trousers and navy polo-shirt were so neat and well-pressed that they looked like a uniform. She gave Isabella's suitcase a brief, curious look before smiling at Paulo.

'Ah, good! You're back just in time to read your son a story!'

'But he says he's too old for stories,' objected Paulo, with a smile.

'Yes, I know he does—unless his Papa is telling them. You're the exception who proves the rule, Paulo! As always.' Her gaze moved back to Isabella and she gave her a friendly smile. 'Hello!'

'Jessie, I'd like you to meet Isabella Fernandes—who is a very old family friend.'

'Yes, I know—Eddie's talked about you a lot,' said Jessie, still smiling.

'And, Isabella—this is Jessie Taylor, who's so much more than a housekeeper! How would you describe yourself Jessie?'

'As your willing slave, Paulo, how else? Nice to meet you, Isabella.' Jessie held her hand out. 'Your father owns that amazing cattle ranch, doesn't he?'

'The very same.' Isabella nodded.

'Don't you miss Brazil terribly?'

'Only in the winter!' Isabella pulled her raincoat closer and gave a mock-shiver, grateful for Jessie's tact in not drawing attention to the baby.

'Isabella is going to be staying here with us for the time being,' said Paulo.

'Oh. Right.' Jessie nodded. 'That's in the spare room, is it?' she questioned delicately.

Paulo's eyes narrowed. Did Jessie honestly think that he'd brought a woman back here in the latter stages of her pregnancy for nights of mad, passionate sex?

He stared at Isabella's pink cheeks and guessed that she'd picked up on it, too.

'Yes, of course,' he said deliberately. 'In the spare room. Is the bed made up?'

'No,' said Jessie briskly. 'But I can do that now, before I go.'

'Oh, please don't worry,' said Isabella quickly. 'I'm not helpless—I can do it myself. Really!'

But Jessie shook her head. 'Good heavens, no—I wouldn't dream of letting you! You look dead on your feet. Why don't you sit down, my dear?'

Isabella hesitated.

'Go on, sit down,' ordered Paulo softly. 'Make yourself at home.'

She was too tired to argue with him, thinking how easy and how pleasurable it was to have Paulo make the decisions.

She sank down onto one of the two vast sofas which dominated the room, and gingerly removed the shoes from her swollen feet. She glanced up to find him watching her, his brow crisscrossed with little lines of concern, and she produced a faint smile. 'You did tell me to make myself at home.'

'So I did. I guess I was just expecting you to argue back,' he observed drily. 'I had no idea you could be *quite* so stubborn.'

'And I had no idea you could be *quite* so domineering!'

'Didn't you?' he mocked softly and, when she didn't answer, he smiled. 'Stay there—I'm going in to say goodnight to Eddie.'

He found his son tucked up underneath the duvet, his eyes heavy with sleep.

'Hello, Papa,' Eddie yawned.

'Hello, son,' smiled Paulo softly. 'Did you get my note?'

'Uh-huh.' Eddie jammed a fist in his eye and rubbed it, giving another yawn. 'How's Bella?'

'She's…tired. And she's going to be staying with us.'

The child's face lit up. '*Is* she? That's fantastic! How long for?'

'I don't know yet.' Paulo paused as he tried to work out how to explain the complications of a very adult situation to a ten-year-old. But children dealt with simple truth best. 'She's going to have a baby, you see.'

Eddie removed the fist and blinked up at his father.

'Wow! When?'

Paulo smiled. 'Soon. Very soon.'

Eddie sat bolt upright in bed. 'And will the baby come and live here, too?'

'I doubt it,' said Paulo gently. 'They'll probably go back home to Brazil once it's been born.'

'Oh,' said Eddie disappointedly, and snuggled back down under the duvet. 'Judy rang.'

'Did she?' Paulo frowned. He had always been completely straight with the women in his life. From the start he told them that he wasn't looking for love, or a life-partner, or a substitute mother for his son. Judy had assured him that she could accept that—but time had proved otherwise and her behaviour over Isabella had only confirmed his suspicions. But Judy was tenacious and Paulo too much of a gentleman to curtail the occasional maudlin phone-call.

'Did she want anything in particular?' he asked carefully.

Eddie pulled a face. 'Just the usual thing. She wanted to know where you were and I told her. But she went all quiet when I mentioned Bella.'

'Oh, did she?' questioned Paulo evenly.

'Mmm.' Eddie yawned. 'Papa—do I have to go to school tomorrow?'

Paulo frowned. 'Of course you do. It's term-time.'

'Yes, I know, but…'Eddie bit his lip. 'But I want to see Bella—and she went rushing off last time.'

'She won't be rushing anywhere,' said Paulo, but he could see from the expression in his son's eyes that Eddie remained unconvinced. And then he thought, What the hell? What was one day out if it helped a ten-year-old accommodate this brand-new and unusual situation? 'Maybe,' he said as he picked up the wizard book which was wedged down the side of the bunk-bed. 'I said *maybe*!' His eyes crinkled. 'Want me to finish reading this?'

'Yes, please!'

'Where had we got to?'

'The bit where he turns his father into a toad by mistake!'

'Wishful thinking is that, Eddie?' asked Paulo drily as he found the place in the book and began to read.

But Eddie was fast asleep by the end of the second page, and Paulo turned off the light and tiptoed out of the room to find Isabella in a similar state, stretched out on the sofa, fast asleep, her hands clasped with Madonna-like serenity over her swollen belly.

It was the first time he had seen the tension leave her face, and he stood looking down at her for a long moment, realising how much she must have had to endure in that soulless house—pregnant and frightened and very, very alone. Her hair spilled with gleaming abandon over the velvet cushion which was improvising as a pillow and her thick dark lashes fanned her cheeks. She'd loosened the top couple of buttons of her dress, so that her skin above her breasts looked unbelievably fine and translucent—as if it were made of marble instead of flesh and blood. He could see the line of a vein as it formed a faint blue tracery above her heart, could see the rapid beating of the pulse beneath.

He heard a sound and looked up to find Jessie standing on the other side of the room, her face very thoughtful as she watched him studying the pregnant woman.

She looked as though she was dying to fire at least one question at him, but her remark was innocuous enough.

'The spare room is all ready,' she said, and waited.

'Thanks.' He turned away from where Isabella slept, and walked into the dining room to pour himself a whisky while he pondered on what he should do.

Jessie had been working for him ever since Elizabeth had died. Sometimes he'd thought that she must have been sent to him by angels instead of an employment agency. She'd been widowed herself, and knew that practical help was better than all the weeping and wailing in the world. She was young enough to be good fun for Eddie, but not so young that she felt she was missing out on life by looking after a child who was not her own.

He also knew that she was expecting some kind of explanation now, and knew that he owed her one.

And yet he did not want to gossip about Isabella while she lay sleeping. He took a sip of his whisky and raised dark, troubled eyes to where Jessie stood.

'I'll be off now,' she said. 'There's a salad in the fridge, if you're hungry.'

'We ate on the way home.' He nodded at the tray of crystal bottles. 'Stay for a drink?'

Jessie shook her head. 'No, thanks—I've got a date.'

'A *date*?'

Her smile was faintly reproving. 'Don't sound so shocked, Paulo—I know I'm on the wrong side of forty, but I'm still capable of having a relationship!'

It occurred to him that Jessie might fall in love. Might even leave him. And, oddly enough, the idea alarmed him far less than he would have imagined. 'Is it...serious?'

'Not yet,' she said quietly. 'But I think it's getting there.'

'Whoa! And there was me thinking you were in love with your work!'

'In your dreams!'

He drew a breath and followed her out to the front door, where he helped her into her coat and handed her her gloves. 'Listen, Jessie—'

She turned to look up at him. 'I'm listening.'

'About Isabella—'

She shook her head firmly. 'No, honestly. You don't have to tell me anything—and I won't ask you anything.' She screwed her face up uncomfortably. 'Well, maybe just one thing—but then you probably know what that is, already.'

His gaze was nothing more than curious. 'What?'

'Are you the father?'

He very nearly spat his whisky out, and it took him several seconds before he was ready to answer. 'Jessie— that's so outrageous, it's almost funny! Almost,' he added warningly and his dark eyes glittered with indignant question. 'You don't honestly think that, do you? That I would suddenly produce a child-to-be? That I would have been having a relationship with Judy, when all the time I had made another woman pregnant?'

'No, of course I don't.' Jessie shrugged and sighed. 'When you put it like that, I suppose the very idea is crazy. But isn't that what everyone else is going to think?'

'Why would they think that?' he growled. 'She's only twenty!'

'And you're only just thirty!' Jessie retorted. 'It's not exactly the age-gap from hell!'

'And I've known her since she was a child,' he said stubbornly.

'Well, she's certainly no child now!' retorted Jessie. After she'd gone, he walked back into the sitting room to stand over the sleeping woman on the sofa once more, mesmerised by the soft movement of her breathing. No, Jessie was right. Isabella was certainly no child.

She'd relaxed into her sleep even more. Her arms were stretched above her head and a smile played around her lips—the first really decent smile he'd seen all day. Though maybe that wasn't so surprising, in the circumstances. Maybe sleep offered her the only true refuge at the moment. And he realised with a pang just how much he had missed that easy, soft smile.

Overwhelmed by a sense of deep compassion, he leaned over her and put his hand on her shoulder and gave it a gentle shake.

'Isabella?' he said quietly.

She didn't respond—not verbally, anyway. She murmured something incomprehensible underneath her breath, and wriggled deeper into the sofa, and the movement made the fabric of her maternity dress cling to her thighs.

Paulo swallowed.

Pushing against the sheen of the material, the bump of the baby could be seen in its true magnitude. She should have looked ungainly, but she looked nothing of the sort—she looked quite lovely, and he felt his body battling with his conscience as he gently shook her shoulder again, but she continued to writhe softly.

He felt desire shoot through him like an arrow—all the more piercing for its unexpectedness and its inappropriateness. And he must have made a small sound, because her eyelids fluttered half-open to stare at him.

And in the unreal world between waking and sleeping, it seemed perfectly natural for Paulo's darkly implacable face to be bent so close to her that for a moment it seemed as though he might kiss her. It was a lifetime's fantasy come true and she stretched her arms above her head in unconscious invitation.

'Paulo?' she whispered dreamily. 'What is it?'

He shook his head, telling himself that she had aroused in him feelings of protectiveness, nothing more. Nature was cunning like that—it made a woman who was ripe with child look oddly beautiful so that men would *want* to protect her. 'It's bedtime,' he responded sternly, but the trusting tremble of her lashes stabbed him in the heart, and made him ache in the most unexpected of places. 'You look like you need it. If you want, I can carry you.'

'Heavens, no—I'll walk,' she protested, wide awake now. 'I'm much too heavy to carry.'

'No, you're not—I bet you're as light as a little bird. Want me to test me it out?'

'No,' she lied, and struggled up into a sitting position. He helped her to her feet and put his hand in the small of her back to support her, just the way he had once done with Elizabeth.

Except that Elizabeth had been almost as tall as him—while Isabella seemed such a tiny little thing beside him. Why, she barely came up to his shoulder.

And yet looks could be deceptive—he knew how tough she could be. You only had to see her astride an excitable horse, expertly subduing it into submission, to realise how strong she could be. He had never imagined that she could look almost frail.

'Come on,' he said softly. 'Lean against me.' Too sleepy to refuse, she allowed him to guide her upstairs and into a bedroom, where there was a large bed with a duvet lying invitingly folded back.

'Get undressed now,' he whispered, as she flopped down on the mattress and sighed.

'Nnnng!' She pillowed her head on her hands, and closed her eyes.

'Isabella!' he said sternly. 'Get yourself ready for bed, unless you want me to do it for you!'

Her eyes snapped open. This was no dream. Paulo was here. Right here. And he was threatening to undress her!

'I can manage. Really.'

He gave her a narrow-eyed look of assessment, only really believing her when she unclipped her gold wristwatch and slid it down over the narrow wrist.

'Goodnight,' he said abruptly.

'Goodnight, Paulo.' He left the door slightly ajar, so that the light from the corridor would penetrate the room if she woke. She would not flounder around frightened in the middle of the night in unfamiliar darkness.

But he was restless. Too restless for newspapers or the stack of paperwork he kept in the study, and which always needed attention. He drank some coffee and showered, and then slipped naked into bed, the cool sheets lying like silk against his bare skin while he lay and thought about the woman in the next room and who had made her pregnant. And how she could be persuaded to return to her own country—because surely that was the only rational option open to her.

He scowled up into the blackness, wondering why the idea of that should disturb him so.

In the end he gave up on sleep and decided that maybe he would tackle that paperwork after all. He pulled on a pair of jeans and shrugged a black T-shirt over his head, and on his way downstairs he paused briefly to look in on Isabella.

She was curled up on her side, facing the door, and from this angle the curve of her belly hardly showed at all. With the light from the corridor falling across the sculpted contours of her face and her lips slightly parted in sleep, it was easy to forget why she was here. Easy to imagine her being in a bed in his house for another reason entirely... Paulo swiftly turned away and went downstairs.

He went through his papers on autopilot, gradually reducing the pile to a few sheets which his secretary could deal with tomorrow. He glanced down at his watch and yawned. *Today*, he should say. Better get to bed.

But he switched his computer on and began playing Solitaire.

He must have been dozing because he didn't hear the front door opening or clicking to a close. Nor did he hear soft footsteps approaching his study. In fact, the first indication that he had a visitor came from the sound of laboured breathing from just outside the door.

His eyes snapped open, his senses immediately on full alert, as he acknowledged that something had aroused him. He willed the aching fullness to subside.

'Bella?' he called softly. 'Is that you?'

'Sorry to disappoint you,' came an acid female reply. 'It's only me.'

He sat up straight as a tall, slim figure walked into the room and frowned at her in disbelief. *'Judy?'*

'Yes, Judy!' came the sarcastic reply. 'Why, did you think it was your little Brazilian firecracker?'

He reached out to click a further light on, his eyes briefly protesting against the bright glare as he stared at the woman standing uninvited before him.

The artificial light emphasised her pale-haired beauty—her long, willowy limbs and the pellucid blue eyes set in an alabaster skin. She wore jeans and an expensive-looking sheepskin jacket. And an expression he recognised instantly as a potent cocktail of lust and jealousy. He kept his face completely neutral.

'Hello, Judy,' he said softly, carefully. 'I wasn't expecting you.'

She raised her eyebrows and laughed. 'You made that obvious enough.'

He kept his voice steady. 'I didn't realise you still had a key.'

'That's what keeps life so interesting, isn't it, Paulo? These little surprises.'

He sighed. 'Judy, I don't want a scene.'

'No. It's pretty obvious from your greeting just what you *do* want!'

'Meaning?'

'Is that woman is staying here? She is, isn't she?'

'You mean Isabella?' he asked coldly.

Judy scowled, ignoring the warning note in his voice.

'You know damned well I do! You thought I was *her* when I came in, didn't you? "Bella"! Well, I'm so sorry to disappoint you, Paulo! How long is she planning on staying for?'

Paulo didn't react. The only movement in his face was the dark warning which glittered from his eyes. 'I don't think that this is a good time to have this conversation,' he said carefully. 'Apart from which, it's really none of your business.'

For a moment her face looked almost ugly as different emotions worked their way across it.

'She's the reason you dumped me, isn't she?' she demanded. 'You were never the same after she came here to see you. I could see it in your eyes that day. You were really *hot* for her, weren't you, Paulo? In a way you never were for me. Not once.'

His mouth hardened as he realised that she had no idea that Isabella was pregnant. And he had no intention of telling her. He carried on as though she hadn't spoken.

'I'm actually very tired, so if you don't mind...'

Judy stiffened as she read the rejection in his features.

'What's she got that I haven't, Paulo?' she pleaded. 'Just tell me that.'

He shook his head. 'Go home,' he whispered. 'Go home now, before it's too late.'

Her eyes lit up as she completely misinterpreted his words. 'For what? Too late to resist me, you mean? Well, maybe I don't want you to resist me. Maybe I want what you're trying to resist, just as badly as you do. What does it matter? I won't tell.' She moved towards the desk and the overpowering scent of her perfume invaded his senses and deadened them. 'Come on, Paulo—what do you say? For old times' sake.'

He shook his head, felt distaste whipping up his spine like a ragged fingernail. 'No.'

'No?' She flicked her pale hair back. 'Sure?' This really was astonishing, thought Paulo. A beautiful blonde begging him for sex. It was most red-blooded men's ideal fantasy and yet all he could think of was that she was going to wake the pregnant woman who lay sleeping upstairs.

'Quite sure. Keep your voice down.' He flattened his voice as the needs of his body fought with the demands of his mind. 'And I think it's better if you go right now.'

'And what if I stay and do…this…?' Her hand swooped towards him and he knew immediately just where she intended to touch him.

'I don't want you to.' With razor-sharp reflexes, he snapped his fingers around her wrist to stop her. *'I don't want you to,'* he repeated deliberately. 'Ever again. Got that?'

She stared into his eyes, like a woman who had never encountered rejection before and snatched her hand back. 'Why not?' she sneered. 'You want to do it with *Bella*, I suppose?'

He didn't have to tell her to get out; the look in his eyes must have done that effectively enough. He just heard her running down the hallway and slamming the front door so loudly that it echoed through the house like gunfire.

He waited until the automatic response of his body had died away completely, and he felt an ugly kind of taste in his mouth. Quietly, he turned the computer off and went to find himself a drink.

Barefooted, he went silently along to the kitchen where he poured himself a glass of water and stood drinking it, looking out of the window into the night sky. Outside, silver-white stars pin-pricked the darkened night and he found himself picturing Isabella's father's ranch in Vitória da Conquista. Where the stars were as big as lollipops—so bright and so close that you felt you could lean out and pluck them from the sky.

He pressed the empty water glass to his hot cheek as he anticipated the fireworks to come. What the hell was Isabella's father going to say when he discovered that his beloved daughter was going to have a baby? By a man she was refusing to name! He was going to be *absolutely furious*.

He was just thinking about going back to bed when he turned to see Isabella standing in the doorway, silently watching him.

She had changed into a big, white nightshirt and a pair of bedsocks and had plaited her hair, so that two thick, dark ropes hung down either side of her face. She looked impossibly sweet and innocent, making the swollen belly seem indecent in comparison.

'Did I wake you?' he asked. He saw the way she grimaced, then tried to turn it into a smile and he pulled a face himself. 'Obviously, I did.'

'I heard…er…noises. Then the door slammed.'

'And did it startle you?'

'Only for as long as it took me to realise where I was. But I probably would have woken at some point, in any case. Indigestion,' she said, in answer to the query in his eyes. 'It's the bane of late pregnancy.'

'I suppose it is,' he said slowly. He stared again at her bulging stomach. 'Would a glass of milk help?'

'Yes, please.'

'Sit down, then, and I'll fetch it for you.' She pulled a chair out from under the kitchen table and negotiated herself into it, wriggling her toes around inside the roomy bedsocks.

Paulo reached into the fridge and poured her a big, creamy tumblerful, then leaned against the draining board and watched while she drank it. He found himself fascinated by the white moustache she left behind, and by the tiny pink tongue-tip which snaked out to lick it away. Who would ever have thought that a heavily pregnant woman could look so damned sexy? he wondered.

His wife had been sick for a lot of her pregnancy. The doctors had told him she was 'delicate'. Like a piece of Dresden china that he dared not touch for fear of breaking her. And yet Isabella looked real and very, very touchable.

Isabella could feel him watching her, and she tried to drink her milk unselfconsciously, but it was difficult. And she could feel the baby moving around at the same time as her breasts began to sting uncomfortably in a way she was certain had nothing to do with the pregnancy. What conflicting and confusing messages her body was sending out!

She put the half-empty glass down on the table with a clunk. 'Did...did Elizabeth have an easy pregnancy?'

Paulo frowned. 'No, not really. It didn't agree with her. She was very sick for the first five months or more.'

Her expectant look didn't waver. Here in the quietness of the night, it was easier to ask questions which had always seemed inappropriate before. 'You must miss her.'

He didn't answer for a moment. 'I did. Terribly, at first. But it was such a long time ago,' he said slowly.

'That sometimes it seems to have happened to another person. We were together for two years, and Lizzie's been dead for ten.'

'Doesn't Eduardo ever ask?'

'Sometimes.' Isabella studied him. 'And does he have any contact with his mother's family?'

'A little,' he began, then suddenly his temper flared.

'What is this, Isabella?' he demanded, suddenly impatient. 'Truth or dare?' Women did not ask him about his wife—in fact, they did the very opposite. Ignored the few photographs which existed of Elizabeth with her infant son. Never asked the child any questions about his mother, as though they could not bear to acknowledge that he had loved a woman and had a child by her.

'You want to squeeze every painful fact out of me?' he grated. 'Yet obstinately refuse to disclose the identity of your baby's father?'

'That's different.'

'Why?' he snapped.

'Because there's no point in your knowing,' she said stiffly. 'I told you. It's over.'

'So why this sudden interrogation? Is this one rule for you and another for me? Is that it?'

She shook her head. 'If I thought that telling you would do any good, then I would.'

'But you don't trust me not to use the information?' he probed softly.

'No, I don't,' she admitted.

For some inexplicable reason, he smiled. 'Then you are wise, *querida*,' he murmured. 'Very wise indeed.'

He saw the way that one plait moved like a silken

rope over her breast when she lifted her head to meet his gaze head-on like that. 'Now go to bed, Bella,' he said roughly. 'You need your sleep.' And I need my sanity.

She paused by the door. He had warned her off prying, but there were some things she really *did* need to know. And if Paulo was in the habit of having late-night visits... 'Did I hear you talking to someone earlier?'

'I had an...unexpected visitor.' He gave a grim kind of smile. And anyway, what was the big secret supposed to be? 'It was Judy.'

'But I thought you said that it was over?' She'd blurted the indignant words out before she could consider their impact. Or the fact that she had no right to say them.

He knew it was a loaded question. Knew it and was surprised by it. No, maybe not completely surprised. 'It is.' He gave her a brief, hard look. 'She won't be coming back again.'

'Oh.' She kept her voice as expressionless as possible and hoped that her face did the same. 'Was it serious between the two of you? I suppose it must have been if she had a key.'

He gave a faint frown, tempted to dodge the question, knowing instinctively that the truth would hurt her. 'I don't do "serious" any more, Bella,' he told her quietly.

She felt her heart plummet. 'No. Right. Well, I guess it's time I went back to bed.'

Paulo's eyes narrowed with interest as he watched

the interplay of emotions on her face. Maybe Judy had been more astute than he had given her credit for.

'I guess it is,' he agreed blandly. 'Goodnight, Isabella.'

CHAPTER FIVE

ISABELLA was woken by a timid knocking on her bedroom door, and she yawned as she picked up her wristwatch from the bedside locker.

Sweet heaven—it was nearly ten o'clock! She stretched beneath the bedclothes after the best night's sleep she had had since arriving in England. How wonderful to have the luxury of lying in. By now in the Stafford house she would have been up and running for three hours. She would have cooked breakfast and loaded the washing-machine and be just about to pick up the vacuum cleaner.

The knocking on the door grew louder.

She sat up in bed and smoothed her hands over her dishevelled plaits. 'Come in!' she called.

A small, dark head poked itself round the door. It was Eduardo. And she could see wariness and excitement on his face.

'Hello, Eduardo.' She smiled. 'Come on in!'

'Hello,' he said cautiously.

'Or should I call you Eddie? That's what Jessie calls you, isn't it? Would you prefer that?'

'Only in England.' He nodded. 'When we're in Brazil, you can call me my real name.' He stood there rather awkwardly. 'Shall I draw the curtains back?'

She sensed his diffidence and widened her smile.

'Would you mind? That would be wonderful—then I can see what kind of view I have!'

The pale, sharp light of winter came flooding into the room as the curtains swished back to reveal the green blur of the distant park. Eddie turned round and Isabella patted the edge of the bed. 'Come and sit down over here. Or do you have to go to school?' She frowned down at her gold wristwatch. 'Aren't you a little late?'

'Papa said I can have the day off—to welcome you,' he added shyly.

'I'm honoured,' she replied softly and patted the mattress again. 'Come and sit down.'

He hesitated for one shy moment, then came over and did as she asked, glancing at the huge bump rather cautiously. 'Papa said you were going to have a baby.'

'That's right.' She supposed he must have told Eddie the evening before, when he'd gone in to read a bedtime story and she had been lying dozing on the sofa. She wondered what he'd said to the child. How he'd explained away the lack of a father. Maybe he'd turned it into a lecture on morality. 'I am.'

'Does it hurt?' he asked.

Isabella smiled. 'No. Why should it?'

'You must have to grow more skin?'

She laughed, and the movement made the baby start to protest. 'I've never thought about that, to be honest. The most painful thing is when it kicks. Sometimes it gets you right—' she clutched at her ribs and screwed up her face in an expression of mock-anguish '—here!'

'Maybe that means he'll be a football player,' suggested Eddie hopefully.

'But what if it's a girl?'

He shrugged. 'Then she can watch!'

'Or be the star of an all-girls team?'

'Nah!' Eddie shook his head decisively. 'Girls don't play football! Not properly, anyway!'

Isabella laughed, enjoying the comfort of the bed and the room, and the winter sunshine which streamed into the room and made bright puddles of light on the crisp blue and white bed linen. It was very obviously a spare room—well-decorated and luxuriously appointed, but with little in the way of personality stamped on it. A vase of flowers might help, she thought. Or would that just look as though she was taking up permanent residence?

'Papa sent me in to ask whether you like tea or coffee in the morning?'

She made a face. 'Your father asked *that*? Tell him that I drink only coffee in the mornings—and then it must only be Brazilian coffee!'

'Ah! Then I must be a mind-reader,' came a murmured boast and Paulo appeared, carrying a tray of the most wonderful-smelling coffee.

He glanced over to the bed, to where she sat with strands of dark-bronze hair escaping from her plaits; Eddie was perched on the bed next to her and Paulo's breath caught like grit in his throat.

They looked such a *unit* sitting there together, that for a moment he found himself imagining what life might have been like if Elizabeth had not died, an indulgence he rarely surrendered to. There might have been brothers and sisters for Eddie, and Eddie might have sat on the bed with his pregnant mother, just like that. He felt a great wave of sadness for the hole in his son's life. 'OK if I come in?'

'Of course it is.' But Isabella had noticed the swift look of pain and wondered what had put it there.

'Papa—Bella says the baby's kicking!'

'Well, that's what babies tend to do.'

'Did *I*?'

'Sure you did.' Paulo nodded, and put the tray down.

He had not foreseen that having a pregnant woman around the place would open up a new channel of thought for his inquisitive son. 'Your mother used to say that you were sure to be a star footballer when you finally made an appearance!'

'But that's what Isabella just said about *her* baby!'

Glittering black eyes connected with hers. 'Oh, did you?' he asked softly, as he lifted up the coffee pot and began to pour.

Isabella found herself wishing that she had leapt straight out of bed and replaited her hair. Or something. Not, she reminded herself, that she was in any kind of condition to go leaping anywhere. And not that Paulo would even notice if she had done. She took the coffee he offered her. 'Thanks.'

He searched her face for shadows, real and imagined, but he could see none. 'Sleep all right?'

'Mmm.' Eventually. She'd heard him moving restlessly in the next room for a while after they had gone their separate ways, and then the milk had made her sleepy.

Eddie looked up at his father. 'Where are we going today, Daddy?'

'Well, Isabella needs to see a doctor—'

'No, I don't—'

'Oh, yes, you do,' he argued.

'But I saw one last week!' she protested.

'Not in London, you didn't,' he pointed out. 'And you need to meet the doctor who will be delivering you. A Brazilian friend of mine—' he stirred sugar into his coffee '—who happens to be one of the country's finest obstetricians! I've already spoken to him.' He saw her mutinous expression and turned to his son with a smile. 'Go and fetch Isabella some crackers, would you, Eddie? Pregnant women need to eat when they wake up.'

Isabella put her cup down as the child jumped off the bed and ran from the room and fixed Paulo with a determined look. 'I am not so provincial that I need to have a fellow countryman deliver me, you know!'

'No. But why not make life a little easy for yourself?' His mocking expression seemed to indicate that it wasn't too late to start. 'You can speak to him in Portuguese and he will understand you.'

'But I'm bilingual!' she replied.

His stare was very direct; the mischief in his eyes unmistakable. 'Yes, I know you are. But I won't feel happy until I've had you checked over properly.'

'You make me sound like a car! Whichever doctor I decide to see is my business, Paulo—not yours.'

'Ah.' He glittered her a look. 'But you've made it my business.'

'No, you did that all by yourself! My father just asked you to look me up,' she argued. 'That was all. *You* were the one who insisted on bringing me back to your home.'

'And by agreeing to come, I'm afraid that you put yourself under my domain. Don't fight it, Bella,' he murmured softly, his eyes gleaming as he deliberately made his statement as ambiguous as possible. 'I feel responsible for your mental and physical welfare—and that automatically gives me certain rights.'

'Rights?' She stared at him, and an odd kind of

excitement began to unfurl in the pit of her stomach. 'What sort of rights?'

He gave a slow smile because her reaction hadn't gone unnoticed. 'Such as making sure you look after yourself—which you haven't been doing up until now. Simple things like eating properly, and getting enough rest and fresh air.' He looked up as his son came back into the room, and his eyes were still glittering. 'Oh, and a little gentle exercise wouldn't hurt.'

Isabella wondered if she was going insane. She must be. His words seemed to be laden with sexual overtones this morning—and the look in his eyes only seemed to confirm it. She put her empty cup down, reminding herself that she knew nothing of men—and even less about a man like Paulo Dantas—the man they called *gato*.

He sipped his coffee and watched her over the rim of his cup. 'Now, *querida*,' he said softly. 'On the subject of baby equipment.'

Isabella looked at him blankly. 'Baby equipment? What about it?'

'Exactly! You don't have any, do you? No crib. No pram. No nappies, even. And even little babies need toys and stimulation.'

She shook her head. 'No, babies need roots and they need wings,' she contradicted dreamily. 'Anything else is just extra.'

'Very idealistic, Bella,' he said drily. 'And it makes for a good opt-out clause if you don't happen to like shopping. But where are they supposed to sleep?'

'Babies can sleep in drawers, if they need to!'

'*Can* they?' asked Eddie, who came back in, carrying a plate of dry crackers.

'Sure they can!' Isabella took a biscuit. 'When people lived in caves, they didn't have bassinets, did they?'

'When people lived in caves, the man's word was law—sounds like good sense to me,' said Paulo coolly. 'And as the man of the house I suggest we go out today and buy everything you need.'

'And can we go to the toy shop, Papa?' Eddie demanded eagerly.

'Provided Isabella isn't too tired.' He frowned as he handed her a cup of coffee. 'And, just out of interest, how were you planning to manage at the other place? Were you really planning to put the baby in a drawer?'

'Of course I wasn't.' She waited while the baby completed its three hundred and sixty-degree turn in her belly before replying. 'Mrs Stafford said I could use the twins' old baby stuff.' Tired-looking pieces of equipment which had been stacked in a disused garage and covered with dust and cobwebs. 'She said they would clean up perfectly!'

'I'll bet she did,' said Paulo grimly. 'Well, why don't you get showered and dressed.' He glanced down at his watch. 'Your doctor's appointment is at midday.'

He was certainly showing a very bossy side to his nature, thought Isabella as she stood beneath the power-shower in her luxurious en suite, which gushed as efficiently as a small waterfall. She savoured every moment of it, washing her hair without difficulty.

She lumbered back into the bedroom afterwards and slipped her other maternity dress on. She'd only bought a couple—unwilling and unable to invest money in clothes she would never wear again. But at least Paulo hadn't seen her in this one before, and its cheerful yellow colour warmed the pale olive of her skin and brought out the red highlights in her dark hair.

Everything took such a long time when you were this pregnant. She sat down heavily at the dressing-table and picked up her hairbrush, wondering if she had the energy to dry her wet hair, strand by laborious strand.

A movement at the open door attracted her attention and she glanced up to see Paulo reflected back at her—and it was with a sense of guilt that she noticed how the dark trousers moulded themselves so beautifully to the jut of his hips and the powerful line of his thighs. Surely she shouldn't be thinking about his *legs* at a time like this?

'Want me to do that for you?' he asked.

'Dry my hair?' The eyes gleamed with the faintest hint of laughter.

He had seen just where her gaze had focussed itself. 'That's what I meant.' He walked over to the mirror and plucked the silver-backed hairbrush from her hand. 'Relax,' he soothed, as he stroked the bristles down through the resisting locks. 'Come on. Relax.'

Relax? How could she possibly do that when his pelvis was on a level with her back, and the reflection of his black eyes was mocking her in the mirror?

But the soothing movement of the brush lulled her into a glorious state of peace and calm. Ironic, really, considering just how precarious her position was. She guessed that this was what they called false security, and let her gaze drift upwards to clash with the hard glitter of ebony once more.

'You know, I'm going to have to ring your father today, Bella. He'll be expecting me to get back to him and wondering why I haven't. And you'll need to speak to him yourself.'

She kept the tremor of nerves away. 'Not today.'

'When, then?'

'Tomorrow. When I feel…calmer.'

'You think twenty-four hours will make such a difference?' he demanded.

'I don't know. I just haven't made up my mind what to tell him.'

'How about the truth?' he suggested sardonically. 'Or is that something which is beyond you?'

'I haven't told him any lies!' she defended.

He gave a short laugh. 'You just ran away instead. Well, I'm afraid that it won't do, Bella!'

She stiffened. 'What do you mean, it won't do? It'll do if I say it will!'

'Not if I decide to tell him myself,' he said silkily.

'You wouldn't do that!'

'Oh, wouldn't I?' he questioned softly, but a note of steel had entered his voice. 'Believe me, I would do whatever I felt necessary to guarantee the well-being of you *and* your baby.'

'Even if it was contrary to what I wanted?'

'Your wants are of no particular concern to me!' he snapped. 'Your *needs* are far more relevant! Have you stopped to think about the things that could go wrong?'

Her golden eyes widened in alarm. 'Such as what?'

He drew in a deep breath. He didn't want to put the fear of God into her—but that did not mean she could bury her head in the sand, either. 'You're young and fit and healthy—but pregnancy carries its own risks. You're an intelligent woman, Bella—you know that. Your father needs to know about the baby.'

He did not want to spell it out, that if some calamity befell her during labour… He gripped the hairbrush so hard that his knuckles whitened. 'That doesn't mean you have to tell him who the father is,' he added gently. Not yet, anyway.

He hoped that she wasn't about to get a rude awakening and that her airy assurance that she would feel herself after the birth proved to be the case. He wondered how she would cope if she fell foul of the baby blues. Or how he would cope... He picked up the hairdryer and blasted the thick, dark mass with warm air until her hair hung in a shimmering sheet all the way down to her waist. 'Let's see what the doctor says first,' he said evenly.

She met his eyes in alarm, realising that whatever she said he would blithely ignore it, if he thought that it was in her best interests to do so.

She thought about arguing with him, but instinct told her that it would be a waste of time. And besides, deep down she knew he was right. 'OK,' she sighed.

He carefully caught up the great weight of hair and tied it at the base of her neck with a saffron-coloured ribbon which matched her dress. 'I think I like it when you're acquiescent,' he murmured.

She met his eyes in the mirror. 'Don't hold your breath!'

The doctor's suite of rooms was in an upmarket patch of Knightsbridge, and Isabella wondered how much this was all costing. But when she tentatively broached the subject of cost with Paulo, she was silenced by an arrogant wave of his hand.

The doctor insisted on conducting the entire examination in Portuguese, despite all Isabella's protestations that her English was fluent.

'But it is the mother-tongue.' The doctor smiled sentimentally. 'And particularly appropriate for the mother-to-be. Do you want Paulo to stay with you?' he added.

Isabella shot Paulo a look of pure horror.

'No, I won't be staying,' answered Paulo smoothly, answering her furious query with an unconcerned smile. 'Isabella is by nature a traditionalist, aren't you, *querida*? She knows how easily men faint!'

She didn't trust herself to reply, just gave him a frozen smile before the nurse popped the thermometer into her mouth.

The doctor was ruthlessly thorough, making little clicking noises as he listened to the baby's heartbeat with an old-fashioned trumpet, as well as the most high-tech equipment she had ever seen.

She dressed again and sat down in front of the doctor and Isabella didn't realise how nervous she was until he looked at her over the top of his spectacles and gave her a look which managed to be both reassuring and alarming.

'Everything is fine—but there is room for improvement! You have not been resting enough!' he announced sternly. 'And you are a little underweight. You must look after yourself, do you understand?'

'Yes, Doctor,' she answered meekly.

Paulo was ushered back into the room and the doctor spread out some shiny black and white ultrasound photos on the desk.

'See what a beautiful baby you have.' He smiled at them both.

Isabella swallowed as she looked down at the tiny limbs. So perfect. A lump rose in her throat and when she looked up it was to see Paulo's eyes on her—the dark gaze oddly soft and luminous.

'A very beautiful baby,' agreed Paulo softly, giving

her such a blindingly brilliant smile that she felt quite dizzy—so dizzy in fact, that she couldn't make out a word the doctor was saying to him.

In fact, the nurse was busy chattering herself. She wanted to know everything. Which part of Brazil did Isabella come from?

'From Bahia.'

'Very beautiful,' the nurse replied. 'The Land of Happiness.' It seemed that she had taken holidays there as a child. She glanced down at one of the ultrasound photos Isabella was clutching, and smiled. How long had she known Paulo for?

'Oh, most of my life,' Isabella replied automatically.

'*That* long?' The nurse gave a dreamy sort of sigh.

'Mmm. Obviously, I was a child for a lot of that time.'

'Ah, of course! He is a handsome man—a *very* handsome man,' whispered the nurse, though Isabella wasn't sure whether this was at all professional. '*Gato,*' she finished huskily, with an admiring look at Paulo's hips.

'What was the nurse saying to you?' Paulo asked her, as they walked out of the clinic towards the car.

'Oh, nothing much,' replied Isabella vaguely. She certainly wasn't going to boost his ego by telling him that the nurse had unerringly hit on his Brazilian nickname. 'What was the doctor saying to *you*?' she asked him suspiciously.

He hesitated, and waited until she was safely strapped into the low, deep blue car before he told her.

'He said that between the two of us, we had created a fine Latino baby!'

She felt a pang of something approaching wistfulness.

'Oh, Paulo, he *didn't*!'

'Yes, *querida*—he did. I suppose it was a natural enough assumption to make under the circumstances.'

'So why didn't you explain that you weren't the father?'

'And what would you have me tell him instead?' he questioned, his voice chilly now. 'That you're refusing to say who the father is?'

'That *is* my prerogative.'

'Though maybe you don't even know yourself?' he challenged insultingly.

Isabella felt the blood rush to her face. Is that what he thought of her? That any number of men could qualify for paternity? 'Of course I know who the father is!'

A look of triumph flared darkly in his eyes and she realised too late that she had walked into some kind of trap.

Paulo's voice was deceptively soft. 'But he doesn't know about the baby either, does he? You haven't told him, have you, Isabella?'

Her lips trembled, but she could not afford to break down. Not now, when she had nursed her secret so carefully and for so long. 'No, I haven't.' She found herself imprisoned in the searchlight of his keen, dark gaze.

'Why not?' She had kept the identity of her baby's father secret from everyone. Because the moment she gave a name to either Paulo—or Papa—she could just imagine the outcome. Somehow they would track Roberto down, demand that he take an active role in her child's life. Isabella shuddered. Never! 'I don't have to answer that,' she said.

'No, of course you don't. But don't you think that he—as the father—has a right to know? And not just a right—a *responsibility* to share in the child's upbringing.'

'No! Because it's over! There's no *point* in telling him!'

But even as she spoke she felt guilt descend on her like a dark cloud. She wasn't being fair to Paulo—allowing him to pay for everything and allowing him to care for her, too. He had rescued her. Given her sanctuary. A sanctuary she hadn't realised she had needed, until it had been forced upon her. And maybe that gave *him* some rights.

Paulo turned the key in the ignition with an angry jerk, wondering why he almost preferred to think that she *didn't* know who the father was. As if it was somehow more acceptable to imagine her having some regrettable one-night stand with far-reaching consequences, than the alternative. Had she loved the man responsible? Did she love him still?

Perhaps her statement that it was over was just a ruse.

She could be using the baby as a way to lever herself back into the man's life. Planning to just turn up and present a child who crooned so sweetly in her arms. Some proud, dark lover, maybe, who would be swayed by the sudden production of his own flesh and blood. It wouldn't be the first time it had happened.

Isabella sneaked a look at the forbidding set of his jaw, and her heart sank even more. To Paulo, it must seem as though she was letting her child's father get off scot-free. Yet it was not quite as simple as that. The situation was bad enough—but if she tried imagining a future which involved Roberto—it made her feel quite ill. A man she didn't love and who didn't love *her*. What effect could he have on her life, other than disaster?

'Paulo?' she asked tentatively, but he smacked the flat of his hand down on the steering wheel in frustration.

'I never had you down for such a coward!' he stormed. 'What do you think is going to happen after the birth?'

'I don't know!' she answered back, and right then she didn't care—even that he had called her a coward—because a band of steel had tightened and stretched across her abdomen, and she felt her face distort with discomfort.

One look at her white face and Paulo's rage instantly evaporated. 'It's not the baby, is it?' he demanded.

She panted shallowly, the way she had been taught.

'No, I don't think so.'

He changed down a gear. 'Sure?'

She nodded. 'It's just one of these—' She struggled to remember the English for the unfamiliar medical term. 'Braxton-Hicks contractions—nature's rehearsal for the real thing.' She pressed her hot face onto the cool of the car window and gulped, hoping that Paulo wouldn't notice she was precariously close to tears.

But he did. He noticed most things. And as a way of bringing his interrogation to a close, her threatened tears proved extremely effective. He felt an impotent kind of rage and anger slowly unfurling in the pit of his stomach, and he was longing to take it out on someone. Or something.

If she hadn't been pregnant he might just have pulled into a layby and treated her to the kind of kiss he felt she deserved, and they both needed. He felt the first warm lick of desire and wondered grimly what masochistic tendency had pushed him towards *that* line of thinking.

If he had been on his own, he might have taken the car to the nearest motorway and driven it as fast as was safe. As it was, he didn't dare—one bump and her face might take on that white, strained look again. He slowed right down and negotiated the roads back to the house with exaggerated care.

Isabella had recovered her equilibrium by the time they got back to the house, but Paulo was busy treating her like an invalid. He made her eat an omelette and salad, then insisted that she lie down for a rest.

'But I'm not tired!'

'Really?' He cocked a disbelieving eyebrow at her.

'I'm fine,' she insisted, even while she allowed him to crouch down by her feet to slip her shoes off. 'Honestly.'

'Well, you don't look fine.' He propelled her gently back against the stack of pillows. 'You look worn out.'

Isabella wriggled her head back against the pillow, and stared up into the glittering black eyes. 'Anyway, you promised Eduardo we could buy toys today—he was looking forward to it.'

'And we can. But only if you sleep first,' he ordered firmly. He brushed a damp lock of the bronze-black hair away from her cheek and carefully extracted the photos of the baby from where they lay clutched tightly between her fingers.

'That's bribery,' she objected muzzily.

'So what if it is?' came the soft rejoinder. 'Remember what the doctor told you.'

He glanced in on her more than once, telling himself that he was just making certain that the pains *had* been a false alarm.

But if he was being truthful he *enjoyed* watching her

as she lay sleeping. And, if he examined his conscience, wasn't it erotic? The steady rise and fall of her breasts, so full and ripe and hard. The way the dark fringes of her eyelashes brushed over the flushed curve of her cheeks. The firm swell of the child as it grew within her.

Look but don't touch. Of course it was erotic.

When Isabella awoke she felt much better. She slapped cold water on her face and brushed her teeth and went to find Paulo and his son sitting at the dining-room table, playing Scrabble.

Paulo looked up and gave her a long, searching stare, then nodded his head as if satisfied. 'That's better,' he murmured.

'Bella!' exclaimed Eddie, his face lighting up. 'Papa said I wasn't to wake you! He said that you needed your sleep.'

'And he was right.' Her cheeks were flushed as she bit back a yawn. 'I did.'

'See how tolerant I can be, Bella,' Paulo said softly.

'When some people might find the urge to say, "I told you so"!'

'Very tolerant,' she agreed gravely, relieved that his black mood of earlier seemed to have subsided.

'And he says we can go and choose toys for the baby if you're well enough. Are you, Bella?'

Paulo was on his feet. 'Shush, Eddie,' he murmured.

'Bella has already had a trip to the doctor's this morning. We might have to put the toys on hold until another day.' Night-dark eyes captured her gaze. 'How do you feel?'

'Absolutely fine. I'm looking forward to it.'

'Very well. We will have a leisurely afternoon in the toy shop.' He rose to his feet like some sleek, black panther. 'On the condition that you take it easy if I tell you to.'

She opened her mouth to point out that he wasn't her personal physician, but the warning gleam in his eyes made her change her mind. 'Very well,' she agreed demurely. 'I'll go and get ready.'

He chose one of the capital's biggest children's stores, where he seemed hell-bent on buying the place up and it was Isabella who had to restrain him.

Having rather distractedly looked round the place at baby paraphernalia which still seemed so *alien* to her, she placed her hand restrainingly on his arm. 'I just need a small pram that can double as a carry-cot, Paulo—nothing more for the time being.'

He stared down at the slim, ringless fingers as they rested on the dark blue wool of his overcoat. 'What about a crib? And a high-chair?'

She shook her head before he could recite the entire contents of the shop to her. 'No, none of those. Not yet. They take up too much room and the baby can sleep in the pram until...' Her voice tailed off.

His eyes narrowed. 'Until you fly home to Brazil?' She tried to imagine it, and couldn't. Tried to imagine staying here with Paulo—and that was even harder. 'I guess so. Oh, look—the assistant is coming over.'

His mouth flattened with irritation as the sales assistant fluttered to dance attention on his every word.

Isabella let him buy a baby-seat for the car, a drift of cashmere blankets and a tape of 'mood-music' to play to the baby.

She was caught between delight and protest. 'It isn't

necessary,' she began, but the look of determination on his face made her give up.

At last they went to find Eduardo, who was totally engrossed in a train set in the toy department. He looked up as they approached, and his face fell. '*Oh!* Can't I stay here for a bit longer, Papa?'

'Sure you can,' grinned his father. 'Come on, Isabella—let's wander round and see what the fashionable baby is playing with these days!'

She'd planned to say yes to only the simplest and most inexpensive of the toys, deliberately telling herself that manufacturers were making a fortune out of bits of plastic. But, even so, they were surprisingly seductive and her attention was caught by a pyramid of stuffed animals in pale shades of pastel.

'And all colour co-ordinated—especially for the nursery,' said Paulo. He held up two teddy-bears, one pink and one blue, and waggled them like semaphores, managing to attract looks of interest from most of the women in the shop. 'So what are you hoping for, Bella—a boy or a girl?'

It was an innocent question which every mother-to-be in the world was asked. But no one had ever asked Bella before. Maybe they had been too embarrassed. Perhaps people thought that an unplanned pregnancy for a single girl meant that you didn't have the normal hopes and fears for your baby. But Paulo's words sparked some complex and primitive chain of emotions which included hope and despair and a terrible feeling of regret. As if they were a normal, expectant couple and Paulo really *was* her baby's father.

Oh, if only, she thought longingly as her field of vision dissolved into a helpless blur of longing. If only.

'Isabella?' His voice seemed to come from a long way off. She tried to say something, but her stilted words came out as nothing more than a jerky wobble. 'Isabella? What is this?'

'N-nothing.' He saw the bright glare of tears which had turned her eyes into liquid gold. Her mouth began to tremble and he acted purely on instinct. They were standing beside a large red play-tent, and he simply flicked the flaps back and pulled her inside, where it was mercifully empty. Into their own private world, and into his arms where she burrowed through the warmth of his coat, letting her tears fall like raindrops onto his silk shirt.

He could feel her warm breath shuddering against his chest as she drooped her hands softly over his shoulders, and he felt an overpowering urge to tightly cradle her.

It was a surreal setting. They were bathed in a soft red light which made the inside of the tent almost womb-like. 'W-we can't stay here,' she husked, a hint of quiet hysteria breaking through the blur of her tears.

'We can stay anywhere we damned well please!' he contradicted on a silken whisper. 'But quietly. Quietly, Bella. Do not excite yourself...or the baby.' Or me, he thought, with a sudden guilty realisation.

Her huge belly was pushing against him, so close that he could feel the baby as it moved inside her. But instead of acting as a natural deterent he found the action one of unbearable intimacy. It was comfort he intended to give her. Not this...this...powering of his heart so that it pounded hotly inside his head and his groin.

He deliberately made the gesture more avuncular, smoothing the flat of his hand down over her hair, fluidly stroking her head as if she were a Siamese cat, while the tears continued to soak through his shirt and onto his shoulder.

And it wasn't until the flow had abated and he had traced one last glimmering teardrop away with the tip of his finger, that he used that same finger to lift her chin, imprisoning her in the sweet, dark fire from his eyes.

'Want to talk about it?' he murmured.

What—and tell him that she wished he *was* the man who had caused life to spring within her? Little could terrify a man who didn't 'do' serious, more than that. She shook her head. 'I'm overwrought,' she said. 'It's a very—' and she gulped '—emotional time.'

'You're telling me,' he said grimly.

'Oh, Paulo!'

'I know.' He tightened his grip. She felt so warm and trembling and vulnerable in his arms. So small. Tiny, almost. What else could he do but carry on holding her like this? This was a hug she needed, he realised. That he seemed to need it too was what troubled him. 'What is it?' he asked her in her own language, feeling her breath warm his chest as she attempted to speak.

'I'm s-so s-sorry!' He frowned, as he wiped a tear-soaked lock of hair away from her forehead. 'You've got nothing to be sorry for.'

'I got pr-pregnant, didn't I?' His stare was laser-sharp. His need to know momentarily overrode his desire to be gentle with her. 'Deliberately?' he questioned. '*Was* it a gamble you took, Bella? As a way of keeping a man who perhaps didn't love you as much as you loved him?'

She gazed at him, shocked. 'No, of course not!' But by a man I didn't love. And she couldn't tell him that, could she? Because if she admitted that, then it would make the consequences of her act even harder to bear. At least love would have justified the whole wretched mess.

His eyes narrowed with alarming perception. 'Even if you *do* regret the act, Bella, you must learn to accept the consequences. Otherwise you will suffer, and so will the baby. Here.' And he smoothed away the last strand of hair, which had escaped from its confining bow.

'Come on, now—we're going home.'

He demanded that Eduardo make sure she stayed sitting on one of the carved wooden benches which adorned the shop's lavish entrance hall, while he brought the car round to the front of the building.

In her weakened state, she watched him. Watched his muscular grace and confident stride. He seemed quite oblivious to the fact that he could stop the traffic.

Literally.

He arrogantly stepped in front of the traffic and no one dared not to obey him as he raised an imperious hand in command. But several cars had slowed down so much that they were almost stationary anyway—eager, no doubt to watch the spectacular-looking man with the brooding features as he helped the pale and pregnant woman into the car.

CHAPTER SIX

'BED!' Paulo insisted, just as soon as they arrived home.

'But—'

'Bed!' he repeated grimly. 'From now on we obey the doctor to the letter. He said you needed rest—and that's what I intend to make sure you get.'

One look at his expression told her that to put up a fight would be a waste of her time and energy, so she crept away to her room, where the bed was almost as welcoming as his embrace in the shop had been. The pillow felt soft against her cheek, and as sleep enfolded her, she remembered the way he had held her, with concern softening the brilliance of the dark eyes.

He brought her soup and toast and fruit for supper, and afterwards she slept on. As if her body was greedily sucking up every bit of relaxation it had been denied during her stay at the Staffords'.

She slept right through the night still tantalised by the memory of that hard, beautiful face and awoke to the sound of silence, which made her think that perhaps the flat was empty. But when she had showered and dressed, she found Paulo lying stretched out on the sofa in the sitting room.

He looked more relaxed than she had ever seen him, his dark hair all rumpled as it rested against a silken cushion. A newspaper was spread out over his bent knees and the jeans clung like syrup to his muscular thighs. Her heart crashed painfully against her ribs and the baby kicked against her, as if objecting. She took a deep, calming breath.

'Hello, Paulo.' He glanced up from the newspaper, thinking how warm and soft she looked, all breathless and sparkly eyed. And how that innocent-looking white blouse provided the perfect backdrop for the thick, dark curls. He found himself wishing that he could reach out and untie the ribbon which confined them and let the whole damned lot tumble down and spill like satin around her shoulders.

'Well, good morning,' he said thickly, and put the paper down. 'Or should I say good afternoon?'

Her breath seemed to have caught somewhere in her throat. 'I overslept again.'

'That's good.'

'Have you eaten breakfast?'

'Not yet. I was waiting for you. Then I started reading and forgot about it.' He stretched his arms and stood up.

'I'll make it.'

'Where's Jessie?'

'She's gone shopping,' he replied, without missing a beat. He had sent the housekeeper out over an hour ago. There were a few things he was planning to say to Isabella today, and he wanted to do so in private. And if Jessie were there she would inhibit him. Because for the first time since Elizabeth's death, he had felt a tiny bit *crowded* by the woman who had worked for him for so long and so tirelessly. And he couldn't quite decide whether it was all tied up with Isabella's presence, or by the fact that Jessie now had a man.

Jessie's attitude had changed. And it wasn't so much the things she said—more the things she *didn't* say. The pursed lips. The raised eyebrows. The knowing smiles.

As if she knew some mysterious secret that she was keeping from him. And he was damned if he was going to ask her what the hell it was.

Isabella glanced at the newspaper headlines, but the drama of world news held little interest for her. She supposed it was the same for all women at this stage in their pregnancy—her world had telescoped right down into this baby inside her.

It was almost lunchtime by the time they sat down to eat, and Paulo waited until she had munched her way through a pastry before delivering the first part of the little lecture he intended to give, no matter how much she fluttered those big amber eyes at him.

'I want to talk to you about yesterday, Bella.' Her coffee suddenly lost all its appeal. 'What about it?'

'You were in a virtual state of collapse in the shop,' he accused, looking at her as fiercely as if she had set out deliberately to do it!

'It won't happen again, I promise.'

'Damned right it won't! Because there will be no more all-day excursions, that's for sure! Dr Cardoso has agreed he will see you here at the house in future.' He pushed a dish of fruit across the table towards her and, to avoid a lecture on supplementing her diet with vitamins, she obediently took an orange.

'I should not have trailed you halfway around London the way I did,' he snapped.

Isabella slowly began to peel her orange, tempted to point out that he hadn't had to drag her screaming, but one look at his face told her not to bother. 'Finished?'

'No. Not yet.' He watched her pop a juicy segment in between her lips and swallowed down a sensation which came uncomfortably close to lust. 'In future, you will rest when I think you need to rest, and you will eat properly.'

She met his eyes with amusement. 'Oh, will I?'

'Yes, you will,' came the silky promise. 'You'd better make the most of this enforced leisure, Bella—God only knows it will be over soon enough!' His eyes were deadly serious now. 'Are you *listening* to me, Bella? Do you understand what I'm saying?'

'Of course I do.' She lifted up the jug. 'Coffee?'

'Please.' He hadn't finished yet, but he let her attempt to distract him.

She poured him a cup, thinking that this was what living with a man must be like. The small intimacies. The shared breakfasts. Her eyes strayed to the triangle of flesh at his neck which was exposed by an open button and she found herself wondering what it would be like to slowly unbutton that shirt, to lay bare the skin beneath and touch its silken surface with the tips of her fingers... And she wondered, too, whether it was madness or just depravity to yearn for someone while she carried another man's child. 'More toast?' she asked, her cheeks going pink with guilt.

'No, thanks,' he said, knowing that she was studying him, and *liking* it—even though he was uncomfortably aware of the irony of their situation. He wasn't in the habit of having breakfast with women. He had always insisted on eating the first meal of the day alone, or with his son, no matter who he had spent the night before with—or how wonderful it had been. It had been a strict rule, necessary to his son's well-being and security. His girlfriends hadn't liked it—but none of them had been willing to risk making a fight of it.

He found himself studying *her*, his gaze mesmerised by the full, tight swell of her breasts.

Sitting there, with her white cotton blouse straining across the bump of baby and without a scrap of make-up on her face, she looked the antithesis of the glamorous women who had passed through his life after the death of his wife. The cool, pale-blonde beauties with their enigmatic smiles.

And if anyone had suggested that he might find himself physically attracted to a woman who was pregnant with another man's child, he might have seriously questioned their sanity.

So how was it that he found he wanted to run the tip of his tongue all the way along that deep cleft which formed such an erotic shadow between her ripe, swollen breasts? He tried to quash the slow, sweet burn of desire as he met her expectant golden eyes but his mouth felt sandpaper-dry.

He glittered her a look of warning across the table.

'Today you *must* speak to your father—you can't put it off any longer. And the truth, Bella—because nothing else will do. He needs to know that you're going to have a baby and that in a couple of weeks time he will become a grandfather.'

A segment of orange slipped unnoticed from her hand.

'Paulo, I told you—I *can't*!' She couldn't bear the inevitable hurt—the disappointment which would surely follow. She loved her father and the bond between them was close. Or had been.

'You can't put it off any longer, I know that,' he said grimly. A combination of frustration and a sudden irrational fear that something might happen to her during the birth made Paulo's temper begin an inexorable simmer towards boiling point. 'Why can't you? What's stopping you? Are you frightened of his anger? Is he such a tyrant that you daren't tell him? What is the worst thing that could happen, Bella?'

'Let me spell out the stark facts for you,' she whispered. 'I am an only child. The only daughter. All my father's hopes and dreams rest with me—'

'I know all this.'

'Then surely you can understand that I can't just let him down?'

He hardened his heart against the misty blur of her eyes. 'It's a little late in the day for that, surely?'

'Your will is very formidable, Paulo,' she told him quietly. 'But even you can't impose it on me.'

He pushed his chair back and stood up. 'No, you're right—I can't,' he said coldly. 'But if you won't tell him today, then I *will*. I've told you what I think. End of subject.' He began to move towards the door.

She looked up in alarm. 'Where are you going?'

'Anywhere, just so long as it's out of here and away from the crazy thinking that masquerades as logic inside that head of yours!' he snapped. He saw her soft mouth pucker, irritated by the way the little movement stabbed at his conscience. 'Call me if you need me—I'll be working in my study. You know where the phone is!' With that he left the room, closing the door behind him with an exaggerated softness.

Left on her own, Isabella was restless. She cleared away their breakfast things and then wandered around aimlessly, putting off the inevitable moment. It was a huge, sprawling house and yet the walls closed in on her like a prison. She forced herself to curl up on the sofa and channel-hopped the TV stations for a while, but nothing grabbed her attention enough to draw her in. There just seemed to be inane game-shows and cookery programmes which didn't seem to teach you anything about cookery.

She found herself looking out of the window at the rain which lashed relentlessly against the pane and a deep, aching part of her knew that Paulo was right. That a baby was not a secret you could keep hidden for ever.

She *should* ring her father. Take all her courage and tell him.

Pity there were no books you could study to prepare for moments such as these. What should her opening line be? 'Papa, you know you always used to talk about becoming a grandfather—'

She shook her head and went back over to the sofa, glancing at her wristwatch. It would be lunchtime now at home, and her father would be tucking into a large plate of beans and rice and meat with vegetables. She dampened down a sudden pang of homesickness. Not a good time to ring. She would try later—after the siesta.

She must have drifted off to sleep herself, because she was woken up by the sound of a distant ringing, and then the click of a door opening, and when she opened her eyes it was to see Paulo standing looking down at her, his face tight and white and strained with an unbearable kind of tension.

She opened her eyes immediately. 'Paulo? What is it? What's happened?'

'I think you'd better come and speak to your father.'

She blinked at him, still befuddled. 'Did he phone?'

'Bella! This has gone on for long enough. You've got to start some kind of dialogue with him—and you can start *right now*!'

She levered herself up with difficulty.

'I'm waiting until after his siesta,' she yawned. 'I'll ring him then.'

He shook his head and his voice sounded odd. Quiet and controlled, but odd. 'I don't think you understand. You're too late. We've moved beyond the stage of being hypothetical. Your father is on the telephone, waiting to speak to you.'

'He can't be!'

'I can assure you that he is.' The urgent pitch of his voice told her something else, too.

'He knows about the baby?' she asked him tonelessly.

'What do you think?'

She rose to her feet, putting her hand out onto the arm of the sofa to steady herself. 'You told him, didn't you?'

His gaze was steady. 'I had to.'

'Oh, no, you didn't!' she breathed in disbelief. 'You were just playing God, weren't you? You decided! You just went straight ahead and did exactly what you thought best—'

'Isabella.' He interrupted her with an icy clarity which stopped her in her tracks. 'Your father was worried sick—wondering why you hadn't got back to him. He asked me explicitly whether anything was wrong. So what did you want me to do? Compound what is going to happen anyway with a lie? How would that make me look?'

'That's all you care about, is it? How *you* look?' He shook his head. 'Believe it or not, I care about you—I always have done. Why else would I have brought you back here?' he put in drily. 'But try putting yourself in my shoes and you'll realise you're not being fair. I owe it to your father, after all he has done for me, to tell him the *truth*! How could I look him in the eye if I had done otherwise? I am thinking only of your welfare, Bella, truly.'

He paused for a moment to let the impact sink in, aware that he was hurting her—maybe even frightening her—but even more aware that it was time she faced up to facts. 'You are acting like a child. It is time to face the music, *querida*.' He gentled his voice. 'Now, your father is waiting, impatient for the answers to his questions. I suggest you go along to my study and provide them for him. Go on.'

She knew then that she could not put this off any longer. She was beaten. And ashamed. She had let them both down—more than that—her stubborness and her cowardice had made a difficult situation even worse.

She stared up into Paulo's eyes, searching for something…anything. Some sign that she was not all alone, and the faint black gleam of empathy there was the only thing which gave her courage to do as he said.

Walking tall and very straight, she went into his study, where the telephone receiver was lying amidst the heap of paperwork which littered his desk. She picked it up with a hand which was oddly steady.

'Papa?' she breathed.

It was her father as she had never heard him before, his voice distorted with a kind of dazed disbelief.

'Bella, please tell me this isn't true,' he began.

'Papa,' she swallowed, but that was all she could get out.

'So it's true!' There was a short, terse exclamation,

as if her inability to speak had damned her. 'You're *pregnant*,' he accused in a low voice.

There was no place left to go. No hiding place. The steel door of the prison clanged shut behind her. 'Yes,' she whispered. 'Yes, Papa—I'm afraid I am.'

In the seconds it took to confirm his fears, his voice seemed to have aged by about ten years. *'Meu Deus,'* he said heavily. 'I should have realised that something was the matter! Your explanation why you wanted to leave college never really convinced me, not in my heart. You were doing so well. *I should have realised!'*

'Papa, I didn't think—'

'No!' He cut across her words with uncharacteristic impatience. 'It is *me* who didn't think—*me* who has let your poor, dear mother down and failed as a parent.'

This was worse than unbearable. 'That's not true and you know it! You've been the best father there ever could have been.' She sucked in a painful breath. 'Papa, I'm so sorry.'

There was a short, strained silence and she could almost hear her father struggling to gain control over his composure.

'You're sorry?' The voice changed. 'But you are not the only one who is to be held accountable, are you, Bella? What of the…father—' he bit the word out with difficulty '—of your baby?'

'What about him?' A shadow fell over the desk, and she looked up into a silent black stare and the hand which was holding the receiver began to shake. 'I don't want to talk about him.'

Her father ignored her. 'Well, I do.'

'Papa—'

'What does he say about all this?' he persisted. 'Has he offered to marry you yet?'

'No, he hasn't. And even if he had I wouldn't want to. Women don't have to do that these days if they don't want to.'

'Please don't tell me what women "want"!' he snapped. 'Maybe your own wishes should not be paramount—you have a baby to think of, in case you have forgotten!' There was a pause. 'Put Paulo on.'

'Paulo?'

'Is he there?'

'Yes, he's here.' Wordlessly, she handed the phone to the man who towered over her, but whose body language was so distant that he might as well have been a million miles away.

She stayed exactly where she was, because this wasn't what you could ever term a private conversation. She had every right to hear what they were saying about her.

'Luis?' Paulo kept his voice impassive, suspecting that Isabella's father would be angry at him for having kept her secret for so long.

'Paulo, how could you do this?'

'I'm sorry, Luis,' he said, genuinely contrite.

'A little late in the day for that, surely?' asked the older man, then sighed. 'I should have *realised* what was happening. Everyone else seemed to.' There was a moment's silence. 'Maybe it was inevitable—she always worshipped the ground you walked on—'

'Luis—' said Paulo, as alarm bells began to ring inside his head. But the older man sounded as if he was in therapy—talking through a problem in an effort to solve it.

'Maybe it was fate. I'm her father and even I thought you looked good together.' Another sigh, heavier this time. 'Still, these recriminations won't help now. These things happen in the old and the modern world. You're together now and that's all that matters. But I need a little time to get used to the idea. You understand. The last thing Bella needs at a time like this are harsh words. Tell her I'll call in a day or so, will you?'

'Sure,' said Paulo evenly.

'Goodbye, Paulo.'

'Goodbye, Luis.'

He replaced the receiver very slowly, and stood looking at it for a moment. And when he raised his head, his eyes were filled with a cold fire which sent a tremor of apprehension shivering its way down her spine.

'What is it?' she whispered.

'Sit down,' he said.

'Paulo?'

'Sit down,' he repeated.

She slid into the chair he was indicating, placing her knees together like a schoolgirl in a class photo. Which was a bit how she felt. 'OK. I'm sitting.' There was an air of seriousness about him that she had never seen there before and her heart picked up a beat. She braced herself for the worst. 'What did he say?'

He stared at her. The way she had lifted her chin— the slightly defiant gesture not quite hiding the very real fear and confusion which lurked at the back of the amber eyes. He guessed there was no easy way to tell her.

'Paulo—*what did he say*?'

He laughed, still reeling from the irony himself. 'That I am the father of your baby.'

There was a moment of disbelief, followed by a stunned silence. 'But that's crazy!' she said, shaking her head in furious denial. 'Crazy! I've never heard anything so—'

'Isabella,' he interrupted, seeming to choose his words with enough care to bring them slamming home to her. 'Just think about it.' He slid into the chair opposite hers, so that their knees were almost touching and even in the midst of her jumbled thoughts, her body still registered his proximity.

'I am thinking about it!' It was the most bizarre thing she had ever heard. How could she be pregnant by a man she had never even kissed? 'I mean, we haven't even…even…' Her words faded away to an embarrassed whisper.

'Had sex?' he supplied brutally, quashing the guilty thought that indeed they had not…just in the fevered bed of his imagination and maybe it was about time he started turning fantasy into reality. 'No, we haven't. How very right you are, Bella,' he murmured. 'It's a sickener, isn't it—to be blamed for something you haven't actually done?'

'So how can he possibly believe it to be true?'

'He isn't the only one, is he?' he snapped. 'That Stafford woman thought I was responsible. So did the doctor. Even Jessie secretly believes it—no matter how much I deny it!'

'But why?'

'I believe it's called circumstantial evidence,' he clipped out. He moved his face closer to hers, his voice low and urgent. 'Point one—you have steadfastly refused to reveal the true father's identity.'

'But—'

'Point two,' he interrupted coldly. 'As soon as you found out you were pregnant, you left Brazil and came rushing straight to England—to *me*. Didn't you?'

'Well, what if I did?' she croaked. 'That on its own doesn't make *you* the most likely candidate, does it?'

His smile was forced. 'On its own, no—it doesn't. But add that to the fact that your father noticed a certain frisson between the two of us, back in February. A chemistry which was apparently remarked on by most of the people there at the time.' He paused, and frowned, because this was puzzling *him*. 'Which was almost *nine months ago.*'

The final damning piece of evidence fell into place and made the whole picture clearer—except that it was not the true picture at all, merely an illusion. 'Oh, my God!'

'Precisely,' he snapped, and his face grew hard. 'Now I'm not going to deny the attraction which fizzed up between us, because only a self-deluding fool would do that.' His mouth twisted in tandem with the convoluted line of his thoughts. 'But nothing more than wishful thinking happened on my part. I did not have sex with *anyone* during my trip to Brazil. I can't speak for you, of course.'

She couldn't look at him, her gaze falling miserably to her lap. She knew what his eyes would accuse her of. That she had lusted after him, but had fallen into the bed of someone else almost immediately. And when it boiled down to it—wasn't that the awful truth?

'Now, the facts may be stacked up against me, *querida*—but just in case your father comes after me with a shotgun in his hand I want you to tell me one thing.'

She knew what his question would be, even before his lips had started to coldly frame the words. A question she had evaded for so long now that evasion had become almost second nature.

'Just who *is* the father of your baby?'

CHAPTER SEVEN

Isabella swallowed. 'His name is R-Roberto.'

Paulo's eyes grew stony as he heard her voice tremble over the name. He shook his head. 'Not good enough. I need more than that.'

It didn't even occur to her to object to that snapped demand. She was in too deep now to deny him anything.

'His name is Roberto Bonino and he—'

'Who is he?'

This was the difficult bit. 'I knew him at university.'

She swallowed.

Paulo stiffened as he recognised evasion on a mega-scale. 'Another student, you mean?'

She felt her neck grow hot. 'No.'

'Tell me, Bella.'

Something in his voice compelled her to look up at him and she knew that her pink, guilty cheeks gave her away at once. 'He...he was one of the lecturers, actually.'

There was a long, dangerous pause. 'One of the *lecturers*?'

'Y-yes.'

Somehow he had been expecting the worst, but the truth was no less devastating in its delivery. He felt the cold, dead taste of disappointment in his mouth. And the slow burn of anger. 'But that's a complete abuse of power!' he snarled.

'He was only temporary—'

'And you think that makes what he did acceptable?'

She shook her head, its weight pressing down like a heavy rock on her neck. 'No. Of course I don't.'

The anger inside him gathered and grew into bitter accusation. 'So was it love, Bella? True love? The kind that fairy tales are made of? Eyes across a crowded room and wham-bam—' his black eyes glittered '—you're in so deep you can't think straight?'

She heard the cynicism which stained his words, and shook her head. There had only ever been one man who had had that effect on her and he was sitting within touching distance. 'No.'

He wanted to grab hold of her and lever her up into his arms, but he forced himself to stay sitting. 'What, then? What exactly *was* the relationship between you? Tell me what happened!'

Still she couldn't look him in the eye—unable to face his condemnation and scorn when she told him what lay behind her ugly seduction. That it had been Paulo who had set her senses on fire. Paulo who had set in place a fevered longing that meant she hadn't been able to think straight. It had been Paulo who had planted the rampant seeds of desire—but had left just before the inevitable harvest... 'I used to go to his psychology lectures,' she explained painfully.

'Psychology? Oh, *great*!' He felt like punching his fist through the wall. 'Do you think he'd ever thought about studying his *own* behaviour?'

She carried on as if he hadn't interrupted, a slight

desperation touching her words now. 'He was more a friend than anything. At least—that's what I thought. We used to go out in a big group sometimes—'

'Didn't he have any friends his own age?' he asked sarcastically.

'Actually, he wasn't much older than most of the people he used to teach, so he fitted in.'

'Yeah, he sure did,' he agreed pointedly, then found her answering blush too painful to contemplate. 'And?' he prompted, but the harsh note of accusation had all but gone.

Isabella looked at him—at the carved perfection of his face with its intriguing blend of light and shade. A proud, beautiful face which now wore an icy-cold mask of disapproval. 'I guess I was all mixed up.' That much was true. She had been longing for Paulo—obsessed by his memory.

'And randy?' he questioned cruelly. 'Surely you're not forgetting that?'

She swallowed down a lump of distaste. 'Let's just say I wasn't completely indifferent—' She saw him jerk his head back as if she had struck him, and tried to be as honest with him as possible. 'We'd both had a few drinks and...' Her voice tailed off, too embarrassed to continue.

Paulo seethed with a terrible kind of rage. He bit the words out as if they were bitter poison while his fist itched to connect with her tutor's pretty, young face.

'You mean he got you *drunk*?'

'No, of course he didn't!' She nearly asked him what he took her for, but she didn't dare. He might just tell her. 'I had a couple of glasses of wine on an empty stomach and I'm not used to alcohol.' She looked him straight in the eye then, challenging him to condemn her. 'So go on, Paulo—call me a tramp! Call me whatever names you want, if it makes you feel better.'

Impossibly, and appallingly, he thought of what *would* make him feel better—and it had something to do with covering the soft, rosy tremble of her mouth with his.

Covering it so that the memory of Roberto's kiss would be as stale as ashes in her mind. He shook his head. 'You're no tramp, Bella,' he said softly. She had told him most of what he needed to know—so why the defensive tightening of her shoulders? 'But there's still something you're not telling me, isn't there?'

She bit her lip and looked away. 'There's quite a lot, actually. But I didn't think you'd want to know.'

His mouth hardened, unprepared for the sudden blitz of bitterness. 'I don't mean every sordid detail of your night with this…this…' He stopped himself from spitting out the only word which was halfway suitable, and one which he would never use in front of a woman. Especially about the man who had fathered her child.

'Were you a virgin?' he asked suddenly, though deep-down he knew what her answer would be.

'I… Yes.' She hung her head as he made a sound as though she had hit him. 'Yes, I was.'

Swallowing down the taste of bitter jealousy, he let his hand reach out to cup her face, his dark eyes luminous with a kind of poignant sadness.

'It should have been me,' he said softly.

Meeting his gaze, she was already close to tears, but she held them at bay for long enough to whisper, 'Wh-what should?'

He let his hand fall, so that it was on a level with her belly and then, intimately, shockingly—he reached out a finger and drew it meticulously down over the drum-tight swell of the baby and Bella gasped aloud as he touched her.

'This. This baby of yours. It could have been me, couldn't it?' he questioned huskily, beginning to stroke a tiny circle around her navel. *'This.'* And his finger undulated over her belly as the baby moved beneath it.

'Mine.'

'Yours? How could it possibly be yours?'

'How do you think? By the *traditional* method of fathering children, of course. I should have made love to you,' he whispered, but he saw that beneath the fine olive complexion, her face looked almost bloodless in response. He let the anger go for a moment and let regret take its place—a bitter, lasting regret that he hadn't felt since his wife had died.

He could barely bring himself to acknowledge the precious gift he had refused—only to have someone else step in and steal it in his place. 'If only I hadn't listened to my crazy, *stupid* conscience!' he groaned aloud.

She stared at him in confusion. 'What are you talking about?'

'Oh, Bella—you know what I'm talking about!' His words sounded urgent and bitter, but his hand felt unbelievably gentle and she let him leave it right where it was, splayed almost possessively over the bump of the baby. 'You wanted me as much as I wanted you, didn't you?' he questioned softly.

She couldn't escape the question burning from his black eyes, even if she had wanted to. And she was through with evasion and half-truths. She would not tell him a lie. She couldn't. Not now, not after everything he had done for her. Was doing for her. Even now.

'Yes,' she said quietly.

'So subdued,' he murmured. 'So unlike the Bella I know.'

She wondered if the Bella he knew existed any more, but by then the moment for sensible debate had vanished and the unbelievable was happening instead. Paulo was pulling her to her feet and into the warm circle of his arms and the thoughtful look on his face gave her the courage to ask, 'So why didn't you?'

It was almost scary that he knew exactly what she meant. 'Make love to you?' He stroked her thickened waist reflectively. 'How many reasons would you like? Because you were only twenty and I suspected that you were innocent, as well as being the daughter of my host?' Or because he recognised the danger she represented, as well as the excitement? A danger to his well-ordered life and its carefully compartmentalised emotions.

'Of course...' And he paused—a slow, dangerous beat. 'None of those obstacles have any relevance any more, do they?'

With a thundering heart Isabella stared at the darkening of his eyes and the deepening colour which highlighted the broad sweep of his cheekbones. And just for that moment it was easy to pretend that he really *was* her lover.

'Paulo!' she gasped, because the baby chose just that moment to kick her very hard beneath her heart, or maybe that was just the effect he had on her.

'What is it, *querida*?' His voice was gentle but he didn't wait for an answer, just bent his head and began to kiss her. And all sane thoughts dissolved as Isabella was left with the sensation of a long-awaited dream being fulfilled.

This had been too long in coming, Paulo thought with an edge of desperation as he lowered his mouth onto hers. He could not recall a hunger of such keen, bright intensity. Nor kissing a woman so heavily pregnant with such raw passion before. For a brief, heady moment he allowed himself the sensation of melting, of their mouths moulding together as though they had always been joined with such perfect chemistry.

But this was *Bella* he was kissing. Sweet, stubborn Bella. And a very pregnant Bella, too. He reached his hand out—supposedly to push her away—but the hand somehow connected with enchanting accuracy over the heavy swell of her breast. And he gave in to temptation. Cupped it. Kneaded it. Fondled it until he felt it peak like iron against his fingertips and he heard her half-moaned response.

Bella felt her knees threaten to give way. Her heart was fluttering and so was the baby—while all the time she could feel the heavy pulsing of desire as it began its slow inexorable throb. She clung onto his broad shoulders and kissed him back as though her life depended on it. And maybe it did.

He dragged his mouth away from hers with an effort and gazed down into her flushed, dazed face. He could barely speak, he was so aroused—so much for his reputation as the cool, controlled lover! 'We have to stop this right now, Bella,' he told her huskily. 'Jessie will be back soon.' And so, he remembered in horror, so would his son.

'And Eddie!' She echoed his thoughts as she frantically smoothed the palms of her hands over her hot cheeks, aware that her hair must be mussed up, her lips stained dark by the pressure of his mouth. 'I'd better go and…tidy myself up,' she gulped.

She made to move away, but he caught hold of her hand, his eyes boring into her as he understood one more reason why she had borne her secret for so long. 'That's why you couldn't bring yourself to tell your father about the baby, isn't it? Because this man—Roberto—abused his position.'

She nodded, causing even more disarray to her hair. 'That's how Papa would see it, yes. He would create a big scene. Can you imagine? He might even attempt to prosecute, and then it would be in all the papers. Can't you understand why I ran to England, Paulo?'

'Yes, I can.' He nodded his head slowly. 'But you've compromised me now, haven't you, *querida*? Your father is convinced that I have sired your baby. And to tell him otherwise would risk the kind of commotion you're so anxious to avoid—even if you were willing to do so.'

'So what do I do?'

His eyes glittered as he considered her question, the memory of her kiss still sweet on his mouth. 'You stay here. With me. And Eduardo. And after the baby is born, well, then…' He shrugged as he gave his rare and sexy smile—thinking that she could work *that* one out for herself.

The arrogance and complacency of that smile brought Isabella crashing back into the real world. 'Then what?' she questioned slowly. 'What exactly are you suggesting?'

'Why, then we could enjoy our mutual passion, Bella,' he purred, seeing the darkening in her eyes and feeling his body's answering leap in response. 'After all, why should I take all of the responsibility of impending paternity, but with none of the corresponding pleasure? Live here. With me. And we will become lovers.'

Lovers.

There was silence in the room, save for the ominous ticking of a clock she had never noticed before. And, while he must know how much she wanted him, something held her back.

Because she'd already made one big mistake in her life—she certainly did not intend making another. And if she allowed herself to fall eagerly into his bed on the strength of that coolly impassive suggestion, then how would he ever have any other image of her than that of a passive sensualist, all vulnerable and needy where men were concerned?

'And just how long did you have in mind?' she questioned acidly. 'Until you've taken your fill of me, I suppose?'

He stared deep into the amber eyes, respecting the guts it must have taken to ask that question. A trace of the old Isabella, he thought—her spirit remarkably uncrushed, despite what fate had thrown at her.

'Who can say, *querida*? Until it is spent. All burned out. Until you decide where you want to settle with your baby. Who knows for how long? I certainly can't tell you.' He paused, watching carefully for her reaction. 'But of course there are alternatives open to you if the idea doesn't appeal.'

She opened her mouth to speak, but the ringing of the front doorbell shattered the spell and he moved away from her. Her eyes followed him as he moved across the room.

He was wearing only a simple sweater with a pair of faded denims. The washed-out green of the sweater only drew attention to the spectacular darkness of his Latin American colouring, while the jeans were moulded to buttocks and thighs so powerful that... She found herself imagining seeing him, every bit of him, naked and warm in the act of loving.

'Oh, yes.' He nodded, his voice deepening as he observed her flushed reaction and her darkening eyes. 'I can see that it *does* appeal.'

Pride made her tilt her chin to stare at him, but pride also made her speak from the heart. 'I can't deny the attraction between us either,' she said slowly. 'But soon I'll have a baby to think about, as well as myself. I can't just leap into an affair with you. I might feel differently after the birth.'

'You might not,' he objected.

Her eyes mocked him. 'Well, you'll just have to wait and see, won't you, Paulo?'

It was not what he had wanted to hear. Nor expected to hear. Isabella could tell that much from the frozen look of disbelief which briefly hardened his outrageously gorgeous face.

But she kept watching him, waiting for the inevitable thaw—and when it came the frustration had been replaced by an emotion he used to swamp her with, but one which had been absent just lately.

It was called respect.

CHAPTER EIGHT

'WHAT'S the matter?' Paulo flicked off the television programme he had been half-heartedly trying to watch and stared instead at Isabella, who'd been shifting her position rather distractedly on the sofa, distracting him in the bargain, despite all his good intentions.

She'd told him that he would have to wait and see and he was going to abide by her decision. Even if the effort half-killed him.

Isabella stifled a yawn as she met the soft question in his eyes, aware that he'd been sitting watching her for the best part of an hour while pretending to watch TV. She'd spent the early part of the evening having Eddie teach her a computer game and now she was paying the price for having sat upright in front of a small screen for over an hour. She shifted around on the sofa again.

'Nothing.'

'Something,' he contradicted, thinking how pale her face looked and wondering if her nights had been as short of sleep as his had. Probably not. She probably slept smug and sound in her bed, knowing that she had him right where she wanted him—dangling on the end of a string.

He sighed, realising that he'd forgotten the last time a woman had said no to him, and the last person he'd ever imagined it would be was Isabella—not after the way she'd come to such swift, passionate life in his arms. 'Come on, Bella,' he urged softly. 'I can tell you're uncomfortable.'

'Her back hurts,' explained Eddie, who chose that moment to wander into the room in his pyjamas to say goodnight. 'It always does at this time of the night, doesn't it, Bella? 'Specially if she sits still.'

'Oh, really?' Paulo shot her a look which bordered on the accusing before rising to his feet to take his son to bed to read him a story. And when he came back he found that she had changed position on the sofa, but still with that same faint frown creasing her brow.

He sat down beside her, registering the way her body tensed as his weight sank onto the sofa beside her and he slowly and deliberately stretched his long legs in front of him, smug himself now to realise she wasn't entirely immune to him. 'So how come my son knows more about your current state of health than I do?'

She shrugged her shoulders uncomfortably, aware of the arrogantly muscular thrust of his thighs. Was he lying in that provocative position on *purpose*? she wondered agitatedly. 'He heard me telling Jessie that I get backache.'

Paulo frowned, badly wanting to reach out and trace the sweet, curving outline of her lips. 'And is that unusual?' he asked huskily.

'No, it's perfectly normal. They told us to expect it.'

'Who are "they"?' he asked softly.

'The childbirth classes I went to when I was au pairing. And the books say so, too.'

'Maybe I should read them, too,' he mused, before asking. 'Is there any known cure?'

Not for the ache in her heart, no. Backache was an

altogether simpler matter. A smile hovered on her mouth in spite of the fact that her whole world seemed to be a maelstrom of swirling emotions. 'Massage,' she told him stolidly. 'It helps but it doesn't cure.'

'Hmm.' He shifted in his seat. 'Turn around, then.'

Oh, sure—having Paulo caressing her skin was exactly what she *didn't* need. 'No, honestly—'

'Turn around,' he repeated quietly. Because at least if she turned away she wouldn't be able to read the hunger in his eyes.

With difficulty she did as he said, wondering if he had noticed the slow flush of colour which had risen in her cheeks.

He moved his thumbs into the hollow at the base of the spine and heard her expel a soft breath as he began to press away some of the tension.

It was crazy—more than crazy—but this innocent act of kneading her flesh felt like the most indecent act he had ever performed. 'Is that—' his voice deepened '—good?'

Any minute now and her thundering heart would burst right out of her chest. 'It's...fine,' she managed.

Paulo's nerves were stretched to the breaking point in an exquisite state of frustration. He wondered what she would do if he slid his hands round to cup her breasts, then sighed. Because he was essentially a man of honour. And that, he thought, would be taking advantage.

Definitely.

'Better?' he murmured.

'Mmm. A hundred times.' She was torn between longing for him to continue and yearning for him to stop.

'Get yourself to bed then, and I'll bring you something warm to drink.'

She shook her head. 'I'm not thirsty.'

'It's a very expensive, very delicious chocolatey drink which I went out of my way to buy you when I was coming back from work,' he coaxed, and injected a stern note into his voice. 'Because chocolate is what you told me you'd been craving, Miss Fernandes—and because I notice you just pushed your supper around your plate this evening.'

'Does nothing escape your notice?' she teased.

Very little, he thought as he steadied her on his arm.

And nothing whatsoever to do with her. She looked like a different woman since coming to live with him. Pregnancy had made her hair shine like mahogany and her skin gleam with radiant, glowing health.

In her bedroom, Isabella struggled out of her clothes and into the nightshirt which made her look like a vast, white tent, and was sitting up in bed when Paulo brought her a cup of chocolate.

He sat leaning moodily on the window-ledge while he looked around the room—noticing that she must have been out into the garden and picked a selection of berried twigs and brightly coloured pieces of foliage and placed them in a tall, silver vase. Jessie never did that kind of stuff. And he liked it, he realised... He liked it a lot.

In the corner of the room stood her bag, all packed for hospital, and beside it a small pile of Babygros as well as a yellow teddy-bear which he had picked up personally after they had had to cut short their visit to the toy shop.

'You're all ready, then?' he asked.

She followed the direction of his gaze and nodded, not missing the warm approval in his voice. 'More than I was before.'

'You were heavily into denial,' he observed slowly, remembering how she hadn't brought a single baby thing back with her that day he had picked her up at the Staffords'. 'So what changed all that?'

'Telling my father, I guess.' She sighed, and knew that once again she owed him her gratitude. Did being indebted to the man mean she could never be his equal? she wondered. 'You were right to push me into it, Paulo. I feel such a fool now for not having the courage to do so in the first place.'

'We're all allowed to be cowards sometimes, Bella,' he said softly, thinking that if she had done that then she would never have arrived here, seeking his help. Would never have slotted into his life like this—disrupting it, yes, undoubtedly, but making it seem more *alive* than it had done for a long time. And he realised too, that her life had not been easy since she had found out about the baby. Not easy at all.

He kept his voice casual. 'How would you like to catch a taxi into the city, and meet me after work tomorrow night? I could show you my office—we could maybe grab a bite to eat.'

She looked down at her bump, horrified. 'Like *this*?'

He smiled and shrugged. 'Why not?'

'What will your colleagues think?'

He gave the smile of a man who had never pandered to other people's opinions. 'Who cares what they think?' He raised his dark brows. 'So, would you?'

'Well, I would,' she admitted, almost shyly.

In the end, she took Eddie along with her because

having Paulo's son accompany her seemed to legitimise her presence. She met most of Paulo's frankly curious colleagues, seeing from their expressions just what deductions they were making about her role in their director's life.

While Eddie was busy changing the screensaver on his father's computer, she took Paulo aside and hissed into his ear, 'You do *know* what everyone's thinking?'

'That I'm such a super-stud?' he mocked.

Her eyes widened and she met the look in his eyes and started to giggle. Well, if Paulo didn't care, then she certainly wasn't going to waste her time worrying about what was, in fact, her private fantasy!

So she settled back and allowed herself to be steered through the building with all the exaggerated courtesy which would naturally be afforded to a rich man's pregnant mistress.

They toured the impressive glass-fronted skyscraper, and then the three of them got a cab to Covent Garden for hamburgers and milkshakes—or rather Paulo and Eddie ate the hamburgers while Isabella indulged herself with a very thick strawberry milkshake.

On the way home, Paulo turned to her in the taxi.

'Tired?'

She shook her head. 'Not a bit.'

'Back hurting?'

She smiled. 'My back is fine.'

He tapped the connecting glass and asked the driver to drive down around by the Houses of Parliament so that they could see the historic buildings lit up by night.

Eddie turned to Isabella. 'What an amazing night!' he exclaimed. 'It's just like being on holiday!'

Yes, it was. But holidays always came to an end, she reminded herself.

The following evening—just by way of saying thank you—she had a martini waiting for Paulo when he arrived back from work, and if he was unsettled by the distinctly *wifely* gesture, he didn't say so.

He sipped it with pleasure and regarded her with thoughtful eyes. 'Oh, by the way, a letter arrived for you from Brazil this morning,' he said, putting his drink down on the table and fishing a flimsy blue air-mail envelope from the breast pocket of his suit jacket.

Isabella stared at it. 'It's from my father.'

'I know it is. Why don't you e-mail each other? Eddie says he gave you a crash-course the other day.'

'I told you. Papa hates technology. He'd use pigeon-post if it was reliable enough.'

He smiled. 'Oh.'

She held it in her hand for a moment. She had had several conversations with her father since the one when he had slammed the paternity accusation at Paulo. She had been expecting his anger to be ongoing, but there had been none. More a kind of quiet resignation. Most unlike her father, she thought.

'Well, go on, then—open it.' He watched while she ripped the envelope open with suddenly nervous fingers and quickly scanned the page, relief lightening her face as her eyes skated over the main portion.

'Good news?' he queried.

'*Kind* of,' she answered cautiously, but then she began to study it in more detail and her colour heightened.

Paulo was watching her closely. 'Want to read it out loud?'

'Not really.'

'Bella,' he said warningly. 'I thought we were through with secrets?'

She made one last helpless attempt at evasion. Or was it pride? 'A woman should always keep a little something back—didn't you know?'

He held his hand out for the letter. 'Please.'

She handed it over.

Paulo scanned the sheet for the source of what had obviously made her react like that and it didn't take him long to find it.

Obviously, I would have preferred for this to happen in a more conventional manner, but I cannot pretend that I am displeased. Paulo is a fine man and a fine father. I could not have wished for a better husband for you, Bella—so cherish him well.

Paulo looked up to find her attention firmly fixed on the glass of mango juice she had poured herself.

'Bella? Look at me!'

'I don't want to discuss it,' she said fiercely, but she raised her head to meet the accusation sparking from his eyes.

'Well, I *do*! Perhaps you've already booked the church and arranged the venue?'

'I have not!'

'But we're getting married—apparently—so don't you think the prospective groom should be informed?'

'Do you honestly think I told my father we were getting married?'

'How should I know?' he questioned arrogantly, thinking that he would like to untie that velvet ribbon in her hair and have it tumble all the way down her back.

Her naked back. '*Now* where are you going?'

She jerked the chair back from the table, her breath coming in short little gasps. 'As far away from you as possible!'

He was on his feet in seconds, standing in front of her and forming a very effective barrier. 'Stop it and calm down.'

'I do not *feel* like calming down!' she told him distractedly. 'I feel like…like… Ow, ow, *ouch*!'

'Is it the baby?' he demanded immediately.

It felt like someone tightening a piece of string around her middle and then tightening it again. Her hands reached up and she clutched onto his shoulders, her nails digging into him. 'I don't *think* so!'

'I'm going to call the doctor—'

'No! No. Wait a minute!' She panted and paused. 'No, that's OK. I think it's gone.'

He dipped his head so that their eyes were on a level.

'Sure?'

Her heart seemed to suspend its beating. She was still, she realised, gripping tightly onto his shoulders. And through the thin shirt she could feel the silken yield of his flesh to the hard bone beneath. 'Qu-quite sure.'

She let her hands fall away, and Paulo forced himself not to grab them back. She was about to have a baby, for God's sake—and here he was wanting to feel her in his arms again.

'Maybe I'd better call the doctor?'

She shook her head. 'To say what?'

'That you had a pain—'

'Paulo, it was more of a twinge than a pain. And it's gone now.'

'Sure?' he demanded.

'Positive.'

'I just don't want to take any chances.'

'Who's taking any chances? The pain has gone.' She spread her arms out as if to demonstrate. 'See? All gone. I don't want to be one of those neurotic women who calls out the doctor ten times—and every time it's a false alarm. Now go away. Don't you have any work to do?'

Paulo shrugged unenthusiastically. He wanted to stay.

He wanted to kiss her. He wanted to do a lot more besides. Maybe it was better if he *did* clear off. 'I've always got work to do.'

'Then go away and do it,' she shooed.

'And what will you do?'

'I'm not planning on going far. You don't have to worry.'

'I'm not worrying.' But that was a lie, he thought, as he headed off to his study. He was—and, oddly enough, his worries were not the ones he would have imagined at all. It didn't bother him one iota that most of the world imagined that he was the father of her unborn child. In fact, wasn't that a supposition he had deliberately *flaunted* by inviting her into his office last night?

No. He found himself wondering what on earth would happen when the baby arrived. He had told Bella that she had a home for as long as she wanted one and now it suddenly occurred to him that she might not want a home at all. Or to be his lover.

As she had said herself, she might feel differently after the birth. Because now that her father knew and seemed to be coming round to the idea—and bearing in mind that she could usually twist him round her little finger—then what was to stop her going back to Brazil as an unmarried mother?

He imagined her leaving with her baby, and instead of a sense of reprieve he was aware of a great yawning idea of emptiness.

When Elizabeth had died he had decided to live his life in the best way he could for their son, completely forgetting that life never remained static. That life *was* change. He frowned as he switched on the computer.

Isabella prowled the house like a thief, restless without knowing why and looking for something to do. She sat down and wrote a long and chatty letter to Charlie and Richie, as promised—and hoped that Mrs Stafford would be adult enough to pass the letter on to her two young sons.

When she had stamped the envelope, she found a feather duster and wandered from room to room, polishing flecks of dust from all the mirrors. Next she cleaned the two sinks in the downstairs cloakroom, even though they were spotless and gleaming. After she had rearranged all the spices in the store-cupboard, she rang the local Portuguese delicatessen and placed an order for a delivery.

'I'd like rib and shoulder and breast of pork, please. Sausage. Linguica. Green cabbage. Oh, and beans.'

'And when would you like this delivered, madam?'

She frowned at herself in the mirror, thinking that she looked especially enormous today. 'Any chance of tomorrow morning?'

There was no hesitation whatsoever—probably because of the delivery address, Isabella decided.

'That shouldn't be a problem, madam.'

When Eddie got in from school the next day, he

came straight into the kitchen as he always did, to find Isabella up to her elbows in cooking utensils. He strolled over to the work-surface, where she was chopping onion as if her life depended on it.

'What are you doing?' he asked with interest.

'Jessie isn't here, so I'm making *feijoada* for our supper.' She smiled.

'What's that?'

'Come on, Eddie,' she chided. 'You remember? It's Brazil's national dish. With lots of meats and different sausages—'

Eddie looked down at all the different pots which were cluttering the work-surface. 'Looks difficult to make.'

'Not difficult. Fiddly. Lots of different things all added to one big pot at different times. See?'

'Can I help?'

'Of course you can help. Wash your hands first and then you can prepare this garlic for me. See this clever little machine? Now—' she leaned over his shoulder '—put each bulb in here—and it will crush it up for you.'

That was where Paulo discovered them when he arrived home from work. Unknotting his tie, he wandered into the kitchen to find Isabella removing a large piece of meat from the pot with Eddie standing glued to her side.

Paulo smiled—as much at the sight of their obvious companionship as the warm, homely smell which triggered off snatches of boyhood memories. 'Mmm. *Feijoada*.' He sniffed, as he walked into the kitchen.

'What's brought all this on?'

'You don't like it?' she asked him anxiously.

He smiled conspiratorially at his son. 'Show me the

man who doesn't like *feijoada*—and I'll show you a man who doesn't deserve to eat! No, I was just thinking that it's a pretty adventurous thing to cook, if you're feeling tired.'

'But I'm not feeling in the least bit tired!' She energetically threw a handful of bay leaves in the pot, as if to demonstrate.

Jet eyes lanced through her. 'So I see,' he agreed slowly. 'And wasn't that polish I could smell in the hallway?'

'Oh, it's Jessie's day off and I was just waving a duster in the air,' she explained airily. 'More for something to do than anything else.'

He nodded. 'Eddie—want to go and get changed out of your school uniform, now?'

'Sure, Papa.' He stood looking at the image she made once Eddie had gone. Her stomach was so big that she should have looked ungainly as she moved towards the cooker—but she didn't at all. She just seemed perfectly ripe and extremely beautiful—even though her cheeks were all flushed from bending over a hot pan.

'You're nesting,' he said suddenly.

She turned round, wooden spoon in hand. 'Mmm?'

'It's called nesting. That's why you're doing all this.' He waved a hand around. 'Cleaning and polishing and chopping and cooking. You're getting ready to have your baby.'

'You can't know that.'

'Yes, I can. Elizabeth did it, too—it's nature telling you to make your home ready for the new arrival.'

She searched his face for signs of sadness. 'Does having me here like this bring it all back?' she asked softly.

He didn't look away. 'A little.' He saw the look of contrition on her face and shook his head. 'It's not a problem, Bella—I came to terms with what happened to Elizabeth a long time ago. I had to—for Eddie's sake. But—' and he narrowed his eyes into a searchlight stare as he saw her face grow pale '—it does give me the upper hand when it comes to knowing what I'm talking about. And that was another one, wasn't it?'

'Another what?'

'Contraction,' he elaborated roughly.

Suddenly an intimation of what was about to happen to her whispered fingertips of fear over her skin. She shook her head and gave the beans a stir. 'It can't be,' she said, a slight edge of desperation in her voice. 'The baby isn't due until next week.'

'And babies never come when they're supposed to.'

'Oh, really?'

'Yes, really,' he agreed calmly, when he saw her attempt to turn a grimace into a smile. 'And for goodness' sake, will you stop pretending that you're not getting contractions, when it's pretty obvious to me that you are?' he exploded.

So she wasn't fooling him at all! At least his words gave her licence to drop the wooden spoon with a clatter and to bend over and clutch at her abdomen as she had been dying to do for ages.

And it took a moment or two for her to realise that he was standing in front of her, his face a shifting complex of shadows looking for all the world like some dark guardian angel sent to protect her. Her eyes were big and fearful as she stared up at him. 'Ow,' she moaned softly. *'Ow!'*

'What is it?' he demanded, his hands spanning her

expanded waist and feeling her tense beneath his touch. 'Another contraction?'

She nodded her head. His hands felt strong and real and supportive, but wasn't all that an illusion? In fact, wasn't everything just an illusion compared to the razor-sharp lash of pain she had just experienced? *You spent nine months imagining that something couldn't possibly be happening, and then all of a sudden, it was. And there wasn't a thing you could do to stop it.* 'Paulo—I'm scared.'

He lifted one hand from her waist to soothe softly at her head, the shiny curls clinging like vines to his fingers. 'I know you are, *querida*, but you've just got to take it easy, remember? Slow and easy. This is what you've been preparing for, Bella. You know what to do. Remember your breathing. And the relaxation—all that stuff you did in your childbirth classes—I know it too, don't forget. I've done it before. I'll be there to help you.' He paused. 'If you want me there.'

A few minutes later, she choked out a gasp at a new, sharper pain. 'Another one!'

Paulo glanced down at his watch. 'That's ten minutes,' he observed, as calmly as possible.

'Is that OK?' she whispered, because everything she had been taught seemed to have flown clean out of her head.

He frowned. This all seemed to be happening far more rapidly than it was supposed to. 'I'd better ring Jessie and get her in to come and look after Eddie,' he said, watching her body tense up again. 'I think it's time I took you to hospital.'

This time the contraction almost swamped her, and the sweat ran down in rivulets from her forehead. And if this was just a taste of things to come... Isabella gripped Paulo's hand, not feeling the sticky moistness from where her nails dug into and broke the skin to make him bleed.

'Don't leave me, Paulo,' she moaned softly. 'Please don't leave me.'

That vulnerable little plea smashed its way right through his defences, and he was filled with an overwhelming need to protect her.

'I won't leave you,' he promised, as he reached for the telephone.

CHAPTER NINE

THE whirling blue light of the ambulance cast strange neon flashes over both their faces and the sound of the siren screamed in their ears as they sped towards the hospital.

Through a daze, Isabella gripped onto Paulo's hand, squirming around to try and get comfortable—but no position seemed to help.

Paulo was trying to stay calm, but it was harder than he had anticipated. He had tried paging Dr Cordosa, but the obstetrician had been sailing and was currently making his way back up the motorway. Paulo glanced down at Isabella, thinking that if her labour continued at this alarmingly fast rate, then Dr Cordosa would miss it anyway.

'How are you feeling?' he asked.

'Hot!' Sweat beaded her forehead. 'Will Eddie be OK?'

'Stop worrying about Eddie—he'll be fine. Jessie is there with him.'

'What about the *feijoada*? It's only half-cooked!'

'Bella!' he said warningly.

At the hospital they were rushed straight into the Emergency Department, where Bella was put, protesting, onto one of the trolleys. Paulo held her hand all the way up to the labour ward and when the midwife arrived to examine her she continued to grip onto it as tightly as a drowning woman.

The midwife gently pushed him aside, speaking to him as if he was a child himself.

'Can we have the father on the other side of the bed, please?'

He was about to say that he wasn't sure that he'd be around for the main part of the action, when he felt Bella's fingernails digging into the palm of his hand again. He looked down at her, the question in his eyes being answered by the beseeching look in hers. His heart pounded. When she had begged him not to leave her, she had meant it, he realised with something approaching shock.

'Sure,' he said, but he delicately kept his eyes on her face while the midwife conducted her intimate examination, and for the first time in his life he actually felt *shy*.

What Paulo wanted for Isabella more than anything was a straightforward birth, but he knew the instant that the midwife raised an expressive eyebrow at her runner across the delivery room and the runner hurriedly left the room that maybe this birth was not going to be straightforward at all.

He could tell that the team was trying to play any drama down, but he knew when two other doctors entered the room that things weren't going according to plan. He quickly read their name badges. One was an obstetrician and the other was a paediatrician. So didn't that mean that both mother *and* baby were in danger?

His heart made a painful acceleration, and he found himself praying for the first time in years. Dear God— he had already lost one woman in his life—surely fate would not be so merciless as to take the other one?

But he must not let his fear communicate itself to Bella. Not when she was being so brave. He watched the look of grim determination on her face as she conquered the rising tide of each contraction and he was reminded of her fundamental fearlessness. He gritted his teeth, frustrated at his inability to help her when she most needed him.

For Isabella nothing existed, save the powerful demands of her body—everything else faded into complete insignificance. She refused the drugs they offered her, but gulped down the gas and air, which helped. And so did Paulo, just by being there. She gripped onto his hand when the contractions grew so strong that she did not think she could bear to go through another one. Whenever she unclenched her eyes, his face swam into her line of vision and she could read the encouragement there.

And something else, too—a kind of pride and admiration which filled her with a powerful new energy.

People had started telling her to push, but she didn't need them to tell her anything, because by then the urge to get her baby into the outside world had become too strong to resist.

'Here's your baby!' called someone.

'Come and see your baby being born, Paulo,' urged one of the midwives.

Paulo couldn't have refused the midwife's request, even if he had wanted to. And he didn't. He knew that it was important for Bella to have someone witness an event which was as miraculous for her as for any other woman—even if the circumstances surrounding it *were* unconventional.

He let go of her hand and walked down the room to see the dark, downy head beginning to emerge and his heart gathered speed as a shoulder quickly followed. He was aware of furious activity executed with an unnatural calm, and then the baby slithered out, but made no sound as precious seconds ticked by. There was more activity, and then, quietly and dramatically, the first tenuous wail of life which hit him like a punch to the guts.

'It's a girl!' said the paediatrician, bending over the baby and cleaning the tiny nose and mouth.

Paulo walked over to Isabella and looked down at her pale face and the hair which was matted to her brow and cheeks. He bent down and brushed a damp curl away, so tempted to kiss her. 'Congratulations, *querida*,' he whispered instead. 'You have a beautiful daughter.'

A great wave of relief washed over her, leaving her shaky and exhausted in its wake. 'Can I hold her?'

'Just for a moment,' said the paediatrician, as he carefully placed the tiny bundle in her arms. 'Her heartbeat was a little low during the delivery and she was a little slow to breathe—so we're going to take her off to Special Care for her first night, just to keep an eye on her. Does she have a name yet?'

Bella stared down at the impossibly small head. The peep of dark curls through the swaddled blanket. And all the dark, frightened thoughts which had driven her half-crazy at the time she'd become pregnant—dissolved like magic. Because this baby *was* magic. A sense of love flooded her. 'She's called Estella,' she said, the overwhelming emotion making her breath catch in her throat. 'It means "star".'

'No, you're the star,' said Paulo softly, but he spoke in Portuguese, so that only Bella understood.

She looked up into his face and saw that his eyes were bright—the warmth and care in them surely too strong to be imagined? As proud as if he really *were* the father. Her lips began to tremble and she looked down and kissed her baby's head.

Bella opened her eyes in the middle of the night and wondered what was different. She sat bolt upright and looked around her. After the delivery she had submerged herself in the most delicious bath and had then fallen asleep, with Paulo sitting like some dark, beautiful guard beside her.

But now Paulo had gone and the crib by the bed remained empty. Fear clutched erratically at her heart as she reached out and rang the bell by her side and the nurse came hurrying into the room.

'Yes, dear—what is it?'

'Where's my baby, please?'

'She's still in Special Care—but not for very much longer. I spoke to them a little while ago, and she's doing just fine.'

'I want to see her.'

'And you can. But why don't you rest for the time being, and wait until the morning?'

'I want to see her,' said Bella with a stubborn new resolve in her voice she didn't recognise.

The nurse insisted on taking her up to the Special Care Unit in a wheelchair and as they drew up in front of the cubicle, Bella felt tears of relief pricking the back of her eyes as she watched the tableau being played out in front of them.

Behind the bright glass screen stood Paulo, and he was cradling the tiny baby in his arms, his lips moving as he spoke softly to her.

And Bella made a broken little sound. A primitive

sound which seemed to be torn from some place deep within her.

The nurse looked down at her. 'Are you all right?'

Bella nodded. *I love him. I've always loved him.*

The nurse beamed. 'You new mothers! Of course you love him—you've just had his baby, haven't you?'

Isabella hadn't even realised that she had spoken the words out loud, but suddenly she didn't care. And maybe Paulo realised that he was being watched or spoken about, because he suddenly looked up, and his brilliant smile told her that the baby was going to be fine.

'I'm going in,' she said to the nurse.

'Let me wheel you—'

'No. I want to walk. Honestly.' Paulo stood and watched while she climbed carefully out of the wheel-chair, watched the proud way she refused the nurse's arm and held herself erect, before walking stiffly into the cubicle and over to where he held Estella.

She looked into the black brilliance dancing in his eyes—eyes as dark as Estella's—thinking that he could easily be mistaken for her baby's father. But he wasn't. And he never would be. 'You've got my baby,' she whispered.

'I know. Can't resist her. Do you want her back? I thought so. Here—' And he held her out to Bella with a soft smile. 'Go to Mummy.'

Very gently, he placed Estella into her arms. The baby instinctively began rooting for her mother's breast and Isabella felt a tug of love so powerful that she stared down at the shivering little head with an indescribable sense of wonder.

And Paulo stood outside the magic circle, watched the first tentative explorings between mother and child, appalled by the dark feelings of exclusion which ran through him.

He wanted her, he realised. Just hours after she'd had another man's baby and he wanted her so badly that it hurt. Now what kind of person had he become?

He glanced up at the ward clock which was ticking the seconds away. It was four in the morning. 'I'd better get back home. I want to be there for Eddie waking up. I'll bring him to visit tomorrow. Goodbye, Isabella— sweet dreams.'

Suddenly he was gone, and Isabella and the nurse stared after his dark figure as he strode off down the hospital corridor without once looking back.

The nurse turned to Isabella and gave her a confused kind of smile. 'Why, the naughty man didn't even kiss you goodbye!' she clucked.

Isabella dropped a tired kiss on the top of Estella's head. 'I think the excitement of the delivery must have got to him,' she said. Far better to think that than to imagine that he hadn't kissed her because he simply hadn't wanted to...

CHAPTER TEN

THE following morning, Paulo arrived on the ward before the night-staff had gone home, bearing a bottle of champagne tied with a pink ribbon.

Three staff midwives looked up as he appeared at the office door and their mouths collectively fell open at the sight of the tall, dark-haired vision in a deep blue suit and an amber tie of pure silk.

'I know I'm early.' He smiled. 'But I wanted to see Bella before I went to work.'

The trio all sprang to their feet, smoothing down crisp white aprons. 'Let me show you where she is,' they said in unison.

Paulo's black eyes crinkled with amusement. 'I know where she is,' he said softly. 'I asked one of the nursing assistants. And I'd like to surprise her, if I may.'

Bella was busy feeding Estella, the baby nestled into the crook of Bella's arm while she tugged enthusiastically at her mother's breast. It was the strangest and most amazing sensation, Bella decided, her mouth curving into a slow smile of satisfaction.

Paulo stood outside her cubicle and watched her, marvelling at how easily and how naturally she had taken to feeding her child.

Breast-feeding had not been quite so popular when Eddie had been born and, in any case, Elizabeth's postnatal blues had meant that he had been able to take on most of the bottle-feeding so that she could rest.

He thought how the baring of Isabella's breast, though intimate, was not especially erotic. Then he saw her remove one elongated and rosy nipple and wondered just who he had been trying to kid.

Bella looked up to find herself caught in the intense dazzle of his black eyes and she felt the tremble of her lips as she gazed across the room at him.

And any idea that she might feel differently after the birth or that her words of love yesterday had been the hormone-fuelled fantasies of a post-partum woman were instantly banished. Because just the sight of his dear, handsome face was enough to engulf her with an unbearable sense of yearning.

He came in and put the champagne down on the locker. 'Hi,' he murmured.

'Hi,' she said back, feeling almost shy—but maybe that wasn't so very surprising. He had seen her at her most exposed—body and emotions stripped bare as she had brought new life into the world.

'I thought I'd pop in on my way in to work.'

And play havoc with her blood pressure in that beautifully cut dark suit. She smiled. 'I'm glad you did.'

He looked down at the baby who had now flopped into an instant, contented sleep. Had Eddie ever been that tiny? he wondered in bemusement. 'How is she?'

'Beautiful.'

Like her mother, he thought. 'Can I take her—or would that disturb her?'

She shook her head. 'Take away,' she said huskily.

He bent to pluck the swaddled bundle from her arms, surprised at the pleasure it gave him to hold Estella again. She smelt of milk—and of Bella—and he felt compelled by a powerful need to drop a kiss on top of the tiny head.

Isabella watched while he cradled and kissed Estella, and in that moment she loved him even more for his warmth and his generosity. I wish he would hold *me* like that, she thought with fierce longing.

'I phoned your father,' he said.

Her heart thudded a little. 'And?'

'He's puffed up with pride—I never imagined that he could go a full minute without saying anything!'

No need to tell her that he had then uncomfortably submitted to Luis's congratulations and endured the inevitable questions about who the child most resembled—Paulo or Bella. 'It's difficult to say,' he had replied smoothly, without stopping to question why the evasion had slipped so easily from his lips.

'How's Eddie?' she asked.

He stroked the downy head with the tip of his nose.

'Excited. More than excited—even the computer doesn't have an edge on this baby. I'll bring him in with me tonight.'

Paulo visited her morning and evening until she and the baby were discharged a week later, and he had an air of anticipation about him as he led her outside to where a large and shining family car awaited them.

With her arms full of blanket-swathed baby, Isabella blinked at the gleaming motor in surprise. 'What's this—a new car?'

'That's right.' He opened the door for her. 'Like it?'

'It's lovely, but what happened to the old one?'

'Nothing. It's in the garage—this is an extra. We need a bigger car now that there's four of us.'

He doesn't mean it the way it sounded, she told herself fiercely, as she bent to strap Estella into the newly installed car-seat.

Eddie was standing on the doorstep waiting to greet them, and he was hopping up and down with excitement. His father had taken him most days to visit them in hospital, leaving Paulo and Isabella feeling distinctly invisible! All Eddie's attention had been fixed on the tiny infant who clung so tightly to his finger with one little fist.

Paulo had found the experience strangely moving, noticing the interaction between his son and the new baby with something approaching remorse. He had always been so certain that Eddie should be the exclusive child in his life—always steeling himself against committing to a relationship again and the possibility of more children. Not that it had ever been a hardship. No woman had remotely tempted him to do otherwise.

But it was sobering to see how his son behaved with the baby—as if someone had just turned a light on inside him. As baby paraphernalia began to be delivered to the house, Paulo found himself wondering whether an immaculate house with a working father and a housekeeper was not vastly inferior to the noise and mess and love which this new addition seemed to have brought with her.

Isabella brought the baby into the house, walking with exaggerated care and still feeling slightly disorientated. She had only been away for a few days and yet she was returning as a different person. As a mother. With all the responsibilities which went with that role. Yet the sense of unreality which had descended on her since the birth had not completely left her, even though Estella was real and beautiful enough.

It was hard to believe now that Paulo had actually held her hand throughout. He had seen her stripped of all dignity—moaning and writhing with pain. He had wiped her brow just before she pushed the baby out and he had even watched her do *that*. But he had not touched her, nor kissed her and somehow she had thought—no, hoped—that he would. Maybe *he* was the one who had changed his mind.

But her troubled thoughts disappeared the moment she looked around her. The hallway was festooned with balloons and a lavish arrangement of scented pink flowers was standing next to the telephone. From the direction of the kitchen drifted a sweet, familiar smell.

'It's the *feijoada*,' explained Paulo as he saw her sniff the air and frown. 'We froze the meal you were making when you went into labour. Eddie said it would be perfect as a welcome-home feast.'

'Eddie's right—it's the very best,' said Isabella, looking at a silver and pink balloon saying 'It's a Girl!', which was floating up the stairs. 'And this all looks wonderful, too.' Her voice softened. 'You must have worked very hard.'

Jessie came out of the kitchen, a wide smile of welcome on her face. 'Welcome home!' she said, and hugged her.

'Thank you, Jessie!'

'Can I have a little peep?' Isabella pulled the cashmere blanket away from the miniature face and sighed. 'Isn't she beautiful?'

Paulo found himself looking at the mother instead of the baby. There was no doubt that she looked absolutely breathtaking—her figure seemed to have gone from bulk to newly slender almost overnight. The nurse had said that because she was so young and fit her body had just sprung back into shape straight away.

She was wearing a pair of saffron-yellow jeans and a scarlet shirt stretched tight over her milk-full breasts. The abundance of copper-brown curls were tied back from her face with a black ribbon and her unmade-up face looked dewy and radiant.

So what was the matter with her?

She seemed so distant, he thought. Detached. Her movements jerky and self-conscious—her only true warmth appearing when she was relating to the baby. Or to Eddie. But certainly not to him.

'Come upstairs and see what we've done for Estella,' he said softly.

'Can I hold the baby for a bit?' said Jessie eagerly. 'Give you a bit of a break?'

'Of course you can!' smiled Isabella but, with the infant out of her arms, she felt curiously bereft.

'Let me see her too, Jessie!' said Eddie.

Isabella's heart was in her mouth as Paulo followed her up the stairs. 'Where exactly are we going?' she asked him.

'The room right next door to yours,' he said, a faint frown appearing as he heard the unmistakable note of wariness in her voice.

But Isabella's nerves were temporarily forgotten when she opened the door and looked inside and saw what a lot of effort he must have gone to. 'Oh, my goodness,' she sighed. 'How on earth have you managed to do all this?'

It was the cutest baby's room imaginable.

One wall was dominated by a mural of Alice in Wonderland—complete with white rabbit and grinning Cheshire cat—while the rest of the walls were the exact colour of cherryade. An old-fashioned crib stood next to the wall, with flounces of lace nestling delicately amidst the pink gingham, while a rag-doll sat with several of her sisters on the gleaming, newly painted window ledge.

She found herself thinking that he had gone to an awful lot of trouble for a stay which might only be temporary and her heart gave a sudden great lurch of hope.

'Like it?' he asked.

She turned to him. '*Like* it? Oh, Paulo—who in their right mind could not help loving it?'

'And are you in your right mind?' he asked her softly.

Something in his tone made the hope die an uncertain death. 'I...think so. Why do you ask?'

He smiled, but there was a cold edge to his voice. 'You are wearing the kind of expression which I imagine the early Christians might have adopted just before being fed to the lions,' he said drily. 'What's the matter, Isabella—did you think I was planning to drag you up here to make love to you already?'

From the look on his face, the idea clearly appalled him. 'I didn't say that,' she said woodenly. She trusted him not to hurt her, to respect her and not to leap on her before she was ready—yet he was hurting her far more by standing on the opposite side of the room like some dark, remote stranger.

He frowned at the reproachful look in her amber eyes.

'Bella, you're tired. And you've just had a baby. What kind of a monster do you think I am?'

'You're not a monster at all,' she said. 'I'm just grateful for all the trouble you've gone to—'

Damn it—he didn't want her *gratitude*, just some sign, some indication that she still wanted him. 'Don't mention it,' he put in coolly.

Rather desperately, she said, 'But it must have cost a lot of money?'

The light went out in his eyes. 'Please don't mention it again, Bella. Let's just call it a small repayment for the kindness shown to me by your father all these years.'

And wasn't that a bit like saying that the debt was now repaid? She wondered?

She wanted to touch him, to run her fingertips along the hard, proud outline of his jaw, but inside she was scared.

She *had* just had a baby and she also had a poor track record where men were concerned. If she started a relationship with Paulo, she had to be very sure that she was doing the right thing. And while in her heart there wasn't a single doubt, she needed him to know that she wasn't acting on a whim when they made love.

If he still wanted *her*—and she needed to be sure of that, too.

Paulo saw the discomfiture on her face and wondered if she felt compromised. 'Of course, you mustn't feel that just because I've had the room decorated you have to stay.' His eyes were full of question. 'You may have already made your mind up that you want to leave.'

She wondered if she was keeping her horror carefully concealed. 'Leave?'

He forced himself to continue, even though the words nearly choked him. She had to have a let-out clause, he decided grimly.

'You might want to go home,' he suggested softly. 'To Brazil. You could take Estella and show her to her father.'

She met the dark challenge in his eyes without flinching. 'But Roberto doesn't want me. I told you that. And I don't want him! It's over—it never really began.' Because he had only ever been a shadowy lover—an unwitting replacement for the only man she had ever really wanted.

'But he might feel differently once he knows about the baby.'

'He isn't going to *know* about the baby!'

'And don't you think he has a right?'

'I think I have a right to choose whether or not to tell him,' she told him softly.

'But your feelings towards him may change,' he argued, wondering what contrary demon was making him put forward a case which was detrimental to what *he* wanted. 'What if Estella grows to resemble her real father more and more—what then? You might find the biological tie irresistible—you might even want him back again.'

She didn't react—would not let him see how much his callous words had hurt her. He'd sounded as though that was what he *wanted* her to do. Maybe, as a father himself, he was now becoming indignant on Roberto's behalf.

She heard the sound of Estella's cry floating up the stairs towards her and in an instant she had stilled, lifting her head to listen. 'Is that Estella?'

'Yeah. Saved by the baby!' He noticed that there were two small, damp circles of milk on her shirt and gave a wry smile, which did little to ease the ache in his groin. 'But mightn't it be best if you change your shirt before you go down?'

She looked down at her damp and rocky nipples and when she lifted her head to meet his eyes, she saw the unmistakable spark of desire. And laughter. 'Just go, Paulo!' she said huskily.

Downstairs he found Eddie sitting on one of the vast, overstuffed sofas, cradling the baby expertly in his arms.

'Are you OK holding her?' Paulo asked gently, and the look his son gave him cut him to the marrow.

'Of course I'm OK! Oh, Dad, look! She's so cute! Loads of the other boys in my class have got baby brothers or sisters—I wish Estella could be *my* little sister! Why can't you marry Isabella, and then she can?'

'Because real life isn't like that,' he said gently.

'Well, real life sucks!'

'Eddie!' Paulo opened his mouth to issue a short but terse lecture on the unattractiveness of swearing, but something in his son's haunted expression drew him up short.

He had lost his mother so young that he had no real memory of her, Paulo remembered painfully. Maybe it wasn't so surprising that Eddie had already forged a bond with this fatherless little infant, Paulo thought, and felt a lump catch in his throat.

The sense of loss had been with him for a long time—long after the pain of bereavement had gone. The random cruelty of life had made him wary of committing to anyone again—but now he was beginning to realise that you couldn't live your life thinking 'what if?' He had once accused Isabella of cowardice, but hadn't he been guilty of emotional cowardice himself?

'Can I take her for a minute, son?' he said gently.

When Isabella came back downstairs, with her hair flowing loose around her shoulders, it was to find father and son being extremely territorial with *her* baby! She looked over at the two males sitting up close on the sofa, their dark heads bent over the sleeping bundle. To an outsider, she realised wistfully, they would look exactly like a normal family.

'Can I use the phone, Paulo?'

'You don't have to ask every time,' he growled.

'Thank you.' She gave him a serene smile. 'It's just that I'd better ring my father and tell him I'm safely out of hospital.'

'And neither do you have to tell me the name of everybody you're calling.'

'I'll remember that,' she said gravely.

Paulo paced up and down with Estella locked against his neck, desperately trying not to succumb to the temptation of eavesdropping into her conversation.

Maybe their conversation of earlier had been closer to the mark than he had imagined. Maybe even now she was talking to her father about the possibility of returning to Brazil... He had brought the subject up and she had grown quiet long enough to suggest that she had given it some serious thought. And why *shouldn't* she feel differently now? That was what babies tended to do to you.

'Paulo?' He looked up to see those delicious curls falling almost to her waist and his lips tingled with the need to kiss her.

'You got through OK?' he asked thickly.

She nodded, thinking how tiny the baby looked in his arms. And how right. 'He said to thank you for the photos, and asked how the hell did you get them over to him so quickly?'

'There isn't much point me having access to all the latest technology—' he shrugged, with a smile '—unless I'm actually going to use it. What else did he say?'

'He's desperately excited. Buying up every pink article in Salvador. And…'

He narrowed his eyes. 'And what?'

Isabella hesitated, glancing over at Eddie and Paulo guessed that she wanted to speak to him in private.

He followed her out into the hallway. 'What is it?' he demanded softly.

She met his eyes with embarrassment. 'Well, since we haven't issued a denial—' she paused again.

'Go on,' he prompted.

She shrugged awkwardly. 'He still seems to be labouring under the illusion that we're getting married.'

'Oh, does he?' asked Paulo slowly.

'I really should tell him that we aren't, but…'

3He looked up, trying to work out what emotion was colouring her voice. 'But what?'

She sighed. Paulo did not need to know that her father thought he was the most wonderful thing since sliced bread. And that the prospect of his only daughter making such a glorious marriage seemed to have erased the memory of her unconventional pregnancy. 'Oh, I don't know,' she hedged. 'It seems to be keeping him happy.'

'Then why don't we keep it that way?' he suggested thoughtfully.

CHAPTER ELEVEN

ISABELLA turned Estella's night-light on and went quietly downstairs to the dining room where Paulo was waiting for her.

He looked up as she came in, his dark face thoughtful as she did up the final button of her bodice, and he sighed. How in God's name had he ever been stupid enough to think that breast-feeding a baby wasn't erotic?

'Is she asleep?' he asked.

'Out for the count.' She slid into her seat and watched while he heaped a pile of glossy black grapes into the centre of the cheeseboard, thinking that Saturday night dinner in the Dantas household was an experience not to be missed.

Because, despite the undeniable masculinity of his appearance, she had discovered that Paulo was no slouch when it came to finding his way round a kitchen. And that, as well as a hundred different ways with pasta, he cooked a mean steak. But then, as he had told her, Jessie might have been around to do the bulk of the house-keeping duties—but she certainly wasn't on call twenty-four hours a day, seven days a week!

He was sitting staring at her now, the black eyes softly luminous. 'So what did the midwife say?'

Isabella swirled red wine around the globe of her

glass and pretended to study it. She certainly wasn't going to repeat the midwife's brisk question word for word! 'Sex-life back to normal by now, I expect?' And Isabella had nodded her head vigorously, because how—*how*—could she possibly tell the nurse the truth? That she had never, ever been made love to by Paulo Dantas. But that oh, she wanted to.

'Hmm, Bella?' he prompted on a murmur.

'Oh, just that Estella was the most beautiful, bouncing baby—'

'Uh-huh. Anything else?'

'And that we're doing everything right.' She heard the word 'we' slip off her tongue and silently cursed it. Just because she continued to play happy families inside her head, that didn't mean the rest of the world had to join in. Even though Paulo seemed to be doing a masterly job of playing happy families himself.

'That's all?'

Isabella put her glass down on the table. 'Paulo, just what are you trying to say?'

He suspected that she knew damned well. 'Nothing.'

'Look, why don't you come right out and ask me?'

'It would shock you, pretty lady.' He gave a gritty smile, thinking that lately she didn't look just pretty— she looked absolutely knock-out beautiful. Like tonight, for instance—in that silky red thing which covered her from neck to knee and yet left absolutely nothing to the imagination. He wondered whether it had been designed for the sole purpose of having a man itching to tear the damned thing off.

'I told you.' She sipped her wine and smiled encouragingly at him. 'I'm unshockable, these days.'

Paulo pushed his untouched plate of cheese aside and

stared at her, thinking that much more of this and he was going to go out of his mind. Because, even though he and Bella and Eddie and Estella had been living the kind of lifestyle which usually featured in the glossy supplements of Sunday newspapers, deep down, the undercurrent of tension between the two of them had been unbearable.

There had been all the frustration of having her so close—but not close enough. Of nights laced with hot, erotic dreams which left him waking up, sweat-sheened and frustrated—despite the inevitable conclusion to those dreams. Of knowing—or hoping—that she was lying there tossing and turning, just the same as he was. Aching with the need to touch her, to lay his hands on a body which was driving him slowly insane. So that going to work each morning had become a welcome kind of escape from the unwitting spell she was casting over him.

She moved with such unconscious grace that he found he had never enjoyed watching a woman quite as much as he did Isabella. There was nothing of the flirt or the tease about her. She was as uncomplicated in her young, strong beauty as any of the thoroughbreds he had seen her ride on her father's ranch.

But a deal was a deal and he forced himself to remember the stark facts. He was older—and far more experienced. He knew just what to do and exactly which buttons to press if he wanted to get Bella into his bed. But the decision had to be hers, and hers alone. And, whilst before the baby had been born he had deliberately flirted with her, he no longer trusted himself to do that.

A distended stomach meant that you couldn't exactly throw a woman to the floor and make love to her like there was no tomorrow. Which was what he had felt like doing earlier when Isabella decided that she was going to dress up for dinner. He swallowed down a mouthful of wine without really tasting it.

Isabella stared at him through the candles, willing him to say something—*anything*—which would bring the subject round to the question of them becoming lovers without her having to actually blurt it out.

'Paulo?' she whispered huskily, her eyes full of question.

'Yes, *querida*?' He kept his voice neutral and his smile bland.

She stared at him in frozen disbelief. Because when push came to shove she needed a little more in the way of wooing. She knew he had promised her nothing other than an affair which would 'burn itself out', and she could accept that. She wasn't asking him to sign the register and produce a band of gold—just give her some sign that he really, really *wanted* her—because she was damned if she was going to beg!

She slammed her napkin down onto the table before jumping to her feet. 'Oh! Paulo Dantas!' she cried frustratedly. 'You are so…so…'

'So?' he goaded, his black eyes laughing even while his body sprang into aching life.

'*Stupid!*' And she pushed her chair back and walked straight out of the dining room, resisting the urge to slam the door behind her—because Eddie was in bed, fast asleep, and so was Estella.

She got as far as the top landing before she heard the sound of soft footfalls behind her, and for some reason the idea that he was silently chasing her through the house was unbearably exciting. She speeded up until she was almost past his bedroom door, when a hand appeared from behind to grab her wrist and to twist her round to face him and she nearly fainted with pleasure when she saw the hunger written darkly in his eyes.

'Stupid, you say?' he drawled softly.

Her heart pumped erratically. 'D-did I?'

'Stupid?' He gave a low, exultant laugh. 'Let's see, shall we, *querida*?' And he pulled her into his bedroom and softly kicked the door shut behind them.

Isabella felt the instant shimmer of arousal as his arms locked tightly around her waist and he stared down at her, his eyes devouring her with a hot, dark fire.

'Oh, *querida*,' he said, on a low groan of submission before giving in to the temptation which had been eating away at him for too long now. 'Bella, *querida*.' He felt like a man who had strayed into paradise unawares as he crushed his mouth down on hers, feeling the rose-petal softness of her lips. He kissed her until he had no breath left and then he raised his head. 'Do you want me?' he asked dazedly.

I've always wanted you. 'Yes,' came her throaty response as she wrapped her arms around his neck and clung onto him like she was drowning and Paulo represented safe harbour. Her gorgeous, beautiful Paulo. 'Yes, yes, yes.'

Paulo couldn't remember a kiss this hot or this intense and he knew that if she continued to generously press her body against him like that, that he would end up taking her against the wall. And he didn't want to just ruck her dress up and push aside her panties, ending up with his trousers round his ankles while he thrust long and hard and deep into her. He groaned.

Well, he did—of course he did. But she deserved more than that.

'Come here,' he said breathlessly. 'Come to bed.' She was barely aware of the sumptuous fittings. Or the vast bed with its cover of rich, earthy colours. All she could see was the intense black light shining from his eyes as he sat her down, and began to unbutton the bodice of her dress.

'I want to touch you,' he said shakily. 'I need to touch you. Every bit of you. Inside and out.'

Bella shivered, unable to look away, feeling the buds of her breasts begin to tighten and the honey rush of desire as it soaked through her panties. She wondered if he could see the love which must surely be blazing from her eyes, but maybe she had better keep them closed.

Love wasn't part of the deal, was it?

Paulo's fingers faltered for a moment as he caught an unmistakable scent of her sex, but he forced himself to continue unbuttoning, even though he would have willingly bought her twenty replacements if only he could rip it off. Her fingers had started to flutter over the silk of his shirt, skittering downwards in a way that made him shake his head.

'No,' he whispered.

'No?' She wanted to be good for him. She wanted to give him pleasure and she had read that all men liked to be touched *there*.

'*Querida,*' he said, speaking with difficulty because he felt seconds away from exploding. 'I've been wanting this for too long.' Because if she touched him there… He peeled away the dress and a moan of rapture was torn from his lips. Her breasts were as full as they had been during her pregnancy, and very, very beautiful. He dipped his head reverentially towards one, and flicked the tip of his tongue towards one hardened nipple which pushed pinkly through the gossamer-fine black lace.

It was like being injected with some earth-shattering drug and Isabella fell helplessly back against the mattress, her hips moving in synchrony with her disbelieving gasp of pleasure. 'Please, Paulo,' she whispered, though she had no real idea what she was asking him for.

The husky plea and erotic action threatened to end everything before it had started and Paulo groaned again. He forced his head away from its sensual plundering of her lips, staring down into amber eyes which now looked black as raisins.

'Easy,' he breathed raggedly. 'For God's sake, Bella—take…it…easy.'

She wondered how she was supposed to do that.

Especially now that his hand was slithering up her skirt, and then he gave a disbelieving little moan.

'Wh-what is it?' she stumbled.

'Stockings.' He swallowed. 'You're wearing *stockings.*'

Isabella heard the deepening of his voice and smiled.

She might just be a girl from a ranch in the middle of nowhere, but there were some things that every woman over the world should know.

'Doesn't *every* woman wear stockings?' she asked him innocently.

'They should.' He groaned again. 'They should.' But then his fingertips had moved beyond her suspenders to the cool, pale flesh of her thighs. And beyond.

Oh! 'Paulo!' she breathed. *'Gato. Querido gato.'*

'You are making this bloody difficult for me,' he groaned as her head fell back and she moved distractedly again. Unable to resist, he briefly touched the warm, damp silk of her panties until he remembered that he was trying to undress her. His fingers skated away and she mouthed a silent prayer of protest, so that one finger in particular came skimming back again.

He could feel her fullness and her wetness and tightness, heard the broken words which escaped from her lips and which made no sense to him. She spoke in a mixture of English and Portuguese, her voice heavy with longing and thick with need.

He gave up and began to touch her with rhythm and purpose, thinking that this wasn't how it was supposed to happen.

Well, maybe part of it was. Hadn't he dreamed of seeing her like this, her body stretched out with abandon on his bed? Writhing with need and with desire and no thought of anything other than pleasure—the wild tumble of her hair painting his pillow with such dark curls.

He gave a small smile as he rubbed his finger against her and she nearly leapt off the bed. He had expected passion, yes. And response, yes—that, too. But this... He dipped his head down and took the blunt tip of her nipple into his mouth, while his finger continued to tease and play against her.

Isabella felt like she had entered another world—a world dominated by sensation. By pleasure. By Paulo. And he seemed to know exactly what to do to make it get better all the time... With something approaching astonishment, he felt her begin to tighten with an incredible tension, which could only mean one thing and he stared down into her face. Saw the mindless seeking of rapture which made her oblivious to everything except what was just about to happen in her own body. He speeded up the rhythm and spoke to her in her own language, sweet, erotic words he had never used before, words which made her melt enchantingly against his finger.

'Paulo!' she called out, and the slurred pleasure in her voice was tinged with surprise.

He smiled as he saw the sudden, frantic arching of her back, the incredulous little gasp she made as she reached that elusive, perfect place and then began the slow, shuddering journey back to sanity.

He watched the gradual stilling of her body, the flush which crept and bloomed like a flower on her neck. The way her lips parted in a helpless little sigh. The slumberous and lanquid stretch, like an indolent cat in front of a fire. And then the thick fluttering of her lashes as her slitted eyes gazed up at him.

'*Oh,*' she breathed uninhibitedly. 'What was *that*?' He had suspected. No, deep down he had known. But her question—with all its implications—filled him with such a heady sense of his own power that it was as much as he could do not to throw his dark head back and give a loud, exultant laugh.

So. Roberto had given her a baby, yes. But no pleasure.

'*That, querida* of mine,' he purred, 'was the pleasure you deserve. The pleasure I intend to give you…over and over and over again.'

'*Again?*' She swallowed, with a greedy gulp.

He smiled. 'As many times as you like. But for God's sake let's get these clothes off.' His smile became rueful. He really *was* going to have to take control here, or he would never manage to get her—or himself—into bed!

And he wanted to. Needed to. Needed to feel close to her, skin on skin. Limb on limb.

He found the side fastening of her dress and slid

the zip down—sliding the silky garment down over the curve of her hips with a hand which shook like a schoolboy's. And it was a long time since he had undressed a woman like this.

Those who had been in his bed since Elizabeth's death had all been icons of experience. So eager. So orderly. Neatly disappearing into the bathroom before returning to bed, all washed and toothbrushed and douched, smelling of perfume and soap and chemicals.

While Bella… She smelt like a real woman. He bent his head to unclip a stocking and again caught the raw perfume of her sex as it drifted towards him, and he resisted the urge to bury his head in the dark blur of curls which was lying with tantalising temptation above the creamy flesh of her thighs.

Later, he thought. They could do all that and more—but later. He dropped the dress onto the floor, and the stockings and garter belt followed, until she was just lying there in her bra and panties.

Her breasts were swollen, pushing against the black lace of the bra she wore and he found himself praying that she wouldn't have to go and feed the baby. But then he remembered that she had slipped away at the end of dinner, and he gave a great shuddering sigh of relief. Now, how selfish is *that*? he asked himself, as he tugged the lace panties down over her knees, trying hard not to touch her—anywhere—because he was holding onto his self-control only by the thinnest possible thread.

'Get into bed,' he said urgently.

'Touch me again,' she begged him, but he shook his head.

It had been too long. He had wanted her for too long.

'If I touch you again, I'll explode,' he said huskily,

and the expression in his eyes made her draw in a shivering breath of excitement. 'Get into bed while I get undressed.'

She watched him take his clothes off. His face was shadowed in the unlit room as first the white T-shirt was removed to reveal the quietly gleaming olive of his muscular torso. The black jeans followed, sliding them down over the powerful shaft of his thighs until he stood in just a pair of dark silk boxer shorts. His movements were naturally slinky and sensual as he peeled off the final piece of clothing.

Isabella's eyes widened. *'Gato,'* she murmured out loud, without thinking, and his smile was one of pure brilliance.

He paused only to tear open a condom and to carefully sheath himself with it and Isabella wondered if it was normal for a man to be that aroused, that quickly.

He drew back the cover and climbed into bed with her, pulling her into his arms, and smoothing the rampant curls away from her face. 'I don't know very much,' she admitted huskily.

'I'll teach you everything I know,' he promised and felt her shiver with anticipation in his arms. Her eyes were as bright as stars and the flush on her neck was beginning to fade. He bent and kissed the tip of her nose, just for the hell of it. And then her lips. A soft, sweet, drugging kiss that went on and on until he could wait no longer.

He pushed her back against the pillow and lay over her, his elbows taking all his weight, while the creamy swell of her breasts pushed alluringly towards him.

'Scared?' he asked.

She opened her eyes very wide. 'Why should I be scared?'

'It's your first time since having a baby. I'll be very—' he swallowed, feeling unbearably moved by the look of trust in her eyes '—gentle.'

Her faith in him was implicit. She felt the moist tip of him pushing against her and she gave an experimental little thrust of her hips, so that he nudged gently inside, filling her completely. And if she shuddered, then so did he. 'Be what you want to be, Paulo.'

He gave up. The questions could come later. Right now, it was her turn. And his. His.

He made one long, slow, hard stroke. And then another. Dipping his head to kiss her, his tongue copying the same, slick and erotic rhythm. Increasing the tempo as her control began to leave her. Watching the opening of her lips in a frozen exclamation as it started happening to her all over again.

And he could no longer wait. Nothing in the world could have stopped him. Nothing. He tensed and steeled himself, aware that this was going to feel like nothing had ever felt before.

And it did.

Oh, it did.

CHAPTER TWELVE

PAULO opened his eyes to find his head resting on the glorious cushion of Isabella's breasts. And that she was trying to slip out from underneath him. He tightened his arms around her. 'Oh, no,' he objected sleepily. 'You're not going anywhere.'

'Paulo,' she whispered. 'I must. I hear Estella and I need to go and feed her.'

He rolled onto his side, and snapped the light on, blinking at the sudden intrusion, but just in time to watch her climbing out of bed, beautifully and un-ashamedly naked.

'You'll come back?' he asked.

Isabella pulled the red dress over her head, not both-ering with underwear. The front fastening of the dress meant that she would easily be able to feed the baby, and then she had better take a shower and... She shook her head. 'I'd better not—it's two in the morning.'

He propped himself up on his elbow, and the black eyes glittered by the lamplight as he watched her. 'So?'

'By the time I've fed her, and changed her and settled her back down for what's left of the night—there won't really be time for me to come back in here.'

If he had learnt one thing and one thing only during

that exquisite interlude, it was that she liked him to talk dirty.

'But I haven't finished with you yet,' he said quite deliberately.

Isabella swallowed as she heard the dark resolve in his voice, but knew that she had other responsibilities than being his lover. She was a parent, too. And so was he.

She bent to pick her disgarded panties and bra from the carpet and looked him straight in the eye. 'I don't think I should be here when Eddie wakes up.'

'You won't be! His room is right along the corridor and he's the world's heaviest sleeper—you know that,' he objected. 'Besides, I always wake first.'

'What if for once he doesn't?'

'He always knocks first.'

'But *we* might oversleep,' she told him softly, thinking that if they carried on the way they had been doing up until half an hour ago they might risk oversleeping for a week!

'Then I'll set the alarm.'

'Paulo!'

'OK, OK.' He sat up in bed and raked his hand back through the thick, dark hair, knowing deep down that she was right, damn her—and yet oddly irritated by her determination. Because at that moment he wanted her so badly that he felt like he would have shifted heaven and earth to have her back here in his bed.

Isabella smoothed her hair down and blew him a kiss.

'Bye.'

'Come over here and kiss me properly.'

'Or?'

He laughed, but the laugh was tinged with sexual danger. 'Guess?'

Her heart thundered in response as she walked over to the bed and bent down over him and he was given a tantalising glimpse of the shadowed cleft between her breasts. Her face and then her mouth hovered into his line of vision and she pressed a sweet, swift kiss on his lips, before going back to the door.

He very nearly said, When will I see you?

Until he remembered that he could see her whenever he wanted. Mmm. He sighed and smiled and snuggled into the pillow and was asleep in seconds.

Feeling hot and sticky and more than a little uncomfortable, Isabella fed Estella, changed her and then sang gently to her for a little while.

In her arms the baby snuffled, oblivious to the ever changing play of emotions on her mother's face. Isabella put her down in the beautiful gingham crib, tucked her in and stood looking down at her for a long moment. She thought about the years to come—God willing—when she would gaze down at her daughter like this.

She jammed her fist in her mouth and turned away, tears burning at her eyes as she realised just how irrevocable the sexual act could be. Out of her desperate attempt to put Paulo out of her mind had come this tiny baby.

And tonight. Irrevocable for a different reason—though there would be no baby. Paulo had made sure of that.

She thought about his tenderness and his passion. The way it had really seemed to be *her* that he wanted in his bed. Not just because she was a body, and any body would do.

Tonight had been irrevocable because it had sealed

the truth in her heart once and for all. That she loved this man Paulo Dantas. Would love him forever. And that made her more than vulnerable where he was concerned.

He had been totally honest with her. He had told her she could stay with him for as long as... What had he said? 'Until it is spent. All burnt out.' Just as he had told her that they should indulge their mutual passion.

Well, now they had. So what came next?

One thing was for sure, she decided, peeling off the scarlet dress and dropping it into the laundry basket. She needed to keep some vestige of independence—if only to prove to herself that she didn't need him around every minute of every day. Because if that happened she would be lost.

The last thing she wanted was to become totally dependent on Paulo—to become addicted to his beautiful, strong body and his quick, clever mind.

Because everyone knew how difficult addictions were to kick. It was better to never get started in the first place.

Isabella woke for Estella's early morning feed and then took a long, long shower, arriving in the dining room for breakfast at the same time as Eddie.

'Hi, sweetheart,' she smiled.

'Hi, Bella. Where's Estella?'

'Guess?'

'Sleeping!' he grinned.

'You've got it in one! You can go in and say goodbye to her before you go to school, if you want.' She saw the warmth on his young face. 'Tell you what—when you get home tonight, you can help me to bath her. Would you like that?'

'Oh, Bella—*can* I?'

'Can you what?' asked a deep, sleepy voice, and Isabella's mouth dried as Paulo walked into the dining-room.

'Hi, Papa! Isabella said I can help bathe Estella tonight!'

'That's nice,' said Paulo blandly and, sitting down opposite her, poured himself a glass of juice and raised it up to her in a silent, sexy toast.

Isabella struggled to hold onto her self-possession, but it wasn't easy. What did he think he was playing at? Usually he presented himself for his morning bread and fruit already dressed for work. Wearing an immaculate suit, a pristine shirt and a silk tie which made him look like a walking advertisement for executive-hunk.

So *why* was he barefoot and unshaven, wearing a faded old T-shirt—having just thrown on *the same pair of jeans that he had worn last night*? And now a bare foot had moved underneath the table and was inching its way suggestively up her leg!

She snatched it away as if it had been contaminated and thought about pouring herself a cup of coffee, except that her hand was shaking so much she didn't think she would be able to make the cup connect with her mouth.

She met the glittering jet of his gaze. 'Won't you be late, Paulo?' she asked him pointedly.

'Late?' he enquired sunnily. 'I'm a director of the bank, *querida*. I can stroll in late once in a while if I feel like it.'

'But Dad.' Eddie frowned. 'You told me that if you're a director you must always set an example—and that you should only ever be late if you've got a genuine reason to be. Like that time when I didn't want to go in because we had a maths test, but you made me.'

'He does have a point, Paulo.'

'Oh, *does* he?' He glared dangerously, and then, drawing in a breath, managed to smile. 'Anyway,' he said casually, 'I thought I'd work from home today.'

Isabella knew exactly what he was playing at—and she wasn't going to let him do this. It was vital to her sanity not to let him invade every waking moment of her day as well as her night.

'Oh, what a pity I won't be here.' She smiled.

The glower deepened. 'What do you mean, you won't be here?'

'Just that I'm taking Estella to see the doctor.'

He stared at her. 'What's the matter with her?'

'Nothing.' Her mouth softened. 'It's just a regular check-up.'

'Well, he can come here—I thought we agreed that!'

'No, we did not!' she said quietly. 'That was before—when I was pregnant and exhausted. I *need* to get out, Paulo—and Estella needs the fresh air, too, because it's good for little babies. Right?'

The black stare iced through her. 'Right,' he said coldly.

She only toyed with a croissant and, in the end, gave up and went to the utility room to find a clean sheet. She was just tucking it into the base of the pram when she heard Paulo come up behind her. She was prepared for him to touch her, but he didn't—what she was not prepared for was the irritation which was sending dangerous jet sparks glittering from his eyes when she turned to face him.

'What's the matter, *querida*?' he purred, thinking that he had never been so expertly turned down by a woman before. And that as a method of increasing desire it was proving achingly effective. 'Been having second thoughts this morning?'

'No, of course not.'

'Then why are you so intent on keeping me at arm's length?'

Isabella looked over his shoulder to check that no one else was around. *'Jessie's* here!' she hissed. 'What do you expect?'

He shrugged. 'So I'll give her the day off.'

'No!'

'Yes—'

'What, so *you* take the day off and then give Jessie the day off—and you and I spend the rest of it in bed together, I suppose?'

He grinned. 'Sounds pretty good to me.'

'Well, I don't think it's a good idea—in fact, I think it's the worst idea I've ever heard!' Well, maybe that was overstating her case a little, but she needed to make him understand how she felt.

There was a long, dangerous pause. 'Would you care to explain why?'

Isabella sighed, because this wasn't easy. She wanted him—she wanted him too much, that was the problem. 'Paulo, I desperately need to maintain some sort of routine with my baby, not launch headlong into a sizzling new love-affair with you.'

'Surely the two aren't mutually exclusive?'

'No, of course they're not... But I think it's important that I'm there for Estella. If she were *our* baby we'd both be gazing at her non-stop, not each other—'

'But she's not *our* baby,' he pointed out, unprepared for a sudden great lurch of sadness.

'No, she's not. That's why I need to get to *know* her— we need to bond—and if I'm in your bed all the time, then we won't.' She looked at him with appeal darkening the huge, amber eyes. 'You know we won't.'

Paulo sighed. The irony was that he wouldn't have it any other way. If she'd ignored the baby while playing all kinds of erotic sex-games with him, then he would have found it a complete turn-off.

'No, I guess you're right.' He sighed again. 'But night-times…and I mean *every* nighttime…those are our times.' He gave her a look of dark, shivering intent. 'Got that?'

'Oh, yes.' She swallowed, and reached out her hand to touch his face, but he stopped the movement instantly, handcuffing her wrist between his thumb and forefinger while he shook his head.

'Oh, no, Bella,' he said softly. 'You can't have it every which way. You can't just love me and leave me, then kiss me goodbye and leave me aching all day.' And he swiftly covered her mouth with a sweet, hard kiss which sent *her* senses reeling, before giving a devastating and glittering smile as she gazed up at him in dismay. 'See? It hurts, doesn't it, sweet *querida*?'

But, before her befuddled brain could begin to think of an answer, he had turned on his heel and left.

By the evening Paulo had calmed down a little, though he conceded that his buoyant mood might have had something to do with his anticipation of the night to come.

On the way home from the bank, he stopped off at the florist and bought an extravagant display of white, scented flowers—'nothing too *obvious*', he had told the florist, who had taken one look at him and suggested red roses—plus chocolates and a video for Eddie.

He arrived home to find the house strangely silent. Eddie was sitting in the study, laboriously doing his homework, and Isabella was sitting by the fire in the smaller sitting room, breastfeeding the baby.

She hadn't heard him come in and carried on, blissfully unaware of his presence by the door, murmuring sweet nothings to the child who suckled her, and he felt a sudden great urge to kiss her.

Instead he said softly, 'Hi!'

She looked up and her heart leapt with the sheer pleasure of seeing him. 'Hi.'

'Good day?'

'Sort of.' She hesitated. 'Paulo—about this morning—'

'I'm sorry—'

'No, I'm sorry—'

'I said it first,' he teased softly, and produced the lavish bunch of flowers from behind his back like a magician magicking a rabbit out of a hat.

'For me?'

'Well, who else?' She buried her nose in the blooms and breathed their scent in. 'Jessie?'

'No, seriously.'

'Paulo, I *am* being serious. She's—'

'Where is she?' He sniffed the air. Yes, *that* was the odd thing. Normally when he arrived home from work, Jessie was crashing around in the kitchen, cooking something for supper. But tonight there were no tempting aromas to signal the arrival of an imminent supper. 'Where is she?' he repeated.

'She's gone out to buy champagne.'

He frowned. 'But we've got plenty of champagne in the house.'

'I know we have. But she wanted it to be *her* champagne. *Her* treat.'

'*Querida*, you aren't making much sense.'

'Paulo—' She drew a deep breath. 'Jessie's gone and got herself engaged!'

'Jessie has?' He shook his head. 'I don't believe it!'

'Well, you'd better. It's true. In fact, that sounds like the door—so why don't you ask her yourself?'

In the distance, the front door slammed and Jessie came breathlessly into the room, carrying a brown paper bag with a foil-topped bottle in it, smiling so much that her face looked fit to burst.

'Jessie, is this true?' he asked, mock-sternly. 'Are you about to take the plunge and get married?'

'Yes,' Jessie beamed. 'It's true! Isn't it wonderful?'

'I guess it is,' he said slowly. 'It's just come as a bit of a shock, that's all.'

'It was a shock to *me* when Simon proposed,' confessed Jessie. 'I mean, we haven't *really* known each other for that long, and...' She gave a self-conscious and slightly apologetic shrug. 'He wants me to stop work as soon as you'll let me. You won't be needing me for much longer, anyway, will you?'

Paulo started, wondering what was happening to the smooth and well-oiled machinery of his life. 'You're not *leaving*?' he demanded, aghast.

Jessie frowned at him. 'Well, of course I'm leaving,' she told him softly. 'I can't keep coming in twice a day to cook your meals when I have a husband of my own to care for, can I? And besides—' she shot a quick smile at Isabella '—I sort of got the idea that I was becoming supernumerary around here anyway. You won't miss *me*, Paulo—not any more. You've got Isabella and the baby here now.'

Paulo opened his mouth to say something, but thought better of it. Now was not the time to selfishly think about his own needs and Jessie had been indispensable to him. She had helped and supported him through all these years—so now he must be genuinely happy for her.

'Congratulations, Jessie,' he smiled. He held out his arms to her and gave her an emotional bear-hug.

Over the top of her head, he tried to catch Isabella's eyes, but all her attention seemed to be concentrated fiercely on the baby in her arms. 'We'd better get that champagne opened and order in some pizza,' he observed thoughtfully. 'Let's make it a party!'

Supper was served amidst much excitement and some chaos in the dining room, where Simon was telephoned by Jessie and summoned in to join them. The tall librarian was clearly nuts about his future bride, and Isabella felt a pang of emotion which felt appallingly close to jealousy. But she fixed a bright smile onto her lips as they all raised their glasses in a toast, even Eddie.

It was late by the time that the newly engaged pair left, giggling like a couple of teenagers, while Eddie was yawning again and again.

'Come on, son,' said Paulo softly, as he shut the front door. 'Bed.'

'G'night, Isabella,' yawned Eddie.

'Goodnight, sweetheart.' She felt oddly nervous as she busied herself throwing away the half-chewed slices of pizza and tipping the dregs of champagne down the sink, especially when she turned to find Paulo standing watching her.

'Leave that,' he said tersely.

'But—'

'*Leave* it, I said.' His voice roughened. 'And for God's sake just come over here and kiss me, before I go out of my mind.'

She didn't need to be asked twice. She went straight into his arms and raised her face tremulously to his, before he blotted out everything but pleasure with the pressure of his lips.

He raised her face to look at him, his brows criss-crossing as he took in the faint blue shadows beneath her eyes. 'You're tired,' he accused softly.

'Are you surprised?' She smiled.

He shook his head, feeling the instant spring of arousal as he thought about what had happened. 'No. I was pretty rampant with you last night—I couldn't keep my hands off you.'

'I noticed,' she murmured. 'Did you hear me complaining?'

'Nope.' He lifted her hand to his mouth and began to gently suck at each fingertip in turn, enjoying the way her eyes darkened in response and the impatient little shake of her shoulder as she squirmed for more. 'Tonight, though, you sleep.'

She blinked up at him in alarm. She had planned to ration her time with him, yes. That was why she had sent him to work this morning. But she had saved the nights exclusively for him. Only maybe he didn't want that any more. Maybe once had been enough to slake his thirst. 'Alone, you mean?'

He gave a short laugh, as if she just suggested some-thing obscene. 'No, with me. In my arms. But definitely no sex.' He told himself that he had resisted women in the past—women far more experienced at seduction than Bella was.

Then wondered just who he was trying to fool.

CHAPTER THIRTEEN

'ISABELLA—there's a fax just coming in for you from Paulo!'

'Coming!' Isabella tucked the blanket around Estella and switched on the musical mobile above her head. 'Thanks, Jessie,' she said, walking into the study to see Paulo's fax machine spilling out paper. 'What does it say?'

Jessie looked affronted. 'I haven't read it! It might be...personal.'

Isabella didn't reply as she leaned forward to rip the finished message off. Jessie wasn't stupid. These days, it was an open—though unacknowledged—secret that she was sharing Paulo's bed at night. A fact brought point-edly home to her when her lost necklace was produced from down the back of the mattress in his room. But at least Jessie had had the tact not to ask any questions when she had handed it back to Isabella. In fact, these days Jessie was more interested in holding her hand up to the light to study her brand-new engagement ring.

Isabella smiled at the housekeeper before reading it.

'Only a few days to go now. Paulo's going to miss you.'

Jessie shook her head. 'I don't think so. He doesn't

need me any more, not really. It's time for him to move on as much as me.'

But Isabella wasn't really listening; she was too busy reading the fax. It was a copy of a newspaper cutting, written in Portuguese, and it was a birth announcement taken from one of Brazil's biggest nationals. She frowned at the date. A week ago. It said: To Isabella Fernandes and Paulo Dantas—a girl.

Luis Jorge Fernandes is delighted to announce the birth of a beautiful granddaughter—Estella Maria—in London, England.

Isabella quickly crushed the paper in her hand and walked out into the hallway when the phone started ringing. She snatched it up, knowing that it would be Paulo.

It was.

'You got my fax?'

'Yes.' She chewed on her lip. People *thinking* that he was the father was one thing, but actually seeing it in print... 'I don't what to say, Paulo—my father had no right to do that. I don't know what possessed him!'

'Don't you?' came the dry response. 'I've got a pretty good idea. He's obviously trying to shame us into getting married!'

It occurred to her that he couldn't possibly have picked a more loaded or offensive word to use. '*Shame* us?'

'You know what I mean. That's how he'll see it.'

'Well, I'd better telephone him right away,' she said stiffly. 'Just to set the record straight.'

There was a pause. 'Unless you want to, of course.'

Isabella stared at the hand which was tightly gripping the receiver. 'Want to what?'

'Get married.' As a proposal it left a lot to be desired.

Even if he *did* mean it—and she couldn't be certain that this wasn't just another example of Paulo's mocking, deadpan humour. Imagine if it was, and she started gushing, yes please—forcing him to hastily backtrack and tell her he'd been joking. 'I won't be blackmailed into anything,' she told him fiercely.

Another pause. 'OK, Bella. But don't ring your father until we've discussed it.'

'Paulo—'

'Not now, Bella. I'm in the office and I'm busy. It's Friday, remember? We'll talk about it when I get home.'

She put the phone down, feeling as mixed up as she'd ever been. How *dared* her father? How *dared* he? And Paulo wasn't much better, either. Idly drawling a proposal of marriage down the phone as if he were asking her whether there was any bread in the freezer, when marriage was a serious undertaking which should not be undertaken lightly! How *could* he?

She felt glad that it was the weekend, and that Eddie had gone to stay the night with a school-friend. The last thing she felt like doing was eating, but Jessie had made a casserole and Paulo would be hungry, so she put a low flame underneath it.

Paulo walked into the kitchen to find her stirring at the pot, thinking that she managed to look a very sexy hausfrau indeed, and was just about to tell her so, when he saw the tell-tale glitter of anger sparking from the amber eyes, and merely remarked, 'Hmm. No point asking for a kiss, then.'

Her anger was threatening to spill over like some horrible corrosive liquid, but she forced it under control.

'Correct.'

He pulled a cork from a bottle of wine, and poured himself a glass. 'Like some?'

'No, thanks,' she said tightly.

He sipped the wine, looking at her defensive body language through the thick forest of his lashes, and sighed. 'OK, Bella—just who are you angry with? Me, or your father?'

'Both of you! And I don't need any patronising proposals of marriage from *you*, Paulo Dantas! Just because Jessie is leaving and you think you'll be left in the lurch! Well, it's probably cheaper in the long run to employ another housekeeper instead of bothering to get married. It will certainly be less trouble!'

'How very right you are,' he agreed coolly, and walked out of the kitchen, leaving Isabella staring after him, feeling...feeling...well, *cheated*. She had wanted a passionate defence of his offer to marry her—not that rather bland indifference, which confirmed her worst fears that he hadn't meant it at all.

She heard him slamming out of the house without bothering to say goodbye or tell her where he was going and, for the first time since they had become lovers, Isabella slept in her own room that night. She lay wide awake, and thought she heard Paulo's door close long after midnight.

And in the long, grey hours before dawn she was able to realise with an aching certainty, just how much she missed him. She missed him lying next to her. And not just Paulo as her lover—even though he was the most perfect lover imaginable. She missed the way he held her during the night. The bits that came *after* the sex. A lazy arm locked possessively around her waist. A thigh resting indolently on hers. He made her feel warm and comfortable and very safe.

She must have dozed fitfully because, when Estella woke at six the following morning, Isabella felt more exhausted even than when she had first brought the baby home from hospital. And there seemed little point in going back to bed.

She wasted time in the shower and spent even longer getting dressed, forcing herself to make coffee and toast and thinking that the sound of movement might bring Paulo out of his bedroom. But it didn't. And she couldn't just barge in there and wake him. Could she? Even if she was sure that he would have wanted her to.

So she wrapped the baby up warmly and took her outside in the pram. The park was almost deserted and it was a bitterly cold day. The trees were all bare now, and the leaves had been neatly brushed up and taken away, leaving a stark winter landscape behind.

But Isabella didn't even register the plummeting temperature. She was trying to tell herself that maybe it was a good thing that her father had brought matters to a head. She was going to *have* to come to some kind of decision about her future. Because she knew in her heart that she couldn't just stay on indefinitely, playing pretend families with Paulo and his son.

And didn't Eddie risk getting hurt too, the more she hung around slipping irresistibly into the role of mother-substitute? What would happen to him when the relationship finally petered out?

Beneath the snug protection of bonnet and blankets, Estella began to stir and when Isabella looked at her watch she was amazed to discover that she had been out walking for almost two hours.

She went back to the house with all the enthusiasm of someone who was just about to sit an exam, and she had just bumped the pram through the front door when she heard the low sound of men's voices coming from the sitting room.

She left Estella asleep in the pram and walked into the room. Paulo stood by the golden flicker of the fire, his face as she had never seen it before. Dark and cold and frighteningly aloof. And then the identity of the other man froze itself onto her disbelieving brain.

The man stood with his back to her, his hair untidily spilling over the collar of an old denim jacket. But she recognised him in one sickening instant.

It had been almost eleven months since she'd last seen him, unshaven and loudly snoring off a hangover. She'd crept from his bed in the middle of the night, feeling that she couldn't have sunk any lower if someone had tied a heavy stone to her ankles and thrown her into the river.

But as a result of that night had come her baby—and although with hindsight she would never have chosen to behave in the way she did she could no more imagine a world without Estella than she could a world without... 'Paulo?' she whispered.

'You have a visitor,' he bit out. 'Aren't you going to say hello, Isabella?'

'Hello, Roberto,' she said flatly, but she kept her face expressionless, because some instinct told her that she was in some kind of inexplicable danger here.

Roberto turned around, and Isabella was unprepared for the revulsion which iced her skin, but still she kept her face free of emotion. She recognised now that she'd been a different woman when she had fallen for his practised seduction. That his smile was weak, not careless. And that he'd taken advantage of her vulnerability and her status as one of his students.

'What are you doing here?' she asked him quietly.

'Why don't I leave you both in peace?' put in Paulo silkily, but Isabella barely registered his words or even the fact that he had slipped silently from the room.

Because she could scarcely believe that Roberto was *here*, standing in front of her, his very presence tainting the place she had come to think of as home. 'How did you find me, Roberto?'

He shrugged. 'It wasn't difficult—thanks to your father's birth announcement. Paulo Dantas is one of Brazil's better-known bankers. And England's, too, it would seem,' he added jealously, as his eyes flickered around the room. And then it was *her* turn to be sized up, and he gave her a sly smile. 'You know, you're looking pretty good for a woman who has just had a baby—'

'Why are you here?' she asked, in a frozen voice.

'Why do you think?' He looked around him. 'Where is she, Isabella?'

Her heart pounded in her chest. 'Who?' she croaked.

'Please don't insult my intelligence.' She opened her mouth to tell him that he flattered himself, but shut it again. Making him angry wasn't a clever idea.

'*Where is she?*' he repeated. 'My daughter. Estella.'

At the sound of Estella's name on *his* lips, Isabella grew rigid with terror, but she did her best to hide her reaction, instinctively knowing that she must appear strong. She must. 'You've only just arrived, Roberto,' she said softly. 'And have had nothing to drink. Let me offer you a little something.'

She saw him hesitate, and saw greed win out over the question of paternity—despite the earliness of the hour.

'Yeah, a drink would be good. Dantas could barely bring himself to speak to me without spitting.' His eyes glistened as they watched the uneven rise and fall of her breasts. 'But I guess I know why.'

'I'll go and get you that drink,' she breathed, and she just about made it to the kitchen before crumpling into a chair, her fingers jammed between her teeth to prevent herself from crying out in real terror.

And that was how Paulo found her. He didn't say a word until she raised her head to look at him, and what he read in her eyes caused him to flinch.

But he needed to hear it from her. 'Do you want him?' he asked flatly.

She swallowed down the nausea. 'How can you even ask?'

He forced the words out. 'Because he's the father of your baby.'

'Oh, Paulo,' she pleaded. 'Please. *Help* me.' It was the lifeless quality to her voice which blasted into his consciousness and made him decide to act. Because through everything that had happened up until now she'd kept her spirit and her courage intact. Even her tears before the baby had been oddly defiant, brave tears. And for Isabella to look the way she was looking at him right now...helplessly...hopelessly... 'Come back into the sitting room with me.'

'He wants a drink—'

'*Damn* his drink!' Paulo contradicted in a voice of pure venom.

Roberto looked up as he heard them approach. 'No drink, I see. But you've brought lover-boy with you instead.' His eyes narrowed with malicious calculation. 'Though maybe you haven't told him how *close* we were, Isabella?'

'You've come a long way, Bonino,' Paulo observed, almost pleasantly. 'Surely not just to draw attention to your inadequacies in bed?'

Roberto flushed. 'A very long way,' he agreed. 'But I figured it was worth it.'

'So what have you come for? Money?'

Roberto tensed and a shrewd look entered his eyes. 'Actually, I came to discuss access to my daughter—'

Isabella sucked in a breath of outraged horror.

'She is not,' interrupted Paulo calmly, '*your* daughter.'

The two men stared at one another.

'She's mine,' said Paulo quietly.

Only the welfare of her baby gave Isabella the strength not to react, but her legs felt unsteady. She glanced anxiously over at Roberto.

'You're lying,' he accused.

Paulo shook his head and snaked out a hand to draw Isabella snugly against the jut of his hip, fingertips curving with arrogant ownership around her waist. 'We're lovers,' he said deeply and, compelled by something she couldn't resist in that deep, rich voice, Isabella raised her face to his. 'We've always been lovers, haven't we, *querida*?'

And in one sense she supposed they had. There had certainly never been any other man who had taken up residence heart, body and soul, the way Paulo had. She nodded her head, too dazed to speak.

'I d-don't believe you,' spluttered Roberto.

'Then prove it,' said Paulo in a cold and deadly voice.

'Go ahead—apply to the British courts. You can start the whole lengthy and exceedingly expensive legal proceedings *and you'll lose*,' he threatened.

Roberto swallowed. 'And if I won?'

Paulo appeared to consider the feeble question, then shrugged. 'Well, it's all academic—because you won't. But you certainly wouldn't get any co-operation from us if you were expecting to take Estella out of the country. Even if you could afford the return ticket—which I doubt, not on a lecturer's salary. A salary you may not have for much longer.'

His eyes glittered like black diamonds. 'If you take this any further, I shall hire the very best lawyers in the land to prove that you are an unfit father. And I don't think I'd have much trouble doing that, do you—in view of your rather *unconventional* attitude to student relationships?'

Roberto licked his lips. 'I think I will have that drink, after all. Then I'll go.'

Paulo ignored the request. 'Are you still working?' he asked, still in that same calm, almost pleasant voice.

Roberto swallowed. 'Sure.'

Paulo smiled, but it was a hard, cruel smile. 'How do you think that your superiors would feel about you abusing your position by seducing students? They might get mad at that, mightn't they? So might the other students. And their parents—now they would be *really* mad, wouldn't they? You see, Roberto, even in the most liberal circles, people don't take kindly to a fundamental position of trust being abused.'

Roberto had started to shake. He licked his lips like a cornered animal. 'What are you planning to do?' he whimpered.

Letting Isabella go, Paulo took a deliberate and intimidating step forward. 'What I would like to do,' he said icily, 'is to beat your face into an unrecognisable pulp before extracting a full and frank confession which

I would then take to the university authorities to deal with. I would like to see you jailed and to make sure that you never worked in a responsible position again. That is what I would *like* to do—'

'Paulo—'

'Not now, Bella,' he instructed softly, before turning his attention back to the man who seemed to have shrunk in stature since Isabella had first entered the room. 'But I don't trust myself to lay a finger on you, you worthless piece of slime. So instead I am telling you to get out of Isabella's life once and for all. And to stay out. And that any mention of your fleeting—' his mouth hardened on the next word '—involvement with her will be rigorously denied and followed up with an exposé you will live to regret. Believe me.' His eyes glittered. 'Oh, and if word ever reaches me that you are forming unsuitable relationships with any of your students again...' He allowed himself a grim smile and shook his head. 'Just don't go there, Bonino,' he warned softly. 'And now get out of my house before I change my mind and hit you.'

Roberto opened his mouth like a stranded fish. He turned to Isabella with a question in his eyes, but something in her face made the question die on his lips, unasked. He swallowed and shrugged, then turned and walked out of the room without another word.

The echoing of the front door closing behind him was the only sound which could be heard for several long, tense moments.

'How can I ever thank you?' she whispered, lifting tentative fingertips to touch the dark rasp of his chin but he shook his head, and she let her hand fall.

'Keeping a creep like that out of Estella's life is

thanks enough,' he answered coolly. 'You don't have to make love to me to close the deal, Bella.'

'Close...the...deal?' She screwed up her eyes in disbelief. 'But yesterday you were asking me to marry you.'

'And we both know what your reply was.'

'I thought it was a joke.'

'A *joke*?' He stared at her incredulously. 'Why would I joke about something like that?'

She met his eyes defiantly. 'Because you don't "do" serious, remember?'

'OK,' he conceded. 'That *was* a pretty arrogant state-ment to make—but it was true at the time I said it.'

'And you made asking me to marry you sound so casual,' she accused. 'Like you didn't really care one way or the other.'

'Bella,' he said patiently, 'our relationship has hardly been the model of conventional behaviour up until now, has it? But if a diamond ring and a bended knee are what you want—'

'They aren't!' she said furiously. 'But maybe you could try convincing me that our relationship isn't going to "burn itself out" the way you predicted! What's the point of getting married, if that's the case?'

He frowned. 'That's not what I said—'

'It is!'

He shook his head. 'No,' he contradicted flatly. 'You asked me how long we would be lovers, and I said that I didn't know—*until it burned itself out*. But it isn't going to, is it, Bella?' he questioned softly. 'We both know that.' He saw the way that her lips trembled, and gave a slow, lazy smile. 'We like and respect one another in a way that goes bone-deep. We click in a way that's so easy. I feel fantastic when I'm with you—and this kind of feeling doesn't come along in most people's lifetime. Believe me, *querida*.'

'Then why did you say it?'

'Why?' He stroked her hair thoughtfully. 'Because I was hurt and frustrated—furious that someone else had been your lover and furious with myself for not having prevented it. And yet, I had this overpowering urge to protect you and look after you. I wanted to ask you to marry me then, but the last thing you needed was *more* emotional pressure being heaped on you. That's why I was prepared to wait—and I thought that once we really *did* become lovers rather than just fantasising about it, then…'

'What?' she asked him tremulously.

'That by then you would know how much I loved you.' His eyes softened as he looked down at her. 'And I was certain that my behaviour since would have convinced you that I've fallen completely under your spell.' He gave a very sexy grin. 'Bella—do you think I'm like that in bed with *every* woman I've ever slept with?'

'Never, ever mention them again!' she warned him fiercely.

He smiled. 'I love you.' He turned and looked down at her upturned face, at the golden light dazzling from her huge, amber eyes. 'Don't ask me how or when or where it happened. It just did.'

She reached up to stroke the dark rasp of his chin.

'I've always loved you, Paulo,' she told him honestly.

'From childhood devotion to adult emotion. But when I got pregnant I felt so bad about myself that I didn't think anyone would love me…'

'But now you do?' he probed softly.

'Oh, yes. Yes! I love you, Paulo!' And she went straight into his waiting arms.

'Cue violins,' murmured Paulo, as he gathered her close and bent his head to kiss her.

CHAPTER FOURTEEN

ISABELLA turned around, the silk-satin of her gown making a slithery rustle as she moved away from the mirror.

'Do I look OK?' she asked uncertainly.

It was a moment or so before Paulo could speak. 'You look...enchanting, *querida*. So enchanting, in fact, that I would like to remove the dress that you have just spent so long getting into—and make love to you for the rest of the afternoon. But unfortunately,' he finished dramatically as he fastened a pure-gold cuff-link, 'I have a wedding to attend.'

'But wedding dresses are not supposed to look sexy,' said Isabella worriedly. 'That wasn't why I chose it.'

'I know—but I suspect,' said Paulo drily, 'that you could cover yourself from head to toe in sacking and I would still be overcome by desire for you.'

'Well, that's good,' she said contentedly. 'Do you think we ought to give Papa a knock? The cars will be here soon and we don't want to be late.'

'I just did. He's dressed in his morning suit, and is entertaining *both* our children. Eddie loves him.'

'So does Stella.' Her father had flown over for the wedding, and it had been an emotional reunion. Isabella hadn't seen him for over a year and a year was a long time for a man of his age. He looked older, a little more stooped and certainly greyer, but his brilliant smile on seeing his brand-new granddaughter for the first time had made him seem positively boyish.

And once Luis had been convinced of his daughter's happiness he had been more than charmed by the comfortable life she shared in London with Paulo and their children.

'No homesickness?' he had questioned sternly.

And Bella had glanced across at Paulo. 'My home is here,' she'd said simply.

Luis had mentioned casually that he was leaving the running of the ranch in the hands of his manager and was in the process of buying a small flat in Salvador.

And that night in bed Paulo had told Bella that he suspected her father might have a romance brewing.

'Do you think so?'

'He mentioned something about it in the car when I picked him up at the airport,' he'd admitted, then studied her face in the moonlight. 'Someone he's known for a long time—but he was waiting until you were settled. Would you mind?'

'Mind?' she'd asked, with a grin. 'Why would I? I'm far too smug and happy to do anything other than shout the advantages of living in a loving relationship from the rooftops!'

'Good,' Paulo had whispered before he'd bent to lick her nipple.

She had also told her father that she would probably complete her university degree. 'One day,' she'd added, but there was no trace of wistfulness in her voice. No sense of dreams unfulfilled—not when she'd everything she had ever wanted right here.

'She's young enough to do anything she wants to

do,' Paulo had said, sizzling her a narrow-eyed look of adoration.

'That's provided he doesn't give you any more babies,' Luis had teased, as he'd bent to ruffle the dark curls of his granddaughter.

Paulo's and Bella's eyes had met across the room in a moment of perfect understanding. As far as Luis was concerned, Paulo really *was* the father of her baby—but they felt exactly the same. He was—in every single way that counted.

She watched him now as he slotted a scarlet rose into his button-hole, and thought that she had never seen her husband-to-be look more gorgeous. *Gato.*

With a hand that sparkled from the light thrown off by the enormous diamond which Paulo had insisted on buying her—'Conventional enough for you?' he'd growled—Isabella picked up her bouquet.

'I guess we'd better go.'

'In a minute,' he murmured. 'But we have something very important to do first.'

Isabella straightened his button-hole and looked up at him in bemusement. 'What have I forgotten?'

He smiled. 'Why, this, of course.'

And he kissed her.

* * * * *

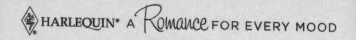

HARLEQUIN® A *Romance* FOR EVERY MOOD

If you enjoyed these passionate reads, then you will love other stories from

HARLEQUIN® *Presents*

Glamorous international settings...
unforgettable men...passionate romances—
Harlequin Presents promises you the world!

HARLEQUIN® *Blaze*

Fun, flirtatious and steamy books that tell it
like it is, inside and outside the bedroom.

Silhouette **Desire**

Always Powerful, Passionate and Provocative

Six new titles are available every month from each of these lines

Available wherever books are sold

'GET ME OFF THIS wretched boat!' Kat said, as a sudden wave of panic washed over her. 'And I mean *immediately!*'

The engineer shrugged. 'Sorry, no can do. You'll have to take that up with the boss. He'll be here later.'

Carlos Guerrero was coming *here?* Kat blinked, feeling as if she had fallen into the middle of a raging sea, without any way of keeping herself afloat. The most important thing was to get away. To run. To escape before...

Before the man who had made her senses scream with longing put in an appearance.

Staring out of the windows to see that the port of Antibes was now just an array of glittering masts and boats in the distance, Kat realized she was trapped. Then she heard a sound which made her heart miss a beat. And then begin to accelerate with excitement.

The distinctive whirr-whirr chopping sound from overhead, which could mean only one thing—a helicopter! And whoever was flying it would surely take pity on her and whisk her away from this luxurious prison.

With a small whimper she flung open one of the doors and hurled herself through it—only to be brought up short by a solid object as she cannoned into it.

A very solid object indeed.

'*Buenas tardes, querida,*' came a deeply accented voice which trickled over her senses like thick, dark honey.

And to her horror, Kat found herself staring up into the forbidding features of Carlos Guerrero.

Kat stared up into icy black eyes which were skating over her with undisguised disapproval. *'You!'* she accused, though her knees had turned to jelly and her heart was thundering so loudly that she felt quite faint. But what woman in the world wouldn't feel the same if confronted with that spectacular physique, clad in close-fitting black jeans and a soft white silk shirt—even if his handsome face was so cold that it might have been sculpted from some glittering piece of dark marble?

'Who were you expecting?' challenged Carlos silkily. 'It *is* my boat after all.'

Will Carlos be the man to tame tempestuous Kat?
And will she ever be able to convince him
she's more than a pampered socialite?
Indulge yourself with this dramatic tale of
ruthlessness, redemption and raw passion
by favorite author Sharon Kendrick!

KAT AND THE DARE-DEVIL SPANIARD

Available September 2010 from Harlequin Presents

HARLEQUIN *Presents*

USA TODAY bestselling author

Sharon Kendrick

brings you a tale of sizzling scandal
and red-hot passion!

Part of the exciting Harlequin Presents miniseries

The Balfour Brides

A powerful dynasty…
Eight daughters in disgrace…

A scandalous saga of dazzling glamour
and passionate surrender!

KAT AND
THE DARE-DEVIL SPANIARD

Carlos Guerrero can't resist his reluctant new housekeeper,
feisty Kat Balfour—he'll put her to work, though he'd rather
put her to bed! But first he must tame this willful beauty….

Available September 2010
from Harlequin Presents

LARGER-PRINT BOOKS!

GET 2 FREE LARGER-PRINT NOVELS PLUS 2 FREE GIFTS!

PASSION GUARANTEED SEDUCTION

YES! Please send me 2 FREE LARGER-PRINT Harlequin Presents® novels and my 2 FREE gifts (gifts are worth about $10). After receiving them, if I don't wish to receive any more books, I can return the shipping statement marked "cancel." If I don't cancel, I will receive 6 brand-new novels every month and be billed just $4.55 per book in the U.S. or $5.24 per book in Canada. That's a saving of at least 13% off the cover price! It's quite a bargain! Shipping and handling is just 50¢ per book.* I understand that accepting the 2 free books and gifts places me under no obligation to buy anything. I can always return a shipment and cancel at any time. Even if I never buy another book, the two free books and gifts are mine to keep forever.

176/376 HDN E5NG

Name	(PLEASE PRINT)	
Address		Apt. #
City	State/Prov.	Zip/Postal Code

Signature (if under 18, a parent or guardian must sign)

Mail to the Harlequin Reader Service:
IN U.S.A.: P.O. Box 1867, Buffalo, NY 14240-1867
IN CANADA: P.O. Box 609, Fort Erie, Ontario L2A 5X3

Not valid for current subscribers to Harlequin Presents Larger-Print books.

**Are you a subscriber to Harlequin Presents books and want to receive the larger-print edition?
Call 1-800-873-8635 today!**

* Terms and prices subject to change without notice. Prices do not include applicable taxes. Sales tax applicable in N.Y. Canadian residents will be charged applicable provincial taxes and GST. Offer not valid in Quebec. This offer is limited to one order per household. All orders subject to approval. Credit or debit balances in a customer's account(s) may be offset by any other outstanding balance owed by or to the customer. Please allow 4 to 6 weeks for delivery. Offer available while quantities last.

Your Privacy: Harlequin Books is committed to protecting your privacy. Our Privacy Policy is available online at www.eHarlequin.com or upon request from the Reader Service. From time to time we make our lists of customers available to reputable third parties who may have a product or service of interest to you. If you would prefer we not share your name and address, please check here. ☐

Help us get it right—We strive for accurate, respectful and relevant communications. To clarify or modify your communication preferences, visit us at www.ReaderService.com/consumerschoice.

HPLP10R

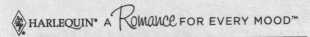

HARLEQUIN *Presents*~

Glamorous international settings...unforgettable men... passionate romances— Harlequin Presents promises you the world!

Save $0.50 on the purchase of 1 or more Harlequin Presents® books.

SAVE $0.50 on the purchase of 1 or more Harlequin Presents® books.

Coupon expires February 28, 2011. Redeemable at participating retail outlets. Limit one coupon per customer. Valid in the U.S.A. and Canada only.